SHALIMAR

SHALIMAR

KAMALA
MARKANDAYA

 *A Cornelia & Michael Bessie Book*

HARPER & ROW, PUBLISHERS, New York
Cambridge, Philadelphia, San Francisco,
London, Mexico City, São Paulo, Sydney

FIRST U.S. EDITION

Library of Congress Cataloging in Publication Data
Markandaya, Kamala, 1924-
  Shalimar.
  "A Cornelia & Michael Bessie book."
  British ed. published as: Pleasure city.
  I. Title.
PR9499.3.M367S5 1983   823   82-48838
ISBN 0-06-039022-0

83 84 85 86 87   10 9 8 7 6 5 4 3 2 1

SHALIMAR

Chapter One

THE boats went out before it was light, the nets were down before the sun came up. They caught sardine, mackerel and prawn. On longer trips, which could stretch over three days and nights, the fishermen took only the older boys with them. The younger ones were sent to school, in obedience to the wishes of authority; but those who rebelled and ran home were only mildly admonished. For there were always jobs a-plenty waiting to be done in a village that lived by fishing.

At no time did Rikki rebel. He took to books as he had taken to the sea. Both gave him pleasure, but the sea had come first. He kept from his infancy a clear, abiding memory of being lowered from his father's arms into a warm, familiar, infinitely blue and embracing element.

'The baby swam! No sooner the water touched than he swam!' The child's father swore to cronies, in accents of pride and joy.

These feelings echoed his son's; and to this enduring memory was added another of similar intensity when Mrs Rose Bridie placed the open, illuminated volume in his hands.

Mrs Bridie herself was overcome. Something in her parched soul was watered, when she looked into the child's suffused face. This warm, golden boy, after a lifetime trying to coax sparks from children mostly made of lead.

She drew him onto her lap and read to him out of the Bible.

*

Mrs Bridie ran her school for the fishermen's children in one shuttered room of their tumbledown house. Sometimes when it was not too hot she taught in the open: she in a chair under a frayed straw hat, the children bare-headed, sitting solemn and square on the baked earth of the Mission compound. There were never more than a dozen. Irregulars.

That the boy was a regular, Mrs Bridie soon noticed, at first unbelievingly, then with a rush of pleasure that she stifled, she did not believe in indulging the passions. She called him Rikki, contracting what her tongue found impossible. She reduced all the children to make it manageable. Sometimes she gave them nicknames.

Once upon a time when there were princes in India, English governesses had done as much for their princely charges. Princes and princesses, growing up to be rulers of sizeable territories, still answered to Booboo or Bubbles. In a piquant twist to history, so did a select few of these far from princely children. These few, however, reclaimed their given names when they stopped going to Mrs Bridie's.

Rikki did not stop. He kept going, and because of what fate ladled out, no one had the heart to claw the child back from his pleasures, outlandish though they were judged. Rikki liked going to the Bridies, and he went. He liked Mrs Bridie's English lessons. The language seemed to unfold before him, daily yielding something fresh and delightful. He loved Mrs Bridie's rich, leather-bound holy books with gilt and vermilion edges to the leaves, which she sometimes allowed him to handle. He loved the stories she read to him out of them, they were so rich, so full of Mrs Bridie's heart. Sometimes when she took him on her lap to read to him, he could hear it fluttering away inside her. When she had finished she would put the book down gently and simply sit, pressing his head to her bosom.

He wondered about the tall, bony woman with her yellowing skin and her tired eyes, who looked so different from everyone around. He wondered about her stories, puzzled over and was charmed by them. He thought about her bosom. So flat, he could feel through the stuff of her dress, not at all like the full globes of his mother. He thought it must be so from never having brimmed with milk for children.

The Bridies were childless.

Rikki wondered why.

Sometimes, when she encountered the child's grave, wondering eyes, Rose Bridie was tempted to take flight, to hide herself before he could strip her body and soul. But then, giving herself a little shake, and doing up the top button of her high-collared dress, she would bring him into focus for what he was: a little boy of five.

To him she was a woman who held the key to locked, mysterious boxes that he barely knew existed, except for the barest outlines that were showing up hazily in the distance. He longed to get at them and prise them open.

If his longings made him learn fast, he also discerned that the process lay as much in himself as it was within Mrs Bridie's power. But while he leapt ahead, her proceedings, he found, did not keep

6

pace. She taught too slowly, he felt, and one day gave out this plain opinion. Mrs Bridie, if ruffled, kept her head. Absorbing the shock, she fell back on morality: namely that he, like her, must think of others besides themselves.

That day, then, that momentous day when Rikki lost the best part of his family, they were doing infants' grammar. Not for his benefit, as he was gloomily thinking to himself, for by then he could read even Mrs Bridie's tomes, and the grammar simply flowed in the wake of the reading. For the benefit of others, namely two dull newcomers who had just bumbled past the alphabet state.

I am
You are
He is
She is —

they were chanting, while Rikki closed up his lips, not deigning to join in this childish nonsense, when his roving eye fell, surprised, on one Muthu who was standing in the doorway.

Muthu, a fisherman's son like Rikki, had not come by choice. They had picked on him to carry the news, on the simple premise that someone had to do it. Muthu might have managed better, except that being at the Bridies handicapped him badly. When small—he was now twelve—he had come to school in this very place, and had developed feelings about the Bridies. He would not go anywhere near, after stumbling through a year or two of schooling; not even if there was a creelful of prawns to sell, for which they were prepared to pay exorbitant prices. It was, he told, that he found their large hands and unusual skins (brick-red, was Mrs Bridie's) alarming; but he was not a boy who took fright easily, he lacked the necessary imagination. The truth of it was they gave him uneasy feelings, as if he was a lump of clay in their hands, and if he did not watch out he would end up like he did not know what.

Now he stood, and shuffled his feet, and could not get out a word; and got on the nerves of Mr Bridie who was putting a door back on its hinges.

Doors regularly fell off their hinges, windows jammed, tiles clattered off the roof at the slightest hint of wind, in the Bridies' ramshackle bungalow. He did the minimum into which his wife's nagging drove him, and retreated thankfully to his table on the

7

verandah and into his own preoccupations. The only reason he was re-hanging the door before it fell off was because of the terrible scraping the children made as they went in and out, which pierced even his absorption. Rather spitefully, he had chosen not to wait until lessons were over; and as he hated giving time to anything save his own concerns, the carpentry was not going well. Now here was this stolid, speechless youth, standing on one leg, a raised foot rubbing the back of his calf like a stridulating cricket.

'What is it?' asked Mr Bridie, sourly.

'I have a message to give to Rikki,' said Muthu, who had rehearsed it well.

'Well, you can't, in the middle of lessons,' said Mr Bridie, with a new-minted reverence for Mrs Bridie's teaching.

Only the nature of the message gave Muthu the strength. He stood on two legs, and mumbled to Mr Bridie.

Now it was Mr Bridie whose strength ebbed. He left the door to hang, and said: 'All?'

'All. Father, brothers, uncle. I have come to tell him,' said Muthu.

God, these people, felt Mr Bridie; and took the name of the Lord in vain but under his breath because of Mrs Bridie at the far end of the room. Then, chilled, he leant against the door-frame, and said, clipping the sentences,

'You walk in here. You want to tell this small boy: From this moment on, you have no father, no brothers, no uncle. My God—' as his fury rose, and his tic came on, 'what is wrong with you people?'

'It is the message,' said Muthu.

'Break it gently,' said Mr Bridie, shortly, and savagely.

'How?' said Muthu, itching to stand on one leg again.

'How?' By now the tic was severe. Mr Bridie winked and blinked, and finally brought out, hoarsely, and now and then going shrill, 'How should I know? You should, you're another like him, aren't you? Only don't let it fall like an axe on his neck, try to remember if it's not too much for you that he is only a little child.'

Then he left it to them, after crooking his finger at Rikki to summon him out of the class.

So it was that Rikki, blown by a strong wind on the Bridies' verandah, learned that the best part of his family were no more. It was the best that Muthu could do about not letting it fall like an axe.

'What happened?' asked Rikki.

8

'A sudden storm blew up,' said Muthu. He swallowed hard, and avoided looking. 'But don't cry,' he said, taking the child's hand in his. 'Your father was a brave man. No one else would have dared to take a boat out, as he did.'

Rikki was too stunned to cry. He was also old enough, at six, to understand about the sea and the demands it could make, as those who lived by it did by that age. So he accepted what crumbs were going, and instead of walking, which he could have done perfectly well, rode home on Muthu's shoulders. Muthu, for his part, offered the ride because it was a long way, by anyone's standards, back to the fishing village. He had also observed that small children had a fondness for riding on their elders' shoulders; and so provided what comfort he could.

Chance and accident, which had thrown them together, continued to operate. Following his original loss, Rikki's mother died, not long after his father, whom she had loved. Muthu's family took him in. It was the wife who proposed. There was something about the child, as she had seen him. Astride her own son's shoulders, one hand clasping his neck, desperate fingers wound into the curls that sprang thick and strong at the nape.

The old man, her husband, did not oppose her. He already had a son and a daughter by the young woman—it was his second marriage; but he would not stand in the way of her wishes, which in any case were not that far removed from his own.

Not that offers were lacking. The whole community had come forward. If not they, someone would have sheltered the orphan. It was a standing arrangement, or a way of life, that went back as far as anyone could remember and beyond that, they guessed. So long as one soul or one roof was left, all of them knew, no one need fear having to scavenge around like a stray dog. It was the one certainty, or assurance, of an uncertain life.

Rikki accepted it as his due, and even birthright, as he was brought up to. But that more than his rightful dues were lavished he soon perceived, as he drew close to his foster-mother.

'Call me Amma, if you like,' she said, busy with the bellows and the charcoal so as not to embarrass the child. 'I *am* your mother now, and lucky to be.'

And as he came to love the warm, loving woman, he did.

*

Muthu, his foster-brother, took the place of his brothers. They fished together. They mended the nets together. They would have gone together to the Bridies, if Rikki could have persuaded. But the older boy would have no truck. He would learn all he needed to from the sea, or his elders, he declared. He would not go near the Bridies, even assuming he could be spared. But there were always things to be done.

While Rikki was spared whenever possible. He divided his time, as they allowed him to, between his village and the strange dot in the landscape that was the Bridie compound. Mrs Bridie, content with the arrangement at first, soon felt it was not good enough. In her view the child deserved all the time she could give him, she would see that he got it. In his view she nagged.

'You've only attended once this week,' she tackled the subject, tapping the open, incriminating attendance register. 'I can't achieve miracles, you know, Rikki.' For his strictures on her teaching continued to rankle.

'Yes I know, Mrs Bridie,' he said.

She could not let it be. 'It's that brother of yours,' she said jealously. She had seen them together. 'He's taking you away from school.'

'It's not his fault.' The injustice roused Rikki. 'It's the prawn-fishing season,' he explained, to this peculiar woman who seemed not to know the plain facts of life. 'Everyone has to lend a hand.'

'And a good thing too,' said Mr Bridie, who had bought two basketfuls, being mightily fond of prawns. He was sitting on the verandah steps and peeling them for his tea, popping the prawns from their skins between a finger and one large thumb. Mrs Bridie could not bring herself to look.

'Food is not,' she pronounced, 'everything in life.'

'No,' said Mr Bridie. But he had seen his wife stand over the cook, supervising closely as he prepared the sauce in which she dipped the prawns before she devoured. So fast too, she could beat him at it any day. 'No, but it's a good part, Rosie,' he said, and grinned, and popped another prawn.

In Mrs Bridie's eyes her husband was a coarse man. No doubt he was, in the way he ate and drank, and in the language that flowed from his blistering lips when yet another slate or windowpane slithered down to ruin; but those same lips let fall the finer cadences of poetry, and his hands were capable of delicate work. He made miniature cathedrals, accurate to the last detail; or ships, complete with mast and sails, which he slid entire into clear

10

glass bottles. The house could fall down, Mrs Bridie felt resentfully, so long as Mr Bridie's ships were launched without mishap. And her eyes grated over the ravaged verandah, torn up to accommodate his pebble mosaic.

What made it worse, it captivated the child, and took him away from his lessons.

Indeed Rikki was transfixed. He was half off the wooden form.

'Will you show me how, one day, Mr Bridie?'

'Why not now, Rikki?' Tossing the ravishing pebbles enticingly. 'Why wait for one day?'

For Mr Bridie, subjected to his wife's attitudes, was alive to the need for allies. He took the boy's hand.

And showed how. His red, prawn-peeling hands grew delicate as he guided Rikki's fingers. Together they knelt, and steered the little polished stones into position.

'What use, Benjamin,' said Mrs Bridie, standing on the verandah, tapping her pointed toe on the scroll-edge of the design that was emerging, 'What use, do you suppose, this craft will be to a fisherboy?'

'As much use, Rose,' said Mr Bridie, 'as your stories. That is to say, as much or as little as he cares to make of them.'

*

That imbibing the craft or art of fishing would be useful, no one in the fishing colony would dispute. It was not even debated. It was a way of life, taken for granted over the generations, no other presented itself or seemed even remotely feasible. Muthu, then, more or less took over, from the men who were no more, Rikki's apprenticeship to their calling. At first they fished the river, far up the estuary where the currents were mild, before they grew turbulent in the race to the ocean. Later it would be sea-fishing.

'When?' Rikki considered he was ready to set off at once.

'Later.' Muthu did not share his opinion.

'Why not now?'

'Because you're not ready.'

'When will I be ready?'

When, when. Muthu, making ready for an ocean trip, oiled his limbs, sifted sand over to give grip, to double-seal against wind and weather. Rikki had copied faithfully. Nevertheless the skin of his palms was rubbed raw from helping with the heavy, salt-encrusted nets.

'When your hands don't look like strips of meat, even before we

11

get going,' said Muthu, shortly. But then he softened and said, 'When you can hold a line with a big fish fighting at the end of it.'

Which Rikki almost could. At least it would not be long. He shivered in anticipation, and completely forgot his galled palms.

*

'Your hands will have to heal before you do any more writing,' said Mrs Bridie, and took away his pen.

'I'm sure I can manage, Mrs Bridie,' said Rikki, longing to have his pen back.

'But that is not to say you can do it properly,' said Mrs Bridie, withholding the instrument. 'If a thing is worth doing, it is worth doing well. You must always aim to be immaculate.'

'What does immaculate mean?' asked Rikki. That he should ask if he did not know had been soundly inculcated, in the process of acquiring English.

'It means pure and good,' said Mrs. Bridie.

It was a sufficient explanation, but inflections he caught made him want to investigate further. He resisted it. He was learning that when there were inflections, little more would be forthcoming. He concluded that certain words were beyond Mrs Bridie. Sometimes he thought she did not understand them herself, but the stock answers she gave suggested that she did not want him, or anyone, to meddle with the meaning. She had two, one of which was, 'That is all you need to know, Rikki.'

Barred from writing that day, he began to read. It was Genesis; and in the course of his reading he found himself stumped. Taking a chance with the pronunciation, he asked; and when she pretended nothing had been uttered, repeated the question.

'What does it *mean,* Mrs Bridie?'

This time she did not even attempt, before returning the stonier of her two stock replies.

'Never you mind,' she said.

If she would not tell, calculated Rikki, there was Mr Bridie. He would always oblige, Rikki had discovered, he did not stiffen, or visibly suffer behind sealed lips like his wife. He approached him when lessons were over.

'What does eunuch mean, Mr Bridie?' he asked.

Benjamin Bridie was about to answer, when he remembered the child's tender years, or at least told himself he ought to.

'Ask me when you're older and I'll tell you,' he said.

*

Rikki did. He was getting on for eleven by then. Mr Bridie explained. Rikki, listening, and turning it over in his mind, was bewildered. No one in his village would have hesitated, or put off this long. What then was wrong, or different, here? Could it be, it suddenly struck him, that Mr Bridie was a eunuch? It would account for his childless state. Rikki wondered, and eyed.

'Oh no,' said Mr Bridie. He saw he was being stripped, and was, besides, close enough to the boy by now to scent out the unspoken. 'Oh no, I'm all there. It's entirely prim Rosie's doing.'

And man and child though they were, they came to that central, inner core on which age, or indeed the body husk, has no bearing whatever. Standing equally, together they contemplated an area of loss. It was to an equal that Mr Bridie spoke.

'Perhaps I'm to blame too. Who knows?' he said gently. 'Perhaps it isn't all Rosie's doing.'

But in moods less high-flown, or truthful, he would continue to call her Primrose. Or sometimes, under his breath, God's bridie.

*

Rikki's perceptions continued to branch, embracing both Bridies, and those distant boxes that he readily imagined were treasure chests, borne on bright, swaying palanquins that were advancing towards him.

Exactly when, he could not have pinned down; but quite soon he understood that it was not faded, scraggy Mrs Bridie who infused him most strongly, but that scraggy redskin Mr Bridie. His large red hands would grow as tender as a woman's when he bottled his ships. Or when he spoke, it could be about almost anything—astonishing oddments that he would let fall, casually, from his travels or reading. He read every kind of book, Rikki, marvelling, was learning; whereas Mrs Bridie conversed purely with the Bible.

Roaming the compound one day, while the class was kept hard at some childish verbs, he came upon a crate filled with books in a disused godown. On the whiskery wood was stencilled Mr Bridie's name in bold, once black, now rusty brown capitals: BENJAMIN BRIDIE. Rather gingerly, because Mrs Bridie handed out what they read, he picked out a volume; and was well into this golden treasury when he saw the shadow fall. Tall, angular—he waited for her stony invective.

Without a word Mrs Bridie prised the volume from his hands.

'Why shouldn't I, Mrs Bridie?' he demanded, boldly. He was

13

not quite so little now.

'It is not suitable, Rikki, for your age,' she replied.

That very evening a padlock was put on the shed.

At that stage he was in her power, he had to accept what was done. The time would come, however, when he simply took whatever his nature needed.

Meanwhile there was Mr Bridie. When in the mood, or coaxed, he would read from his books, or recite from a well-stocked memory. Or, sitting on the verandah steps, after they had done with the mosaic for the day, he would tell, richly, rivetingly, of pirates and emperors, of India and Greece and the glory that had washed over them and receded, of the splendours of Granada, or of Rome, which had once touched and glanced off this very coast. And would pull out a coin to show. Dented, green with age, yet it moved Rikki. It moved him to wonder.

Mrs Bridie could move him too, but it was more on her account.

'Primroses?' she said when he asked. 'They are little yellow flowers that come out in the spring, Rikki.'

'In England?'

'Yes. Spring in England,' she said, gently, and he saw the mists gathering, 'is a very lovely season.'

'Will you ever go back, Mrs Bridie?' he asked.

'Perhaps. Who knows?' Her hands lay like withered leaves in her lap. 'But we've been away so long,' she said.

'We're staying on,' said Mr Bridie, and laughed, grimly.

'We soldier on,' said Mrs Bridie, dabbing her eyes, which tended to water if the light was strong. 'But I must say it isn't always easy.'

Perhaps her husband didn't always make it easy.

'Two old sweats, Rikki, left behind when the hosts retreated,' he said, laughing boisterously, and he slapped his thigh. 'You see before your very eyes, my boy, the relics of a bygone age.'

'The Lord's Will be done,' said Mrs Bridie, less piously than usual, but still quite gently.

Did it sustain her? he began to wonder, noticing the bones that jutted, and the prickly heat which sprang up every hot weather and kept her twitching irritably under the coarse cotton dresses she favoured.

But she would grow still when talking of England, or describing chalk cliffs which had been a last sight, or telling of Scotland her birthplace and Mr Bridie's. And there would be a dew: a hint of it on her unlikely, leathery skin. Listening to her he received an impression of something filmy, soft veils over what she related, as if her memories were confused and she had taken to inventing much-loved, once-known landscapes now lost to her forever.

One day she told him she was a Viking. Not English, not Scottish.

'Look, Rikki. See how flaxen it is,' she said, teasing out a strand of hair from her bun and holding it up to the light.

He gaped. Flaxen would have streamed silver, in this light. The strand was a dingy grey.

Some gentleness, however, prevented him from saying so.

Another time she transformed him.

'Foreign blood, somewhere. The colour of your eyes, Rikki,' she said, holding him by the shoulders, gazing deep.

He knew what colour his eyes were: between grey and gold, according to the light. But pale eyes were not unknown along this stretch of coast.

'No, Mrs Bridie,' he said.

'I'm sure,' she insisted.

'I have my father's eyes,' he said. That memory stood out clearly.

'But his were handed down,' said Mrs Bridie, and spoke severely of vanished sailors whose behaviour had made a mockery of the teachings of the Bible.

He thought her slightly dotty.

It was a last observation from her that very nearly convinced him.

He was fourteen, and whipping up egg-whites for Mrs Bridie because, she said, Cook was sulking, having just given notice. When, in a lull—he was holding up the whisk, to test if the froth was firm enough for her purpose—all of a sudden she said,

'He would have been like you, you know, Rikki.'

'Who?' He could hardly guess whom she meant.

'If I had had a son,' she replied, looking him full in the face.

He had to look away. It was manifestly impossible, judging from the way she flinched if poor Mr Bridie so far forgot himself as to touch his wife. It was equally inconceivable that a child of her flesh should be anything but the colour of her flesh. Fair once, it was faded over the years to a dull, slightly curdled yellow.

Whereas his own—Rikki smiled to think of his own smooth,

15

clear browns.

Mrs Bridie, he felt, was an unwarmed woman.

While it was the warm, gold-skinned child she had come to love that was returned to Mrs Bridie in the last few moments of her life. His name was the last word that those gathered round the bed thought they heard.

Mr Bridie rapidly followed Mrs Bridie, but kept his thoughts to himself even when he knew he was dying. He died not of a broken heart, but of botulism like his wife, both having eaten from the blown tin of salmon. Having consumed less, he lingered longer. They were buried together, on the same day, in the small cemetery where Indian soil had taken care, over three centuries, of the bones of the missionary English.

*

It went out on the grapevine. Rikki waited till the drums were quiet before he set forth. He went to the Bridie compound, and from there was directed by solemn bodies to the graveyard where he stood and looked at what had been done.

'You shouldn't have buried them like that,' he reproved. 'She could never bear him to touch her, you know.'

The clergyman thought the boy was overwrought, and did not know what he was saying. Tears were indeed pouring down Rikki's face as he walked away, carrying the gifts they had left him in a neat bundle under his arm as Mrs Bridie would have liked. She had been at great pains to show him how.

Chapter Two

THEN he got over the Bridies. He accepted the finality of death as he had to, and without rancour; and laid them, gently enough, to rest. Early experience, in any event, had taught him to come to terms. As for the books they had opened, these too were closed. He himself acknowledged the seals that had been placed on them.

Amma was glad. Let no one say she rejoiced over death, never that, no; but it was a relief to have back her foster-son from that Mrs Bridie. The stringy woman had lured him away, she felt, more often than was fair, and a little too often for her liking. Because, was he or was he not a fisherman born? Besides which it was pleasing to have the affectionate, clear-eyed child by her: restored, she put it to herself, to the bosom of her family.

Rikki certainly felt it to be so. It was his family, he had no other. In this loss, as before, he turned to them: to his loving mother, and his small lively sister, and to Muthu. They sailed the same boat. They swam together, Rikki better at it, going further, staying in longer, early aptitude had not abandoned him. His brother a plodder, keeping to his depth, soon wading ashore and, stocky legs firmly planted, shaking himself dry like a dog.

While Rikki swam in a sea banded green, blue, the most innocent, milky turquoise hues where it washed over the hidden reef. Round the reef, lazily, smiling, swimming well, very well—

'Aren't you afraid?' asked Muthu.

'No. I know it's there.'

So did Muthu; but one might get swept.

And together they laboured at earning a livelihood, or took pleasure in a coracle, going round in helpless circles on a placid river until trial and error taught them to manoeuvre the awkward craft. Or they hunted lizard, cruelly, with catapults and stones, until the lust subsided. Or went in gangs past the ruined castle on the hill the English had left behind them, cheekily past the barky old Sikh soldier who had been left in charge; and on to the crest to gather berries in the casuarina wood. Or, half-daring, half-afraid, to taunt the ghosts of girls whose laughing voices drifted through the trees.

Descending the hill, and rounding the bay, there were the crab-runs. Crabs raced, violet in the last rays of the sun, for their bolt-holes, in a desperate bid to escape predators. Predators pelted after, intent on prey, sprinting along the phosphorescent sands.

Coming home at dusk, both of them starving, there was rice and a fish stew bubbling on the fire. And since the catches had been good, vegetables and a coconut chutney. And their mother, wreathed in clouds of steam, presiding over the lot.

Complaining, too.

'Where have you been, the pair of you? Almost dark and—'

'We hunted crab.'

They had indeed, and to prove or mollify produced the two aged specimens, less spry than their brethren in nipping into sandholes.

The dressed crab went in the stew, not enough to add anything but a little flavour, but a good flavour.

'Ah, lovely!' Amma sighed over the aroma, and doled out with a generous hand, most generous with Rikki. Because her own pair had two parents apiece, she reasoned it out somewhat tortuously, whereas the boy—

'Eat,' she urged. 'Eat and grow up big and strong, so that you can master the sea.'

Apu, her husband, listened. Women, he felt.

'No one,' he said at last, 'no one can . . .'

A temporary illusion, that mastery of the sea; perhaps necessary to a way of life, he thought, or might even have said; but he was not a man of many words.

Amma hardly noticed him. She rarely did. He was that old, maybe twenty years older than herself. In any case she hadn't the patience to wait for his pearls of wisdom. So slow, before he could form up and deliver. She went on with what she was saying to the boy she had taken under her wing.

'So that if your mother rose up from the ashes,' she told him, 'she would not be able to point the finger of reproach. She would not be able to say: "What have you done to my child? Is that ugly scarecrow there the cherished one whom God entrusted to your care?"'

Rikki laughed. He was bulging with good food and her attentions. No one could have pointed to him as an uncared-for starveling. None of them starved. When the fishing was bad they went hungry, and ran up debts. In good seasons they ate well, and it washed out the misery.

When she said it again he laughed again, but differently. He was older now, beginning to go to sea, and his skin was glossy with

18

health. Her care, and the massages with oil, had accomplished that. From his parents, or somewhere along the line, had come the gift of beauty. It had no great bearing, he was largely indifferent; but he saw mirrored in their eyes that he was a good-looking boy.

*

There was less time now for crab and coracle, more time for the fishing. Always that.

'Well, that's life,' said Muthu, busy with the pile the nets had scooped up, converting leaping silver into produce for the market. Gutting the fish, cleaning the cavity, tossing the fillets into the creel—he reckoned to do it before he could count to five, but hoped to improve if he could work out a way of reducing the number of moves it took him.

'Don't you think?' he said, not because he was not sure himself, but there was something about Rikki.

'Yes,' said Rikki, and honed the blade until it showed blue, and tested it against a thumb. 'Yes, it's life,' he said, and slit open the fish, slicing cleanly, seeing the dots that sprang, outraged, scarlet, in a row in the wake of his blade.

'I wouldn't change it,' Muthu laboured on, he thought he saw a way to gut and clean in one move. 'Not if I could. Would you?'

'How could I?' Rikki smiled at the ridiculous question.

'Just suppose.' Muthu wanted to be reassured, for no particular reason.

'I don't suppose anyone,' Rikki was chuckling now, 'is likely to consult either one of us.'

Chapter Three

ACTUALLY there had been, for the record, much prior consultation, and jetting to and fro, before the change was set in motion. The prism of involvement was broken down to its primaries, and each aspect scrutinised with care, and balanced on meticulous, even judicial scales, before the project was accepted in principle, and the surveyors went out.

Sober, professional, neutral, knowledgeable, even their tough approach did not prevent these men being touched by what they saw. This incredible coast, unaware, dreamy, a slight air of being shelled out of time, the coastline created for sheer envy—it crept even into the solid reports. Also it begged to be built on, perhaps in response to the global yearning for escape. Escape, or possibly no more, or less, than a retreat into once-known, once-loved and familiar landscapes: a memory that lay deep in the bone.

In this setting, then, AIDCORP were to build the luxury pleasure complex which at blue print stage, with rare unity, and not entirely cynically, got to be called Shalimar by everyone concerned.

Much later there were those who would call it a holiday camp, or even, when driven, a tourist trap; but generally speaking the honeymoon period persisted.

The Atlas International Development Corporation, to give it its full name, had been founded by Herbert Boyle immediately after the war; though there were those, opponents and rivals, who held he more or less fell into it. Boyle, straight from school into jute in Calcutta, had volunteered for Army service, while retaining his interests in sandbags and such. He might have saved himself the trouble, for in the meantime the empire was folding, his services were no longer required.

Demobbed, adrift on a labour market assuming international proportions, Boyle digested the fact that the day for soft options was over. He set about looking for ventures to engage those talents that had already rewarded the young man so handsomely in Calcutta.

So of course did others; but Boyle had the advantage over some,

20

in that he had already shaken the pagoda tree. If timing is important, so is capital. Boyle had no need to go round cap in hand. The Army had given him a nucleus of the necessary skills. He started at once.

From the beginning a characteristic of AIDCORP was its willingness to go anywhere, do anything. Have passport, will travel, Boyle, ingenuously translating, would say—like many another demobbed officer, and disarmingly enough. But it soon became apparent that the Major, florid and pugnacious from his years in jute and the Army, absolutely meant it.

Quite possibly, then, the company would in any circumstances have done well enough. But whether by accident or design AIDCORP in due course included men who saw clearly where the future lay. It lay in fulfilling widespread and wistful longings for progress: progress out of a wretchedly unacceptable poverty and backwardness into something that decency could stomach. The prerequisite for it was believed to be, initially most ardently, industrial and other development; for which capital, technical skills and expertise, all were in short supply. AIDCORP would plug the gap.

AIDCORP built anywhere, everywhere, almost anything, for anyone, with a virtuosity as dazzling as its politics were bland. To put it plainly, it never allowed private feelings to interfere with business. To put it even plainer, it consisted, with an admirably distilled purity, of purely technological mercenaries. It was not of course, the only such entrepreneur; but it was among the best in the field. The field, as it happened, were all those slabs of terri- tory where there had been a discernibly lopsided development in a century and more under, presumably, fully developed governments and governors of accomplishment.

That it should be askew was enshrined in the situation. Exigencies of trade and the military called for ease and speed of movement. Consequently roads-railways-bridges were built; and were to figure prominently when the credit-debit ledgers were subsequently opened. This being demonstrably insufficient, a fairish slice of the world started looking for ways to round out, and got to be called the developing nations.

There were those who, observing the inflow of high-powered energy, and the extravagantly well-padded enclaves from which it operated, were afflicted with a sense of *déjà-vu*. The less inhibited indulged in loud, if hackneyed, descriptions. It was nothing but the old carve-up: the same old imperialists at it again, only this time

21

disguised as technocrats. And they saw their case proved by the balance sheets.

Perhaps so. More simply, it was simply an effect of empire, now working through.

Empires, on the whole, are not won or run for the benefit of the original inhabitants. To assume otherwise is romantic thinking, or naivety of a noble order, or the end product of the solicitous unconscious after prolonged hassles with a niggling conscience. Empires, like any commercial enterprise, operate for the benefit of the shareholders. Apart from a sprinkling in the uppermost echelons, it is a lucky original inhabitant indeed who is allocated a share.

More usually all these aborigines were shunted off into second place, which also became the place for their natural aptitudes. Where, in any case, was the sense or profit in fostering local skills, when the newcomers could supply all the talent that was needed? Where the money, for this costly business? And where the need, say, for machinery manufactories, when ships loaded to the gunwales were daily unloading such hardware?

In a crude if simple operation of cause and effect, the newcomers grew more skilled with practice, the indigenes less.

When the conquering wave receded it was a matter for woe, certainly, that the shore was not over-peopled with the able, but not a matter for astonishment. Opportunities, then, were galore, the time was ripe for free and able enterprise.

Meanwhile homegrown governments had grown vigilant.

If, ineluctably, there had to be foreign involvement, it would be kept as minimal as possible; and this time round they would write the rules. No deal went through but bristled with clauses and conditions. There were checks and controls, prohibitions, restrictions on the export of profits, insistence on fixed quotas for the employment of local labour, restraints on the import of overseas personnel—the contracts were infuriatingly crammed with small print. Withal it was not unknown for entire companies to be bundled out, bag and baggage, without a vestige of civilised regret or compensation. Also without any vestige of hope that a frigate would sail into a neighbouring ocean to put matters right.

There would be no place for all this historical minutiae, except that a primary ingredient of history is human beings. For the most part Boyle did not think in these terms, except perhaps in nostalgic moments, when he sat on a verandah musing on past glory, or when he found himself needled by some tedious effect. As he himself trenchantly expressed it, the small print nearly drove him barmy.

AIDCORP could have gone under. More sensibly, for Boyle was sensible despite being driven, it chose to survive by evolving with the times.

AIDCORP itself could hardly have disentangled, when it took stock from wherever it currently operated, whether it was an import or part of the environment. The chairman, Boyle, was certainly English; but half a dozen nationalities were represented on the Board, and could be cited or produced in each zone of activity. As many were dotted among the senior executive.

As for the workforce, local recruitment was the norm. Contractual obligations aside, it was less fraught than bringing in expensive, and cantankerous, foreign labour. The obligatory, unassuming locals could be clustered round the hardcore of AIDCORP-trained veterans, and operational efficiency maintained by the permanent staff.

In most senses of the term, AIDCORP was a multi-national.

When, therefore, broad smooth motorways were called for by an African State, it was Kramer who went out, co-operating closely with a fresh young African trainee-executive who was also the chief of his tribe. Uijtterlinde, the Dutchman, happily back on familiar territory, speaking the lingo like a native, was jointly responsible with a national conglomerate for a couple of their dams. Pierre Laborde was in Djibouti, something to do with moles and harbours. He did not speak the natives' language, but then the natives obliged by speaking his, enough to get along. For there were all these affiliations. The fabric had been permeated, even if empires had shut up shop.

For Shalimar, accordingly, Boyle assigned himself. He had an affection, deep and genuine, for the country in which he had made his fortune. He knew it well, and undoubtedly his Indian connections would be invaluable.

Then there was Cyrus Contractor, a fellow director, and indisputably Indian, despite repudiations now and again from his wife, whose usefulness in his own country went without saying.

And there was Tully, also a director, who was very English indeed.

In welcoming, some eight years previously, this latest entrant to the consortium, Boyle had concentrated on his capital, with which the young man was handsomely endowed. Only in certain moods would he dwell, rather shiftily, on other qualities that had

23

recommended Tully to him as a member of the Board of Directors.

As far as Tully was concerned, AIDCORP might have been tailor-made. One or two things, perhaps, not quite heart's desire: but as a realist he allowed they were inevitable, given that perfection is not of this world. It was with a sense of adventure that he started, but then as he himself acknowledged, he came from a fairly long line of adventurers.

Tully, to begin with, had not been earmarked for India. Some, like Laborde, thought him eminently suitable; but Boyle had been tepid. He was not sure why. Except that in honest moments he grasped that, basically, he did not want to risk being upstaged by a man of his own race who might also be said to have a lien on the country. They got on well enough, Tully a man after his own heart and all that, but—. Anyway, he was elsewhere engaged. Just finishing a project, entitled to his furlough after a long stint in Iran, Boyle was unprepared to ask the man to sacrifice.

Then the world as usual erupted. Boyle, who should have been free for the Indian assignment, was needed to take over in Oman—anguished appeals from a personal friend, a relative of the Ruler's. There had to be a rapid series of switches—not too difficult, all could do each other's jobs, and indeed each mustered a variety of skills, so absolutely vital in the tropics. Finally Tully was allocated to Shalimar, and would take up as soon as he could, alongside Cyrus Contractor. And Boyle, unwilling to forgo India altogether, made it clear he would join forces later, when he was free.

Chapter Four

THE village observed, with interest, the activity. Men came and went, important-looking in shoes and spectacles, carrying cases and supple canes with silver mountings. Motor-cars bounded along the cart tracks. A lorry, loaded with canvas. They watched, when not busy elsewhere, tents blooming in the coconut groves. They were told to assemble, to discuss matters and learn what was to happen. Assembled, they listened to the earnest speaker.

'A city? Hereabouts?' Boggling slightly.

'More like a village.'

'Another one?'

'Yes. Let me explain.' Conscientiously. Perspiring.

Sitharam, man of the country, and AIDCORP veteran, trained in Bombay and Cincinnati, explained with care and invited questions. A short, roly-poly, patient man, mouth like a sabre-cut but only from the *pan* to which he was excessively addicted, in fact he was the mildest of men.

He had to fall back on henchmen for the rough dealing, of which, thankfully, there was little.

Except for the awning.

There was one, belonging to the village, a striped affair of great age and respectability and even some dingy remnants of grandeur. Communally owned, it was lent out by its venerable custodian for ceremonies that took place in public, in the open, like a coming of age or drawing the lottery. Useful for keeping off the sun and cooling the emotions when heated, it was just what AIDCORP needed. Being early days, it lacked these basic amenities. Sitharam sent henchmen to negotiate, and hid himself.

Chetty, the henchman, large, dark, far from handsome, growing less so by the minute in the eyes of his audience, negotiated. That is, in his meaning of the term. In fact he simply seized the valuable property. Or meant to, but now the shrivelled custodian, expanded into something surprisingly close to a bulldog, hung on like one.

But Chetty was a powerful man.

'And remember,' he hectored, loftily, and dust and feathers flew as he wrenched the unwieldy bundle out of the custodian's hands, and hoisted up on a muscular shoulder, 'Remember it is *your* interests we shall be discussing. You should consider it an honour that any of us are prepared to sit and discuss under your moth-eaten cotton.'

For Chetty, aside from muscle-power, was also a master of inversion.

*

The old man was brought in to consult. He was the headman, to whom should they refer if not him? But Apu's headmanship was based upon a different set of values, pertinent to a different kind of living. He did not have answers to their questions.

But he was invited, and came, and felt he could have answered better but they were bundling him along, it was not easy. Or if they had asked differently, he could have told. Where the shoals were running, just from catching the chatter of a bird, the shrill of excitement in it. Where was best to set the crayfish traps. And he told, eyes gone gentle and milky, of his boat, which he had built to be the finest on the coast, and his sons saw to it it still was.

Nothing useful to be gained from the old dodderer, they saw, while continuing to make efforts.

'What grows here?' Apu, seated obediently under the awning, repeated. Pondering, he could have listed palms, casuarina, silk-cotton—. He chose to say cactus.

'Prickly-pear,' he said. Because it did grow in abundance.

And: 'Yes, there are willing young men.' Because it was only too evident. Fishermen were pledging their services. They lined up to turn into coolies, at such time as AIDCORP might beckon.

Then Apu roused himself and said clearly: 'This is our territory. The waters are ours, to a five-fathom depth.'

It had always been so. He himself wondered why he now had to lay claim.

'No one disputes it. Tell them so,' said Cyrus Contractor. He had come specially to attend the meeting, and sat on a chair on the portable dais that Chetty had had trundled in, with his personal interpreter standing alert at his side. 'There is no intention whatsoever to purloin their waters. But tell them,' he said, in his soft voice, to convince others as he was himself convinced, 'we must all learn to share what is God's gift to us all.'

The old man heard, but said nothing.

'Is it not so?' The interpreter prompted, on his own initiative.

26

'Yes,' said Apu, and massaged his arms, and went away, walking slowly between Muthu, his son, and Rikki, who was no less.

Contractor watched him go, and more or less echoed: poor old dodderer. In fact he was the same age, fifty, as the oldie, only not so worn. For although the cares of the consortium were in all conscience onerous, still the living was better. Contractor could count on three excellent meals daily, tenderly presided over by his wife, exquisitely served. Apu never counted on more than one, though the seasons could be kind, when they often ran to two. These meals too were excellently served, and his wife would dish out to him first, and give him the biggest dollop after Rikki. Rikki, who would always—it made Apu smile—polish off to the last scrap, he had a healthy appetite. And had grown up strong and healthy, that was the crown and garland of his old age.

*

'What are they going to do?' asked Amma, in between pounding up the chillies, the moment her husband got back.

'Town people,' said Apu. He would never make them out. They themselves, he felt, must feel like fish out of water. For despite a lifetime, now and then he could be touched with pity to see these creatures, beautiful in their cold, silver mail, gasping and floundering as they came up in the nets.

'Yes, we know that,' said Amma, and stopped pounding. The red dust hovered. 'But what are they going to do?' she asked.

'They are going to build,' said Apu.

'What?' asked his wife.

'Who knows?' said the old man.

It would have grieved Sitharam, who had painstakingly explained about phases 1, 2 and 3: Villas in 1, Hotel in 2, refinements in 3. But, perspiration beading his brow, he had already noticed their attention wasn't always gripped.

Indeed their thoughts tended to wander off these abstract deliveries. Time enough to be interested when brick was laid on brick. Meanwhile they had other things to think of.

As for Rikki, cities grew, victorious cities like Akbar's, moulded to the wish, gilded to fit the vision of an emperor.

'But why did it have to die?'

Settled on the Mission verandah, chin cupped in a palm, looking up at Mr Bridie whose red was beginning to flag and turn yellow.

'No one really knows, Rikki.'

'But what do they think happened? What do you think, Mr Bridie?'

'Well, Rikki, perhaps the planners forgot about water. Cities can't flourish without, even for an emperor.'

Nothing could, the parched man saw written in the child's clear eyes. But the reflections were in his own eyes too, which gazed upon the boy.

Akbar's city. Rikki had forgotten its name and there was no one to remind him. But a similar city was rising: his imagination supplied in extraordinary detail.

Chapter Five

TULLY's imaginings had gone to work too.

Over the country, though it could never be wholly unknown or virginal to a Copeland-Tully, whose tree went back to Clive.

Working over the people, who nowhere or at any time were predictable: a vivid and volatile kaleidoscope, Alaska to the Indies one never could tell for certain.

Wondering, in particular, about the man he has come to meet. Liaison officer, according to the fable. In fact, basing this on experience elsewhere, a vigilante drafted in by an alert authority to oversee the activities of the multinational. And *inter alia,* if optimistically, to dovetail AIDCORP into India. Or, it could even be, to check the enduring magpie instincts of empire-builders like the Copeland-Tullys, whose name would carry before him like a standard.

How *they* indulged these instincts to acquire virtually a subcontinent remains a secret, locked in the past, though his own Tully relative—who should know, having been man on the spot—has a key to the mystery clutched close to his heart. Reveals, when pressed, that the empire was acquired in a fit of absentmindedness, which is enough these days, in Tully's opinion (at this point in time he was very young and intemperate), to land anyone in front of magistrates on a charge of shoplifting.

'Toby, you know, likes to shock us.' Some frosty great-aunt, commenting.

'Not at all, Aunt. The way I happen to think.'

'Flippancy happens to be the fashion. The age gets what it deserves, quite rightly.'

Quite so. Flippancy is the carapace donned by the age in place of the old heavy armour.

The men are a lot less chilly.

'That's going a bit far, isn't it, my boy?'

Grandfather Copeland, fishing in his trout stream, the vision that had sustained him in those last stark years when the beloved ward, India, had at last turned on them all. Protesting, now, mildly over a shoulder.

29

'Yes, a bit. Sorry.'

Take back anything for the dear old man, who had taken it in turn with Grandfather Tully to care for young Tullys, whose own father had died, from war wounds, by inches and lingeringly, eight years after the war was over.

Back, then, to this vigilante character.

Crammed full of experience, memories, and reflections, like Tully.

Of a different order, however. He hailed, unlike Tully, from what that young man had persisted in calling, to the annoyance of his clan, a recently occupied country.

But then, in a sense, the lash was self-inflicted. As they brought out, from cabinets lined in mulberry velvet, or from military chests laid up in attics, the treasures of the past. Uniforms, and albums, specially minted coins, or medals specially struck, or a photograph of funny old Great-Uncle Edward in full regalia signing the treaty with the wily Ameer—all these objects commemorating a power and a glory that were gone. Bringing them out, shyly, to show to the child; who very soon scented out the plum jobs that accompanied the deprecated regalia, and the pride that marched alongside these faded relics. Nosed out their obverse too: the humbler pie handed out to the people of an occupied country, even if they didn't actually strangle the losers on the steps of the Viceroy's Palace.

For Tully, as his smarting relations observed, could be very tiresome, even to the extent of raking up the less edifying aspects of an earlier swashbuckling.

'Let me assure you, Toby—' Grandfather Tully, this time; another of the eminences that had ruled India. All of them anxious for him to get it right, before taking up an Indian assignment, in these changed times.

'One simply did not, I assure you, think in those terms.'

'They seem appropriate enough.'

'My dear boy, India was *never* an occupied country. Mistake to imagine. *They* never felt that.'

'How does one know?'

'I hope not. My friends—and I like to think I still have a few—assure me they didn't.'

'Bound to, aren't they? Common decency.'

'You may be right, Toby. I daresay you may. But I think not. I hope not. I mean, it was never brutal, was it?'

'I don't know. How *does* one?''

30

'Well, not like Czechoslovakia. Not at all like. Well, not since the Mutiny. Went over the traces then, I grant you. But not since. At least, I hope not.'

But it still couldn't have been roses—not all the way. Not from their angle. From which this vigilante character, Tully felt, might well judge.

Listening, however, his ears pricked for nuances, Tully had to admit the man sounded reasonable. At least over the telephone.

'Where shall we meet?'
'Your scene. You say.'
'At the bar?'
'Ideal, if there is one.' (In this wickedly desiccated State).
'There is, in the basement. It's called Shiraz Wine Cellar.'
'Didn't know it functioned.'
'For you, it will. We're not fanatic about spreading the gospel.'
'I'll be there. At six?'
'Six is fine.'

At six precisely comes the owner of the voice. Slender, lounge-suited, black-haired, identifying red rosebud boutonnière, Tully's own vintage (for which he is duly thankful), holding out a civil hand.

'Heblekar.'
'Tully. Toby, for short.'
'Mine's Heb, for short.'
'No first name?'
'Yes first name. But doubt you can manage that many syllables.'
'Let me surprise you.'
'All right. But to tell you the truth, I like it as it stands.'
'As it stands, then.'
'Good. Good flight?'

Tully, who had flown tortuously from Bombay to Delhi, believed he had seen the wings flapping. Juddering along, his suspicions had time to harden. Namely, that the suave fleet was reserved for the pampered and critical who travelled the inter-continental routes, while the natives as usual made do. It amounted to a plain and simple case of national pride, observable—as Tully had observed—in its more acute forms in Third World territory previously deprived of the privilege.

'I'm not complaining,' he said.

31

'Not the type?' A flicker of an eyebrow.

'I'm the type all right. It's just that—' diplomacy in the strain, not for nothing, '—it got so interesting.'

'Yes. It has that effect on me too.' Heblekar smiled and relaxed.

Perched on bar-stools, slewed round to face each other, each resting an elbow, porcupine quills standing at the ready were laid flat. Both sets.

'You know,' says Tully as they mellow, and after some close study. 'I've seen you somewhere before. Distinct impression.'

'I expect you have. In a sort of way.'

'I can't think where.'

'Devapur State.'

So that's where: it comes back. This man, or his near double, full frontal in a silver frame on a drawing-room table—

'Thought I had. Seen a sepia,' says Tully, 'of your old man—'

'Great-uncle.'

'—in a frilly-frilly turban.'

'Next to yours in a fancy hat.'

'Fancy?'

'Plumes. Cockerel.'

'Ostrich. Only the best, I assure you.'

'Well! Live and learn,' says admiring Heblekar.

'Well, well,' says marvelling Tully. 'So this is what viziers' descendants do, these days.'

'Yes. Civil type. Admin. Can't fall lower. What about you?'

'The same. Out in the cold hard world. World doesn't owe one a living, now it's stopped being a colony.'

'Right. You could not be,' says sympathetic Heblekar, 'more absolutely right.'

And they mused on the past, like old men; but being young men, only for a little. Except that Tully had to remark on it, from the frisson that ran down his spine.

'Just think,' he said. 'We've known each other all this time, so to speak.'

'This time, right,' said Heblekar, after thinking. 'In those times doubt if we'd have cracked a bottle together.'

'Have we?'

'We have,' said Heblekar, and hospitably called for replenishments.

*

In his luxury suite in the hotel turned straight out of the Hilton mould, pot-familiar (except for Shiraz smouldering in the basement) from his global travels on behalf of AIDCORP, Tully pondered on mundane matters.

Namely, where to park himself while Shalimar was under construction.

Not that he was fussy. Pleasure domes in Xanadu involved—no less for Tully than the great Kublai—subsisting in caves, in hide-covered tents on the edge of bleak deserts, wind-lashed, sand-blasted, whacking at flies, feeding on stringy goat while harrying the slaves, watching the great project take shape—routine stuff like that.

Tully was perfectly prepared. Usual white man's burden, now shouldered by conglomerates like AIDCORP.

Except that, in this particular desert, Arthur Copeland had built his dream castle and called it Avalon.

'Not that one wanted to be buried there or anything—not away from one's own country, Toby, one wouldn't have wanted that...But a retreat, somewhere one could unwind, be oneself, perhaps.' His eyes, still a piercing blue, mist over. 'Took a long time to build, you know.'

'How long?'

'Years, Toby.'

Not only the building, but getting hold of the land. Lease extracted in slow time, with infinite patience—water wearing down stone—from his friend the granite Dewan. Paranoid about mercenary-settlers, this otherwise sensible man. Full of horrid stories about entire nations being taken over by this caucus planted (according to his theories) in the body politic to ensure precisely this havoc. Able to cite examples from history, worse still, and rather too fond of doing so.

But in the end...

'A little place by the sea. Spent some enchanted times there, Toby. Quite enchanting. The children loved it.' Esmond, whom the war had claimed, and Sophie too, really, the zest for life had gone out of her with the slow dying of her husband. So, there were the two young boys, who took the place of his own lost children.

'Would you have liked to stay on?'

This child, Toby, always questioning. It made the old man wonder.

'Oh no, my boy,' he said. 'Not to settle. No, never. Never permanently. But strange country, India. Wraps itself round you

33

before you know where you are.'

'Like a python?'

'Dear me no, Toby. Much pleasanter. Too pleasant. I might never have escaped.'

'Would you have minded?'

'Not escaping? I think so, my boy. It would have altered me from what I am, and I'm sure I wouldn't have wanted that.'

'But you wouldn't have known.'

'That was the danger, Toby. Or perhaps I should say that was the price that would have been exacted. But—' softening, '—give Avalon my salaams, won't you. And the old country. Some day when you get there.'

'I shall get there.'

'I've no doubt you will. When you do,' very gently, an arm about the child, 'be careful, won't you. Because it can be perilous, you know, as perilous as staying on.'

'Why?'

'I don't know, Toby. At least—' carefully, '—each of us has to find out for himself. Because you see, my boy, it gives back. Whatever it's given, I've come to believe. It always knows, better than we do. Subtle country, India. Yes.' Intent on the rose-bed, and the lavender. 'Yes, quite a little minx.'

It made young Tully the more determined.

*

Made a bee-line, as soon as he could. Heblekar, the Dewan's descendant, naturally the best informant. Asks him at dinner, over the coffee and cognac, the day after first meeting which has encouraged such freedom.

'Avalon?' says Heblekar, candid from brandy. 'Of course it's around. Things don't vanish just because you lot have left the country.'

'No. Human fallacy.'

'Yes.' Heblekar accepts the apology. 'It's near the site. Overlooks the bay—built for the view, I imagine. On the hill here.' He sketches on the snowy cloth. 'You can't miss it. Catches the light quite a bit. Carrara, you know. Specially shipped.'

'*Carrara?* With your own quarries not a stone's throw?'

'True. Have to be some slinger, though. But in those days—strange shibboleths, weren't there?'

'I don't know. Not all of them.'

'Well, native anything assumed below par. Not everyone, of

34

course, but—'

'Not my grandfather. Not one for shibboleths.'

'Well, don't suppose he was entirely his own man.' Heblekar offers charitable reasons, takes his arm. 'Why don't we adjourn to my pad? Got a couple of sketches you might like to see.'

When he had pored over the map, and the artist's impression in watercolour which gave a better idea than the faded photograph in the Copeland album, Tully came out with it.

'Can I? Will you wear it?' he asked.

'Why not? No problem,' said Heblekar.

'No question,' said Tully, 'of water dripping on stone?—I quote my relative.'

'None whatever. In his day, possibly. But those days,' said tranquil Heblekar, 'are over.'

And Shalimar being a common destination, they fixed up then and there to travel down to the site together.

So there it is, the little place by the sea where Copelands can be themselves.

A country mansion that plays at castles, touches here and there of Mediterranean abandon, perched on a little hill. The beach below fine-grained, grading finely down to the sea; water-slides, cling-film transparent, laid on the sand all the way to the waterline where they glide into one another and turn into ocean. Tracks, time-faded, race down the hill into the sea, which reflects blues right back to oriels, fan-lights, glassed-in galleries, a gazebo with a crystal dome.

Landward, the undefended side, a path of crushed stone, fortified by gates. Crunching up there comes a breath of sea just over the feathery crest of trees that crowns the hill. A copse of casuarina, laid carpets of berries and needles, a brindled shade. Tully sits down, sniffing, happy, feeling at home, a little overwhelmed as well. Heblekar squats beside him, on his heels.

'Just say when.'

'Have you cleared it?'

'With the Minister himself.'

'Thanks.'

'No sweat, I *told* you.' Heblekar bounces a little, nervously, on haunches converted into a limber chassis. 'Take some doing up, though,' he frets.

'A bit.'

No point in glaring denials. Ruined walls, fallen urns, broken

35

columns—nothing like fragmented Carrara for pointing up decayed splendours. Dumb indignation of a fine order.

'More than a bit.' Heblekar stops bouncing up and down and turns severe. 'We deserve to be caned.'

'What for?'

'The way we let things slide. Quite disgraceful. No excuses.'

No rhubarb either, about the state of the economy. Tully warms to his companion who is picking needles, eyes well down, off his corduroys.

'Nothing,' he says cheerfully, 'that a lick of paint won't cure.'

And catches Heblekar's look, which leaps over every communication barrier. No slouches, the Brits, is what it says, transposing freely into brisk new idiom. Not when the chips are down.

Tully was not too weathered, or hardboiled, not to savour the compliment.

Chapter Six

ALONG the coast the serious work was beginning. The villagers heard the rumbling, and soon breathless children came running to tell of lorries snaking in, or of mountainous, earth-moving machines grinding across the countryside. Fishwives laid down their whetted knives, and, shading their eyes from sun, stared at the glinting metal. Fishermen, the flighty ones, were drawn by the peremptory drums, *Rum-tum. Ek-dum!* drubbing up recruits all day long, for Ramalingam's drums were compulsive. He had won and kept his post as Commissioner for Labour Recruitment by the demonstrable efficiency of his thump-out.

Lives which, looking back, had tended to the monotonous, were now packed with interest.

In the village the young men vied to see who had done best. Paid, *pro tem,* at piecework rates, they totted up their earnings at each day's end. In no time a lottery was mounted. Up went a blackboard in the open, now that the awning was unavailable, with the chalk handy for the scores all fair and square after a count-out in public. As much ferment was generated as during the annual lottery.

When there was time to spare Rikki, and others, sauntered down to the market square for a look. Sometimes Valli accompanied her older, tolerant foster-brother. Or rather she danced along, her small, pointed face alight with excitement. For she had wheedled from her father, and had wagered the entire sum on a certain young man winning, and could hardly wait to collect.

And everywhere rang loud and cheerful cries of *Bakshee, sa-ar!* which had been learned via Chetty, who had by no means intended to teach anyone. Like other things, it just happened.

Sitharam was embarked on communicating, and failing to, as he saw. His audience saw the perspiration beading, and one or two soft-hearted stole away and presently came up with offerings of tender-coconut milk.

Chetty noted, and remembered in his time of trial. He was after a punkah he had seen with his own eyes, and the grim custodian was flatly denying its existence, because *he* needed it to swish over heads at weddings and such. Chetty, pausing to rally his strength,

37

recollected the incident and beckoned an urchin.

'Ai, baccha,' he said. 'Fetch me tender-coconut. If you're double-quick, I give you *bakshish.*'

He got his drink in double-quick time, bakshish changed hands. The exchange, freely proposed, might be said to be fair. Soon, however, the bakshish tag was firmly tacked on to courtesy; and sometimes quite blatantly to nothing whatsoever.

'Bakshi, sa-ar! Bakshi!' Children, and youths too, clamoured barefacedly; and those who had a smattering, from the Mission school, were able to offer variations on the theme. 'Ai-vant-munnee! Munnee, sa-ar, munnee!'

Tully had been blooded almost as he landed in Bombay. The experience continued at every stop on the tourist route he had taken time off to follow. The moment he left the precincts of whatever resplendent hotel it was, where towering guardians mopped up the riff-raff, he was beset. Judging from these cities, Tully believed it to be a way of life, an impression amply confirmed by his hosts when he returned to his roost in Delhi. He listened to their advice, and learned that life would be hell if he weakened; and having heard them out, adjusted to local customs in his own way as he had a habit of doing. Each time, before setting forth to sample the Indian air, he filled up with silver for distribution; for as a rich and reasonable man he saw no reason to be niggardly. Copeland-Tullys had never suffered from the vice: he did not see why he should start the rot. He saw no reason, either, to disappoint handicapped children.

Blithe young beggars rose with the lark—or more factually picked themselves up off pavements where they had been slumbering, to lay siege. They surged round, smiling and whacking their naked bellies, smiling just as widely when he turned out his pockets to show them.

'That's the lot. Now scram.'

Smiling back, amused by these cheeky besiegers, by the sense of a compact between them. He sharing out. They scarpering: their side of the bargain honourably kept as if honourable seals were appended to the truce.

Having perfected the technique, Tully brought it with him to Shalimar, or at least to the spot where it was scheduled to rise. Overnight he made sure of the small change before raising the tent-flap—they were under canvas, after some hilarious attempts to billet themselves on the locals.

38

As expected that morning, his second in Shalimar—the first had gone to Avalon—that morning he was in the thick of it when he noticed the boy, or youth. He had noticed him briefly the day before, for his fluent English—he had come bearing some message for Contractor from the headman. But then it had been under the awning, the talks sticking, the boy in the usual village turnout of neat, patched tatterdemalion.

Without such lumber he presented differently.

He was standing alone, back to a boat drawn up on the beach, no more than a few yards away; but he created silence and distance. Amid cries of *Bakshi-sa-ar* and *Ai-vant-munnee* that flew, with the children milling around, without holding apart he manufactured an aloofness of mind that he appeared to need. While, quite simply and openly, he watched. Half leant against the boat, ankles crossed, naked except for a loin-strip. The sun, just coming up, struck golds and browns off a polished, well-moulded shoulder that rested against the prow.

Tully paused to admire; and would have admired longer but for certain feelings: a slight jolt as of one who is catapulted willy-nilly out of his role or niche. For, as he was perceiving, he the observer was under even stricter scrutiny. If he observed Indian mores, his own were not to escape. In the situation that had now developed, from squinting down the microscope he was the victim squashed on the slide.

Intrigued by the fantasy, after recovering his equilibrium, Tully might perhaps have explored further but for a crowded schedule. Taking over at the last minute, he had a busy day—busy times—ahead. Restoring the ruffled linings to the pockets of his shorts, which he had just demonstrated to be empty, he resumed his tour of the AIDCORP acres.

Tully's perceptions were accurate. Rikki had certainly been intent, engaged as he was in comparing colours and tints. Before distempers turned him a dingy yellow towards the end, Mr Bridie had been a reddish man in the parts of him that showed. But when a sleeve fell back, or he sat slack on the verandah steps, or, rarely—for it was only when Mrs Bridie was absent—he came out in a singlet instead of a shirt, Rikki had seen that the fabric was of a pure, most tender dye. Just such milky hues were visible in Tully, at hairline, at the line of thighs revealed by the khaki as he walked, above a wash between pale umber and honey the sun had laid on his legs.

For Rikki had developed a profound interest in pigments, and

39

would spend hours matching the mosaic chips to colours that existed, Benjamin Bridie could not help concluding at times, only in his head.

Tully, that was who it was. Rikki knew, like everyone else: an efficient grapevine ran through the village. He went over in his mind, while preparing for the fishing trip. Unstoppering the flask, resuming the oiling, rubbing oil into tender patches that remained in spite of the weathering. Any spot he missed, experience had taught, sun and wind would rake out and brand as a reminder not to be careless. The oil flowed from the tips of his fingers, supple, gleaming, over his flesh.

By now Tully was on the periphery, except for brief recollections of having been noticed by him. Rikki was not unduly surprised. He had discovered people did notice him: his own kind, as well as people like the Bridies, of whom Tully was one.

Certainly Mrs Bridie had been warmed. The palest blues crept into her faded eyes when they fell upon the vivid child. But she would not have chosen to express it in terms that seemed apposite and proper to Tully.

*

The working day over, the sea invited him. It would be warm, after sunning itself all day. Tully, from childhood summers in Cornwall, was used to cold seas, but, never one for hairshirt, never turned down bounty that tropical travel on behalf of AIDCORP had made so amply available.

Now he fetched a towel and headed for the beach. It was deserted, presumably evening meal time, he could see thin blue smoke drifting over the thatched huts of the fishing village. The sea, peopled all day, stretched calm and empty. Intending to make the most of the light, and seclusion, he stripped quickly, and leaving his clothes neatly piled on the towel, waded into the water. It was only then that he saw he was not alone, and recognised in the lone figure the boy he had earlier noticed. Astride a catamaran, behind the line of rollers, he could hardly be seen. But then he rose, the gold light falling, and stood finely balanced, a statue on a waterborne plinth.

Presently, tiring of this pose, he stretched out his arms, and, heel over toe, initiated a tightrope act. Mincing delicately along the length of this log—catamaran by courtesy only—he was clearly enjoying an exercise in equilibrium which he had turned into playtime.

40

It amused Tully. He had to stand where he was, and once again admire, in words of some extravagance that Mrs Bridie would have avoided. This pagan bronze, with a missionary accent.

Rikki became aware of Tully only when he saw him swimming out. Swimming well, he conceded, and straddled his log to watch him tackle the breakers. But when he was through that barrier he began to wonder if Tully knew about the reef. The evening was calm, there was no danger, but coming on it unaware might be jarring. Tully meanwhile was still heading out to sea. Launching off the log, Rikki swam to intercept, calling a warning as he went.

His voice carried clearly. Tully stopped swimming and trod water. Used to the Atlantic since knee-high, he knew enough to pause when advised; and also enough to know himself outclassed. Good swimmer he was, but the boy was of an altogether different stripe. Swimming in long, clean strokes, with a grace that suppressed all notion of effort, he had made the sea his element.

But then of course it was. He was a fisherman's son, and lived by the sea with a fisherman's family. Tully had been curious enough to enquire, and had been enlightened by Heblekar.

Rikki meanwhile was alongside.

'Mr Tully,' he said. 'You must be careful. There are rocks here, you know.'

Tully did. AIDCORP carried out exhaustive surveys before launching its projects, as any concern would, as almost anyone would know. Not to, argued a quality of unflawed innocence that touched Tully. He smothered the crisp yes-I-know that hovered, and said instead, 'I'm glad you told me. We must do something about it.'

'What?' asked Rikki, slightly astonished.

And they bobbed together in the glassy, bottle-green swell between breakers while Tully explained.

Chapter Seven

RIKKI thought about it. A marker buoy, anchored all those fathoms down, to the order of men like Contractor and Tully. Powerful men, who directed the powerful AIDCORP, whose mighty operations were daily revealed. And from time to time he could not resist, but had to abandon whatever he was doing, to go and take a look. As Apu saw, and wondered what it was made the boy so restless. Looking at the unmended nets, and the traps not baited, now and then blaming himself for not providing an anchor as, perhaps, the boy's father would have done. He could, he supposed, exercise restraint. Apu backed away; a reluctant fisherman would only bring bad luck. Truth to tell, however, it was not in his nature to compel.

While Rikki wandered in AIDCORP territory, gazing down into vast holes in the ground smelling of newly-gashed earth, looking up at enormous S-shaped hooks that dangled from steel arms, touching the flanks of shining new machines, awed by the whole grand, unceasing business.

It sucked him in. Mesmerised, he drew nearer; and was snapped up by the Commissioner for Labour Recruitment, though he put it differently.

'Ey, you,' said he, 'you would like to be tea-boy, no?' For Ramalingam saw the training would be useful. English-speaking youth would be in demand later, for the restaurant and shop.

Rikki was not sure. But there he was, installed in a wooden shack, behind a huge tea-urn, dishing out the tea for two hours daily according to the bargain they had struck.

He found it a pleasant change. He polished up the tea-urn, winking at his absurd reflection in the curved, distorting surface. His hands caressed the pottery, thick, glazed, chipped, but still a world away from his mother's tin-pot collection. When not rushed he would go outside, and peering up admire the tricolour flag that floated above his shed, which the lieutenant had had installed.

The lieutenant, young Ranji, seconded by the military in aid of the civil power, namely Heblekar, was enamoured of flags and his country. They would be everywhere, once Shalimar was built. Meanwhile he made a start with the tea-shed that catered for

42

AIDCORP's taskforce.

'Looks good,' said diplomatic Heblekar. He thought it absurd for the tatty shed. He envisioned it, rather, flying in splendour over, say, the Red Fort (as it did). But he would not engage with his proud, impetuous junior.

Muthu, in a different sphere, was more truthful.

'The tea is good,' he said, wiping his lips with the back of his hand, 'but in my view it is not a job for a man.'

For in his view, and experience, women served.

Rikki's opinion was not dissimilar, but he was in love with the novelty.

'It's something to do,' he said, somewhat lamely. 'And I only come here to serve in my spare time. When there isn't much to do,' he went on, working up to boldness, and not strictly accurately since they made him clock in at regular hours.

It baffled Muthu.

'There's always something to do,' he said, helplessly. He did not know what was to be done about his brother. Now and then he sucked his teeth, and ruminated, and shot a side-long glance or two. No, he never would make out.

*

Then it was not only the strength, the great cast-iron grids and tubes and towers and gaunt skeletons of steel. There were also pretty things to see. Little villas blossomed fawn and pink and white-washed, crushed shells in the chunam wash, in certain lights they sparkled. Strung along the beach, their trim aprons all but lapped by the ocean. Tiled in celadon, copper-red, ochre, some thatched. Not like the villagers' plain and sturdy, but thatching with wheatsheaf designs, and ripple and deckle edges.

For Contractor had gone out of his way to encourage the thatchers, paying for workmanship of this quality out of his private pocket. And he would stand a little when he had time, and pushing back this topi gaze awhile and find it soothing, and say to himself in his soft way, 'It is good to see the old crafts kept alive.'

While Rikki was charmed by the soft colours, or by the glitter at sunset and sunrise. And would come at these hours to see it strike up. He thought it beautiful, and might not have moved on from there but for Tully.

It was the end of the working day—the sirens were sounding. Tully, en route for his tent, came upon Rikki riveted, like a pillar, in front of a villa.

'Hullo, Rikki. What are you up to?' he said for no particular reason, for it was clear the boy was up to nothing whatever, beyond contemplating the glittering cube.

'I was just looking,' said Rikki, withdrawing a hand that had been about to touch. Grain, like pigments, interested him.

'Just looking. Can't we tempt you to buy?' Tully said the usual sort of thing, cheerfully and without thinking.

It made no sense to Rikki.

'Are you joking, Mr Tully?' he asked, coolly.

Tully was nonplussed, an unusual experience for him. Odder still, he found he was not joking.

'No, not at all. Tell me,' he said, recovering, 'what you think.'

'I think it's beautiful,' said Rikki, standing back a little. The sun, striking oblique but hard on the pristine surface, created dazzle.

'Do you? Really?' asked Tully, also standing back, and shading his eyes.

'Yes,' said Rikki. 'Why? Isn't it?' he had to ask, although at this point, between heat and light, the villa almost shimmered.

'Well, I suppose,' Tully said, to his own surprise, 'it depends on the eye. All kinds of muscle there.'

And his gaze, clear of dazzle, held Rikki's, seeming to him to suggest possibilities for his own development. He felt his sight was being stretched, but on a rack, a sense that half excited, half frightened him. So that he disengaged.

'To me it looks,' he said, as light as the image that floated up, 'like a meringue.' Smiling at a memory, affectionately. For this particular villa was pink, an effect that could be achieved elsewhere by a drop or two of cochineal. Or pounded insect, as he called it before he learnt the name of the dye, and even after, to see the look of horror dawn on Mrs Bridie's face. Sometimes she would cork up the bottle, while he held his sides.

'Yes. Just like a meringue,' he said, silencing Tully who had not quite believed his ears.

Meringues continued to bother Tully. Meringues? In this village? It was so outré that after leaving it a week or two he had to ask.

Lounging in the doorway of the tea-shed, sampling the brew as was his custom, he said, offhand,

'Do you know what meringues are, Rikki?'

'Yes,' said Rikki.

44

Because Mrs Bridie had a passion. She begged him to whip up the whites because she had taught him and he was so good and reliable, whereas none of her successive cooks were. Unlike Rikki none of them stayed long enough to be properly instructed. When batches came out of the oven she was generous, spreading the tinned cream lavishly, handing her assistant, as fast as he could demolish them, pale-brown shells (pink when he desisted from pounded insect) that melted in the mouth.

He had to come out with it.

'I should know, I used to make them,' he said, somewhat smugly, 'the most delicious meringues, Mrs Bridie used to say.'

It solved one mystery, while raising others.

'Are you saying,' said Tully, curiously, leaving the pursuit of this woman till later, 'the villas seem like meringues to you?'

'Yes,' said Rikki.

'Sweet, light and crumbly?'

'Not crumbly,' said Rikki.

'But that,' said Tully, 'is their prime quality, Rikki. As you should know.'

Rikki admitted it, a meringue expert could hardly do less; but clung to his view: Not crumbly.

Since he had seen them building, and underpinning, the solid foundations, the piles thumped in by gigantic hammers—

'You should know, Mr Tully,' he said, 'they are too well built to crumble.'

'Yes, I suppose,' agreed Tully.

When, coming out to survey the villas in question, and the evening advancing, it seemed to both that what they were scanning was not merely the structure, but had come to include life-giving properties. Perhaps it was an effect of the light. It swirled about the walls, hinting at such ingress while abstracting from stability.

Tully admitted it, a trifle obliquely.

'Not everything we undertake,' he said, 'is a raging success.'

Some took fire: Alexander's city was a prime example; but then he did have a special touch. Others, also rising instantly to insistent wands—

'Sometimes,' he said simply, 'cities die, for unknown reasons, however soundly built.'

'Like Akbar's victory city,' said Rikki.

'Yes,' said Tully, and some intensity that he caught made him wonder.

45

Indeed, inwardly Rikki was smouldering, seals of wax were beginning to melt. After a lifetime (it was barely a year) here was another like Mr Bridie. One who could speak if he chose, like Mr Bridie, who would toss aside the tools, and stop cursing the obstinate, rusty hinges, and begin telling about cupolas and domes.

After that stretch of near-silence.

'Can you remember,' he said, hugging the possibilities to himself, and testing to make sure, 'what it's called?'

'What what's called?'

'Akbar's city.'

'Well, I ought to be able,' said Tully smiling, 'considering it's only a few weeks since I was there.'

And he named the city.

It riveted Rikki. Tully had seen, unlike Mr Bridie.

'Never been flush enough to gallivant around, Rikki,' the withered man would say, rattling the coppers in his pocket, 'but I could tell you stone by stone, untravelled as I am.'

But Tully had travelled. Rikki was convinced, for whatever reason, that stone by stone he could tell of an emperor's dream, on which his eyes had rested.

Tully noticed the blaze, and was moved, without knowing why.

*

Amma, in her way, was also beguiled.

She would leave off grinding the spice, or salting the tiddlers for home use after the bigger catch had been sent off to market, to watch them carrying in shrubs in bud, or well-branched trees, in containers.

'All ready-made,' she told, awed, and could not help the envy sparking up. In her patch she had to labour at it, coaxing up the seedlings, and feathering in the pollen before the blossom would set.

Or she would stand in the doorway of their hut, marvelling at the villas.

'As pretty as anything.' Over a shoulder to her husband, who would not comment.

'Sparkles like sugar-candy, don't you think?' She wanted him to.

It alarmed Apu. He could not provide anything like these sugared almonds.

'What,' he said, 'has it to do with us?'

46

It made his wife bridle.

'Right next to us, it *has* to do with us, what do you mean?' she asked.

So forceful, the old man felt. But then she was that much younger. Perhaps it was wrong, a second marriage, he thought, not for the first time. But without it there would not have been his pretty, spirited little daughter, or his solid, dependable son.

He turned to him now, and the two of them spoke of the day's catch, and plans for the coming season; and now and then Muthu was troubled by thoughts of how he would manage. One could not say it, but the old man was not—. And Rikki, well, Rikki—.

When the scamp himself was spotted, by Amma.

'Rikki,' she hailed, the sight of him always cheered her. 'There you are at last! Whatever kept you?'

He gave her a hug. 'I was talking with Tully,' he said.

Amma was not surprised a bit. She had always known he was a saucy one—mixed with the Bridies and all, and got up to all manner of high-falutin' things—no, nothing in it to surprise her.

After they had eaten the brothers sat on the charpoy outside, giving their parents time to settle. Muthu's throat was knotted up, but he felt it was time to broach the matter.

'Soon be the mackerel season,' he said.

'I hadn't forgotten,' said Rikki. Actually it had slipped clean from his mind.

'Need every hand. You know the old man,' said Muthu, low, 'is not what he was.'

'I know,' said Rikki.

'But what,' said Muthu, 'about your tea-job?'

'My tea-job? I'll give in my notice,' Rikki answered the appeal at once, and generously, 'first thing in the morning.'

*

First thing in the morning—not his, AIDCORP's, which began at the more civilised hour of 7.30—he sought out the Commissioner for Labour Recruitment, who was sitting at his desk, or so he called the bamboo edifice.

'I've come to give notice,' he said.

'Ey, you can't do that!' said Ramalingam.

'Why not?' asked Rikki.

It was irrefutable. The Commissioner had to re-think, while tapping the bamboo with his ruler.

'Why?' he asked.

'Because it's the mackerel season,' Rikki gave his reason, which seemed to Ramalingam utterly senseless.

Chapter Eight

THE mackerel gave themselves up in shoals. At times they appeared to be impelled, perhaps by sheer weight of numbers, to suicide. This was one of them. The boats came in loaded to the gunwales, riding low with the catch. Silver pyramids of fish built up along the shoreline. Women streamed out to gut and clean, and sang as they laboured. Nets flared as they were furled out to dry, sun lighting up the droplets of water. They shone, flecked with the scales and flakes of mackerel, like mirrorwork veils.

Tully, intending a closer look, went round to Heblekar's cabin to invite his company. By now they had graduated from tents into cabins with mod cons like portable loos, instead of trench latrines, and table-fans that ran on batteries, since punkahs had proved unprocurable.

'Care to come?' he said, parked on the table—Heblekar occupied the only chair.

It turned Heblekar queasy. It was against his creed to cut short life, even of fishes. In the interests of public relations but actually to spare himself embarrassment, he ate what hostesses put on his plate. Prudence warned, however, that the fragile, cultivated ability would disappear, were he to observe the process. He confessed this very private matter to Tully, as perhaps he would not have done elsewhere, or to others.

But deserts, or the wilderness—they were a good fifty miles from a town of any size—deal in extremes. They could have fled each other with silent shrieks. Instead centripetal forces, which can also manifest in such milieux, had begun to draw them together.

'I know what you mean,' said Tully, and perhaps he too would have been less forthcoming elsewhere. 'Wouldn't care myself to see a calf butchered. But it doesn't stop one relishing an escalope.'

And strolled off for a look, and to be educated, as it happened, in village economy by Rikki.

Rikki was reckoning up his earnings while he worked—what the fish would fetch, what his share of the proceeds would amount to, when he saw Tully walking down the beach. And felt an impulse, which he throttled. He had no reason to approach, no request or plea. And Tully was a director, as he well knew, and some had

49

taken to impressing on him. Rikki went on with what he was doing.

Hand over hand, coil on coil, expertly twisting, the coiled rope grew into stooks. Stood like stooks of corn, stiff with salt, glittering, salt crystals catching the last few rays. Tully settled down to watch, to compare with other scenes, not dissimilar, in another continent.

While Rikki's impulse, refusing to die, grew. Tully was alone. In the midst of throngs a man was alone. If he was not to be left so, he, Rikki, would have to act. His territory, his move. Not up to Tully, who had chosen to leave his own, or AIDCORP's, precincts.

Presently he could not resist. Wiping off coir fibres and salt, he made straight for the catamaran on which Tully was sitting.

Arrived, however, he found not a thing to say. It had been an impulse of friendliness, that was all. He had no words, and no way of telling how it would be received. He stood tongue-tied and uncertain.

Tully had to help out, and was not incapable. He said, easily, 'Tired, Rikki? You must be,' and waved him down.

Rikki's stiffness went, he squatted companionably on the warm sand.

'Yes,' he said, 'I didn't think of it, but I am.'

'One doesn't when one's working,' Tully agreed. 'It only hits you later.'

'Where?' asked Rikki.

'Where?' This unusual boy. 'Oh, in the small of the back, usually,' Tully answered, 'but sometimes here, across the temples.'

'It's the same with me.' This co-suffering delighted Rikki. 'But I'm glad,' he said, 'there's been all this work. It helps pay off what I owe.'

When it was fully paid off, he would buy his own boat... but first he would settle up for what he owed: all the money on the boat his father had not finished paying for, plus the accumulated interest. When he went down, and the boat with him, money-lenders had soon made plain who collected the debt.

'You see,' he explained, 'I have a huge debt.'

'Huge, Rikki?' Huge debts? A boy of fifteen if that? It seemed unlikely to Tully.

'Yes,' said Rikki, briefly.

Tully did not press.

'Well, you've had a field day.' Waving at the spoils. 'Looks as if we shall be feasting forever,' he said, somewhat ruefully. Fish already tended to loom over-large on the menu.

'We shall not,' said Rikki, with the faintest accentuation of the 'we' that nevertheless registered on Tully. 'Only a part is for feasts. The most part is for trade.'

'Trade,' repeated Tully. It was a detail that should not have escaped him. Trade was the foundation on which rested the formidable Copeland-Tully pile. Though—he smiled to himself—hardly anyone was pleased when, narked by some plummy relative, he issued reminders. And, recalling, he was amused by the aunt who surfaced, from all those leagues away, features iced with dismay above the Cashmere and the pearls.

'We used to be traders too,' he said now, to Rikki, undeterred by distant aunts. 'We've been coming here for quite a while.'

'Your forbears?' said Rikki. The Bridies too had made such claims, while disclaiming the commerce.

'Among others. Merchants to begin with,' said Tully, 'eager to trade for the good things of life, I suppose you would call them.'

'All this way,' said Rikki, moved to wonder. Mr Bridie had an armillary sphere, and would jab a finger at space between the metal rings, to show the skies under which he originally dwelt. 'All this way to trade.'

'And barter,' said Tully.

'We barter too.' Rikki deserted the sphere for earthly matters. 'Sometimes through our sangam,' he thought to inform, 'we barter directly, to get a fair deal.'

'For what?' asked Tully.

'Hides and charcoal,' said Rikki. Oil too, he remembered. Only a few drops were left in his bottle, he would have to do some bartering soon.

Hides and—Tully laughed. 'Rikki,' he said, 'I imagine these merchants were after a bit more than that.'

Rikki turned it over in his mind, carefully, even craftily.

'Boys?' he said.

'Boys,' repeated Tully, and was slightly thrown, as he would not have been in more soigné company, but recovered almost at once. 'Yes, I'm sure boys were part of the cargo,' he said.

And again thought he caught a flicker.

Indeed, Rikki was testing to see. There were aspects to Mrs Bridie that would have dislocated him if incorporated in Tully, who was of her kind. It would have flawed a man who could advance a horizon, or a dream, as Mr Bridie had been able. That Tully

51

could, Rikki had glimpsed. It was a quality he could hardly have borne to see sullied, as it would be in a man who was less than whole.

Tully, feeling his way, could only arrive at the obvious. Innocence, he saw, bore more than one aspect; while accepting that as yet he had some way to go. Quite some way, he was beginning to suspect.

Chapter Nine

In his sweltering cabin (largest in the camp, AIDCORP's topmost echelon believed in such hierarchy) Cyrus Contractor uncapped his Sheaffer to compose a letter to his wife.

My dearest Zavera, he got as far, when the scent she favoured flooded in. Then he could no more continue but sat, very still, overcome by her fragrance, which still had such power after a quarter of a century of marriage.

It had to abate, before he could resume.

Then, taking up his pen again, he was stumped for what to write. There was so much going on, he did not know where to begin: a hundred things, as he could see, staring moodily out of the window. But at length he was inspired, and this time the Sheaffer ran away with him.

Things are going well, he wrote rapidly. *Herbert* (Contractor and Boyle were on these terms) *has not joined us yet—he is coming out later—but T. Tully and I get along well. I remain well, as I hope this finds you. I hope to see you soon, the hotel foundations are laid.*
Your affectionate husband.

Here he paused, and after looking round to make sure he was not observed, quickly and furtively added SWAK under his name.

He would have preferred not to perpetrate this childish deed but that he knew it gave Zavera pleasure.

Contractor would have gone to much farther lengths to please his wife.

Zavera Contractor was in Bombay, at her sister's. She had fled away from Delhi after bidding adieu to Cyrus, and after corresponding with her sister to make all sorts of arrangements, because she could not bear to stay in the house without him. Lovely house though it was, designed by Mr Goldman the distinguished architect. She always said his fee was worth every pie. How can you expect style, if you are not prepared to pay for it? she often said to her Indian friends, who were apt to support this folly.

53

Mrs Contractor was Indian too, her documents made it clear. Zavera cheerfully paid no attention to anything her passport might claim, or her husband's either. 'It is only a scrap of paper,' she would say with a flick at the false thing. 'Our roots, you see...' And she would tell how they were tried and true Persians, ancient, Zoroastrian, and not to be muddled with the modern Persians who were not what she would call well-behaved.

It made her husband wonder. Mostly he felt he belonged. The great seas of Hindusthan had washed over for centuries, and if they had claimed him, like many another, he felt no call to protest too strongly. But there were times, confrontations with what seemed to him typical Indian ineptitude, or caste brawls, when the grain he shared would surface. Then he was glad to acknowledge explicitly, welcoming the feeling of difference, of constituting an alien, well-ordered, superior and impregnable island—emotions which brought him close to his partner Boyle.

Zavera Contractor took an affectionate pride in her roots, her husband, her daughters, in her house and her sister's too, on Nepean Sea Road which had the most salubrious views in the whole city. But she preferred her own. Only, when Cyrus was away, it felt so lifeless and empty.

Perhaps it was too big, she sometimes thought, for one woman, not counting the servants. All these suites of rooms, in which she could hear her footsteps echoing as she toured daily, for she did like them kept up, sadly unused though they were. And her mind, towards evening, would begin to slide towards her daughters, who might have occupied these suites, if things had turned out differently. Then Zavera would lay aside whatever she was busy with, and allow her fair, plump hands to lie idle in her lap, and fall to thinking, tenderly, of her children.

Such lovely girls, Nadia and Nargiz. So Westernised, and both married to Westerners, and living in the West. One in Ohio, one in Washington D.C. They had visited, once, it was not easy with the kiddies. And she had been over, once, what with the currency restrictions that was not easy either, although the girls always said all expenses on us, Mummy-ji. But how could one take advantage? Still, there were the photographs, which they were so good about sending.

Zavera took them with her, in a special portmanteau, wherever she went—wherever AIDCORP had landed Cyrus, but after he had tamed the jungle sufficiently for her to join him.

On this morning of her departure, she passed the photos one by one to Mary-ayah, who was packing—she would not have trusted them to anyone else. Ayah was accompanying her to Bombay, or she would have been quite lost. So was Joseph, she would not have known what to do without him either.

At which point the faithful servant manifested with the silence of long training, bearing a silver salver.

'Tapal, memsahib,' he announced, quietly pleased.

'For me, Joseph?' Zavera's heart gave a little flutter.

'Yes, m'm. From Sahib,' said the kindly man, 'from—' Some dump although squinting closely as he was he could not decipher the rustic postmark. He simply handed over.

'Oh, Joseph. Thank you,' said his mistress, with a grateful smile that amply rewarded. It was what had made him agree against all sense to accompany her, after Bombay, to this benighted village in the deep South which no one in Delhi—he had enquired—had heard of. Truth to tell, however, for most of his life Joseph had gone everywhere with peregrinating Contractors, and invariably against his better judgment.

The door had barely closed behind him before Zavera had read all the news, all six lines, and was confiding to Mary-ayah.

'Sahib is well. Hotel is nearly ready.' Well, the foundation stone had been laid.

'Memsahib is happy,' said Ayah.

'Yes,' said the memsahib simply, being incapable of concealing her emotions.

*

Indeed, foundations had been laid, and not only the hotel's, for by now AIDCORP was working at full steam. Employing a smallish army, building in double quick time sheds, cabins, access roads, ablution blocks, inserting plumbing, stringing telephone lines, setting up the complex infrastructure of a modern city, of which Shalimar was a microcosm. Its surface open, visceral reds and yellows showing. Skyline cluttered with cranes, steel hawsers, mountains of grit, of sand, of chipped granite. Smoke rising, thick, white, black and foul when the censors slipped. Steam, hissing up from vents, smelling of oil and machinery.

Men, behind everything. AIDCORP had its own cadres, but could use all the casual labour it could get. It began paying over the odds and half the fishing tribe came in and solved the labour problem. The problem transferred to the colony, which split. It was the trawling season and no one could remember the boats not setting out as a fleet, bound together for safety and profitable working. The fishing fraternity swore at the renegades, accusing them of halving the catch. Those who had reneged stole away, beached their boats high and dry and stopped up their ears against cries of desertion, and worse; much worse. For they continued to think of the ocean as their mother, for all that they had left her. It hurt to hear an umbilical union described in obscene terms.

'The place is—is not the same.' Apu struggled to put it into words, himself unsure if he meant place, or people.

Or would stand, when summoned, by some desk or table to give his counsel. He was headman, his presence proclaimed it, if somewhat emptily. But gave his opinion.

'The place is changed,' he said.

'Is not all life change?' said Sitharam, gently.

While the Commissioner snapped his fingers for the tom-tom men. *Rum-tum!* went his peremptory tattoo. *Rum-tum. Ek-dum!* all over the place.

And since when have men been able to resist the call of the drums?

Except that at sea one did not hear. At sea, where the sounds were different, some measure of tranquillity returned to Apu.

*

Day after day the catch turned out poor. They ate so meagrely, the cramps were beginning. These were not unknown, but good seasons made them forget. The suicidal mackerel had spoilt them all.

'Wish there was more to eat,' said Rikki, hungrily.

'Who doesn't?' said Muthu, tartly.

'I'm only saying.'

'Well, don't.'

Muthu went on working.

Rikki toed a meagre creel.

'The rate we're going,' he began, heartfelt. His debt hung heavy, his boat was receding.

'Well?' said Muthu.

'We're not getting anywhere,' said Rikki.

'What do you expect? The spirit is sucked out of the entire fleet,' said Muthu savagely, crouched by his father's boat, butchering the fish. He would take it out on someone, or bust.

'Don't blame me,' said Rikki morosely. 'At least you have your

56

father's boat to inherit. What about me?'

'What about you?' said Muthu, putting down his knife.

'I could get my tea-job back,' said Rikki.

'Tea-job,' said Muthu. 'Tea-job. Tea-job.' Hitting with the flat of one hand, wet fish fillet in the other going *Fluck! Thwack!* across Rikki's face.

Rikki could have hit back, he was stronger; but it was his elder brother. He picked himself up, wiped blood from a cut lip.

'Yes, tea-job,' he said, thickly.

Parents dared not ask the cause. Tempers flared, they understood, at times like these. But these times would pass, and they could wait, they imagined. They were silent.

Even Valli managed it. She pressed her lips together tightly, and glanced no more than twice at the smitten cheek and lip. She too knew, being twelve years old, that when the boats came back empty it could happen that men flew at each other like fighting-cocks. Soberly—she had a tendency to skip and sing—she took up her share of the household tasks.

Chapter Ten

TEA-JOB kept repeating in Rikki's head. But he had to wait until the swelling was down and he could speak properly. Daily, examining his mouth in a broken sliver of mirror propped up on the window ledge, he exclaimed to his smarting reflection, 'I will! I will!' fiercely, clamping his jaws together to keep up steam.

Presently there was no reason for inaction. He waited a few days more, in case, throwing glances at his brother, but there was no move from that quarter. Muthu was closed up. Perhaps he, too, struck flint daily. And there was nothing to tempt with, the skimpy fleet was returning with skimpy catches.

Rikki chose his hour. He meant to be early, before people grew fretful, and miserly with favours. But his feet were weighted, or something. It was past noon when he arrived at the awning under which, moth-eaten or not, a good deal of business got transacted. In one corner stood Heblekar's table—he had soon fled his superior, but sweltering, cabin. In another the Commissioner's bamboo contraption was erected, behind which officiated the bulky Ramalingam.

'What do you want?' snapped the Commissioner, with a baleful eye, the moment he saw who had entered. He had no patience with unruly youth that stopped work when it felt like it. Youth, moreover, that had just brushed past the belted peon as if that functionary did not exist.

'My tea-job,' said Rikki.

'Ey-hey, do you. Tea-job is gone,' said the Commissioner, accusingly.

'Any job, then,' said Rikki. He was easy, so long as the easy money flowed.

'There are no vacancies,' said the Commissioner, starting off officially, but rising shrill as his feelings got the better.

Rikki simply did not believe it. After all that tom-tomming? He stood planted, a fair impression of a tree.

The shrimp of a peon, by the entrance, was endeavouring not to be seen. He would not have cared to be called upon to chuck out.

Heblekar had a better notion of responsibility, not to mention having to justify his appointment. He pushed aside his papers and strolled over to deal with the situation which was ballooning up.

'I'm sure—' smoothly, this dovetailer of AIDCORP into India, '—you can fit this strapping youth in somewhere?' he invited.

'Later on, possibly,' said the Commissioner, to a principal. To the petitioner he said, 'What are you waiting for?'

'My tea-job,' said Rikki.

'Tea-job, tea-job!' repeated the Commissioner, rather like Muthu, but slightly more controlled. 'Deserter, vamose!' he grated.

Vamose? What did it mean, exactly?

'It means go away.' Ramalingam gave up all thought of control. 'What is the matter with you, eh? Are you a madman? Are you trying to drive me mad?' he cried.

'No. I just asked,' said Rikki, turning to leave. It was a habit, dating back to the schoolhouse. Mrs Bridie encouraged all her pupils to enlarge their vocabulary. In any case he was glad he had asked, *vamose* was the sort of word that would always come in handy.

Outside, high noon, after the filtered light of the awning it was blinding. Hardly anyone was around, at least not in the open.

Except, as often happened, Tully, who was out on his rounds.

Striding along in sandalled feet, an open-neck shirt, his hair a thick, burnt-gold shield that would protect, Rikki was ruminating, better than the topi that Contractor and Ramalingam would ram on at first stroke of the sun.

When Tully came up.

'Hullo, Rikki. Any luck with the job?' he asked.

'What job?' asked Rikki. In his ruminations, he had forgotten.

'The job you were after,' said Tully, patiently.

'No,' said Rikki, wondering how he would know about this, but assuming a man in his position would know everything. Certainly Tully did his best, although in this case he simply happened to have overheard.

'No, no job. You see,' he explained, 'the Commissioner is angry. I do not think he understood about the mackerel.'

'Perhaps not,' said Tully.

'He is,' said Rikki, 'walled up.'

'Yes, perhaps,' agreed Tully, and now they were walking in step. 'It does take a little time to work the grudge out of one's system. So,' he asked, 'what next?'

Rikki did not know, except that all the time his feet were

c   59 carrying him to the rosy cloisters of silk-cotton trees which at this time of year were in full flower.

It was a rose shade that fell from the trees: not a leaf on the branches, only crimson canopies one after another opening over columns of tall, pale wood.

They sat, Rikki at ease on the petalled ground, Tully relaxed after he had scraped around and found a fallen branch. Easy as he was, his frame would usually insist on a cushion—some sort of middleman—between him and the earth.

'Didn't know this place existed,' he said, when he was free of these earthly distractions, 'and we flattered ourselves it was a pretty thorough survey.'

'Yes, it's hidden away, you'd have to know,' agreed Rikki. A concealing forest of palmyra, and a dip in the land, saw to that. 'Besides,' he said, 'it's just ordinary trees, you'd hardly notice until it comes into season.'

'But when it does,' said Tully. By now he was engulfed in these rich falls of crimson. 'It's just like a cathedral,' he said, 'only whoever put in the stained glass was drunk on one colour.'

'Not one. Lots of shades,' said Rikki absently, absorbed in wood, the work of children, or of men without work. Clasp-knife out, he began carefully whittling.

'Variations on a rose theme,' said Tully, watching him, picking up the softwood shavings and turning them over in his hand. 'Is it good for toys?' he asked.

'Toys? I don't know,' said Rikki. 'It's good for floats, though.'

'Is that what you're making?'

'Yes.'

If he kept at it it would help buy essentials, like rice. Floats always sold, if only to the tallymen who would sell them back when times improved. 'Besides,' he said, 'it's something to do.'

But to Tully, now, somehow it seemed to be the wrong thing.

'It's not what you ought to be doing at all,' he said. 'That's where you ought to be,' pointing in the right direction, although barely a glimmer was visible from where he sat. 'On the high seas, fishing.'

If it sounded romantic to him, as it did, still Tully would not dismiss it out of hand. He had found truth and romance sharing the same bed too often, for such summary or sophisticated dismissals.

'Fishing,' repeated Rikki, listlessly. The way he felt, it had to come out. 'I am done with that. I want a proper, steady job,' he

60

said.

'Are you sure?' asked Tully.

'Yes,' said Rikki, whittling. Certainties were flying like the wafery wood. 'And even if I wasn't—' And fell silent.

'If you weren't?' Tully had to nudge.

'The sea is in no mood to give anything,' said Rikki, and laying his knife aside, linked his hands loosely. 'It happens, they say, when people leave, when there are—there are—' he could hardly get it out, 'desertions.'

'I've heard it said,' said Tully.

'Yes, there's a lot of talk,' said Rikki.

'Not here. In England,' said Tully.

Strains not that different had sounded there too, in a small fishing village they went to in the summer, as children.

Those distant, Cornish eyes, foreign even to English children, reflecting an Atlantic twilight, sometimes the ruins of a mineral landscape. Come halfway round the world, he was finding, to stumble upon their counterpart.

He did not know how to proceed, except through childhood.

'It was a little port. . .we went every year,' he said. 'It's supposed to be very English, messing about in boats. We certainly loved it.'

'It's not difficult to understand,' said Rikki.

'I'm looking for a boat. An old love,' said Tully; and it was. 'Will you build me one?' he said.

'Will you trust me to?' asked Rikki.

'There'll be reasons not to,' said Tully, 'when you supply them.'

The rose light was intense. It picked on a fallen pod of some past harvest, lit up floss still wound inside the split case, overlooked by some careless, or glutted, bird. Mostly there wasn't a strand to be seen. Fledglings for miles around bedded down on silk.

Rikki scraped petals over the find, with a toe, slowly.

'Mr Tully,' he said, formally, but gently. 'You must not invent jobs for me.'

'One cannot invent old loves,' said Tully, as gently. 'The most you can throw at me is that I'm paying back some scrap of what I owe.'

'You owe me nothing,' said Rikki.

The innocence was piercing. Tully could only rebut in a general way.

'You could say that, I suppose. But—' eyes down, fiddling with

61

wood shavings, '—most of us feel something is owed when a child loses its father. Up to the rest of us to make good, no matter whose child.'

When he saw it was going out of his grasp into the personal, and perhaps elsewhere would have drawn back. Here, he went on.

'Not that one ever can, wholly...though in my case they did make a fair job of it. You see,' he said, and was subdued by the past, its enduring strength, 'I didn't really know my father either, you know.'

Rikki flinched. In the rose light, in the forest of silk-cotton, chill winds blew. Dreadful, shrouded shapes were carried in. They could mangle him, if he was not infinitely careful.

'My father was a brave man,' he mumbled, in the teeth of his dread, so hunched up no one could have heard properly.

But it was hardly to do with hearing, or perhaps Tully's hearing was acute.

'I know,' he said, and dropping this subject took up another. 'Begin right away, you can pilot me up-river,' he said briskly. 'I've always wanted to explore.'

Chapter Eleven

THE chill winds abated, they could not blow icy forever.

Rikki flew, the moment the rains were over, to put the work in train. He selected the timber himself, watched it hewn, chose his builder, harried the man, and presided over the laying of the keel. He would have dragged Tully to watch the ceremony, but Tully was occupied with other business which seemed, to Rikki, of utterly no account, by comparison.

'In thirty days,' he laid down.

'Ask for the moon,' said the jovial shipwright, one Hassan, and laughed heartily.

'I know what can be done. I am my father's son,' said Rikki.

'So am I,' said Hassan, and went on smoothing wood, woodshavings flew like curled feathers before the cutting edge of his adze. 'But I'll give you this: it's bedded in the bone, I know it's in your line.'

'I've just told you that!' said Rikki, fretfully.

'I'll see what I can do,' said the tolerant man. 'Hurry things up as far as I can, seeing it's you. But you can't rush this kind of job, you know. All done by hand, hand-beaten, hand laid. But,' to console the distraught youth, 'it'll be finished within your lifetime, I promise.'

The boatyard, from being a place of unattainable joys which he tried to avoid for that very reason, became for Rikki a haven of bliss. He haunted it. By day, as soon as chores would allow, he raced to the boatyard, and rooted there, made a nuisance of himself. The shipwright, jealous of his reputation, had to prise the coir roping from the hands of this eager apprentice. Or would unplug the holes, and patiently re-caulk, while assistants removed the resins and tree-gum to a place of safety.

But it was going well. Rikki was happy. When the busy day was done, he sat happily on the string cot outside their hut, and turned it into Tully's boat. It would be as his own, he resolved, rocking. It deserved, and would receive, as much devoted attention.

Tully waited for a price to be put on all this devoted labour. He waited in vain. In the end he had to decide what to pay Rikki, who

63

by now had named himself Tully's assistant.

*

'At least it's in our line,' allowed Muthu, grudgingly. He meant, even if one went over to AIDCORP.

Rikki overlooked the grudging tone. He was too peaceful to want to bicker. He went on with his rocking.

'I hope it pays well, at least,' said Muthu. Since that had been the object.

It did. Tully, after waiting, paid fairly—lavishly, by local standards. But Rikki scarcely thought about it. He would have worked for Tully for nothing.

However, since he had been asked, he obliged.

'Yes, very well,' he replied.

Tully also commented, after a brief visit to the boatyard. Rikki, finally, had virtually dragged him, using purely moral chains.

'Seems to suit you,' he said, 'rather better than being tea-boy.'

Rikki was brimming over, boatyard smells were strong in his nostrils.

'Tea-boy is all right for some,' he said, airily, and immodestly. 'But someone like me—well, even my mother, you could tell she didn't think much of it, although she didn't say a word.'

'She sounds most forbearing. A most unusual woman,' said Tully, smiling.

'She is very nice,' said Rikki warmly, with the warmth his mother could always kindle. 'If you were to meet her, you would think so too.'

'I'm sure,' said Tully.

'I will take you to our home, you can see for yourself,' said Rikki, hospitably, but recklessly, he himself realised. He had to think hard to extricate himself. 'When I have time,' he said.

'But you do have time,' said Tully, reasonably.

'After your boat is built,' said Rikki rapidly, to divert Tully; and Tully, who was keen on his boat, was diverted.

'When will that be?' he asked.

'You can launch her first of next month,' said Rikki, 'but owing to the necessity for speed the timber is still young, the boat must not be sailed very far until the new season.'

He spoke firmly, handing out orders waterman to landlubber, back in his own element, conscious of his own power, and revelling in superior emotions this exercise bred.

*

64

'When will you ask him over?' enquired Amma, busy with her quern, soft white clouds of risen flour wreathed around her. 'Let me know in good time, and I will prepare a feast.'

For hospitality to strangers in their midst figured cardinal in the village code, as in many another wilderness.

Rikki did not jump at her offer. He knew there was a canyon between her festal fare and what Tully could summon to his board. Prowling round the new city that was rising, he saw the spoils coming in, faraway place-names stencilled on the crates: turtle from the Andamans, teas from Assam and Sri Lanka, quail, lamb, pink-grilled salmon bedded in ice, and lush scarlet berries on rafts of straw—rare and sumptuous fare garnered from around the land, fit to grace an emperor's table.

Neither Tully nor anyone else ate like emperors. These imports were by way of sampling the dishy bait that could be procured, when the time came to lure tourists to Shalimar.

But it was plain to Rikki he could command like a prince if he wanted to.

'All in good time,' he said, eyeing his unworldly mother.

*

'I thought,' said Tully eventually, when the promised invitation failed to materialise, 'you were going to ask me to your home.'

Rikki hummed. He did not wish to reveal the extent of their dilapidations, which were going from bad to worse, and were now spectacular. With prices shooting up every day it was inevitable—unless one had opted into Shalimar. Those who were in could afford far above what they were used to. Those who baulked, like Apu, could not afford even the minimum they had been accustomed to buy.

Tully did not insist. It was not in his nature; or perhaps he had a glimmering.

Meanwhile there were diversions, suggested by Rikki.

'The wrestling, you must see,' he said. 'The great Sandhu is the challenger, there is no one to match him. Let me take you, I'm sure you will enjoy it.'

'What about your family?' asked Tully. He had some notion it would be that kind of occasion.

'They can look after themselves quite easily,' said Rikki, meaning that Tully could not.

It was a novel sensation for Tully, who more usually looked

65

after several hundred men. As he also enjoyed most sports, he accepted the invitation with pleasure.

Chapter Twelve

SANDHU was the champion of the South, winner of innumerable bouts, on the way to becoming All-India champion. When he told people so they believed him. They prepared him for this peak, lavishing love, faith, devotion, money. His fame reflected all the way back to his birthplace, which was given a greater respect than any of the surrounding hamlets. He was a mountainous man, dressed in a leopardskin which left a powerful shoulder bare, who shook the earth when he stamped with a massive foot, and was renowned for the baby-rock treatment he meted out to opponents before finally routing them.

People come from far and wide to support their man. He repaid them amply. He brought his own trainer, his masseur, a camel-load of special sand to sprinkle the testing ground, his own special glory. Two strong men advanced before him, carrying his shining trophies. Two strong men marched behind, one bearing a gold bowl of high lustre, the other a tripod of polished ebony. Settling him down they anointed his flesh with reverent hands, and the ceremony due to their hero. Gleaming and supple he rose to the sound of cymbals and drums, rippled his muscles to warm up the crowd, promised them pleasure, the show of their lives, a kill.

Everyone knew he kept his promises. Everyone who could come, came.

'Is it always like this?'

Tully, squashed in, given a privileged stand plus a garland, surveys the unbelievable mêlée.

'Always, always!'

Rikki bounces with the crowd. Heblekar, likewise invited and honoured, is also bouncing with the people. Tully would feel left out, except that voice and touch are generously ushering him in, whisking him swiftly into the bubbling mixture. In less time than is believable he has abandoned his country's colours, and with it his restraint, and is bouncing with the rest.

'Mr Tully.' A sober note, amidst the revelry.

'Yes?'

'You will break the stand, and injure yourself, if you leap about

67

like that.'

His youthful guide, somehow mindful of the tenderfoot in the flock, on the lookout for folly. The privileged platform is certainly less sturdy than the baked earth on which the others are roistering.

'All right, I'll control myself.'

But it's easier said than done. The air crackles with excitement, it is impossible to dodge such electricity. The two men in single combat generate power, circling, feinting, grappling, locking, tackling. The crowd, not merely roistering but informed, follows every clinch with praise, applause, advice. Its relish for the finer points notches up to ecstasy. Tully shares it. New to the art—lost to its finer points—nevertheless he is swept along with the rest.

'Now watch this.' Rikki breathes, rather than speaks.

The crowd barely breathes, as they come to culmination. This murderous cuddle, in which Sandhu converts his opponent. The man visibly shrinks to the size of a doll as he is lifted and cradled in Sandu's mighty arms. Held and rocked, slowly, faster, helplessly, he is dashed to the ground in the grand finale.

He lies on the earth, thumping out his life. Or so it seems: he, too, has sworn to give value for money.

A deep silence falls as Sandhu advances, plants a foot upon his grounded adversary and simply stands, without humility or vengeance, a neutral god. There is indeed a touch of the divine about the victor, whose mighty foot proclaims for all to see that it could grind this puny opponent into the dust, but refrains.

The gongs begin. Echoes are still clashing as worshippers surge forward to raise up their man. When transfiguration is completed. It is not a man whom their shoulders enthrone, but a ringing bronze deity. Hands clasped, carved eyes unseeing, carved breasts gleaming, he is borne along on this devout, human palanquin.

The smell of sweat flows in his wake, strong, pungent, a potent aroma that works up the passions. The mood begins to turn again, from reverent to earthy. There are bawdy catcalls, whistles, uproarious song. The women have already retired. The men are rioting. There are war-dancers among them, quite clearly, as well as pea-shooters. Round shot flies, stinging hot flesh. Flowers are thrown in wide arcs, leaves, garlands, glinting crystals of sugar-candy.

Money.

Coins are chinking onto the ground, a rain of nickel and silver.

The champion's acolyte speaks.

'In olden days our rajas bestowed silk purses bulging with gold

68

coin,' he says, reproachfully.

'To dancing-girls. And where are the rajas?' says Heblekar, but he obliges, gracefully, he has graceful ways, he un-knots a silk scarf he is wearing and shapes it into a lotus and shakes silver into its cup. Tully copies, bundles up tatty notes, all he has, into a cotton handkerchief and—turned to a fine peony, he can feel the ruddy colour rising—thrusts the clumsy parcel into the great man's hands.

Rikki is equipped too frugally for such flourishes, and anyway it is not his station, but he has already flung silver pieces, no less, into the arena. All is acceptable and duly accepted, but it is the lotus on which the high mark of favour falls, which is borne away resting tenderly on Sandhu's murderous, cupped palm.

*

'Flinging money like a sahib,' said Muthu, awed. Right and left, he had observed. 'You must earn good money,' he said to his brother.

'I told you I did,' said Rikki.

'Yes, he does, and he is not mingy with it either,' said Amma, placidly, folding away the embroidered silk she had worn to the wrestling, with which Rikki had lately presented her.

Whereas Muthu naturally could afford no such flourishes.

Natural it might be, but the thought nagged all evening, and emerged as they were preparing for the night.

'What,' said Muthu, 'are you paid all this money for?'

'For my work,' said Rikki, bashing the lumpy kapok.

'It looks to me like a lot for a little. It looks,' said Muthu, ponderously, 'like easy money.'

It seared Rikki. He thought so too, when he bothered to think at all. He stopped working on his pillow.

'What stops you?' he asked.

'I like to earn my money,' said Muthu.

'Do you think I don't?'

Rikki was furious by now. He shouldered his sleeping mat and marched five steps to the uttermost corner of the hut. He would have slept on the charpoy outside if the wind had not been gusting so strongly. He wished he didn't have to share quarters with a disagreeable clown.

*

First thing next morning he bought a hamper of fruit and went

69

with it to Ramalingam's tent. Ramalingam was sitting outside under a thatched lean-to, breakfasting.

'I know,' he said at once, keenly, morning air always sharpened him up. 'You would like a job, now that the boat is finished.'

Rikki admitted it, while handing over the hamper.

'Let me think,' said the Commissioner, sipping coffee, free hand rummaging in the straw for a ripe papaya or banana to finish off with. 'Yes, I know. Can you swim?' he said.

'Can I—!' The man was batty, or blind. 'I can,' said Rikki, mildly enough, considering.

'Prove it,' said Ramalingam, who was not a Labour Commissioner for nothing.

They fixed up for the claim to be tested.

Some weeks later Ramalingam, duly convinced, sent for Rikki. 'There,' he said.

There was nothing, only a hole in the ground to which he was pointing. It was like Mr Bridie, jabbing at space on his armillary sphere.

'Yes?' said Rikki, trying to be intelligent without feeling it.

'That,' the Commissioner, who was not deceived, explained patiently, 'is the swimming pool. When it is filled, it will be a major attraction in Shalimar. And you,' said he, 'can be life-saver.'

Life-saver, for those in peril in this harmless pit that yawned for water within sight of the sea?

'There is no need,' said Rikki, and he too was patient. 'There are no rocks, no depths, and no currents. If you tried you could not drown in this kind of pool.'

'You do not know the kind of people who will use it. Their stupidity,' rejoined Ramalingam, libellously, 'is monumental.'

'Even so—' began Rikki.

The Commissioner did not wait for him to finish.

'You are made for the job,' he said crudely, looking over the applicant, and taking in various selling features. But then his eyes fell away. For Rikki had an effect, as many were beginning to notice to their cost. Not of turning them into better people; but of glimpsing themselves as they had once been. An earlier Ramalingam, the Commissioner understood, would have been incapable of inserting these meretricious sub-tones into his dealings.

Meanwhile Rikki had reached his own conclusions.

70

'It is not a proper job. Not for me,' he said, not without some high disdain, his shoulders spoke frankly.

It stung the Commissioner. He sent his youthful self packing.

'Don't come bleating to me then, when you next feel like working,' he said, forcefully.

It made Rikki think again. He had been about to leave, but now turned back.

'I must have Tully's permission first,' he said. 'I am his assistant, even though his boat is finished, until he releases me.'

'Do that.' Victory quite restored the Commissioner. 'But don't try any fruit-business with him,' he advised, not without some pity for this neophyte. 'Pipsqueaks like you cannot buy people like him. They are big fish, who only accept corporation-size bait, or else mini token gifts. Take my word,' he said, wise from experiences of his middle years: the sahib concerned had taken him by the scruff and bunted him along the verandah and out. 'There is nothing in-between, except himalayan ructions.'

But, thought Rikki, was not the Commissioner a big fish too? He gave that impression.

'Are you not a big—' he began.

'I am. But I am not so proud. Did not that poor lady, the mother of God, no less,' said Ramalingam, who had a smattering, from Loyola College which he had attended, 'accept the gifts they brought her? Mind you,' he pointed out, 'they were adroitly mixed. Gold and myrrh are kingly, but anyone, even a beggar, is allowed to offer incense.'

In his view fishermen were next door; and in this was not far out, except that fishermen, while penurious, did not beg.

*

Rikki had to enlist the aid of his foster-sister, the cactus thickets being the women's preserve, to secure the mini gift he had in mind.

'Why, have you got a girl?' asked Valli, giggling, showing a full row of small, sharp, pearly-white teeth.

'Never you mind. Just get me the flower,' said Rikki.

'It's not easy, you know. You always get your fingers pricked,' said Valli. 'What will you give me if I oblige you?'

'A kiss,' said Rikki.

'Oh no, that won't do, not a rich boy like you,' said Valli, tossing her plaits, flouncing her skirts—all manner of saucy rejections.

71

'A bottle of scent,' said Rikki.

'Oh no,' said Valli, and stopped her saucy nonsense, her lips were curved and sweet. 'I just wanted to see. I'll do it for you for nothing.'

Armed with the flower Rikki flew round to look for Tully, before it could wilt or something in his sweating hands. He found him at last, bent over one of the scores of machines that laboured for Shalimar. But now, unaccountably, he found himself holding back, seized by a strange reluctance to offer the sweetener.

So he stood, watching Tully work, convinced afresh that he actually loved these metal monsters, considering how often they would work for him after stubbornly resisting everyone else. Now and then he shifted around, because after all he had to deliver.

Tully, busy as he was, felt the presence. And felt it to be squalid, being good at interpreting emanations. And ignored as long as he could, but was presently driven.

'Rikki,' he said, straightening up. 'What are you sidling around like that—like a blessed crab—*for?*'

It revived Rikki. The flower ceased to be anything, except itself.

'A present for you, Mr Tully,' he said gaily, and sprang his surprise, producing the gift he had tucked well away behind his back. 'A flower—it's quite rare, there's only one bloom in each season.'

But there had not been enough time for conversion to be completed.

The flower was a flower, but nothing could have been more obvious than its original purpose. Reversion could not hide that kernel from anyone, except perhaps a novice. Tully was far from.

'You're not, by any chance,' he said, coolly, 'trying to bribe me, are you?'

'No, I'm—I'm not,' said Rikki, chattering a little as he remembered he was. Thoughts that had evaporated, re-formed uncomfortably.

'You were, if you aren't now,' said Tully. 'Why can't you just say what you're after?'

'Nothing,' said Rikki.

And they stood, and Rikki felt himself dwindle in the eyes of another man.

'All right then, I'll tell you,' he said, subdued. He wished, now, he had been open with Tully, as Tully was with him. Instead of trying to buy his permission, and even, it did occur to him, the

72

man himself, and the integrity locked up in the term. 'I have built your boat,' he said. 'The work is finished. But I still take your money, which I do not earn. Now the Commissioner has a job for me, which I cannot take until you release me. It is not a proper job, in my estimation,' he had to add, in all honesty, 'but it will save my face.'

'That is important, of course,' said Tully, eyebrows up. Two arcs: very superior, he could feel.

'Yes,' said Rikki, simply.

Tully considered. Travel round the world, he felt, still somewhat uppish, to find identical lunacies.

In himself too, however. The same honesty that had propelled Rikki into the open was nudging, reminding of face-saving operations of his own.

'Very well,' he said.

The matter disposed of, Rikki was free to remember the gift he had brought.

'Is it not beautiful?' he said, anxiously, holding out the flower.

'It is indeed,' said Tully, accepting the bloom, to Rikki's vast relief.

'It has a nice smell too,' he volunteered, and waited for Tully's reaction; which Tully saw no reason to withhold now. He bent his head and sniffed.

'M-mm, lovely,' he said, as anyone might have done, but it served to firm certain conclusions of Rikki's.

*

'Did he like the flower?' Valli, all agog, came dancing up to meet her brother.

'Whom do you mean?' asked Rikki.

'Tully, of course,' said Valli, with a pirouette.

'Of course he did.' Rikki drew on his accumulating store of evidence. 'He is as human,' he said, 'as you or me.'

Chapter Thirteen

He is a human being like us!

Tully, parked on a fallen tablet with AVALON incisively cut in the stone, virtually heard, yet again, the words of discovery. Chuckled over the hoary old sentiment, issuing mint fresh from each pair of astonished lips as scales drop.

Visibly, in the boy. Eyes questioning, uncertain, opaque behind the topaz, suddenly clearing, admitting him, Tully, into the community.

Why, under the skin he's not that different!

Compliments human beings pay each other. Most, anyway. Though there was one eccentric who held out to the end. This man—crony of his mother's—believed that the natives of Africa never grew up. Treated them like a Victorian papa: kindly, but standing no nonsense from the children. His houseboys loved him. Winked at each other over his head, indulged the old man's notions, conspired to see to it that he went to his grave with his delusions intact.

Not everyone is that lucky. Moments of revelation, thrilling, murderous, lurk round every corner of a foreign strand.

His foreign corner might have been anywhere East of Suez. Crowds, heat, mélange of smells, of races. It was in fact Hong Kong, leasehold bastion to Britain, offshore outpost to China. He, riding in a rickshaw for a lark, swagger stick under his arm, all the aplomb of an officer in a colony of even these tenuous dimensions. A yellow cadaver of a man, calves like shrivelled pears, propelling the bicycle that hauled the contraption.

Paid off at the end of the journey the man hung around as per usual, exaggerating his wheeze, whining for extra. Tully, briefed by old China hands that to yield was fatal ('strip you clean, nearest thing to a plague of locusts, believe me, old boy'), nevertheless found it pleasanter to fork out.

'But I'll bet my last dollar,' he said, white, severe, twenty-one, some salvationist gene up on its hind legs, 'it won't go on food.'

'You win,' said this humorous cadaver, and held out a shameless hand for more money. 'Me need fix,' he said, grinning vilely, vile breath of a ruinous system.

74

And they both stood outside history, watching its workings. Battles fought before either was born. The Opium Wars, which a sizeable slice of Tully's countrymen hazily imagine were waged to put down the odious Chinese opium merchants. Cadaver's history is nil, but he does not need it, he is the living evidence.

Suddenly, from the different poles of their experience, the two innocents converge. Blinking at each other, exchanging confidences.

—Hey, you're a man too!

—Just what I've been thinking!

—Ah, so! So what would *you* do?

—Same as you. Run like hell. Probably same escape chute, since you ask.

Both grinning, one hundred per cent comprehension behind their complicity, while Tully emptied his wallet.

Years since that oriental episode.

Eight years orbiting the world. Landing eventually, as could almost have been predicted, in Avalon. A ruin, begging for restoration, eloquent appeals in every fallen stone impossible to ignore at any age.

'Master Toby! What are you doing there?'

What *should* he be doing, way down a crater, dust in his hair, surrounded by building bricks incomparably superior to anything in the toy-chest?

'I'm building a castle, Nanny.'

'Come along, Toby. It's time for your tea, we've been looking for you everywhere. Yes, you may just plant the little flag on the turret first.'

Poor Nanny, her features gone forever, only her toes remained firmly fixed, in shoes with the black cherry buttons, planted on the edge of the abyss opened by Hitler bang in the middle of London.

Square, fair, inexpensive *au pair* Inge next, though they still hung on to Cook. The Copeland-Tully resplendence flickering, but still enough to provide embers, infinitely warmer than other people's entire hearths, for the sons of a subaltern who had died fighting for his country.

He would never have said so. Almost certainly curled up in embarrassment when posters said it for him. But plainly he believed in, and fought to preserve, his country, in particular its greatness, when that greatness was already on the slide. As others glimpsed, nothing like peeking from abroad to provide these

75

illuminations. Glory waning with loss of empire, a few wisps of moral leadership to provide a fig leaf, the country settling into position as a province of Europe—an offshore island that superior Europeans once doubted existed, and if it did if Caesar was all there, wanting to invade such a miserable land, making a meagre sense only if he was after pearls for his mistresses (assuming his gem-detectors were sound).

Tully smiled. Hasn't thought about Julius in years, not since Gaul-is-divided-into-three-parts was etched with infinite boredom into the lobes of his brain. A visionary, though, whom Copeland-Tullys would have saluted as soul-mate. Same genius in the genre. Building imaginatively, compulsively, one way or another, buildings of one kind and another, some not without grandeur.

Grandeur, unquestionably. Not always the squalid pillboxes of acquisition, subjugation, and intimidation. Not by any means.

Around the globe, then, along with the roads-railways-bridges, a girdle of empire and its edifices: sub-places, citadels, mansions, fortified manors, follies, forts in the Negev, in Outer Mongolia, and residences as delightful as Avalon, with the merest soupçon of bristling castle. Something in the strain, even of that small boy forever constructing turrets out of London rubble—they learnt to look first in bomb-craters and building lots when he went missing.

Tully slid off his perch, picked his way through imposing rubble and up the steps, walked along the terraces and into rooms and out again, inspecting this peach of a ruin. Christened Avalon, built lovingly in the days when India seemed embedded in empire forever like a jewel set in Celtic gold. Falling apart now, the way people do when the reason for being goes missing. Quite a bit of renovating needed here, but these days he has more at his disposal than a spade and a child's pair of hands: all the formidable resources of AIDCORP, in fact.

AIDCORP built briskly, crisply, cleanly as far as possible, not beyond using pre-cast for speed, if asked to, thinking only briefly of men who thought nothing of spending sizeable chunks of life fussing over a single finial; but prepared to, if the money was forthcoming.

Money. Into the modern continuum of time-is-money.

AIDCORP got on with the job. Across the bay it was in full stride. The hill on which Avalon was perched provided ample views. It was like a general that he stood, on a height, looking down on Armageddon. On which they would impose, smoothly and efficiently, a shape and an order that would eventually give a new look to the landscape.

Elsewhere, however, the view that stretched was in a different class, set in different country.

Perhaps it was his giddy situation, but now Tully was pleased to think it could well be his own. Ancestry provided links, the generations that had been conceived and born in the country, it would not be too fanciful if some part of it had entered. Given time, he felt, he could slide in as easily as anyone born—

When the boy began to loom. Rikki, to whom this landscape belonged, whose claim was fuller, more rounded than his could ever be. Into which, being sprung from it, he effortlessly slots. His air, light, views. Rights, grave and nebulous, that they actually write into the dry parchment of title deeds. His landscape.

Tully's thoughts, freewheeling so far, began to revolve around the word. Perhaps, again, it was the somewhat dizzy height that caused the meaning to fluctuate. Not content with externals, it had gone underground to embroil with the interior. Very soon he could not have said, any more than Apu, if it meant places or people; while he veered to the view that landscape could embrace human beings as easily as crags or a headland.

And standing there, absorbed in the interplay, the landscape did seem at one with the boy, it led his thoughts back to Rikki. Warm, sunbrowned, eyes capable of dreaming, hinting at a purity haunting as a country glimpsed in a state of extreme grace, or delirium. Coupling it with honesty as naked and illuminating as himself. Fully capable of asking directly, and taking what he wanted—facets of vice in the average canon, substantiating into virtue like a wafer in a mouth no less, and perhaps no more, innocent than Adam. Utterance shamelessly blatant at times, at others restrained by a fastidious and touching grace.

Even over something as ridiculous and as desperately coveted as a pair of swimming flippers.

Tully, smiling, watches light gathering in a hazy cone over to the East, slowly grows aware that he is not the sole observer. The boy has come up the hill. Keeps his distance and calls, ready for flight if not wanted, looking for welcome, but not pressing a claim.

'Mr Tully?'

'Hello, Rikki. Come on up.'

'Are you sure?'

'Yes. Come and admire the view with me.'

The boy comes, rather shy, walking delicately in this private enclave, stands beside him.

77

'It's nice here,' he ventures.

'I think so.'

'It belongs to you now, doesn't it?'

'Yes. For a spell, while I'm here.'

'On earth, do you mean?'

'Well, that too, of course, but actually I mean here in India.'

'I often come here, you know.'

'I didn't. But you're welcome.'

'Even now?'

'Any time. Don't want you to be a stranger in your own land.'

Rikki melts, settles on the terrace steps preparatory to confiding his past, warmed by it, by the sun which is just lighting up the Copeland marble.

'When we were children,' he said, 'we loved to play on this hill. Sometimes in the casuarina wood, just over there—do you know where I mean?'

'Yes.'

'But only us boys. The girls were afraid, they said it was haunted.'

'Unlikely.'

'Why?'

'Well, perhaps by children. It's a happy place...my mother used to play there, you know.'

'Was her name Sophie?'

'How on earth—?'

'It's cut in the bark. Lots of the trees.'

'I believe she had quite a few admirers.'

'She must have been beautiful.'

Eyeing him, glancing off to something else when his eye is caught.

'This place must have been beautiful, once.'

'I imagine it was, in its heyday.'

'Heyday?'

'At its peak of glory.'

'Must have been a long time ago.'

'It was. Years ago, when my grandfather built it.'

'When it was lived in.'

'Yes, I would say that's fairly important for buildings.'

'It would have been warm then,' said Rikki, touching marble which was only just warming up under the early sun. 'You are going to live here, aren't you?'

'Yes.'

'Straight away?'

'No.'

'Why not?'

'Don't fancy living in a ruin.'

'Do you call this a ruin?'

Walls, after all, are standing, and entire rooms that would keep out the weather.

'Well, I'm spoilt I know,' said Tully, 'but it seems pretty tumbledown to me.'

'Mr Bridie's house,' said Rikki, under some compulsion to tell, 'was forever tumbling down, but he didn't mind. He just lived there. Both of them did.'

'Well,' said Tully, 'people are different, aren't they?'

'I suppose so.'

'I like order,' said Tully, and ran a hand over mortar extruded from layered brick like a slipped disc, squeezing out painfully between vertebrae. His fingertips grated over the crumbly extrusion with a psychic as well as a physical aversion.

'I think, you know,' he found himself saying—oddly, to one who could have little conception of these matters, 'that was one reason, perhaps the only respectable one, why we took over your country, to impose our order on what seemed to us your confusion.'

Indeed this area was virtually unknown to Rikki. He turned to what he knew.

'Mr Bridie,' he said, 'was from your country.'

'Yes. But he seems to have stayed away too long,' said Tully. That ever-present danger, or temptation. 'It alters people,' he said.

Rikki had all but documented the ruinous surface changes that overtook the Bridies, especially towards the end. The inner re-structuring he could only guess at, never having seen the original assembly. That it was shaken, he understood, from what they let fall, the accusations they threw at each other; while still having little idea of the nature of this destructive internal bombardment. Despite all, what mattered to Mr Bridie he had guarded, that much was plain. Somehow in the midst of confusion and decay, he had kept his private recesses, or refuges, intact.

Rikki framed it as well as he could.

'The sap was gone from them,' he said, 'but Mr Bridie's ships—you could have sailed in them, they were so full of life. And the mosaic we made—it was powerful, I see that now.'

Things became clear, with the passage of time. Or perhaps it was the passing of childhood.

'Though at the time,' he said, 'it had a kind of beauty, that was all I could see. If I looked with his eyes.'

'And if you looked with your own?' asked Tully.

'It was his design. I made it for him,' said Rikki. 'It took me a long time, of course I was proud of my work, it was done by my own hands. But sometimes,' he said, 'I could hardly bear to look.'

Sometimes it haunted, the face of a tortured man.

'Why not?' Tully had some sense of edging, unwillingly, nearer to a mystery rooted in him too. Sometimes it brushed, in the terror, or urgency, of separating combatants so closely grappled as to be one.

'There was so much pain,' answered Rikki, re-tracing to bring back the feeling, 'it became like pleasure. But you see, that was what he wanted. It gave him pleasure.'

Silence fell, there on that hill. Nothing stirring, not a blade. A void so empty, it could only create, it was a creating condition. Out of which Tully said:

'What would you have wanted?'

'I don't know,' said Rikki. Childhood was over and far away. 'But if it was now—'

'If it were?'

'I would want my design to give pleasure. . . a different kind of pleasure. It would be a loving design,' he said absently, shoving debris around, stone fragments moving into helix and ammonite shapes on the terrace. 'I'm not sure what exactly, I would have to think about it,'

'Why not,' said Tully, and pursued a rare, impulsive firefly, 'think about it now?'

'What for?' Rikki shrugged. Where was the point? 'The Bridies are dead and buried,' he said.

'But I'm not. I think,' said Tully, thinking exuberantly, 'a mosaic would look quite splendid in Avalon.'

'It would,' said Rikki. 'But—' recovering from this hallucination, 'you don't mean—'

'I do.'

'Really?' Face suffused, longing to believe, belief still suspended.

'Yes. Why not?' said Tully, gently, contemplating Avalon, the immense canvas of this once-loved retreat, one part of which will be delivered into caring hands. 'It's ideal,' he said practically, 'there's enough stuff lying around, it would be criminal not to use it.'

Where, exactly, would be decided later, and jointly.

Chapter Fourteen

SHALIMAR and Avalon, a-building.

In their different ways. Shalimar crisply, with targets to meet at each stage, and bristling with penalty clauses that worked like goads. No one—least of all Tully, with his capital at stake—could moon over it. But he could afford to be pernickety over Avalon. Not quite fussing over every finial, those days were gone; but circumspect.

Shalimar villas were induced birth—some smoothie medico, getting things moving, wanting his weekends uncluttered. Avalon grew, wrapping mother-o'-pearl round its fallen grandeur, in the hands of craftsmen imported by Contractor, closely supervised by Tully.

Rikki, marvelling, but also questing for a site, followed at Tully's heels along the magnificent terraces, down wide, shady verandahs, into and out of lofty, echoing rooms. Touching travertine and chalcedony, wonderingly, their surfaces responding to his hands, repeating their names after Tully. Seeing with Tully's eyes, with a growing clarity.

'You'll be happy, won't you,' he said, 'when Avalon is ready for you.'

'Yes,' said Tully. The cabin palled, no question, but that more was involved than degrees of comfort he accepted. 'The place suits me,' he boiled it down.

Rikki accepted this reduction, but would continue to tease at it for further meanings, in silence.

Picking at his mind, as Tully perceived, in an effort to get to know the man behind.

And vice-versa: this too he admitted.

A two-way deal, getting to know one's fellow. Advancing beyond language to contemplation. Contemplating another human, most complex of beings, each engaged in a voyage of discovery no less strenuous, or ravishing, than a physical adventure. No wonder, then, that the best generals, field or soul, were not merely the hardiest of men, but those most able—or matchlessly gifted—at working through to the silent syllabary of another.

In search of the mind, then. Mind not overfond of letting on, even at its most loquacious. Especially then. Lurks behind the brain, into its substance and forever beyond, intercommunications of infinite subtlety. God, or whoever, was never merely a stunning creator, but a cold, cold-blooded scientist. Man on his quest has to get along with subliminal flashes—a look, a tone, a silence, an air. Eye to these peepholes in the screen which can, with luck, open out to reveal unknown, spreading savannahs.

On this particular morning discoveries included the mundane. They were walking, single file, along a track, shrunk from some original broad plan by invading scrub, that meandered about the Copeland pile.

No purpose in these coils and twists, as far as Rikki could see.

'What do you think, Mr Tully,' he said presently, as they emerged from yet another baffling figure-of-eight, 'they were thinking of, when they made this path that goes nowhere?'

'Pleasure,' said Tully, supplying the answer without difficulty. After all, he was descended from the mind that had devised. 'It's what is known as a Walk.'

'A walk, leading nowhere?' When Rikki walked, it was with a purpose—towards a boat, say, or the beach. Some definite goal.

'If it led anywhere it would lose half its charm,' declared Tully, it seemed self-evident to him. 'It's meant for people to wander in, as the mood takes them,' he explained.

'I see,' said Rikki. Somewhat tight-lipped, but willing for new conceptions to wash over him, while not quite won over. 'Is this for pleasure too?' he said doubtfully, as they came upon a bleak wooden bench, several slats missing, set in a rough embrasure cut in the hill.

'Yes. It's a View,' said Tully, firmly. Here at least he could adduce support. And he pointed out the legend carved in the wood. PROSPECT POINT it read, the letters were faint but visible.

They sat perilously, one at each end to prevent the rickety structure see-sawing, peering at a dense thicket of well-grown cacti.

But under the intensity of their gaze the solid object lost its certainty, its uncompromising outlines wavered and grew fluid; the thicket, insert with splintery sea-blues, dissolved before their eyes to reveal a wide, cut-sapphire expanse of ocean. It could have been a trick of light, or even a reversion to original intention, in which both were involved.

'One can easily see,' said Tully, presently, 'the whole ocean at one's feet, from here. In spite of the cactus.'

'Yes.' Now Rikki was with him. 'Sometimes we see what's there, sometimes what isn't.'

'Perhaps they're two sides of the same face,' suggested Tully.

The same face could look serenely on creation, preservation, and destruction.

'I think they are the same kind of power,' said Rikki.

A power that could play over lesser areas too, raising palaces, or reducing bushes, come to that.

*

It was in the course of some such wanderings that Tully was inspired.

They had walked up the hill to the mansion, empty now, the workmen had gone, a last flare of twilight was touching up the peak. Going up the steps, and crossing the verandah, they came through into a room—like a crystal box, it seemed to Rikki. So full of light and glass, difficult to tell where light ended and glass began—it captured him utterly. Tully recognised a conservatory of sorts; but then some Copeland cavalier demurring, he conceded it was more like a not-so-miniature Kew. It incited him to extravagances of his own.

'This could be the sun-room,' he said, richly, to his captive, but receptive, audience. 'A place where the sun can be properly worshipped.'

Put that way, Rikki saw it immediately; but his recollections, too, were raising objections.

'Mrs Bridie,' he said, 'said people who worshipped the sun were unredeemed heathens.'

She would, poor old duffer, felt Tully of this unknown carpist; but as she belonged, however tenuously, to his own kind, he suppressed the commentary.

'I still think it ought to be the sun-room,' he said, a sentiment with which Rikki absolutely agreed.

This decided, they moved out of the solarium, Tully's mind crammed with pictures of gardens that would bloom, to be viewed with advantage from the sun-room, after the murk of ages had been scraped off the glass, whose crystalline state only Rikki's mind had conjured up. In this mind, now, orchards were enlivening the crystal. From instant seed implanted by Shalimar, whose blossoming results his mother had envied, he virtually saw the ready-grown trees fruiting on the hillside in full view of the

83

sun-room. Or at least melons, ripening on the vines.

When they entered the room that led off the solarium-to-be.

Heretofore both had been capable of skilful conversions, the worst havoc wreaked by time and the elements could be seen as boons in disguise. But this—

'What,' said Rikki, hushed, the circumstances did warrant solemnity, 'could you possibly do with this place?'

It was a room of considerable dolours upon which they jointly gazed. The ceiling was rent. The roof let in light, the wind, past rain, bits of sky. Rusty brown waterstains tear-dropped down the walls. Watery snail trails criss-crossed a depressed floor, a recent downpour had left several puddles.

'This,' said Tully, inspiration once more descending like a dove, 'is going to be the impluvium.'

'Pluvium?' repeated Rikki.

'It's the old name for it. An indoor pool, built to be fed by rainwater,' said Tully.

'Built for the rain to come *in*?' Rikki could hardly believe.

'Yes.'

'Right into the room?'

'It was meant to. They found it refreshing.'

Rikki gaped. 'In our village,' he said, 'there are any number of pluviums. No one feels refreshed. It drives our people frantic.'

They were laughing. The plight of these frantic wretches turned to high comedy. It was left to Tully to rescue them from these lamentable depths, which at length he did.

'But this will be different,' he said, soberly, and could not resist some embedded instinct, whose childish elements he conceded, to show the peasantry what could be done. And he drew, with a toe and puddle water, a courtyard round a pool, with shrubs in tubs, and a fountain.

'You will see,' he said with a flourish, 'how charming it can be made.'

Rikki followed well enough, while his own plan burgeoned. He waited, courteously, until Tully was through before he proposed:

'Round the pool, Mr Tully,' he said, 'I think would be the right place for your mosaic.'

'It would,' said Tully, the possibilities were evident. 'What have you in mind?' he asked, to be amiable more than anything. He was perfectly satisfied to leave it to the boy.

'I don't know yet.' Rikki sought and sat down on a dry upland. Hugging his knees, chin sunk in the bony cusp, eyes brilliant, looking up at Tully. 'I must think about it. There is a lot of thinking to be done.' he said.

Tully could appreciate. Avalon, too, had taken a long time to rise.

Chapter Fifteen

HEBLEKAR observed that Tully was flourishing, and reduced it to some such phrase as the climate agreeing with him. At least he did not develop heatstroke or heat rash, or line up the diocalm tablets on his bathroom shelf—symptoms diffused widely in Delhi's diplomatic coterie, in Heblekar's experience. He, too, was finding it less disagreeable than he had feared. This aboriginal stretch—as viewed from the capital—did from time to time yield surprising bonuses.

'It's nowhere as bad as I expected.' He confessed as much to Tully, whom he had gone to round up for dinner. Tully, with his maps and machines, was apt to be casual.

'What did you expect?' asked Tully, shelving a promising sketch plan.

'The usual discomforts.' Heblekar grimaced. They were all present, and loathed by him. 'But somehow the place makes up. Something about it, isn't there,' he said, 'like—like—' He hardly knew how to give a name.

'Like Eden?' Tully helped.

'Wasn't brought up on your myths,' said Heblekar, 'But yes, there is a quality.'

And as neither could pin down better, they rose to sally forth to dinner.

Dinner, like many another institution, had evolved in Shalimar. At first they had dined exclusively, in a solitary state dictated by dietary vagaries. However, men being social animals, especially in a desert, this faddy splendour was soon ditched. Soon there was a large, circular, airy tent, and slung from ingenious AIDCORP props a brand-new punkah of local manufacture, and to operate it a lissom punkah-wallah recently graduated from the ranks of fishermen. Under this canvas, and waited on by servitors minutely briefed as to what dish for whom, they dined relaxed and in something like comfort. Even Sitharam, most particular of mortals, succumbed, finding the mess tent preferable to chewing on his own on brinjals and rice in his tiny, blistering-hot corrugated cabin. Heblekar might claim to spy a fly, or the odd grain of sand in his soup; but he too was near-content. As for
86

Contractor, he flowered, more or less silently as was his way, in company.

The atmosphere was conducive. All-male, free and easy, the flavours of a regimental mess were established in no time at all by the lieutenant, Ranji. The aura clung to the young officer, lately and heartbreakingly snatched from his regiment. He imparted an ambience which his fellows found agreeable.

Ranji too. He rejoiced in juvenile bawdy, which had them in stitches, in a way that the raconteur found eminently satisfying. Or he would tell, richly, of battles, especially like Cannae, in which the imperial might had taken a thrashing; discovering in Heblekar, and even Tully, an interested and imperturbable audience. Or Cyrus would listen with an admirable patience as he described, with the aid of chessmen, the tactics behind the scattering of the Persian hordes at Issus...Only sometimes, despite congenial company and the military derring-do, the lieutenant would think, wistfully, of the pleasure of ladies' night, and the regimental band playing, and the delight of asking some charming gazelle in organza for the next cha-cha-cha.

This too he freely confessed, his was a frank nature. And in doing so touched a chord.

All of them missed their wives. All of them were accustomed, from the nature of their operations, to the absence of women in greater or less degree. All of them, fulfilled by exacting jobs, understood such fulfilment was fundamental to their nature, even ranked first. It could not prevent them yearning for their women.

'It won't be long,' said Contractor, a trace huskily, and put down his knife and fork, and fell silent. Sometimes, when he thought of his wife, his throat would go dry, and he would feel himself drained of vitality. Especially since the flight of their daughters he depended on his beloved Zavera. She poured life back into the denuded pitcher.

'Soon the villas will be ready,' Sitharam took up for his chief, whose unfailing courtesy to his thin-skinned, tremulous deputy had been repaid with an unshakeable devotion. 'And then the ladies can join us,' he said brightly, and sipping his Vimto was glad for others' sakes. He himself had no great hope. His shy wife, by comparison with whom Sitharam was a lion, could seldom be persuaded to sample the hurlyburly of AIDCORP life—as she called it, her toes curling up at the very thought.

'Well, roll on,' said Heblekar, heartfelt. In his case there was not only an adored wife, but an adorable infant, from whom the call of duty had plucked him. Or so he liked to think, although only stern representations from the parents-in-law had prevented the infatuated Heblekar from installing the pair in a tent. In lieu, he dotted his living quarters with snapshots, and photographs framed in silver, rosewood, and (lately) wood from the breadfruit tree fashioned into supports by the local carpenter.

Whereas Tully, who also had a wife, had merely a snapshot which he kept in his wallet. This he now produced, in view of the conversation, and passed to Heblekar.

'Your wife?' Heblekar took the dog-eared thing, and studying the subject, strongly felt it deserved better. 'She's beautiful,' he said.

'Yes, she is rather,' said Tully, stuffing the snap back in his wallet in a way that made Heblekar resolve to commission the carpenter straight away.

'Will she be joining you?' he asked.

'Corinna?' said Tully. She would come. Would she stay? He hardly knew. Only this time he hoped. More than anywhere else, at any other time, it had become important to him that his wife should understand, and share, what was of value to him. 'I very much hope so,' he said.

Then the conversation became general. Heblekar had plans to inveigle the Minister, when Phase 1 was completed: his august presence would give the venture a boost. Ranji, listening, was already composing the copperplate At Homes to summon certain slim beauties to grace the occasion. Contractor hoped aloud his wife would have arrived by then, to add a woman's inimitable, finishing touch. Which made them all chuckle. Masters of the meticulous, each aspect of their work necessarily brought to a high finish, all of them knew that their own, men's, touch easily outclassed any woman's. But they happily paid the fair sex these compliments.

*

As the building advanced, and the wilderness retreated, their thoughts turned more and more to their wives. When the longings became an ache, they turned to exercising the muscles, and so forth.

At eventide Tully would come upon Heblekar, standing upside down outside his cabin, practising yoga, or sublimation. Or Heblekar would perceive Ranji, in white buckskin breeches and glossy riding boots, mounting a one-man expedition to deprive some protesting yokel of his scraggy pony. Or ordering the labour as if they were troopers, himself a resplendent captain of hussars.

'What for?' he dared to ask one day, though usually he avoided tangling. 'I mean, it's just a village,' he said, narrowly avoiding being hypnotised by a deal of dangling and sparkling accoutrements.

'What for? Esprit de corps,' said Ranji, informatively, but somewhat scornfully, as he rather doubted it would mean much to a civilian type.

Whereas for Tully it was swimming, until they could get round to cricket.

Chapter Sixteen

WITHIN hours of arriving Tully had, as it were, appropriated the sea for his own. He all but saw it as a duty, as an islander, to steep himself in it, convincing himself and anybody he could buttonhole of the special relationship between Englishmen and the sea, whose summons they were as duty-bound as lemmings to obey.

Up in his eyrie (by now precariously habitable) he heard the irresistible summons: the sea calling, clear as a bell. Tully answered religiously, with punctilio, every morning. Up each dawn, stripped for action, towel streaming over a shoulder like a scapular, feet barely touching the ground, the earnest religious streaked down to the shining sea.

This particular dawn it turned out different. Zooming down to the path, gulping in ozone in great draughts, sea-dog Tully cannoned into dawn-riser Rikki who was freewheeling up.

Ankles, arms, towel, net, entangled forever they fell. Objects rolled, strange, bewildering football shapes bouncing down the surprised hill. Gourds and greenery, it seemed to Tully's unbelieving eye, seized from the rampant exuberance of a Kabuli market: but was he, perhaps, concussed?

The boy's words, however, carried perfectly clearly.

'Mr Tully,' he said, severely, 'why can't you look where you're going?'

'If it comes to that,' said Tully, equally severe, not even ashamed of a slanging match of such childish proportions, 'why can't you?'

'How could I,' said Rikki, exasperated, impatiently kicking free of fish-net, twisted vines, clods of earth torn from balled roots, and other such items. 'How *could* I, carrying this load?'

'What *is* it?' said Tully, baffled.

'It *was*,' said Rikki, pointedly, 'your orchard.'

'Orchard? Here?' Tully's gaze, wanting the insights afforded by crystal rooms, wandered over tussocks of tough dune grass, over slopes liberally seeded with rocks, among them hewn boulders bearing traces of whitewash, once boundary stones to the Copeland holding. 'I don't think,' he said mildly, 'it's possible.'

'It is. You agreed,' accused Rikki. 'Have you forgotten?'

'I said orchard?'

'You did,' said Rikki, inner eye bent on various hummocks over which Tully's pumpkin and watermelon vines would sprawl.

Those that were left.

He would, he saw clearly, outer eye roving over broken fronds and greenery littering the slope, have to beg some more off his mother. And pay her for these further inroads into the family foodstore.

'Do you mean,' said Tully, catching the drift of these mumblings, 'you robbed your own patch?'

'Of course not. I asked my mother,' said Rikki indignantly. 'Besides, they will grow again. My mother is good at growing things.'

'But meanwhile?' Tully, having nosed around, had some idea of local living.

'I paid her. She can afford to buy in the market more than she ever grew,' said Rikki. 'Anyway, she *said* take.'

'I expect you twisted her arm,' suggested Tully.

'I did not,' said Rikki. He had not laid a finger. 'I just asked her,' he said.

Tully let this pass, to move on to the more obvious. Or what should have been.

'Orchards need watering,' he pointed out, thinking of the solitary well that just about supplied the mansion. 'Have you considered that?'

Rikki had. He had in mind for the raising of this vital fluid certain machines in the AIDCORP armoury, whose workings had particularly fascinated.

'You have water-pumps,' he said.

'So we have. But pumps without water,' said Tully, patiently, to this peasant, 'are mighty useless things.'

'I know. But see what I have brought you!' said Rikki.

And a smile of seraphic quality overspreads his countenance as he produces the forked twig and hands it over to Tully.

What is known in the trade as a divining-rod, in which Tully has about as much faith as in alchemy.

'Does it work?' he said, doubtfully.

'Does it not!' said Rikki, glowing with faith. 'The dowser makes a very good living, *all* the wells around here, for when the river goes dry... He didn't want me to have his dowsing stick,' he said, 'only I'm a friend, so he had to be obliging.'

*

Tully took his time over it. When he finally allowed himself to be persuaded he alternated between marvelling at himself, bastion of AIDCORP, placing himself in the hands of this terracotta boy, and the unusual equation which made the working of some highly sophisticated machinery dependent on the twitchings of an unimpressive twig.

They requisitioned a whole morning, one Sunday, for divination.

The two diviners are prowling, both deploying their twigs with fervour, but one of them somewhat deficient in the necessary faith, the other a trifle languid. Coming up for noon by then, and it seems as if they have been plodding over this arid stretch forever.

'On a day like this,' began Rikki, presently.

'Well?' said Tully, resolutely adjusting the vivid neckerchief he was sporting, which, somewhat like a pith helmet, had assumed the quality of a defiant badge.

'It's a good day for fishing, that's all,' said Rikki.

'I've never been a fisherman,' said Tully.

'You could be. I would teach you,' suggested Rikki.

'Perhaps I'll take time off for lessons, one of these days,' said incautious Tully.

In a flash this youth, archetypal native, has downed tools and is lounging on a convenient hummock as a preliminary to inducting him.

'Not now!' snapped Tully, wiping sweat off his brow.

'Why not now? Mr Tully,' said Rikki earnestly, 'you look hot.'

'I am hot. But I believe—' yanking, hard, he isn't going to let this indolent underling get away with anything, '—in doing things properly, one thing at a time. Come on, up.'

The boy rises, clearly amazed by this single-minded ferocity, unruffled by rough handling. 'All right,' he says sweetly, 'but you're tired, I can see that. You sit and rest. I'll look for your spring.'

And does, while Tully squats, simmering, on the vacated hummock. Up and down, like a tranced sheep.

'Look,' he says presently, softly, not crowing though he is fully entitled. His twig is dipping strongly.

'Water?' breathes Tully, coming out of his trance, preparing to be thoroughly ashamed.

Rikki refused to permit it.

'Water,' he confirms, beaming ear to ear, his pleasure clearly arising less from confounding doubting Thomas than from pleasing his tart employer.

And they stood, so pleased with each other and the outcome that there was no more to be said, but both heard the waters bubbling in the spring. So much so that Sitharam had to stomp a little, and clear his throat, to gain attention.

'Mr Tully,' he said, puffing slightly, he had found it a stiff climb. 'Mr Heblekar's compliments, and I am to tell you the Minister is able to come.'

'The Minister?' Tully blinked, still in his watered orchard. Nor, emerging, had he any great use for ministers and ministries. 'What for?' he demanded.

'What for?' Sitharam blinked too. 'He was invited, sir.'

'Oh ah yes, I remember now. Fine. Great. So glad,' said Tully, in accents of ringing truth, where *can* he have perfected such art but in Albion? 'So glad he is able to come.'

'Yes. It is an honour. He is coming on the seventh of next month,' said Sitharam, blissfully unaware and happy, 'when Phase 1 is completed.'

'Let's hope it will be,' said Tully.

'It will, Mr Tully. Shalimar schedule is split second to contract. It is going like,' said Sitharam, and took flight with the lieutenant's aid, 'a military clock.'

'So far.' Tully entered a caveat.

'By God's will,' said Sitharam, marvelling that he had to be reminded, and by a Westerner at that.

And took himself off, spectacles flashing, slightly roly-poly down the hill, to harry the female labour force that, earth baskets balanced on its head, in line formation irresistibly reminiscent of sacrificial processions to Tully, is bringing in humus and loam in which Shalimar's instant gardens can flourish.

Chapter Seventeen

T H E Minister would have thanked them, and politely regretted his inability. Invitations came by the cartload, he could not accept them all. Then certain names were brought to his attention.

Heblekar. Scion of a family whose head, the Dewan, had come laden with books for the Minister, then languishing in prison. He had not, of course, been Minister then. He was a gaolbird, and the book bearer was en route for high if uneasy office in the Principality; and both had lamented each other's lot. Yes, something was owed, if only for these priceless gifts.

And Tully.

The Minister retrieved the invitation from his Out tray and studied the signature which might (almost) have been familiar; and felt a turmoil—was it really yesterday's? He could hardly believe, it boiled up so strongly. But presently subdued it, and turned to the alert young man who was standing by for instructions.

'Consular, did you say?' he questioned, though it was hardly necessary.

'Yes, sir. Grandson, both sides,' confirmed the efficient private secretary.

'Accept,' said the Minister, briefly, and named a date when he would be touring the district.

*

Contractor wrote off at once to his wife.

Our villa is ready. I think you will find it comfy. Please come soon.
Cyrus. SWAK.
P.S. The Minister is coming.

This somewhat string-of-sausage prose might have been a love-sonnet, as far as Zavera was concerned. She placed the letter by the crinolined porcelain lady on her dressing-table, and took it up again a dozen times to re-read, although by second reading she had it off by heart; and now and then gave a peck to the yellowish re-cycled paper. Then when these waves had subsided she sat,

94

pink and flustered, thinking about the hundred-and-one things she had to do. Because she was not only rejoining her husband. She would also be supervising, if not running, the Shalimar complex, including the hotel-to-be. She would nurse them along until they were flourishing concerns, as she had already done with other AIDCORP ventures, before handing over the orderly reins. It was in recognition of these services that Boyle had once again proposed, writing all the way from—Oman, was it? Zavera could not remember, but would not have dreamed of not obliging.

It meant there were these hundred-and-one things to do.

Consequently Zavera's cavalcade barely avoided bumping into the Minister's.

Whereas, therefore, she had fully intended to conduct the great man round, it was Zavera herself who had to be given a guided tour.

*

If the Minister was intrigued enough to undertake the awkward journey, Tully too was beginning to muse, having progressed beyond his first healthy, antipathetic response to bureaucracy. What would he be like, this man in power—elected to his position of power by the people, unlike, say, Copeland-Tullys, whose immense power had rested upon their own convictions, unsustained by a single popular vote? Would this man know? Would he care to bring it up?

Presently he tackled Heblekar, while acknowledging that an effort of imagination would also be required of him.

'What's he like? A flipping old VIP,' replied Heblekar, with the cheerful irreverence of any civil servant for a Minister. Then he saw, by the way Tully continued to loom in the doorway, that it would not do. It was even, he allowed, not quite fair.

'Well, he was what used to be called a troublemaker, got shoved into prison for it. He spent a good part of his life there,' he said.

'Is he that old?' said Tully.

'Yes,' said Heblekar, glad that the point had been taken without his having to spell anything out. 'As old as the hills,' he expanded.

Which, as Tully duly noted, might well provoke predictable, perhaps inevitable, reactions.

Meanwhile Shalimar went blithely ahead with its preparations. Flowers bloomed. Specks were dusted off the brand-new, unsullied pastel villas. The electricity was functioning well, so well that illusions of grandeur flourished—namely to illumine the entire

95

complex, whose boundaries were defined by the engagingly simple process of planting stakes, to which coloured lights could be strung with a corresponding ease. There was to be a band—courtesy of Ranji's comrades; and comrades too had been dragooned into lending support, and young beauties enticed...The lieutenant inspected minutely, and issued crisp orders, and where he could not, dropped hints of the extreme desirability of at least a modicum of elegance.

He need not have fretted. All were prepared to take trouble, every rung from executive down.

Rikki was as anxious as anyone, once he realised he would occupy, as life-guard and waiter, a position of some prominence. Having inspected his wardrobe, he soon concluded he had nothing fit. He approached the Commissioner, but that man was a realist.

'Who cares what you wear?' he said.

Well, Rikki did; and said so.

'Then wear a shirt and your usual,' said the Commissioner, and flicked him away rather as if he was a tiresome housefly.

Certainly Rikki was made to feel. It did not deter him from persisting, though he carefully chose his next target, and what he assumed was a propitious moment.

'Mr Tully,' he broached the matter. 'I have nothing to wear. For the Seventh,' he clarified, that being the date on which energies were beamed.

Tully heaved a sigh. It was a Sunday. He believed in Sundays, for acquiring an all-over tan, and other such important matters.

'Wear what you're wearing,' he advised.

There was silence, of a kind. It oppressed Tully. This soundless whingeing, he felt, but was not going to do anything about it, it became clear to Rikki.

'What I'm wearing,' he said hollowly, and with utter truth, 'is next to nothing.'

Tully shifted a shade impatiently, a bit like a petulant Diogenes, he himself realised. But it is true that Rikki's shadow was keeping the sun off his body.

'One dresses for the climate. Next to nothing is right for the climate,' he asserted.

Annoyingly, in Rikki's opinion. Though he often practised what he preached—unbuttoned shirts, or none at all, and now lolling, in nothing but a cod-piece, in a deckchair on the beach. But in his cabin were cases stashed full of clothes, as Rikki had seen, whereas his own choice—. Going over the three darned shirts, Rikki all but wished he had not spent his savings (all but the hoard reserved for his boat) on a wristwatch, and that silk for his mother.

'I suppose,' he said gloomily, for he was not that keen on the khaki stuff, 'I could borrow one of the peon's costumes.'

'For heaven's sake!' Tully stopped lolling. 'Here you are,' he said, and sacrificed his pillow, or rather his discarded shirt which had been pressed into this service.

'For me?' Rikki, fielding expertly, held the rumpled shirt against his collar-bone and smoothed out the folds. 'Are you sure?' he asked.

'Yes, if you like it,' said Tully, ruffled. It was his hair, and perhaps also he missed his pillow.

Rikki did like it. Tully had not yet had time to mangle the thing, as he usually did, into looking like a labourer's singlet. Though buttons as usual were missing—Rikki saw he would have to cajole his sister. But the quality of the cotton was unmistakable.

'I like it very much,' he said. 'And—' by now he was into the shirt, 'it fits me very well.'

'Good,' said Tully.

'I will,' said Rikki, revolving, the shirt-tails were flying, 'wear my quartz watch as well.'

'Yes, do,' said Tully.

'And my flippers,' said Rikki, producing his much-treasured gift, which accompanied him wherever he went.

'If you do,' began Tully. It would make him look hideous, like a flatfooted platypus if not worse. Why, he wondered fleetingly, were human beings bent on inflicting such gratuitous violence on themselves? Pink hair, or European women gauntly essaying saris. Or one saw Eastern charmers, incongruous in jeans, unspeakable viewed from behind. 'If you do you will trip over your own feet,' he said instead, being good at persuasion, which involved following a fairly sound instinct he had for detecting the human chinks in armour.

Rikki had no intention of falling and making a spectacle. In fact he had been practising his waiter's walk, with wine glasses balanced on a tray, as Tully had observed.

Chapter Eighteen

AND, on the seventh, there they all were dressed up in their very best; the Commissioner in terylene, Contractor in tussore silk, Tully in—

Heblekar has not seen anything like it, not since Bombay: corduroys suave, slinky roll-neck, shoes polished, hair gleaming, a gleam that suggests no less than a curry-comb, after months of living rough.

'My-my, pretty,' he says.

'Not done so badly yourself,' returns Tully, slightly stunned by Heblekar, who has abandoned his frayed Levis and floats, very Indian, very graceful, in a cloud of pure white mull with resplendent gold edgings.

'But the palm, don't you think, must go to Cyrus,' says Ranji, handsomely overlooking his own red-and-gold military splendour.

Cyrus blushes and disclaims. 'The ladies,' he says, and transfers the compliment with a coy little wave to the newly-arrived contingent in butterfly gauzes.

When the VIP responsible for all these convulsions was spotted bowling along the autobahn (as they called it) on the last leg of the journey. They moved forward in a body to greet the Minister.

So this was a casualty of empire, thought Tully; and would tread with care, until he discovered how scarred.

This austere patrician, slender-boned, silver-haired, an aquiline nose, an air of stillness, a friable quality to the bones giving false clues, something more reliably suggesting strength in that still containment. But outwardly an old, frail man, in a Nehru coat buttoned up to the neck, an ascetic black garment that supplied the only sober note in their galaxy.

Men like him, felt the Minister, as he singled out the Englishman. Men much like him, clad in dazzling white duck perhaps, rather than these corduroy casuals; and there would have been a cocked hat, or at very minimum a solar topi. Same authority, minus the power, other than what was on display, or could be deduced from the rising complex.

When even as he advanced along the strip of red carpet the

98

Minister froze—some part of his interior.

Same breed, and the same impulses animated this man too, to build, to tidy things up, to shatter and put together again as he thought fit, a fitness implanted into other minds so as to present as an original conception.

When all these sinister thoughts of casualties and implants were swallowed up as the AIDCORP reception party meshed politely with the ministerial entourage; or at least they shifted onto lesser planes of obsession; and they walked en bloc and amiably towards the dais from which the Minister was to deliver a short, if obligatory, speech.

This dais, custom-built, decked in flowers, had been wheeled to the little cobbled square—they were beginning to call it the piazza—in the middle of Shalimar, and thoughtfully provided with a pair of shallow steps and a sturdy handrail, in addition to the microphone. The party ascended safely, and had arranged itself on the rostrum as if for a group photograph, when the lieutenant, whose moment had come, gave the signal. Drums rolled, flags unfurled, and the regimental band crashed into the national anthem.

All stood—not least the Englishman, as the Minister duly noted, and was appeased in what he considered gross, but irrepressible, regions of the soul. For only yesterday—it was surging up again—such rites had taken place in an occupied country and participation had been less than voluntary. Ah yes, those yesterdays, and the contrasts with the present! Sweet in the nostrils, perhaps intemperately so, the old man felt, in one whose youth had long been left behind. Here the Minister clouted his intemperate spirit; but could not control the spiked libation that poured like a powerful balm over those ancient bruises. He was glad to see Tully on his feet.

Tully was aware. The charge had winged him. Something there, he phrased it to himself, and took care to stand to attention almost as rigidly as Ranji.

But then, the times had given him practice.

Been around, as Tully would say, to darkest corners of the globe, or erstwhile provinces of haughty empires, where, now, the chrysalids are thrusting up to imago: at their proudest, most vulnerable, most touchy, in ominous display beneath glistening casings. Tully has a softness for the genus, which makes him willing to meet its demands, however way-out they seem. To understand is to oblige.

It was not difficult, then, to emulate that stickler, the lieutenant.

99

Indeed, by now a guardsman could not have faulted Tully.

Obliging, and prepared to be, the Minister observed, as he began his speech.

Ladies and gentlemen, friends—the diplomatic phrase deftly embraced management, labour, and several scores of guests, not all of them invited (some had come from quite far up-coast and inland). Phrases, soft as flannel, rolled over the assembly. Great pleasure . . . bid our guests a hearty welcome . . . benefits of tourism to the economy . . .

And certain assurances being owed to minorities, he gave them.

I am sure I speak for all my countrymen when I say we shall spare no effort to extend to all our friends from overseas that courtesy and hospitality to which strangers in our midst are entitled, irrespective of colour, race, or creed. That is a tradition—not ours alone, but also, he said gently, *a hallmark of civilisation, of which I trust we shall not be found to be wanting.*

When goblins began to tweak.

Whatever may be our own experiences elsewhere, he found he had to add; and could not but glance, being only human, from the corner of an eye at the hairy representative of racists beside him to see if he would squirm, just a little.

It did not even occur to Tully. Under the woad, in the course of his overseas travels, he had of necessity grown a skin like an armadillo. Besides, he had a fair notion, the ministerial cupboard would have its quota: which cupboard could swear to housing no skeletons? If he wished, he too could rattle. Tully shrugged, imperceptibly enough, but it was enough.

Obliging, but holding his own, the Minister decoded; for the years of necessity had rendered him, too, sensitive to such nuances.

Equilibrium accordingly returned, since the duellists had laid down their weapons, or at least retired with equal honours. And in this they were aided by Sitharam, at whose instigation a mechanical device, disguised as an umbrella, had been hoisted up over the rostrum; which now let fall a shower of rose-petals.

It was the signal for the next item in the agenda. The Minister stepped down, and supported, not only for show, by solicitous, smart young aides, and escorted by a platoon of Shalimar upper strata, began his inspection of the complex.

It was, basically, a feat of imagination: to leap from rudiments to the glory to come. To discern the Asoka, the hotel already ringingly named, in a collection of skeletal steel to which the Commissioner was directing attention. Or fountains where a trickle spouted from a hastily assembled basin. Or the rills that Contractor planned would flow through these pleasure grounds, in response to a beloved wife's Persian leanings. Yet, if he heard the waters plashing, he was not alone. All paid tribute, in their different ways, to what was essentially a flowering of the will. It blazed, against an incomparable backdrop of ocean.

'You have done splendidly, Mr Sitharam. All this is quite delightful,' declared Mrs Heblekar, warmly. She was rather delightful herself, in a lemon chiffon sari and a wisp of blouse that set off a bare, slender midriff to perfection.

Sitharam was overcome, by praise and the young enchantress.

'It is nothing,' he gulped.

'But it is! You must have worked like Trojans,' breathed Mrs Heblekar.

Sitharam was unsure about this race, but knew he had laboured mightily.

'We have,' he said simply, 'all worked hard.'

The Minister, too, admired the evidence of industry and the imagination as ardently as anyone could have wished; but was concerning himself with one particular aspect.

'I trust, Mr Tully,' he addressed the stranger in their midst, 'you have not found our country too, what shall I say, intractable?' Many did, to his knowledge. It drove them up the wall.

'Not at all,' said Tully, cheerfully. 'In fact—' brushing stray rose-debris from his shoulders, 'I—enjoy being here.'

'But then you are what one can, can one not, without being too literal, call an old India hand?' suggested the precise Minister, with informed precision.

'One can indeed,' agreed Tully. 'But—' smiling, spreading, the Minister saw, ingenuous, rather fine hands; eyes of a deep, remembered blue, and this too was coming back strongly; '—what can one do? One's progenitors... inveterate travellers, down to the last man. Pirates too, given half a chance. But who wouldn't? I mean, it is an irresistible combination.'

It was, put that way.

The Minister was moved to smile, and also to admire the calibre of a protagonist who would never surrender wholesale, or abjectly,

101

but always with reason. While his own mind, he admitted to himself, was proving less felicitous, and much less controlled than usual. It darted, and fixed upon aspects he would have preferred to leave alone. At one stage it swooped on the fishing settlement—not the squalor, that was inevitable; but certain deficiencies that should have been remedied.

'You see, Mr Tully,' he found himself saying, or accusing, 'It is not too easy, to do all that needs doing in our country.'

'No. Not when there's as much to do as there is,' agreed Tully, who was not blind.

'Would you say so?' said the Minister, curiously.

Was it craftily? wondered Tully. The prison cell continued to unsettle him. As he could not be sure, he answered simply.

'It's evident. It must be,' he said, 'one hell of a problem, shifting the sludge of centuries.'

Centuries? It acknowledged some division of the blame; and encouraged the Minister to vanity. But he was also needling, he recognised. For whatever reason, perhaps goblins, the impulse would not rest.

'We have not, I am happy to tell you, Mr Tully,' he said, somewhat flatly, 'suffered a famine, of undue severity, since Independence.'

'More than we can say,' said Tully, who saw no reason not to, and besides, he like the Minister was well informed. 'Half a dozen whoppers in our day. Our Civil Service ought to have been carpeted. Would have been, anywhere else.'

'You would say so?'

'Certainly.'

They walked on. The Minister had no more darts to hurl, or possibly the goblin contingent had been sent packing.

So far Heblekar had hovered, in case. Now he saw the mood was set fair—or at any rate that Tully could look after himself—he detached from the party to escort Mrs Contractor at her request.

So far from it being a social ramble, however, as he had frivolously supposed, it was turning out to be touring with a purpose, and in depth.

They have already inspected the store-rooms. The kitchens are now under scrutiny. It is the hub, as Zavera well knows, and is determined to impress upon her flighty escort who has actually proposed to by-pass.

'It is most important,' she says, halting him at the doors. '*No* enterprise can succeed, if kitchens are not up to standard. They
102

are, Mr Heblekar, vital.'

'Oh, absolutely,' says Heblekar, to whom kitchens are a complete mystery, which he leaves to his wife and the servants.

'Absolute cleanliness is also essential. That is why,' says Mrs Contractor, as she marches him in, and mesh doors twang to behind them, 'I am glad to see there is wiring against bugs.'

'Yes. Good move,' says Heblekar.

'Yes. Wire screens are vital in the tropics. But Indians, Mr Heblekar,' says Mrs Contractor cosily, as she can to one who, though an Indian, she can see is civilised. Civilised Indians, every bit as much as Parsis, are among Zavera's best friends. 'Indians *will* neglect the Detail, you know, Mr Heblekar!'

'I know. Our people do have that weakness,' says weak Heblekar, hoping that no one will overhear this treachery.

'One bug and you can start off an epidemic,' says Mrs Contractor, round-eyed, solemn as an undertaker. 'Then where will you be?'

Heblekar hasn't the slightest. He shakes a despairing head, and grasping an elbow firmly pilots his charge away to the refreshment tent where others can share the burden.

The tea-tent, or rather marquee, was splendid. Ramalingam had gone off to a city not unused to splendour to procure it, since the village awning was now mangy beyond endurance.

A tent à la Tamburlaine, as Tully had already remarked, it matched its mood perfectly to the monarch, otherwise the Minister. The stout, lurid canvas would easily have repelled the hordes of Christendom. The silken underbelly, of a rich burgundy hue, lulled one whose musings had returned him to a bare prison cell...In this atmosphere it was not long before strange conversations were wafting across to Heblekar, still unshakeably involved with Zavera.

'I remember,' the Minister was saying to Tully, with whom there was also an unshakeable involvement, 'His Excellency— Gilbert Tully, was it not? known in certain circles as the filbert—'

'The cultivated cob, also known in family circles as our nutty grand-pop,' Tully was revealing family legendry, which should have been decently veiled, if Heblekar was hearing aright.

'Now he—' the Minister was clearly enjoying himself. '—did not care, Mr Tully—indeed, I may say was most reluctant!—to sign the order for my detention. I had almost to persuade him, in

103

order to protect him from top blimps in Delhi!'

Ah, heady days! The air is almost iridescent.

Heblekar would have liked to loiter here, but is still in thrall to Mrs Contractor.

'Do you not think, Mr Heblekar,' she says, a hand on his sleeve to secure attention, 'we could arrange a little sport, like clock-golf, for example, for the ladies? Since there is cricket for the gentlemen.'

'Is there?' It is news to him.

'There will be.' Zavera understands the ways of men. 'So should there not be something for the fair sex?'

Heblekar is mumbling—not up to him, not his brief, of course all in favour, but—. When his wife takes pity.

'Everything,' she says, her lily hues turned rosy over her Kola. 'Everything is here, it is a masterpiece of planning.' And lavishes a tender glance on her beleaguered husband.

'Except one thing,' says Mrs Contractor.

'What can that be, my love?' asks her husband, anxiously, and lovingly.

'A Tower of Silence,' says Zavera, addressing the pagan Heblekar, whom she cannot expect to be *au fait* with such matters. 'It is most important for our Zoroastrian community.'

'One hopes there will not be many fatalities,' says pale Heblekar, 'among our Zoroastrian visitors.'

'But should not one plan for contingencies? Although there is controversy,' Zavera frankly admits, 'if that is the best method of disposing of our dead. Some persons believe diseases can be spread, if the vultures drop pieces of the corpses. Such nonsense! Don't you think, Mr Heblekar?'

'What do you think?' Heblekar bags Tully, as a Western neutral, to referee.

'Think about what?' Tully is still in the nutty past.

'About whether Towers of Silence are hygienic.'

'I have never known a country breed problems of such quintessentially Euclidean quality,' says Tully, and beams upon Mrs Contractor, convincing her that seldom has she met such an extraordinarily attractive and sensible young man.

All were happy, including Tully, although he could have wished for his wife to be present. The villas were ready, other wives had joined their husbands. But he had learnt to be philosophical. Corinna was not predictable. She would arrive, and depart, as it

104

suited her restless temperament.

*

Rikki, meanwhile, after an admiring glance at the marquee in passing, had taken up his designated post. This was at the outdoor pool, now filled, to which the guests would be ushered at dusk for a breath of fresh air and drinks.

'Which you can serve,' said the Commissioner to his willing labourer, with the happy air of a man conferring favours bent round to benefit himself. 'You have tea-stall experience, and I will arrange a crash course in bar service. It will save searching for another waiter.'

So now he stood, the graduate, arranging glasses on the loaded trolley, chopping unnecessary limes to pass the time, which had stuck. Now and then he strolled, bare-soled on the turquoise tiling that bordered the pool, asserting his role of life-saver that shared with the limes a certain unnecessary quality. For he still could not conceive that anyone would need saving from these clear depths, while continuing to be proud of the role that swimming prowess, and physique, and doubtless his bar technology, had secured for him.

He was engaged, fastidiously, and cheating only a little, in apportioning due weight to each of these ingredients in his success, when he became aware he was not alone. He was not, of course: the ministerial entourage alone amounted to scores, even if for the moment they were ensconced. But the lone horseman riding up the beach encouraged a sense that here on the edge of the sea only two of them existed. Dismissing this romance, arisen from his somewhat lonely station, plus certain propensities of his own that he readily admitted, he went forward to extend the courtesies as per his training to this woman, as he now saw it was. Almost at once he guessed, in spite of the horse that was the meanest of jutka ponies, that it was Tully's wife. Airs that directors wore like invisible diadems could also be sensed on their wives. Nevertheless he asked, for want of anything better.

'Are you Mrs Tully?'

'I am. Who are you?' she said, and so directly that he was caught off-guard.

'I'm the life-saver,' he floundered. 'At least—' catching the glimmer, which after all he shared, 'that's what I'm supposed to be, of course when there are people in the pool.'

At present, of course, it was singularly free of suicidal entrants.

'Really I'm the pool attendant,' he said. 'Also—' cautiously, of this new art, 'I serve drinks.'

'I could do with one,' she said. 'Here, catch.'

She was sliding off her mount. The reins were coming at him, a bundle of leathery thongs smelling of horse and exertion that he just managed to grab, and hold. At this point he should have reeled off what was on offer—he had practised enough; but what with a handful of leather, and the unexpected, his mind was wiped clean as a slate. He could only stand, awkwardly, convinced that his joints were visibly enlarging.

She saved him. If she was a little stiff, it was not caught from him but a consequence of an ordeal survived.

'I'm exhausted, we seem to have been riding forever,' she said, pulling off the cloth wrapped round her head like a turban, shaking her hair free. It was long and silky, he saw, a woman's flowing hair: the turban, and the shirt and trousers she was wearing, had led him to suppose a horseman.

'A drink,' he said at once, lashing his deplorable limbs. This weary traveller, and he, rooted, when every instinct urged such basic duties.

'That would be lovely. And,' she said, 'you could live up to your name then.'

'What name, Mrs Tully?'

'Life-saver,' she threw at him over a shoulder; and laughed.

His awkwardness returned. His joints were butting, developing clubheads. But at least they were on the move, it would not be so shamefully visible. She led. He followed, towing the creaking pony up to the pool as ordered, and right onto the gleaming tiles.

Well, if she said.

'Yes, why not? He's as parched as I am,' she did say, absently, sitting on the lip of the pool, easing the silk shirt clapped to her shoulder-blades, kicking off her dusty shoes. Milky feet were revealed, turquoise veined, red in spots where the leather had chafed—it absorbed him, he would have continued to stare except that he had been told it was not polite, by Mrs Bridie.

When her shriek made him focus again.

'God, that hurt!'

'What?'

'Look.'

He did, and saw the fiery blisters on the backs of her heels which his earlier inspection had missed. They would smart like anything, he readily understood, in water to which huge doses of chemical

106

had been added. Clucking his sympathy he took her feet in his lap, and dried them with great care with his waiter's napkin. By now he had completely got over his awkwardness. It had gone in performing the natural, even tender act, restoring an ease that came naturally to him.

'Is that better, Mrs Tully?' he asked, presently.

'Much.' Smiling at him. He smiling back at what belonged to Tully, whose claims were absolute; while applying the salve procured from a first-aid box that roosted discreetly inside a decorative kiosk efficiently planted beside the pool.

When he began to feel uneasy. Some unquiet was flowing from her even as she sat quietly (he had told her to) and submitted to his ministrations. Something sharp and crystalline that she gave out—although it could also have arisen from the glittery tiles—that would raze him if he stumbled. He had to control an impulse, it rose powerfully, to drop her feet back into the stinging water.

Yet why? This smiling woman—Tully's wife, moreover. He castigated himself, and dug out more ointment to make the pain better soon.

If Corinna felt these less than agreeable rebuffs, she dismissed it as nerves, after a fraught day. Now she was thankful for the way it was ending: by the edge of a pool, and a tender boy with his balm.

They continued smiling at each other.

This was the delightful, if impromptu picture that greeted the party that strolled down to the pool at sunset.

The director's wife—again, no one doubts it, for she has an air—is recuperating by the water, tended by a youthful servant. Beside them a rustic pony, moored to chrome rails, pressed to drink, is jibbing at unfamiliar smells that rise forbiddingly from the pool; and is being coaxed by both humanitarians. The air is charming, if distinctly unusual.

The sophisticated party kept its poise, while interested to see how the director, in this piquant situation. Though not really doubting.

Tully didn't turn a hair. Shalimars, like Xanadu, in all periods of history breed the bizarre. Copeland-Tullys are perfectly versed.

'Minister,' he said, coping well, very cool, very English—it was expected. 'May I present my wife?'

The thirsty party, after holding its breath very slightly, resumed its urbane activities.

The Minister presided, orangeade in hand, from the depths of a

107

cane chair with flowered cushions into which they had thrust him, and from which they would have to haul him out too. No matter: there were capable men about. Young, bright, able, like the attentive lieutenant. Like Heblekar the civil servant, member of a select service, revamped as the Administrative Service, as it had to be, so over-civil-icy and unbearable had been the old Civil Servants whom Haileybury and Winchester had sent out on the P & O steamers. The Heaven-born, as caustic wits had dubbed them. And before long these divinities, with a subtlety entirely their own, had inverted the snub into a compliment...But they were gone, like the race chosen, they only half disbelieved, to rule all others. Long departed, leaving these young men to come into their own.

As he, too, had done, though a little late in life. Participant in the global, disconcerting turnaround that transformed bandits into Ministers, while the soubriquet was returned with compliments.

Western bandits.

It made the Minister jolly to think. He would have frolicked here a little more, but duties pressed on hosts and guests alike.

'May I refresh your glass, Minister?'

'That would be most kind...a quite delicious concoction...but not, I hope, imported?'

'Oh no, sir.' The young man is highly disdainful. 'Our own manufacture. Including the can.'

'Good. Excellent.'

The Minister sipped his orangeade, while sampling the stronger wine that was beginning to flow, squeezed from the grapes of memory and the presses of the mind. Unable to resist, for under its influence the turnaround was acquiring a perfect clarity.

Turnaround, or immemorial dance, in which the figures engaged in a writhing, desperate embrace before rulers and ruled changed places, dancing to the beat of time.

Time, the flattener of empires, and bogies.

Successive nursemaids had threatened the Minister—in his childhood, naturally—with Ingrezi devils. Confessing this in a rare, mellow moment to Tully the Elder, that eminence had confided in turn that his own childhood rebellions had been quelled by blackamoors held over his turbulent head by Nannies. Further back, he told, it had been old Boney.

Ogres of the past, each to its era.

The past is a different country; but his age, or condition, were dissolving the frontiers as the Minister sat in his cane, and allowed himself to drink deep. Then he saw them as plainly as the writhing dancers, crossing oceans, or pouring down the passes into the fertile plains of Hindusthan to take possession. Greeks, Turks, Persians, the French, the English—what matter the name, or the guise assumed, for an act of intrinsic violence? Each taking it in turn, the routine of invasion.

An ancient pursuit, or lust, which blew back on the hot winds, as the country in turn took possession. Those who withstood ejection, were received into the marrow. Stayed on, and in time were absorbed into the measured flow of Hindusthan, immense, indifferent, ineluctable. A drop in the ocean, or an episode in a long, continuing chronicle.

When they escorted him out of Delhi and into exile, it was not to the steppes of their origin, but towards Delhi, that the eyes of the failing Emperor turned. All the way, to Allahabad, to Mirzapur, to Calcutta, to Rangoon, Abu Zafar Siraj-Ud-Din Mohammed Bahadur Shah Ghazi, last of the house of Timur, looked towards Delhi.

Lieutenant Ommanney, who commanded the escort of Bengal Lancers, in between some jackal hunts en route caught these backward glances; but was not so crass as to suppose it was the marble tomb. What the old man craved was closer to the core, contracting into ever more dense and burning matter as he neared the end of the journey: to rest his bones with the bones of his ancestors in a country they had conquered, whose conquest they became.

Captain Davies, into whose custody the prisoner was eventually delivered, as much as Lieutenant Ommanney understood the matter well. A bespoke plot in the land of his birth had long been readied to receive his mortal remains. However, he had his orders, issued in good time, concerned with the interment of the last of the Mughal Emperors. If he understood the cruelty, still the officer was under oath. He scrupulously executed his commission.

When it was done he wrote:

Abu Zafar expired at 5 o'clock on Friday. All things being in readiness he was buried at 4 p.m. on the same day, in the rear of the main guard, in a brick grave covered over with turf, level with the ground. A bamboo fence surrounded the grave for some distance. By the time the fence is worn out, the grass will have again covered the spot and no vestige will remain to distinguish where the last of the great Mughals rests.

109

Both one now. Prisoner and guard, following each other and the immutable laws of change, were both gone to dust. While on earth the dancers were not idle.

The Minister stirred, and sipped his orangeade, rather flat by now; and slowly re-surfacing, moved on to matters connected only by filaments, filmy, tenuous, relentless as a spider's web.

What if, change being inherent, the old power was declining? If the great gold sponge, once so effective, was itself being consumed, its substance broken by subtle agents to permit its own absorption?

The Minister mused. Far from resorbent gold sponges, it was supermarket shelves, more or less identically stocked, that he somewhat prosaically visualised. Sunk in his chair, head resting motionless against the flower-patterned cushion.

Still as a lizard, Tully saw. An unblinking reptile on sunwarmed stone, some ancient rock cracked open by a stray wildflower. The world revolving remotely, somewhere out there, outside its still, dual centre.

For the Minister, surfacing rapidly now, the comparison was different. It framed itself in the homely phrases of a Georgian diplomat he had once entertained, as he half-looked at Tully. Walks like a duck, talks like a duck, must be a duck, he said to himself.

When, inevitably, their eyes met; and in these more truthful pools they dissolved the images. Both were looking beyond reptile and bird into human depths, with the crystal eye of honesty. Frontiers, too, were back in place, at least for the Minister who had dismantled them. This was the present, the past was past. And as he had been reminded, the descendant of even an extremist like Jenghiz had his excuses. Nor would he go so far as to equate Tullys, though if he had conveyed that impression—

As he had, he recognised. And the young man had met his bellicose attacks not merely with skill—that one expected—but with good humour, a feat that went beyond what one could reasonably expect in the performance of duty. While he, who should have known better—

The Minister gave a low whinge, a sheep in a snowdrift, needing a strong arm. At once aides were at hand, on either side, but hauling carefully in case they broke the feeble creature. Once up and on his feet, however, the Minister waved them aside and made his own way, straight, and steadily, to his target.

'Mr Tully,' he said, and stood, rather frail, but determined to go through with it. 'I hope you will forgive an old man's
110

hectorings. Provoked, I need hardly tell you, by experience. It makes one suspicious, which is an unworthy emotion, and unpardonable in one as old as I am.'

'Think nothing—I mean, it's—it's—' Tully, unusually for him, was stuttering; his mouth refused to be mealy. Nor could he pretend, in the face of such driven honesty. He had to pause, and in the end draw it out of himself. It could come from nowhere else.

'Time has a way,' he began, and continued with gathering confidence, 'of catching up. If one's human. And who isn't?'

'So it does. So one discovers,' said the Minister. He had been helped, or perhaps they had helped each other. His own, old man's thoughts continued to cluster in the soft, transparent evening.

'You know,' he said at last, 'His Excellency used to say—I can almost hear him now—the country gives back in exact proportion. Devilish clever, I seem to remember, was the expression he chose.'

'I've heard him.' Copeland, like Tully, had let fall something similar, as they walked together beside the clear waters of a trout steam. 'It obviously made quite a dent,' he said.

'The country?'

'Experiencing it. But I don't know about clever,' said Tully, and smiled. Giving back as good as one got seemed to him a perfectly predictable, if not human, response.

They could not take it further. Aides, now, were moving in to take charge. They did not want to drive back along unlit roads, and perhaps get lost in the bush, as they termed it. In no time the Minister was once more in custody.

*

'Went off well, don't you think?' said Heblekar.

'Reasonably.'

Tully and Heblekar were recuperating, sharing a bottle in the darkening pavilion, now that the show was over. Mostly; there were the usual limpets who would cling until the last flicker. The Minister had gone, tucked into an aged Ambassador that sped like an unbelievable deer, once its worn treads had experienced the unbelievable bliss of AIDCORP's brand-new autobahn. Some elements must have lingered, however, perhaps in the burgundy silk, now slipping to black tulip hues. Presently Heblekar admitted it, if somewhat wryly—a tenuous recognition.

'Always a strain,' he said, and stretched. Darkness, shaken up, flowed and settled around his cloud of muslin. 'A strenuous business, entertaining VIPs.'

111

'Yes.' Trace elements had affected Tully as well. 'At times,' he said, 'it was quite alarming.'

'That old man?' It was going too far for Heblekar.

'Not the man.' Tully retracted, partly. 'What he brought with him, I suppose. The past has a way of reaching out, at times.'

Quite unscrupulous, the agents it would use.

'The past?' Heblekar was peaceful as he was. 'R.I.P.' he said, with feeling.

'If only,' said Tully, also with feeling. 'But it's not that easy, is it? The Greeks understood that.'

'They were odd. The most joyous, but haunted, race,' said Heblekar. But what race isn't? his mind was already asking.

'In the end,' Tully said, smiling—the solution had endless appeal, 'they were prepared to rustle up help from above, to sort out the tangle.'

'Perhaps we'll be driven too. Some divinity, descending from the cloud-machine to short-circuit the cycle,' said Heblekar, smiling as well.

They amused each other. Between them they were also raising ghosts, and assorted eerie forces, helped along by the rustling silk. Both jumped, when the shape appeared. Soundlessly—its feet were bare.

It was Rikki.

Surprised, almost out of his skin, to see the two figures looming up. Enveloped in gloom, when there could have been sparkle. A vast electric chandelier, with its own special generator thrumming away like a humming top—

He pressed the switch.

'I was told—the empties,' he said, gesturing, blinking in the vivid light of at least a hundred candles.

'Yes, of course.' It was too much for Tully as well. He stood up. 'I ought to be moving,' he said.

'So must I.' Heblekar rose as well. 'I'll see you on your way,' he proposed.

Outside it was scarcely dark, by comparison. Starlight, and a sheen that come off the sea, that silk and canvas had shut out. Nevertheless a solicitous watchman stood ready.

'Where to, sahib?' Swinging a hurricane lantern.

'Do you think we need him?' Tully watched the sketchy ellipses described by the wick; it would have to be much darker, before it made any impact.

112

'Not unless you do.' Heblekar dismissed the man. 'Enough light to get you up safely.'

They followed the coastline, round the bay, left it to ascend the hill. Midway up, this considerate bench, for the elderly, or subjects consenting to bewitchment.

'Shall we? A wrap-around view from here,' said Tully, not without a soupçon of pride, for he had restored the original, panoramic vistas to Prospect Point. The cactus had been cut back, the encroaching thorn-trees trimmed.

'I was just about to suggest it,' said Heblekar.

They sat, decently; the bench's see-saw properties had been cured. At their feet a spread of sea, beside it the illumined city of Shalimar, girdled with the necklace of lights.

'Modern cities, at night,' said Heblekar, not unused to them, but succumbing.

'Sheer magic.' Tully could not but agree.

The glow irradiated the horizon.

Soon, however, it seemed to both observers that older settlements were emerging, and even beginning to compete. A few low watts, flickering here and there, were putting forward claims. Presently it was the fishing village, elbowed aside and somewhat eclipsed by its coruscating neighbour, that occupied a central position from Prospect Point.

Unable to deal with it as it was—the subject was strong, and loaded—Heblekar took on the manageable.

'That boy,' he said, 'did rather well, don't you think? I must say he seems to be coming along very nicely.'

'I've noticed,' said Tully.

Fingers that could fashion intricate macramé out of hemp were proving, as Tully had indeed noticed, equally deft at twisting lemon peel into butterflies that perched delicately upon frosty rims. Naturally they would be; but he had thought fit to comment.

—Doing famously, Rikki.

—Really, Mr Tully?

A surge of feeling, lighting up the tawny skin.

—Yes, really.

He eliminated the undertone, after admitting there had been one. This time he genuinely praised a skill so outré, considering his circumstances, it could only have come after some determined adjusting of older fidelities and processes of the mind. Not to mention hours of practice.

'I told him so, in fact,' said Tully.

'I meant to. Deserves credit—I mean,' said Heblekar, 'a fisherman's son...'

'Yes.' Tully was absorbed in the scene, the shifting emphasis on objects as night advanced. They might have rested on invisible, finely balanced scales.

When Heblekar, moved, possibly, by these changes, said a curious thing.

'It's not territory, so much, these days, is it?' It sounded odd, even to his own ears.

'What isn't?' Tully was jolted, without specific reason.

'What one takes over.'

'Land, do you mean?' Tully raked up the old obsession, while other possibilities scrabbled for entry. 'But that isn't on, not that simply, any longer,' he said, with a confidence that diminished even as he spoke. 'Well, mostly it isn't,' he amended.

While Heblekar's thoughts rooted elsewhere. He was on to something that went even deeper, he felt. 'But there are other things, aren't there. Nowadays,' he said, 'it's a different kind of takeover, isn't it?' His muslin flowed, softly, in the navy darkness.

'Well,' said Tully. It would take effort to follow this trail, he saw. 'These days we do things more subtly. CIA-style,' he submitted.

'That subtly, who needs protection?' Heblekar laughed too. 'No, I meant we do it—seductively, I would have said.' Although he would have been hard put to say who the seducer was, what was suborned.

Tully was in equal difficulty. The matter was too dense. It would yield, he felt, only to the instincts, at this late hour.

By now the eclipsed settlement, kindled up between them, might have been illuminated—the tip of some iceberg looming up in frozen seas, reflecting an arctic glimmer.

It was a warm evening, however; and very still. The thin jingle, beaten on a tinny triangle by the watchman, carried up clearly from the piazza.

'I must fly. My wife,' said Heblekar, rising and stretching.

'And mine,' said Tully.

Corinna had gone to bed, earning early retirement after the most charming genuflections that had everyone virtually yearning to construct a litter. She would probably be asleep; but would always wake, and make available to him her lovely, plangent flesh.

*

The villagers, too, had to go over the event. Late though it was,

114

for people who would have to be up betimes.

'Did you see?' breathed Valli. Her eyelids felt heavy as anything, but she would never be able to sleep, she was certain.

'Who could avoid?' said Muthu, with some truth.

'From *inside* the cordon,' said Valli, who had been allowed— Rikki had approached the Commissioner, at her request. 'It looked quite different from there, I assure you. Such a privilege,' she said, to her log-heavy brother, 'it's a pity you didn't ask Rikki, I am sure he would have fixed it for you. Wouldn't you have, Rikki?'

'If Muthu had asked,' said Rikki, yawning.

'I wouldn't have dreamed,' said Muthu. He would have died, his knuckles were declaring, sooner than appeal to this fixer.

'I mean, if I thought you had wanted to,' Rikki tried to patch up, though he was fit for nothing but sleep, he felt strongly. For he had not only collected the empties, he had washed up every glass and ashtray. There was a machine, but it roared like a lion. He did not trust, and was even a little frightened by, what went on inside that lead-white lion of a box. Suppose all that was left was a quantity of chewed-up glass?

For Valli, however, sleep was still the last thing. She was still wandering in Shalimar, among the flowers and lights and the gentry, within the crimson ropes of the cordon.

'Right next to one, the fountains, and everything, and—' she sighed, 'all those lovely lords and ladies, in their lovely robes.'

'Men and women,' said Muthu. 'What is the matter with you?' he snapped at her. This star-struck, absurd girl.

'The matter with you,' said Valli, making her shoulders as sharp, and scornful, as she could, 'is, that you are simply incapable of appreciating beauty.'

'Shalimar is beautiful.'

Amma was stirred. It was the lights, the brilliance had quite captured her. 'Yes, it has given us—' her mind picked over luxuries that brimmed from this fountainhead, 'electricity,' she said, squinting up at the light that shone from the rafters.

The same light, and its source, had affected her husband. It was rather stark, at this hour. It made him feel tired and old, he suspected he looked older than he was.

'But it has also,' he said, 'taken from us...some things...' But he was mumbling, unable to catalogue these losses with any certainty. It hardly made an impression.

'So nice, after putting up with that lantern,' which she had

115

speedily relegated to a corner. 'One never got rid of that kerosene stench, it got right under one's nails.' Amma sighed, and splayed out her worn, but now odour-free fingers. 'And the glass was so dingy—rub till your arms ached, you couldn't get it clean. Never was enough light to see by.'

And pressed her knuckles to her drooping eyes.

'Time we were all asleep,' she yawned.

The old man already was, or seemed to be, muffled up to his ears in his threadbare cotton against the light. It sizzled from the naked, solitary bulb, a blinding pear at the end of its flex. Obedient too.

Amma gave a mental pat, as she reached up for the switch. It was childish of her she knew, but the little slavish click it gave, no matter whether pressed for light or darkness, was still novel enough to register and please.

Chapter Nineteen

Now that the villas were ready, together with essential ancillaries like restaurant, bar, and places of amusement, Shalimar began to inveigle the tourists. After exhaustive discussion, initiated by Zavera, it was decided that these raiders, or prey, should always be referred to as Visitors. As she said, with perfect truth, tourists detested nothing so much as being classified tourists. So why not be obliging? Accordingly, they were. Except that the locals, outside these decisions, were already calling them Shalimaris.

While Shalimar, now, was sometimes called the Camp. Why not? That was what it was. It offered a temporary accommodation. But Zavera, for one, could not tolerate such perversity. A camp, to her, smacked of canvas ruggedness: a far cry from what was on offer. Also, it could not be said to appeal.

Whereas Shalimar undoubtedly attracted.

Sitharam was pleased to see the villas filling up. Phase 1—he was devoted to his Phases—is satisfactorily concluded, he would say to himself, and indulge himself a little. Sitting cross-legged in his quarters, on his lap the rosewood box his wife had given him, its lid raised to reveal the neat, lined compartments in which nestled the lime, the betel leaves, the scented nuts, which he would presently combine into a delectable little parcel and pop into his mouth. The success of Phase 1, and the *pan,* were eminently soothing.

Young Ranji, too, should have been delighted by the flow. Why could he not take it as it came? Any Visitor is some kind of compliment to the host. Besides, it was the very *raison d'être* of Shalimar. But as he watched the Visitors it attracted, of whom a fair share inevitably came from abroad, there were some mixed-up emotions.

'Where are our own people?' he demanded. Ignoring ex-princes, contractors, film stars, and other such stellar types who were in fact, but could not ideally be included in the muster of citizens. 'That is what I should like to know,' he said, fiercely, to Heblekar.

Well, at Shalimar's prices, felt Heblekar. He jingled the coins in his pocket.

'Then prices ought to be whipped into line,' declared Ranji, absorbing the unspoken, perspiring under his collar.

Heblekar could sympathise. This intense young lieutenant, with his principles, and his pip on a shoulder. He brought out the infallible, universal balm. 'Well, foreign exchange. . .the country needs all it can get,' he soothed the crude sensitivity of the very young, while some sardonic, inveterate purist droned from the Persian: *I wonder what the vintner buys, one half so precious. . .?*

'I'm sure you understand that,' he said, robustly, after repulsing this minstrel.

Ranji did; despite his fierce mustachios and considerable military hammering he maintained a fairly firm grasp on reality. Furthermore, he could not resist an appeal on behalf of his country. Ranji had yet to grow out of saluting the flag, whenever possible. It approached imperial, and even transatlantic, proportions. By now the tricolour flew, to his order, in the sandy patch in front of the tattered awning; in the bar, the restaurant, over the budding hotel; and would eventually stand sentinel behind the desk in his office, when they finally gave him one.

*

Others besides Ranji and Sitharam watched the flow into Shalimar.

Rikki was riveted, although his perceptions took on a different dimension.

To him it seemed as if the little beach villas, in a phrase he overheard more than once, were beginning to bloom, as one by one they filled. Flushed into life, he felt, by human entry, like bodies infused with spirit. It could not be otherwise, he had some inkling. Buildings needed these injections of human warmth before they could live and breathe. Avalon, he suspected, despite some advantages that dated from its founding, would grow stone-cold, the lately revived marble would fall back into ruin, once Tully withdrew.

Unless his presence, generating elements of durability, became haunting.

As could happen, he understood. Sometimes hands, if inspired, could induce a permanent glow in the stone. Very soon he was comparing with what happened elsewhere, in the cave temples nearby. Fires smouldered there, sometimes the rock was subtly fanned, he felt a distinct heat. Then he too would begin to glow, like the figures carved in the stone, in whom life was being

118

sparked. Then, half-suffocated himself, he would see them start to breathe, a pulse beating in the hollow of throats, tendrils of hair breaking free from elaborate coifs, and jewels flashing on polished breasts and on girdles that danced in the pitted rock.

Coming out blinking into ordinary light he often wished, barely admitting such presumptuous longings, he could coax a single ember of such incandescence into the embellishing of Tully's pool-room.

The pattern was emerging, but had not come clean in his mind yet, he was still playing around with possibilities. Sometimes, when it seemed close, he would haul his materials out of various pergolas scattered around Avalon in which they were stacked, and stagger off, bent double, to the impluvium. And fragments of travertine and serpentine, chipped off cracked slabs and chiselled and polished by himself, would pour onto the floor in shiny mountains, from the grimy gunny sacks into which he loaded his iridescent treasure.

He could have spent hours.

However, there were claims on his time: as lifeguard, as waiter, as washer-upper, as Tully's boatman (though largely in fancy: the boat was still landlocked). But whenever he could, it didn't matter when: the assurance came from Tully's own lips.

'Do you mean that, Mr Tully?'

'Of course, Rikki. Any time, the place is yours.'

For, curiously, Avalon's grandeurs did not diminish the boy, Tully had begun to notice. In its quirky way the mansion seemed to bend over, willing to extend a coveted membership beyond Copeland-Tullys to this unusual entrant. Tully had not the least wish to interrupt the process.

So, when he was free, Rikki would dash, straight up the hill, through the sunroom to the pluvium, before the inspiration dulled.

But that day in the crystal room, just as he was about to burst in, he caught sight of them: Tully and his wife.

They were standing, face to face, not speaking, not touching.

But if they touched, he had a sense, they would fuse together and fall, right under those glass walls, in that transparent room, with the sun pouring in on fired clay.

Or, just as easily, they might fly apart at first touch, unable to bear such intensity. There was nothing in between. There was nothing else. The sense was overpowering.

119

Transfixed before the glass he felt he would never break free, he was caught forever. But of course he did, finally, and without them noticing his presence, or departure.

Thereafter he grew circumspect. Before venturing he made sure one or other was absent, which luckily, he felt, was often the case. Or if not, he ground up the cindery path in borrowed chaplis instead of skimming in bare feet up the dizzy hill track. No one, with a vestige of hearing, could have been left unaware that Rikki approached.

Having arrived, however, he found himself creeping round Avalon, for reasons he whittled down to Mrs Tully.

It was the way she walked around. Restlessly, in rope sandals, pointlessly into and out of rooms, into the pool-room where he was working.

For at last it was beginning. Sometimes it blazed up in his mind. At other times there was nothing but ashes, reducing him to despair. But some pale fire lurking, which could be fanned up, if he kept at it.

He was so abstracted as he worked at it, he did not know she had entered until she spoke.

'Can I look?'

He edged the gunny forward.

'There's not much to see, Mrs Tully.' For if she, or anyone, looked now it would be blighted forever, a bud picked before its season.

'What there is.'

Standing, edging aside the gunny with the toe of her sandal, looking down at his work.

He could see, with her eyes, the foetal thing. After all, even he barely presumed to discover, in those stumps, the buds of limbs that would grow and perhaps achieve strength, and even beauty.

'I've only just started,' he said defensively, while his own assurance began to ebb.

'Never mind that. But,' she said, 'whatever is it?'

'I'm not sure yet,' he answered, evasively, and yet there were grains of truth in it.

'It's so—I think it's too pale, that's what's wrong,' she said, frowning a little, arching her neck. Its strong, beautiful lines were fully revealed, her flowing hair caught back in a broad silk band of vivid yellow. 'Why not something a bit more—?'

'What?' he challenged, rather than asked.

'Lively,' she said. 'Make it bright and bold.' Standing over his
120

design, one foot tapping. Except for her youth it might have been mouldy old Mrs Bridie all over again.

It made him stubborn, and wary.

He would not put out his fire, but he left the mosaic alone. He would return to it when she had gone and he could be free again. For he sensed she would not stay. There was a fraying in whatever rope tethered her that he felt almost physically. He did not think it could hold her long.

Meanwhile he kept out of her way, presiding over the swimming pool in Shalimar, or watering and tending Tully's hillside orchard. There was a gardener these days, seconded from the growing Shalimar establishment by the Commissioner, personally. He was, however, a stately person, a one-time servitor of Maharajas, used to cosseting the amaryllis, or at a pinch would condescend to cantaloup. He knew, he admitted, little about pumpkins or bitter gourd, or such other homespun vines. Rikki knew even less, but he pestered his mother for tips. Her transplanted vines flourished, less by his efforts or her applied advice than from their own healthy, ingrained impulse to conquer the earth. Vigorous conquistador tendrils overran the somewhat lumpy hillocks Rikki had raised. There were hints of blossom, if one looked closely.

Tully came out, or was brought out, to exclaim.

'Goodness, Rikki. We are doing well.'

Though he did wonder, if every hint came to fruition, what on earth one would do with this profusion of pumpkins. It never occurred, as it might have done to a poor man, that he might sell his produce. Rikki was a poor man, but it did not enter his head either. Every blossom was already a fruit, ripened by the sun, a bloom dusting the skin. Piling them up in his mind he saw the mellow pyramid as an offering, or even a thank-offering, to be laid at Tully's feet.

Meanwhile, as Tully saw, the mosaic was marking time. Abandoned, he would have concluded, but for the sacking that covered one section, pointedly weighted down with some hefty lumps of rubble. He did not peek—those forbidding weights—but he did finally ask.

'What's happened, Rikki? Sticking, is it?'

'No.'

'In that case—'

Because one liked order. A trim surround to one's impluvium, now complete in every respect, except for water. Instead of those perishing gunnybags that stood around, stinking of jute and

121

cement—misshapen bags at that, all manner of angularities from what they were stuffed with.

Rikki was stuck now, having admitted he wasn't. No amount of casting around brought up convincing explanations, what with the true one lodged in his gullet.

'It's Mrs Tully.' He was driven at last. 'I can't think of anything she would like—' (he hadn't even tried, and had no intentions) '—and I don't think she likes what I'm doing.'

'What the hell—' Tully was surprised by his reaction, '—does that matter?'

'Well, it does.' Rikki grew mutinous. All very well for Tully, it was his wife. 'I can't explain,' he said, and turned his back on his questioner. Thick as two plates, he felt, resorting to the rich vernacular of Shalimaris when driven up the wall by the servants.

But Tully's skin was quite thin in an area concerned, after all, with his wife. He had little difficulty in expanding the somewhat tight explanations offered by Rikki, which some instinct of his had wound round Corinna.

Deny it as he would—Tully did, it was a matter of importance to him—there was no denying she introduced strains. The house, murmuring agreeably after decades of neglect, also gave back the grist of her presence, her somewhat irritable footsteps as she trailed around the place, the little exasperated whirrs of her lighter—there were distracted notes in the turtledove.

It jarred, not least on Corinna.

As she stood, looking up at an irrelevant rose in the ceiling, or through a window down the flinty slopes of the broody hill.

She felt bored to death.

It was the pony, if anything, that saved her sanity. It had done so once already, rescuing her from the motor-car that was bearing her to Shalimar. At least that ancient vehicle meant to, but had given up the ghost en route. Needless to say in the middle of nowhere—a good many such stretches in the sub-continent; while the driver and his mate tinkered and prayed, equally uselessly. She would have given thanks for anything that moved, and the only thing—a snail, inching its way across an infinite landscape—was this peasant and his cart.

Somehow, despite applied pressure on one side and reluctance on the other, they parted friends. The peasant had never been richer in pocket, or in heart, which responded readily to Corinna's considerable, genuine charm. While Corinna's heart had been immediately stricken with love for his maltreated, pathetically

122

thin beast of burden.

But this creature was filling out nicely, and could be ridden for pleasure, without feelings of cruelty towards a defenceless animal. So she rode with the wind in her hair down the hill to Shalimar.

Their return was different. She walked him slowly up, reins slack in her hand, plenty of time for him to nibble at thorns, and for her to look around.

One of Toby's specialities, she saw, and here in the most acute form it had ever been her lot.

She gave it a month, rather less than she usually allowed for AIDCORP wildernesses, for herself. It was about as much as she would be able to take, she understood from the start. He, she could easily see, would not complain if he had to serve out a life sentence.

'Do you like it here, Toby?'
She knew, but continued to be curious.
'Yes.'
'I mean Avalon. Living here.'
'I know what you mean. Yes, I do.'

It deepened her wonderment. It was his extreme capacity for enduring boredom, she supposed, neglecting any possibility of involvement with a landscape.

He might have explained, except that it was too private a feeling, and would evaporate before any attempt at enclosure and presentation. He, too, did not think it would be long before she fled. His hopes of winning her over this time were flagging—perhaps they had never been more than a case of hope rising eternal. But he would have liked her by his side.

He, in turn, questioned her.

'Do you, Corinna?' Watching her as she lay, translucent with lamplight, on the rosewood fourposter.

'Do I what?' Curled into her silk wrap, one hand lost in drifts of lace.

'Like being here?'
But she was tired of that.

'So-so.' Sighing, languid—an indolent swan, but turning. Sliding out of silk, silk and lace in an abrupt heap, lovely arms inviting. 'Come to bed, darling.'

Luckily he never needed a second invitation; and the molten experience made it easier for both of them, postponing franker exchanges.

Chapter Twenty

DESPITE a residue of vexation, for he did want to get on, Rikki managed to dump Mrs Tully. Or rather he relegated her to a corner, much as his mother had done with the tiresome lantern. She was stood in this niche, sharing it a trifle oddly with Mrs Bridie, and Mrs Contractor, and sundry other powerful female characters with which, it seemed to him, Shalimar was riddled.

It was his youth, he supposed. These women who gave orders, who expected him to jump to it the moment they parted their lips, were twice and thrice his age. He could not overcome some traces of his upbringing that lingered, that frowned on taking the hatchet to his elders. But where, he wondered crossly, were the younger ones with whom he could engage on equal terms, even if they were sacrosanct Shalimaris?

By which simmering point he had completely forgotten the youthful Mrs Tully.

Some such thought flickered through Heblekar's mind as he watched the comfortable ranks of blue-rinse ladies. But then, and quite soon, realism floated up those jolly, Siamese twins: youth and poverty, women and longevity, senility and wealth. Money-money-money, hummed thirty-year-old Heblekar, from *Cabaret*, a lyric that had made a deep impression on his mind.

Both of them exaggerated. There was a sprinkling of young women: air hostesses, relaxing in sun-'n'-sand; girls, sharp as any silk-route merchant, buying for gilded Occidental emporia, taking time off in Shalimar between exhausting hassles in Varanasi or Jaipur; journalists who came for the colour, and tacked on a story. Miss Lockwood was one of these. She wished to interview Rikki, in depth, against the background of his family. The contrast, she felt, was so-o intriguing.

Rikki refused. He was touchy about his family. The way they lived was their business—not to be recommended, certainly; the cracked mirror was a daily irritant, the charpoys were a disgrace—these days various lamentable features reared up like mountains, after years of unnoticing. But he would not have it exposed, no matter what she paid—she had flourished first cheque book, and then, assuming, wrongly, it meant nothing to a village

125

youth, actual banknotes. Rikki barely deigned to look. Even Tully, to whom he would deny little, had not been allowed. Besides, what did one's family's abject state have to do with one's own resplendence, did this Miss Lockwood imagine? He strode off, his polished shoulders just this side of insolence.

Round Arjuna's Walk (Tully's inspiration), across the bubbling Yamuna (Contractor's rill), along the Avenue of Palms (Sitharam's pride and joy), and so to the Gaiety Theatre (a temporary baptism, until they mutually hit on something happier) next to the Brindavan Gardens.

Yes, a theatre, in, almost, his village!

In which Valli—*his sister!*—was to perform.

Rikki had to marvel, before proceeding to execute her commission. This was to inspect the interior, and convey to her the minutest details, among them the size of the stage and the positioning of the lights which was essential knowledge for a dancer.

By this time he had ceased to lower, his lively, talented sister eclipsing earnest Miss Lockwood.

*

It struck Tully too, each time he passed the building. A garrison theatre, he felt—the sense came over strongly—built to entertain the troops while on a stint at some bleak frontier. A touch of cheer, as they laboured at some great wall or border fort to repel the barbarian invader.

More than perchance—he pursued the engaging reflection—the theatre would have been incorporated at blueprint stage of wall or fort, as routinely as in modern holiday camps. An indispensable part of getting away from it all, as AIDCORP knew, not being inexperienced. People came for peace and quiet; and very soon were unnerved by the silence. Eccentrics of course—always those. But they would never support the 9:1 tourist-servitor ratio—the data came from Heblekar. In classy joints like Shalimar nine suave souls danced attendance on each sojourner, was how he chose to put it. As it was also the hard, expensive fact, eccentrics—Tully supposed—would have to learn to live with their fellows, or herd.

'Hello, Mr Tully.'

An unexpected figure, emerging from the wings.

'Oh, Rikki. Looking over the place?'

An inveterate inspector, this boy. A connoisseur's eye, some

126

times. Sometimes a magpie's, seduced by any bright trash.

'Yes. I was asked. My sister—' in a rush '—is going to give a dance performance.'

He had seen her: a slender twelve-year-old, skipping along—seemingly incapable of anything as sober as walking—in Rikki's wake.

'You must tell me when. I'll book the best seat in the house,' he said.

'Which is that?' One knew where it was, in a cinema, or the shamiana where the Gubbi travelling company put on the Ramayana. The Gaiety was an uncertain quantity.

'The middle of the third row, I believe,' said Tully.

He would attend—it was something to look forward to. Shows at the Gaiety, while entertaining, were a shade repetitive.

Ramalingam also rejoiced, not in the dance or anything like that, but in being able to provide entertainment. Entertainment, together with Recruitment, came under his aegis. He had already done well. There was the disco, nightly. Gonsalez and his Brazilian Ensemble played at weekends. There were guitar and sitar recitals by virtuosi. And there was Miss Carmen Alvarez, of Bombay and Andalućia, expert at spirited sevillanas and the castanets. But Visitors had ideas, in Ramalingam's experience: strange yearnings they had, like pregnant women: they yearned to sample the ethnic. And what could be more ethnic, the Commissioner asked himself unanswerably, than a fisherman's daughter?

One of his spies, set to work early, had spotted the girl. A genuine, taught by the local maestro, adept at folk dancing, and inspired performer at religious festivals, reported this reliable man. Ramalingam took his word, adding to it his own astute conviction that if the locals on their own ground passed it, one need enquire no further.

*

Valli was preparing, and excited. Between interminable chores she practised the steps, and a number of eloquent gestures. There was the skirt of orange silk worked with gold thread, which had been a solicited gift from her affluent brother. There was also a hurdle to get over.

She had to work herself up to it, and throw out advance hints, and it was the nearness of the thing that finally pitched her into asking her father.

'Shall I?' She was subdued—it was not her nature, but the effect he had. Sitting on the mat with the reedy, unravelled fringes. As heavy as a buddha, but unsmiling. It oppressed her.

'You see,' for this was another pressure, 'they want to print the notices, I have to answer soon.'

And she smoothed a seam in the bright silk, and waited for him, it was his answer that was holding up everything. As he kept silent she had to continue.

'They pay well.' At her age it was not the money but a sop that she offered, standard coin of exchange among the older and wiser. '*Very* well,' she stressed.

'Maybe they do. But what—'

What was being sold, what bought? Apu wondered. It was a feeling, he could not frame it as a question. Then how could she answer in so many words, when he was stumped? The old man sat, his slack fingers unravelling the mat still further, gazing at the wall that was crowded with tableaux—an invisible stage, on which family groupings were visible. Perhaps, he felt, he was too old, and she was too young. An afterthought child, conceived in a faltering embrace long after the others, whose innocence would channel his punishment for carnal pleasures enjoyed so late along the road. These thoughts, too, turned into a scourge. What kind of man was he, thinking of himself, when his daughter was in peril? Some halting words began to be uttered.

'A young girl...exhibiting yourself...it's not right...'

'What else, at every festival? Don't we—I and the others—exhibit ourselves then?'

'But that is done to praise the divine.' His certainties were falling back into place, he could speak without stumbling. 'There is a great difference between—'

On and on, felt Valli. Tears wet her cheeks, as she listened to him dismantling her future.

*

'Persuade her,' said Contractor, to whose august ears, via his deputy, the matter was eventually brought.

'It is not the girl. It is her father,' explained Sitharam.

'Persuade him,' suggested Contractor.

Sitharam spared himself. He did not think he would succeed, where the powerfully persuasive Ramalingam had failed. He left it to the girl to work out her destiny. Meanwhile, fortunately, there was Carmen Alvarez, who was perfectly willing to double her appearances.

*

'How I wish I was a boy! You're so lucky, Rikki, you can do what you like,' said Valli.

She had recovered. She was not to flaunt herself, as her stuffy father put it, but was working soberly as a sales assistant in the Shalimar Gift Shop & Emporium. Her parents had given permission, their energies had been sapped. A good many villagers had experienced a similar drain, after *their* battering.

'Why? Aren't you doing what you like?' enquired Rikki.

'I am. But it's only second-best. I would have preferred, you know—'

'Yes, I know.' For he had come upon her one day, in the theatre, embracing the damask curtains one last time, before they rang down on her forever.

'To dance.' She told him anyway, and did a twirl, one of her celebrated, right in the middle of the shop. 'Because when I dance it gives pleasure to—to whoever is watching, and the pleasure reflects right back. I dance divinely then, and I know I look divinely beautiful too, although,' she heaved a sigh, 'really I'm only passable-pretty.'

'But aren't you happy?' asked Rikki anxiously. Looks, after what they had done for him, had soared up on his register; but the heart, that imperative organ, he still put first.

'I'm as blithe as a bird. It's a pleasure to be here, I just love it,' said Valli, and lovingly re-arranged the shells and coral-berry necklaces on her counter. 'It makes such a nice change, after slitting fish open the whole of one's life,' she claimed.

Rikki was happy to hear it. Much relieved, he went his way.

*

Like Valli, Rikki had found a new source of pleasure. He was learning a new craft, it even approached art.

He was a willing and voluntary pupil, to his utter surprise, of Mrs Tully's. It happened perfectly simply, but with a radiance all its own.

He was flitting around on the heights of Avalon, surveying the field below from various vantage points to see if he could spot Mrs Tully. He could then bank on an hour or two of privacy, which he badly needed. For he was suffering from that artist's bane: an urge to put right, immediately, a certain flaw in his handiwork that had

129

swum up in his mind during sessions of exhaustive contemplation. But he would not begin, until he could be sure of absolute privacy, and heaven knew how difficult, not to say impossible—

He was deep into this theme when, in the scoop of bay below Prospect Point, he saw her flying along on this magic carpet. Nothing less could describe the stuff of undulating sapphire, with its fringe of curling silver, on which she was borne. Herself a sapling in silver, balanced like one. He forgot it was Mrs Tully. He even forgot his artist's urge. Rooted he stood, with his eyes on stalks.

Quite soon he was skimming down the breakneck path to inspect the marvel, which turned out to be a girl and her raft. It kept its lustre, however. He noticed neither her lank, dripping hair, nor the somewhat ungainly way in which she was wading through the shallows with the surf-board, but was aware only of having been a spectator at a display of extreme and extravagant grace. It overcame even his feelings for her.

'That was a fine performance, Mrs Tully,' he said warmly.

'Thank you, Rikki.' She responded at once to such unstinted admiration, and with some grace. 'But it's not me especially—I mean, it's the sea that does most of it.'

He couldn't let this pass.

'But if you didn't know how—'

One would tumble about like an inert log; it would not be like riding the bristling crest of some magnificent animal.

'It might be more difficult,' she laughed, and agreed. 'But when you know how it's very easy.'

How easy? Like swimming was for him? Like mending fishing nets, or mixing the drinks? Carving lemon-peel, or floats from pale, silk-cotton wood?

There was, these days, a host of comparisons.

'Easy as anything.' She sensed he was fumbling around possibilities. 'You would learn in no time. Would you like me to show you how?'

For she too, as others had been, was moved by the longings so transparently exposed by this would-be initiate to the world of sophisticated arts.

'No,' he said, or half-said. His shyness had returned, while his yearnings mounted.

'Yes. Come for a run.'

'Now?' He was both defeated and triumphant.

'Why not? No time like the present. Besides,' she said

practically, 'you've only got a few days, before I leave.—What? Yes indeed, I'm off soon.'

Because the month she had given herself was already proving too long.

There was only one surf-board, they had to take it in turns. Rikki, board under his arm, walking behind her, was suddenly and forcefully returned to his Bridie period. She, bony wrists jutting from the long-sleeved cotton, leading the way to the schoolhouse. He following, with a parcel of books, all chosen by her, carried according to her instructions. He had balanced them on his head, to start with; it was the way one carried weights. She removed them one by one, calmly but firmly.

'Not like a coolie, Rikki. I've told you before. Like a scholar, neatly, under one arm.'

Sometimes he obeyed her absurd instructions. Sometimes he rebelled, piled the books in an impudent tower and minced along behind her.

These moody reflections, however, completely dissolved once they entered the sea. Here he was, certainly, under instruction, and bound to obey Mrs Tully's commands, but these irksome bonds were cords of silk, to the radiant pupil he became.

On land, meanwhile, the old feelings remained, flinty, obdurate. He felt she had no business to be in Avalon, and if he had known when she was leaving, would have counted the days. The sea was always a different matter.

*

Sometimes, on his way back, Tully caught a glimpse. Under a westering sun, this extraordinary pair. And stopped to watch, mesmerised by the two, youth and young woman, who are playing the ocean. Literally.

Each in turn scampers up with the frail balsa raft, takes up a strategic position in the swell and waits with a crafty eye on the breaker that has *its* crafty eye on them, is curling up powerfully for the smash when its opponent outwits such notions. Shrieking like a banshee, careless of foam and thunder, the nimble reveller leaps aboard his craft and volplanes in at breakneck speed on the crest of the heaving blue mountain.

Of the two the woman is superior. She has poise, confidence, command, comes up superbly from initial crouch to upright and

131

holds the position. Balancing finely, she rides the skimming plank with her body, guides it in subtle diagonals, her footwork is dazzling. The boy is less adroit. He can match her for balance—years of catamaran have evolved a superb internal gyro—but he gets his timing wrong. He doesn't always catch his wave, which runs away from him. Left stranded, he wallows in its wake, belly-flopped, clutching the flying balsa which has turned pedestrian—his chagrin carries clear across the distance.

But in time, it is clear, he will master these classy techniques.

'Coming along nicely, Rikki.'

Rikki, chest heaving, was too breathless, or moved, to respond.

*

Mrs Tully told him much the same, and generously, one morning when he was tending the orchard.

'Keep practising and you'll be better than me, Rikki, by the time I come back.'

'Will you be coming back, Mrs Tully?' he enquired politely.

He didn't care; he didn't care for her. On her horse, boot in a stirrup, looking down at him. Or worse still drifting around, getting in the way. Besides, now he was launched he could get along on his own.

Provided, of course, he had the matchless plank—a Californian Malibu, he had learnt.

He felt no compunction in asking for it boldly, looking back with surprise, as he did so, to a past when he would have been incapable. Although at the last minute he did feel some compulsion to qualify the request.

'Until you come back, Mrs Tully,' he said. He had, just about, registered her reply that she supposed she would.

'Oh no. You keep it, Rikki. I'm sure I can get another,' said Corinna, smiling.

Chapter Twenty-one

THE house looked empty for a bit, then shrugged off her absence, it seemed to Rikki. It belonged to Tully, he felt strongly; he had raised it from ruin and given it life, it would not notice other comings and goings.

The crooning was starting up again. Working in the pool-room he could hear the sea murmuring in the bay, and birdsong from the casuarina; and working on, felt the glow reflected in as an evening sun warmed and gilded every pane in the glass room.

He was thankful to have received back the freedoms of Avalon.

Tully for his part missed his wife acutely to start with, then less, then got used. He would have liked her to love what he did. As it was, he accepted her absence, as he was accustomed to doing. For Corinna was not one for enduring in one of his deserts. Never had been, as deep down he had always known, though he tended to forget, and in this was helped by the long months of separation. Never pretended to be. A different breed from, say, his Copeland grandmother. Sticking it out year after year in some steamy province or outpost of empire, sometimes in the seething capital of one or other State. Loathing every minute, a lifetime of loathing.

'We felt we had to, Toby,' she said, to the boy leant against her knee as she turned the mottled grey pages of the family album. They were poring over it together.

'But didn't you enjoy it, Grandmama?' He caught the joyless inflections.

'Perhaps,' she said, looking down into eyes as deeply blue as her much-loved husband's, unnerved by hints of a similar recoil from her attitudes, already perceptible in a child of nine. 'Perhaps not always,' she admitted, looking away from those disturbing depths.

Or not at all. Listening to her it came over clearly. Orphans, senses already sharpened by loss, came that much closer to generations that should have been once removed.

'As far as possible, one stayed with one's husband. One's place was by his side,' she said, quite simply.

He saw, with adult eyes, it had been simple: no drama, only a sense of duty, not once declared for what it was. While from the same standpoint he saw that this, too, must have been clearly conveyed in so close a relationship as marriage.

What did a man feel like, tied to a dutiful woman?

His relationship with his wife, he felt, held elements of sanity by comparison, and a good deal more honesty. And these pleasing aspects he clung to.

So he saw her off at the airport, and became conscious in turn of turtledove notes reviving in Avalon, and turned to, among other things, the pool-room that was making progress.

Or at least trimmings were, there was quite a glimmer to surrounds, fewer sacks sagged in corners; while essentials—namely water—were missing.

He tackled Heblekar, ruining, in the process, a somewhat mellow session they were having with the chess, and some port wine, on the terrace.

'When does it rain in these parts?'

Heblekar had only the vaguest. One was not a peasant, to have an intimate knowledge of monsoons and such. In Delhi one retreated to one's apartment, or if caught out, hailed a taxi. It was not a compelling subject.

'Why do you want to know?' he asked, tiresomely, in Tully's opinion.

'Just do,' answered Tully, tiresomely, in Heblekar's.

'Who wants it to?' he fell back. 'Visitors would sue—I mean, sunshine and blue skies virtually guaranteed in the brochures.'

'I know that.' Tully grew truculent. The cloudless sky was an affront, flaunting itself through the deliberate cut-out in the ceiling, an insolent blue lozenge. 'It's just that one likes to know these things.'

'I'd tell you if I knew,' said Heblekar, 'but I don't—' coldly, '—grow crops myself, you know, it's never seemed a necessary piece of knowledge.' That, he felt, was the trouble with the British. Never allowed for class division in others, while riddled with it themselves. A persisting dichotomy in thought processes. Mother (not quite, though coué-ism induced them to believe) of democracy, but practising the most acutely annoying despotism to the farthest colonial dot while empire lasted, and giving aid and comfort to home-grown despots from Chile to Persepolis when that sun had set.

Wouldn't know a South-West monsoon from a zephyr if it struck him in the face, felt Tully, simmering.

They let it pass. It was a pleasant evening: sea-breezes, and the

134

game was drawn, their chess-playing skills being about equally abysmal.

'You see,' said Tully presently, pushing a hopelessly compromised pawn around, 'the pool's bone-dry.'

'I'll tell you what,' proposed Heblekar, abandoning his pawn to its fate. 'I'll do a rain-dance.'

Any chance of success and he would take the ridiculous man at his word, felt Tully. 'You've no idea,' he said—not even smiling, really quite forlorn, the amazed Heblekar observed—'how empty it looks.'

How could it look filled? What else *could* it look?

'What's wrong with tap-water?' Heblekar was mystified. Shalimar bulged with mod cons, even if this aloof mansion's supplies were limited to one well. 'Get the mali—well,' catching an incredulous eye, 'three or four malis, to fill the thing. No shortage of labour in these parts.'

But it would not do for Tully. An impluvium deserved rain-water. Simply tipping in the stuff from kerosene tins would be like drenching the cabbages with water from a font. Or—by now he was thoroughly confused—vice-versa.

There were times when Tully and Heblekar each suspected the other of some lack of soul.

Rikki, meanwhile, was entirely happy—no clouds on his horizon. The orchard was blooming, work was progressing, the flaw that had been nagging away had been dealt with, and he could even say, modestly, that he was beginning to master the Malibu. These days he could plane in on a wave and wipe out (for he had even picked up the argot) at will, before it broke round his ears in a soup of thunderous white water. Or ride his wave, managing a dizzy diagonal or two before he fell. Sometimes, it is true, he was seized and dumped—huge dumper waves he had yet to learn to handle—huge bruises on his flanks to show for it, and ricked muscles; but it happened less and less frequently. And these days there was the gymnasium and the massage parlour which—courtesy of Shalimar—took care of his injuries without charging a single paise.

Yes, Shalimar: free with its gifts and its services, and its rewards for service. He had quite a nest egg tucked away, together with a list he was drawing up, of desirables already acquired, or to be acquired, from this golden pile. Besides this there were luxuries, ladled out with Shalimar's casual, lavish hand: sherbets for which

135

the craze had died, bounty left over from barbecues and fiestas that he carried home in a hamper, there was so much of it.

His mother unpacked the creaking baskets he brought her with the utmost care.

'Such delicacies... and so generous with the leftovers,' she sighed, and sampled the goodies, now and then smacking her lips over some succulent morsel. 'And you're a good boy, Rikki, you never forget your family.'

Her responses warmed him. He loved this warm woman who had undertaken to become his mother and fulfilled the undertaking to overflowing. He loved striding in with the bulging hamper and depositing it at her feet with an almighty *crump!*

But, for whatever reason, he found himself dodging the two men—in particular Muthu, his brother.

That day he was not so successful. The basket was open, his mother was peering and exclaiming, when the two of them appeared. They should have been on the high seas, according to his calculations, but here they were, crossing the threshold, settling themselves by the hearth. While his mother—thick-skinned or something, he felt, his warmer emotions curdling slightly—went on exclaiming.

'And this—smells so nice—what is it, Rikki?'

'Caviar,' he said, briefly. There was a thimbleful, in a boat of waxed paper wearing a frill.

'It looks so costly.' She could tell, from the very container.

'It is. Extremely.' Cost a king's ransom, the Goanese cook, who had once been a chef on a P & O liner, had impressed on Rikki while doling out with a salt spoon. Didn't come every day, a special even for Shalimaris, he had stressed.

'It's fish-roe.' Now Muthu was prodding, with a toothpick. 'That's all it is. Fish-roe.' Hardly a novelty, his sensible voice hinted; and perhaps it wasn't, for fishermen.

'It's caviar.' Rikki would not have the rich stuff downgraded. 'From the Caspian Sea,' he could not resist adding. The name alone would have made sawdust delectable, to anyone but his stodgy brother.

'Why not call it what it is?' Muthu thought it right to insist.

It made Amma sigh. Really, the things men could find to war over.

'What does the name matter? It doesn't alter the taste, *that's* for sure,' she said, and sighed again. 'Just let us eat and be thankful.

Luxuries like these—when could *we* ever afford to buy?'

'Yes, luxuries. Perhaps it's not wise...' obscure misgivings moved the old man, 'for us to get used, being as we are...'

But words never came easily, he soon dried up.

Feeble, his wife felt.

'Why not, when we have the chance?' she said, robustly, as she distributed in salt-spoon proportions. 'We get unused soon enough, so why worry?' She laughed. 'People get used to anything when they have to.'

But it could be grievous, the old man felt, while not really thinking of himself. And he could not, or would not, eat.

It only meant more for the others, thought his wife, although she would not be so unkind as to say so.

Soon Rikki, chafing and irritable, was casting round for excuses to leave. He felt no wish to linger, in an atmosphere that jammed at every point. He was sick of his brother, of the cheerless reception his best intentions met with. Sick of the mangy hut, even the thatch was tattered. These days he scarcely regarded it as his home, and would hardly have bothered to return, he felt, except for his mother.

Presently he found the excuse he was looking for, which in fact was a perfectly valid reason for departure. He was booked to give a swimming lesson, and by now he knew the importance of punctuality. So he walked briskly, glancing now and then at his wristwatch, along the coast, and into the precincts of Shalimar, and up a drive of washed shingle to the new and burgeoning Hotel Asoka to rendezvous with his pupil.

By which time his skies were blue again, lurking clouds despatched by some natural blitheness, and a contemplation of his pupil, Mrs Pearl. To think of her made him smile, with affection.

The beginning of their friendship had not been auspicious.

He was stationed, as usual, by the swimming pool that afternoon. As usual he was thinking what a non-job it was, presiding over so mild a scene, when he noticed the woman, a new arrival at Shalimar. Grey curls with blue lights in them, a dumpy figure not improved by the flowered costume—a glance and he had placed her firmly in the brigade of aged and authoritative ladies that overflowed the Camp.

But they were circumspect.

Unlike this woman who, wearing water-wings, and clearly nervous, was about to jump in at the deep end. She had closed her eyes, and pinched her nostrils together with beringed fingers.

137

Even so he was not unduly anxious—water-wings, after all. But he did take the precaution of peering in, and saw the flowery splodge lodged on the bottom and showing, to his horror, no sign of ever surfacing. He hauled her out, of course, pulling a back muscle in the process, for she was a heavy woman; and sat her on the edge of the pool, and lectured.

'You *know*—I've told everyone—you must *not* swim on a full stomach.'

Fright made him severe, as well as unjust. Not even a Shalimar lunch could make one sink like a stone.

'I know. I'm terribly sorry.' She sat, humbly, a dripping, rubber-tyre lady. This meek, and fairly unusual, attitude made him relent slightly.

'Shall I call the nurse?' There was one: smart Miss Gonsalez, sibling to the band-leader, in a crackling white uniform, who looked after those felled by the climate.

'Thank you, no. Caused enough stir as it is.'

There had been a stir, of West of Suez proportions. Now even that ripple had subsided, as there seemed no prospect of a drowning. People returned to the pool, or to their sun-beds.

'Are you sure you're all right?' He was still barking, but beginning to put himself in her place: that massive slab of turquoise water, pinning one down like a tombstone. At first he had thought only of himself: the terror of losing his lucrative post.

'Yes. You were so quick,' she said. Like lightning, at fifteen. At fifty one's reflexes were best not mentioned. These figures, chosen for effect, were a little out. Both of them were, as Mrs Pearl knew perfectly well, a year or thereabouts older. 'A little shaken,' she said, 'but no worse, thanks to you.'

He fetched her a brandy—a portable bar was parked beside the pool—and her robe, and wrapped it round her shoulders.

'There.'

'That's much better. You know,' sipping aquavitae, and quite mildly, 'I don't think it was the lunch,' she said.

'I don't think it was,' he agreed handsomely. Amazing how pleasant it was, not having a corpse on one's hands. It made him positively genial.

'It's a myth, then,' she pursued, 'that one bobs up three times, before drowning?'

'I don't know. But I don't think—''he had to smile, 'you should depend on that. It would not be wise.'

'I relied on those wings.' She had to laugh. 'But of course

138

they're useless—waterlogged, probably. I've had the perishing things since I started learning to swim, and goodness knows that was in the year dot.'

'You mean you can't?' he had wondered.

'Not a stroke. Isn't that terrible? I mean,' she said, 'to someone like you.'

Born to the sea, anyone could see with half an eye. Moreover she had seen him, shearing across the bay in the early morning, clean dolphin lines in the shining sapphire.

'Some of us can't swim,' he said, truthfully enough, some fishermen preferred to die quickly; but it was said mainly to make her feel better—as she readily perceived, and smiled.

'But you can. I've seen you,' she said. And was presently confessing: 'I'm a hopeless case I know, but I've always wanted to be able.' A small, persisting ambition.

They fixed up for lessons there and then.

So now he stood, on the polished flagstones, in the swept and garnished courtyard which not long ago had been a beach. Some streak in him, akin to Tully's, approved the orderly scene: the neat flower-beds, the steps that swept in matched flights up to the verandah, the immaculate white of balusters and railings. But when it slipped over into beauty—a seat of alabaster, sheltered by a pierced marble screen, scented by an urn overflowing with scarlet roses—he was tranced.

Mrs Pearl had to nudge the sculpture.

'Rikki.'

'Mrs Pearl.' He had to blink once or twice before the spell would give way. 'Of course, your swimming lesson.'

'Yes.' She fell into step beside him. 'You were miles away, Rikki.'

'I was thinking,' he said.

'Of cabbages and kings,' she said, companionably. He could take it up, or not, as he chose.

'Of how quickly it's happened,' he said. 'A few months ago there was nothing here, you know—just beach and sea.'

'And what would you do,' she asked at a tangent, 'if once again there was nothing?'

At once she saw it was an impossible question. How could anyone tell what one would do, until one knew the circumstances? But he answered without hesitation.

'Then once again I would be a fisherman, that's all,' he said

139

simply, and laughed at her preposterous question.

By now they were at the pool—deserted, it was tea-time. She had picked the hour, preferring not to be seen as she essayed the breast stroke—an indecent act, she felt, at her age. It was his time off, but he kept it from her. Some sympathy for this lonely woman, or delicacy, made him understand her feelings. If only he could have poured the art into her sluggish limbs instead of these humiliating lessons, he felt—. As it was he could only demonstrate, and paddle alongside, and hold her up when she gulped and sank, one hand supporting her quivering, but indomitable, diaphragm.

If she had detected dolphin notes, he soon perceived that she was an earth woman, who would always be out of her depth in water. They both persevered, while she in addition was moved by the extraordinary patience, and beauty, of this boy who came to her hotel daily, smiling, willing, often encouraging her to what she could only describe as indulging herself.

'You mustn't,' she said one afternoon, overcome by these feelings—she was not swimming, or even trying, merely lounging in the pool, 'just let me wallow. I would, you know. The water's so lovely and warm, I could stay in forever.'

'Then you must,' he said cheerfully. 'I shall be here, and you will be quite safe.'

'No,' she said, and heaved herself out. 'I won't allow it. I'm sure you have better things to do than nanny an old woman.'

Though she had no idea what. Shalimar and the supplanted colony ran more or less cheek by jowl, but were nevertheless clamped off from each other at blood level by some invisible surgical wizardry.

Rikki had; but he swept these things aside.

'It's a pleasure,' he said simply, and it was not merely the standard phrase drilled into every Shalimar employee, but rose from a genuine feeling.

Why could not Mrs Pearl accept equally simply? Surely she was past believing that everything calls for payment in cash, a somewhat frenetic trading as if life was a corn exchange? she asked herself. But these sound promptings did not prevent her from behaving like a corn merchant.

It was not done too easily either. She had to hunt for her sponge-bag, buried in a vast clutter of things she found it necessary (Rikki had noticed) to carry around with her, and rummage in the
140

steamy depths. . . But at last she extracted what she wanted, and thrust it at him somewhat convulsively, and closed his fingers over the moist banknote and patted his fist.

By now she was beyond words.

Rikki remained calm. He returned the money, and said, politely, 'No, thank you, Mrs Pearl.'

'Why not, Rikki? Time,' she blurted, 'is money.' She did not think it was. Time was mysterious stuff, not an issue from a human mint.

'I'm paid for my time,' said Rikki. And even for his time off, he had discovered. He was earning more than he had ever done in his life—more than his father and brother put together.

Mrs Pearl accepted defeat, temporarily. She knew she would try again, after bolstering herself up for the attempt; and in a burst of honesty understood she would do it to still her rich woman's conscience. Perhaps it was the disturbing country, but she was finding that both riches and conscience rested less easily.

One night, weeks later, Rikki was serving in the cocktail bar when he saw her beckoning and went over to take her order. She was sitting alone, drinking whisky and knitting a woolly jumper—not without difficulty, for the wool was wet, the whiskery ball sat in a puddle of whisky-soda slopped on the table.

'What would you like?' He mopped up some of the mess, and waited.

'Another tot and here you are enjoy yourself,' she said in one fell sentence, and without ceremony pushed it into his hand—not one note, this time, but a roll. Scanning it with an experienced eye he saw it must contain at least a thousand rupees. He gasped and handed it back.

'No, really, Mrs Pearl.'

'Why not?' She glared at this man who was rejecting her conscience-money. 'Is my money polluted, or something?'

'No, of course not—but maybe another time,' he said.

'Why not now?' She challenged. 'Do you think I'm drunk?' She had, of course, deliberately pickled herself for the deed.

He could see she was. Toddy drunks were common in the colony, when the fishing was bad. The cocktail bar had enlarged his experience, widening it to include the women. These days he could have told a drunk, male or female, at a hundred paces: but of course a waiter could not tell a Visitor.

His silence drove her to confession.

141

'Well, I am,' she said belligerently. 'How do I know? Because I never drop stitches when I'm sober.' And she held up her knitting, which was, in all conscience, lamentable. It could have been a net, as easily as a jumper. 'But old fuddled Pearl,' she almost wailed, 'knows what she's doing.'

'I'm sure,' he soothed, while he looked round for help. There were bouncers; one for men, and one, the suavest of mortals, his musculature concealed under the sleekest, most flattering satin, who eased the ladies back to their villas. But never one in sight, needless to say, when wanted.

Meanwhile she had stuffed the bankroll into his cummerbund.

'So am I sure,' she said, and rose above the fumes to even higher reaches of honesty and self-knowledge. 'I'm old. I'm rich. I'm alone in the world except for one niece by marriage. It pleases me to give. Why can't you take?' Her voice pealed as she reached the question mark.

He was bewildered. He himself did not know where he drew the line. Sometimes he took, felt free to take, to *ask* and take. Sometimes he could not. He played it by ear, by feeling, some kind of internal, or spiritual, antennae at work.

'I will. Later.' He postponed dissection, and disinterring the wad slid it neatly into her knitting-bag and pulled the strings tight.

Chapter Twenty-two

WITH Tully it had resolved into simplicity. He asked, or was offered, or refused. There was no sense of strain.

Except that day with the brandy.

Supplies of various kinds came up the hill twice a week, and were stored in the cellars, or the vast underground ice-house, vintage '05, that Avalon boasted. Tully chose to offload himself, not caring to have the place swarming with servants. He carried up what he needed—cold chicken, bread, beer—to stack in the larder or in his fridge. Sometimes Rikki helped.

Perhaps it was the bottle in his hand, jewelled, coldly beautiful, that led him to ask.

'No,' said Tully, after verifying what it was. 'You're too young to start.'

'I'm eighteen.' Which, he had heard, in Tully's world marked off the men from the boys.

'You told me sixteen.' Tully had been told, for there had been a birthday, precisely a week old. He remembered it well because of the sweetmeats Rikki had conveyed from his mother, which had required chasing with alka-seltzers.

'By mistake. I'm eighteen,' he said, sweating a little.

'You're lying,' said Tully plainly, for indeed it could not have been plainer.

'I only want to *taste* it!' cried exasperated Rikki.

'You do that. In Shalimar,' said Tully, washing his hands. 'It shouldn't be too difficult. You look after the trolley, don't you?' A well-stocked trolley too, parked beside the pool, keys entrusted to the pool attendant.

'But that,' Rikki recoiled, when the sense finally percolated, 'would be stealing.'

Tully could have wept. Out here these were the expected perks, householders allowed for them in their budgets as routinely as building firms, where he came from, costed the free holiday for housing chairmen. But this boy—

By now he was out of patience.

'Up to you. All yours,' he said, and plonked down a bottle. 'Help yourself, when you feel up to it.'

But Rikki was squeamish, or finicky. He would have his

143

transactions wholehearted and sweet, or wanted no truck at all. He picked up brandies, sodas, sherbets (he loved sherbets, and Tully had laid in a stock to refresh him while he toiled) and clanked off up the stairs.

It was different with the implements needed for embellishing Avalon's impluvium.

Rikki had a set, a bequest from Mr Bridie.

'You may as well have them, Rikki.' Because Benjamin Bridie was old, old beyond his years—exile did that to a man. 'I don't suppose I shall have much use for them now,' he said, looking down at his ageing hands, objectively enough. Fingers that were no longer capable of the delicate work they delighted in, and would always hold aloof from less. Hands with little grip left in them, covered with old skin, withered, yellow, speckled brown. Gravemarks, children called this autumn confetti; and were told to hush. 'Yes,' he said, pale eyes caressing the tawny boy, this vivid apprentice who had overtaken his master. 'No more ships and bottles for me, Rikki. But you—'

'What would I do with them, Mr Bridie?'

'Who knows? Life is a strange business, you never know what you'll be called upon. . .'

This to a fisherboy. Bridie himself saw some absurdity, without Mrs Bridie to point it out for him.

'Our Lord has mysterious ways,' he said vaguely, and as certainties improved, 'An artist deserves the right tools,' he said with conviction. 'You hold on to them, Rikki.'

Rikki did, he lavished care. But the baize in which they were wrapped, long before he took possession, had been nibbled by Bridie's bandicoots (as they were known: fatter and sleeker beasts, from feasting on Bridie stores, than country cousins who lived off the villagers' rations). More holes than fabric, it barely held the tools. Salt air corroded the metal, cutting edges grew blunt, no amount of greasing and honing restored their pristine keenness.

'I could do with some new ones, Mr Tully,' said Rikki, frowning over a blade.

'Yes, I can see.' A ruinous collection, offending every canon of efficiency. 'Make out a list,' said Tully.

Rikki soon did, and handed it over to Tully, who entrusted the shopping to a peon. He could not spare the time, Rikki could not afford the trip into town. Actually he could, but after a lifetime of counting the small coin, could not believe in such affluence.

144

At length the goods arrived.

It was like setting out a picnic for Shalimaris, felt Rikki, as he arranged various gleaming implements on the work-bench.

'But there's ever so many,' he said doubtfully. Chisels alone had arrived in four sizes. 'I'm sure I didn't—'

He suspected the peon, a weak creature at best, had been overpowered by hard selling.

'I expect I did,' said Tully, slightly offhand.

'What for?' When Rikki wanted to know he asked, with, mostly, a cavalier disregard for feelings. It was unsettling, even for those who were becoming acclimatised; even for Tully, whose clan were specialists in the cavalier.

'Well,' said Tully, after a pause, and still a trifle dodgy about it, 'one or two notions of my own, you know.'

It was in fact a small and persistent ambition like Mrs Pearl's, running alongside AIDCORP's grandeur, more extravagant flow, just keeping its head above water. Starting with the building rubble, and suppressed by dusty au pairs, it flared again in a school which, with the aloof prodigality of nature, and perhaps an equally classical perfectionism, did not care if a thousand fledglings fell by the wayside, so long as one swan, hopefully a Marlowe or a Wren, spread its wings. It believed in fostering human foible, however wayward; as it could afford to, being soundly founded. Tully—gargoyles at this stage—it took in its stride. It would not go so far as to pledge its own battlements, but it provided the wherewithal, together with a craftsman drafted in from a convenient cathedral. A 1:1 teacher/pupil ratio, in any case, was regarded as understrength, if anything.

Perhaps it was Rikki who provided the encouragement, humped over his work, muttering, tormented. Perhaps it was all that Carrara and Flanders marble, shipped in with Copeland abandon and a high disdain for parsimony, glinting through the sacks stored in godowns and pergolas. At any rate here was the cherub, already blocked out, and destined to step out of the marble into the centre of the pool.

Which still lacked the magic ingredient.

'The rains, Rikki,' Tully tackled his assistant and co-worker, 'are overdue, aren't they?'

Rikki grunted; he was busy.

'Aren't they?'

'They'll come.'

'So will Christmas.'

'Yes.' Rikki could not but endorse the sensible proposition. All things in due season, as Mrs Bridie had been fond of saying. She couldn't wait for Christmas, however. Or made it an excuse. By September the Dundee cake had been ordered, and all through the months thereafter they were concocting the meringues between them, batches emerged daily from the dented oven, spongy and pale brown. But they crisped up wonderfully, if only one could wait. He often wondered that Mrs Bridie could not, especially with her uncertain teeth, they invariably lost to unfirm meringue.

'What I mean is,' Tully spelled it out, irony was lost on the peasantry. 'When will it rain? *If*,' he said, crescendo, 'it ever does?'

Such frenzy, felt disapproving Rikki; and sighed for his work, and sat back on his heels. 'One must be patient,' he counselled.

Tully could be infinitely patient; patient ad nauseam, Boyle, his partner, sometimes found it. He would take his time arguing the merits of permanence in structures with some nomad-recruit hooked on the absolute self-sufficiency of a yurt. (Not that Tully wasn't: something about these fold-up-and-go dwellings.) But it irked Boyle, who went more for the Pyramid style. He believed in overseers who could crack invisible whips over the heads of the labouring files, with a sound like pistol fire.

Sometimes he was vindicated. Some men, like some women, respond to the flick of rawhide. Boyle and Tully each gave the other his due. Possibly AIDCORP would not have been the flourishing concern it was, if it had not provided the choice in a world hung, as ever, between carrot and stick.

When it came to his pet scheme, however, Tully's patience crumbled like greedy Mrs Bridie's. He could not wait, it went against the grain, which was English. Perhaps, to do him justice, there was no reason to wait. Soon Ramalingam was on the scene, and hired labourers began to arrive by the lorryload to pipe in supplies.

For Rikki, watching proceedings with his usual keen interest, the project came as something of a revelation.

Shalimar had been raised up with an equal speed and thrust, but it was an enterprise of that powerful giant AIDCORP. This was one man's private whim, less basic to needs than the sinking of a well, or even the burnishing of Avalon. Tully wanted water, and water he would have, no matter that it had to come from the springs that watered his orchard on the far side of the hill. Tully did not care how far they were. He would, Rikki saw, have what he wanted. He would alter the landscape, if necessary, split open any country as if it were his oyster.

As he could, it lay within his power, and the power of men like him.

At times like these Rikki felt the division between them, between one man and another, their minds, their reach and sway, the reality of the distance between himself and Tully. *Distance?* Notes of incredulity sounded as well. Distance between them, chipping at marble in the pool-room together, sharing the light, and emotions? Where was the reality, what was vapour? Presently he had to lay down the chisel and simply sit, wondering, looking full-face at Tully.

'What is it, Rikki?' Absorbed though he was, Tully could not ignore the glance. It would be opaque, he could tell even without looking up. Absinthe gone cloudy, after additives.

'Distance,' said Rikki. 'There is an ocean between us,' he said, flatly.

Tully, not being born yesterday, had to admit it. But, oddly, he found he had to work at it to believe in the solid admission. For was there an ocean? Really? Actually? His incredulity echoed Rikki's. For there were times, long serene stretches in which they were within touching distance, when they touched. He was aware, then, of things going on, at levels not subject to corruption, from which rose feelings of authoritative clarity: a quality of simply being that washed over them like water or light, and merged them into the one landscape.

Chapter Twenty-three

SHALIMAR was a little world all of its own, Mrs Contractor often reflected, cosily, as she allowed thoughts to browse over the amiable landscape while she sat, in her suite in the Asoka, in a comfortable, flowered housecoat. She had moved in the moment the place was ready. Beach villas were all very well for those who liked that sort of thing, but she did not, particularly. Thatched, some of them; and first thing in the morning, the sea, lapping at one's toes. (She exaggerated shamelessly; the sea kept its distance.) But the villas were very popular, and people must have what they wanted, felt Mrs Contractor indulgently, wriggling her toes in her fluffy mules. And what nice people came as a result! The nicest, most charming people were drawn to Shalimar, it made all one's efforts worthwhile.

Mrs Contractor sighed, happily. She presided happily over her fair domain. She managed everything, and rather well, if she said it herself. Certainly no flaw, or corner, could hope to escape her attention as she toured the grounds, or, from the Asoka, issued the order of the day.

At seven o'clock punctually it was Miss Chari, the housekeeper, who also did the flowers. She was a dark, slight girl, with pleasing manners, whom Mrs Contractor had personally selected out of twenty-five candidates for the job. Looking her over, as she stood respectfully in the Shalimar silks (azure and argent borders to a spotless white sari and blouse), Mrs Contractor could not but congratulate herself on having chosen well.

'Shall we have red today, madam?' Miss Chari opened proceedings.

For between them they decided on the *leit-motif* for the day, to co-ordinate mood and decor. Floral arrangements, the napery, the linen—entranced Shalimaris woke to patterned breakfast china that matched the posy of violets or rosebuds on the chota-hazri tray.

'We have had—let me think—pink, for two days, isn't it, Miss Chari?'

'Yes, madam.'

'Then we'll have red...roses, you were thinking of?'

148

'Hibiscus, Mrs Contractor.' Miss Chari chanced her arm.

'Yes, hibiscus, the hedge is full,' approved Mrs Contractor. 'But what kind of leaves—' as her mind filled with nasty pictures. 'I don't want those spiky things, Miss Chari, that you put with the oleander.'

'Fern, then, madam?' Miss Chari weaned herself away. She had been thinking of spikes, after a brush with a chela of the Ikenobo school. 'Dark green, to bring out the red.'

'Yes. Excellent,' said Mrs Contractor benignly. The girl would yet learn, under her training. 'Make sure the malis—you know what they are—but we must have nice fresh sprays.'

'Yes, madam.'

Then it was time for a shower, and a light breakfast with Mr Contractor, before Mrs Contractor moved on.

On her morning round, under a parasol, in a crisp morning sari. For she would *not* be seen, except by servants, in a housecoat. So sloppy, and bad for discipline, and did nothing for one's figure. Round the gardens, and the fountains, a peep at the Emporium to see if the window dressing caught the eye; and so to the kitchens by 9 a.m. sharp.

For everything depended. One knew cuisine could make or break. The most promising ventures had simply gone phut! because the cooking was not up. Besides, tourists—she gave her wrist a little slap—Visitors marched on their stomachs.

The servants prepared for memsahib. They laid out some kind of *bazaar,* after tottering forth at some unearthly hour as memsahib ordered. Fresh this, fresh that. Vegetables picked that morning, and dew must be visible on the fruit as they were unloaded from the lorries. Meat, luckily, had to be hung. But the fish. Lifted fresh from the sea—straight off the beach—kept basted with water—the more delicate must be bedded on ice—

But always a problem, fish. Too much of this, too little of that, and *who* would eat this thing that gave up little but a mouthful of bones? Buyers and sellers alike grew sullen.

'Tell me, Joseph.' Mrs Contractor had arrived, and stood, and spoke, patiently. 'Tell me what we are going to do with all this mackerel—' she tapped a creel with the ferrule of her parasol, '—when it is prawn cocktails and scampi on the menu?'

Joseph did not know. He had hauled the culprit along to explain—the chief fisherman, at that, because it was by no means a first offence.

149

'Well?'

Mumble-jumble.

'What?'

'He is saying, memsahib,' Joseph unravelled, 'low season for prawns.'

'He said that last month!' Mrs Contractor felt she had a right to feel indignant. 'Tell him this month is *high* season.'

Mumble-jumble.

'*Now* what is he saying?'

'He is saying, memsahib, only what the sea is giving, they catches.'

'But they don't catch the right things!'

'Next time they will. Now you take mackerel, memsahib.' For Joseph could not help pitying the desperate old man.

'But, Joseph—mackerel cocktails!' wailed Mrs Contractor.

Now the chef stepped up. He was the one who would have to cope, and be summoned to the dining-room by irate diners to explain what his kitchens had dished up. In any case he—an artist, an ex-P & O chef—had his reputation to consider.

'Too much oil, memsahib.' He prodded mackerel flesh, and oily droplets undoubtedly oozed.

It decided Mrs Contractor, who had been veering. No, she would not lower the standards of *haute tourisme,* as she believed it was known.

'We will buy, any amount. We are not poor,' she declared. 'But we must have *guaranteed* quality, *guaranteed* quantity. Tell him that, Joseph. And,' this was a particular trial, '*all* the guts must be taken out, even one tiny piece can spoil the flavour.'

Otherwise she would simply have to fly in from Miami. Cleaned to perfection, packed in ice, straight into the walk-in freezers—no. The government was troublesome about importing, for some stuffy reason. Well then, Bombay. Yes, that was the solution.

But before she turned away she found it necessary to say, for whatever reason, what was very true: 'If no one comes to Shalimar, let me tell you, you will *all* be out of a job!'

And when she had moved on a few steps, she sent Joseph back to pay for the fish she didn't want. She didn't know why, unless it was that poor fisherman with his wretched mackerel. Although she was fairly certain Shalimar, as usual, employed a member, or two, from that family. *And* paid fat wages, fatter than what they could get for their greasy fish.

*

If Shalimar was a little world of its own, there was a little world *within* that world that was also rounding out nicely, felt Mrs Contractor. In it dwelt what one might call the regulars, as opposed to Visitors who came wrapped up in package tours and could only stay for three days, or a week, or just sometimes for a fortnight if they had booked with the most élite and expensive tour companies. One hardly got to know them before they were gone, and there was the bearer with a bunch of flowers, or on her desk a little flask of Chanel 19, so acceptable because you could not get French perfume for love nor money. No way, as the young people said.

But bitter-sweet, the gifts and departures.

Mrs Contractor sighed. She loved all these fleeting guests, she loved fussing over them, advising them what to do, where to go, what to eat, ushering them into coaches for excursions, and reviving them when they returned with jugfuls of lemon squash, and trays bearing cool moist muslin squares to freshen their steamy faces.

'Because,' she told them when they thanked her, 'would you not do the same for me if I were a stranger in your country? No, no, no, it is nothing, it is simply Do unto others.'

At which point she invariably grew quite radiant.

Goodbyes, on the other hand, were hateful. She would not think of them. But when it came to it—'Au revoir,' she said, firmly, as she stood on the verandah steps, and the hotel's luxury coach pulled in under the portico. Her eyes often pricked.

'But you should expect. In a business like this.' It really flummoxed her husband. 'You are too soft-hearted, my love,' said Mr Contractor.

'You are perfectly right, Cyrus,' sighed Mrs Contractor. She knew she was. She could not help it.

It was cheering, then, to think of those who were staying, not going.

Like Mrs Lovat, who was writing a book about India, and had therefore booked in for three months at Special Reduced Rate. And Mr Patterson, the photographer, who was doing a visual study, also three months, S.R.R. And Mrs Pearl, who had simply fallen in love, and declared she would stay as long as they let her.

'That is years and years,' Mrs Contractor beamed at her.

'Then years and years it is,' beamed back Mrs Pearl.

Then, there were those whom she would term the inner circle. Heblekar and Sitharam and Tully, and that nice boy Ranji, and pretty little Mrs Heblekar in saris of butterfly chiffon—so different

151

from her husband in his horrid blue dungarees. Mr Boyle too: her old and dear friend Herbert, who would soon be arriving, and then there were his friends the Tremletts, old India hands, whom Herbert had very kindly invited for an extended visit, and who had already arrived.

Yes, they made up a delightful, cosy little band.

Mrs Contractor thought of them as her brood, much as she did the Visitors. She looked after them with an equal care. At least she did her best to, but one or two proved resistant. Sitharam, for instance, born in some small Southern town, assuming he knew better than herself who came from the capital. And Tully, who tended to ignore her advice though he should have known better—and at this point in her meditations she did catch him drinking workmen's tea in the works canteen, which she had come to inspect.

'Mr Tully, I have told you before. It is not wise.' She thought it not quite, as well.

Tully did not do it to flout Mrs Contractor, particularly. Or to prove machismo. That it would hardly do, since he was blessed with a cast-iron stomach, reinforced by innumerable jabs. He did it to keep the AIDCORP labour force happy. If workers liked their brew hot, sweet and bright orange, he was quite prepared to sample it from time to time to ensure they got what they wanted.

'Not wise?' Tully raised an unconvinced eyebrow. 'If you're suggesting that tea—anything—brewed under your supervision is unsafe, then I'm afraid,' smiling at the concerned woman, 'I must simply refuse to believe you.'

So pleasant, Mrs Contractor felt, and such a good-looking young man, and an *impeccable* family.

Mrs Contractor melted like butter, but would not allow herself to be swayed.

'You are too charming for your own good, Mr Tully!' she scolded. 'Suppose you get typhoid from the milk?'

'Isn't the milk pasteurised?'

'Of course it is.' She almost bridled.

'Then why?' One hand helpless. The other firmly holding the mug, as she saw. 'Our workmen don't get typhoid.'

'You are not a workman!' She felt quite shrill.

'Ah, then,' he shifted the battleground. 'I could count on being very well looked after in the Spa.'

For there was not only a distant Tower of Silence (unused, happily). There was also the Spa, under which inspired name
152

lurked the small, spick-and-span hospital which had arisen in the very first phase of building, to look after the casualties of peace.

Mrs Contractor would not, or could not, argue any more. She smiled, and managed a civilised 'Cheerio!', and resumed her little tour, while she resolved, severely, she would get Herbert Boyle, the moment he arrived, to have a word with the young man.

But she could not be severe for long. Soon she was dwelling on happier things, the cast of her mind was towards the pleasant. She thought, as she walked towards tiffin (it was time: how it flew!) of the evening, when she would sit with her friends on the cool verandah, and there would be agreeable conversation. About the Kashmir Lakes, or New York, or they would discuss books, or India, with dear Adeline Lovat who came from Newark, N.J. Or perhaps plan an excursion, or some other little diversion, with everyone contributing suggestions, and eventually they would all plump for the same thing, which she had suggested in the first place. Yes, one always looked forward to evenings in Shalimar.

Chapter Twenty-four

WHATEVER Mrs Contractor's opinion of the woman, Rikki found Mrs Lovat a trial. It was like Miss Lockwood, in a more acute form. She wanted to see how he lived, he would not let her. She insisted. He grew morose, reflecting it could go on for months. It redounded to Miss Lockwood's credit, in his view, that she had only stayed a week.

'No way,' he said finally, and rudely, in defiance of every Shalimar precept, and even of his own nature which inclined to the obliging. He hoped to place the matter beyond further discussion, and therefore used the most advanced language in his enlarging repertoire to make her understand.

Adeline Lovat was baffled; and the commonplace, though blunt phrase undoubtedly grated.

'Why not?' she asked, or even challenged, the surly youth.

Rikki stood. To confess why would have been even worse than pushing her over their mangy threshold into the grim hut. He glared at his persecutor, with her wiry hair, and her piercing black eyes, and her impossible questions which he would not answer.

She would get nothing from him, she saw, resentfully. Then some angel of grace lent her a few wisps, which she grasped.

'I don't want to pry,' she said simply. 'It's just that your country fascinates me. I'd like to find out as much as I can, that's all.'

So that he found it was possible, after all, to respond.

'What do you want to know?' he asked, not too ungraciously.

'I'll take anything you give,' said Mrs Lovat, perfectly sincerely.

But she would and she wouldn't, Rikki discovered.

She wanted to learn about his country, and he, also with the best will, either could not get past certain blocks in his nature, or did not know how to enlighten her.

Because, he asked himself, what did he know of his own country? He, who had never gone more than a few kilometres beyond the borders of his village? While a voice did whisper, reinforced by memories of old, fading conversations.

'Another half century, Rose, and we'd still be rooting.

154

Presumptuous, to imagine we can penetrate very far. Just touch the tip of the womb, once in a blue moon—any little boy born in this country could do better. Truths in the blood, you see, my dear Rosie-posy.'

For Benjamin Bridie had raised the needling of his wife to an art, in the exercise of which he would not scruple to use sexual imagery, which he knew she detested.

Rikki allowed it some validity, in the painful process of self-analysis he was now undergoing; while he also understood he was too young, or unskilled, as well as unwilling, to extract such elusive essences and present them bottled and stoppered into Mrs Lovat's wistful palm.

He resorted, instead, to comparative shallows. He sang, in a thin tenor, the old sea-shanties, into her tape-recorder. He told her the old stories—tales from his childhood, and sea-lore, which he found many people besides himself found haunting. His former life, in a way, and all still there, rather surprisingly considering, he himself felt.

'And Manimekhala,' he finished that particular story—he was half under its spell by then. 'At times she would swallow up whole ships, and all the merchants in them.'

'Was Manim—was she a whale?' asked Adeline Lovat, who, bred up on Jonah, was prepared to go that far.

'No, a woman, a divine woman.'

'An interesting legend,' thought, and said, Mrs Lovat.

'It's true,' said Rikki, flatly.

'Oh, non-sense, Rikki!' she protested in her American English.

He was used to the accent, there were several Americans in the Camp; but somehow the way she said it made it sound worse than nonsense, as if it was utterly senseless.

Then he told her about the Emperor of Hindusthan, whose great-great-great-grandmother had been seduced by a moonbeam, and again she questioned.

'Do you believe that, Rikki?' She really wanted to find out.

'Yes.'

'But it's pre-posterous!' It was wrung from her. She badly wanted not to think he was that credulous.

All his hostility returned. Could she not imagine? How, then, did she get to her truths? He began to wonder about the books she wrote.

Mrs Lovat wrote books about India which were admired

everywhere, except in India.

'They don't like my work,' she herself confessed, wistfully, sometimes with a touch of bitterness, for she did try, and could never make out why it had to be so. Sometimes she put it down to a lack of humour, for she saw the funny side of the country, and wrote about it. But how could that be true, when most of her Indian friends laughed easily? she asked herself, and more than once, she was by nature an honest woman. In Shalimar, in all honesty, she had not found the Heblekars wanting. As for Sitharam, he often went into giggles, fits like a schoolgirl.

All the same her novels were not liked.

'I can't figure out why,' she said.

She would not let it worry her too much, but it was hurtful.

*

Rikki reported her to Tully, before she could report him to the Manageress for discourtesy or something. Discourtesy was a grave matter in Shalimar, over which Mrs Contractor might preside, but she would also listen to Tully, as he had very soon spotted.

This precautionary measure, however, was also part of the growing, and intensifying, and agreeable exchange between them.

'She has no imagination,' he repeated his earlier conclusion, and went on to offer an explanation. 'It's all dried up. It's her age,' he said.

Rikki was 16 or 18—after their last argument he had lost track. To him 30 was getting on. Tully, nudging 30, could agree that 40 was getting on, but not that it was quite as desiccated as Rikki appeared to think.

'Well, I suppose she is getting on,' he conceded, after a mental apology to the small, gentle woman. 'But why,' he had to pursue the matter, which was involved: belief in the truths of legendry could suggest either aborigine or philosopher, and those who told the fabulous truth had never since antiquity been treated as other than dealers in pulp fiction. 'Why do you want her to think you *actually* believe?' It was the best he could do with the difficult subject.

'Why not?' Rikki was grinning away. 'Old stupid,' he said, cheerfully.

As they were engaged in the cheerful, both soon put aside the tedium of women.

It was a jolly, naval exercise; a maiden voyage for Tully's boat on which, the weather being promising, the two breezy sailors had embarked. They were sailing upriver.

156

By now Tully was not sure it *was* his boat. Rikki shared the same doubt. They were managing, or not managing, together. Tully, baptised in boyhood in Cornish waters, no one could have termed a novice; but he was intrigued by the craft, which to him was of novel design and unusual construction. He was less attentive than he should have been. Rikki was less nifty, from lack of sleep; he had been serving till the small hours, as usual on a Saturday night. The boom had already slammed him twice.

Luckily for them, the boat knew a good deal about sailing. Its construction was classic, bred up from Indian rivers; and it had been built by a sound builder. Hassan had listened to all the contradictory demands that flew round his head—it must be safe as a coracle but look like a swan; race; be a river-boat; ocean-going; the attributes of a fishing sloop as well—in fact a many-sided wonder.

And calmly proceeded to execute an old, proven design.

The man was sound in realms beyond boat-building. If a foreigner drowned, he knew well, there would be more outcry than if a bargeload of the locals went down.

He made the boat virtually impossible to capsize.

In defiance of all the boat and builder could do, Tully and Rikki succeeded in capsizing it.

The manoeuvre that precipitated them was Tully's. They had just sailed past a creek, when he was seized by a desire to explore it on the instant. Rikki was agreeable, but recommended coming round in a circle since the wind had freshened. Tully was less patient, and intent on testing his boat, or his nautical skills. 'Gybe-O!' he sang, or something equally incomprehensible to his crewman, who was also the master. . . Between them the boat came stern to wind, the main sail began flapping violently, the swinging boom whammed Rikki a third time; and the boat heeled and went over.

The creek, fortunately, lay near. They swam, towing the boat with them, and hauled it on to the shelving beach, and sat exhausted and dripping on the sands. Everything of course was wringing; the canvas, the food in the salvaged picnic basket, Tully's shoes, his towel.

In Rikki's view, towels were dispensable. He had often tried to put this view across to Tully, without success. Now, his eye said, you will discover for yourself.

Tully had no desire, but also no option. He sat, after spreading his gear out to dry, and tried to feel not only naked but shivery.

But it was not easy. The sun shone brightly. A sea-breeze soft as fleece, warmed by sunshine, polished his limbs as engagingly as an odalisque. A towel, however fluffy, might indeed have rasped, in these circumstances.

'Perhaps,' he admitted to his companion, 'we don't need as much clobber as we think we do.'

Rikki was ready to agree with anything, he was in that mood; while he sat, with his wristwatch pressed to his ear, listening for the tick. For it had been thoroughly soused, one couldn't help feeling anxious, although it was guaranteed waterproof.

Soon, however, the day stilled all this neurosis, helped along by canned beer and bars of chocolate that had survived the ducking. Birds sang, or stalked past on haughty stilts with knees hinged backwards—excruciatingly, from human view-point. Frogs plopped up, and saw with dismay, and sank with smothered quaarks! There was a lilt and lap of water in the creek.

'How peaceful it is.' Tully lay upward to sun, arms enshrining his head, lashes feathering in tender, unflawed blues.

'Yes.' Rikki nibbled a stem; spears of tough dune grass had thrust up here and there through the fine white sand.

'If only,' said Tully, 'one could be sure it'll always be like this.'

'It's always been like this,' said Rikki, 'for as long as I remember.'

'That's no guarantee, is it?' said Tully.

'No.' Even guarantees were worthless, as Rikki was discovering. His watch had ceased to tick.

'Seems a shame,' Tully could not help but toll the common, age-old bell, 'that a place like this should ever be spoiled.'

'Why should it be?' asked Rikki.

'No reason.'

'Then it won't be.'

'But—' Tully was aware of going back on himself, 'there are reasons.'

'What?'

'A need. People have a craving. . . the desert seems to call, we all need the wilderness from time to time.'

From which one sprang: the secret thickets beckoned.

'If people need, they should have.' It was so simple; Rikki closed his eyes.

'But you see,' for now despite everything it had begun to nag, 'that's where it starts.'

A thickening of the cervix, imperceptible at this stage: the site,

158

unless there were remissions, for later invasion.

'Do you mean Shalimar?' Rikki opened an eye. Pure instinct led him to ask.

'What do you mean?' It jolted Tully. Sophistries, polished up in daily dealing, coped with sophisticates—a Minister, a Ranji, even Heblekar. But this was Rikki, his ruthless simplicity annihilated the easy, diplomatic answers. 'Perhaps I do,' he said, and this too was in a sense a discovery: covert admissions in the mind sliding into overt delivery. 'But,' he defended himself, 'we give what we're asked to give.'

'Why do you, if you don't really want to?' Rikki opened both his eyes. Useless to try to sleep, he saw, with Tully in this mood.

'Because—' Tully sat up. He was beginning to feel quite exposed, even chilled. He looked round for his towel, which was drying on the upturned hull of the boat, but it was Turkish, and thick, and clearly still soaking. He resigned himself to nudity. 'Well, I suppose,' he said—because what else could explain it, in the state he was in? 'To earn a living' lost every vestige of meaning, in this climate. 'I suppose once we have set the juggernaut rolling, we don't seem to know how to stop it.'

Now they were into Rikki's territory, he took advantage.

'When my mother was a girl,' he began, dreamily. Dreams and reality often telescoped in these realms; when some imp of his own creation caught hold of him. 'My real mother,' he said, and sat right up. 'You don't think I'm a foundling, do you, Mr Tully?'

'I know you're not.' Tully was moved. These haunting anxieties, unnecessary, self-willed, with which people seemed determined to scourge themselves. 'You've told me scores of times. But foundlings,' he said, 'can be loved as dearly as one's own children.'

'She cherished me. Now when she was a girl,' Rikki, reassured, felt able to continue, 'there were people who would throw themselves under the wheels of Jagannath's chariot. They felt, you see, that they had to sacrifice themselves.'

Tully eyed him again, sharply, and again met a gaze of such lucid candour that made him feel ashamed. Nevertheless this hare too had to be pursued.

'Are you advising me,' he said, 'to throw myself under the chariot?'

'Why should you?' Rikki was both wide awake and utterly astonished. 'These people, in my mother's day—their souls were possessed. You are not,' he said and hoped, 'so crazy.'

159

'Tell me,' said Tully, with a distant curiosity, 'these crazy souls—did they ever manage to halt the chariot?'

'Oh no.' Rikki laughed heartily. 'The wheels just crushed them, and the chariot went on.'

Tully had to laugh too. He felt he recognised the picture: pathetic, but comedy of a distilled order that might well appeal to a god as much as it did to humans like themselves.

'It's different now.' Rikki continued on a discernible note of regret. 'These days there is crowd control, and the police thwack those who become possessed. All the same—'

'What?'

'They are remembered,' said Rikki, very faraway now. 'Once a year, when the day comes round, their names are chanted, and they let off fireworks in the village square. Everyone admires them, after all these years.'

'What I love,' said Tully—he felt, or had been rendered, quite helpless by now. 'What I love about you is the labyrinth you invite me to enter.' Every time he parted his lips, almost; and innocently, Tully was convinced.

'Labyrinth?' Rikki knew the word; but Mrs Bridie had forbidden Mr Bridie to venture into the meaning. She distrusted pagan adventures, preferring him to keep to the New Testament where things were better controlled.

'A maze. Something like this.' Tully drew in the sand.

'And?'

Tully told the story. Rikki listened, now and then exclaiming over resemblances to certain tales in his own repertory. Myths, re-affirming a common ancestry, sailed round the globe and connected under a sun now well past the meridian.

Things would be dry, even a towel of Turkish opulence.

'I suppose we ought to be moving,' said Tully at last, tipping sandwiches, baked hard as dog biscuit now, into the creek.

'Why?' Rikki bombarded the triangles of bread. Intrepid frogs, charging up for manna, retired glumly before such mindless shot.

'I'm hungry, for one thing.'

'I'm starving.' But it could be shelved. 'What else?'

'Things to do.'

'What?'

'Well,' said Tully, for it paled by comparison, 'there's a party.'

'For Mr Boyle.' It galvanised Rikki. 'I forgot! How could I forget! I was told—' Rapidly, bundling into his clothes, jamming cans and plates into the picnic basket, basket over an arm, wings

160

on his heels as he readies for flight.

'What about the boat?' Tully, not to be hustled, just gets his oar in.

'It's quite safe. It's yours, no one will touch it. I'll see to it later.'

'Why not now?'

'I shall be late. To serve. If I'm late, you know, Mr Tully, they will *fine* me. A *ten-rupee* fine.'

Cheeks positively hollow at the thought, and the firm smack of Management evident in the fine sprint he puts on.

Chapter Twenty-five

BOYLE had indeed arrived, long after scheduled date. He had been held up on the very tip of the Arabian peninsula by the natives; usual postwar phenomenon of the locals getting above themselves.

Not a plane to be had, not for any amount of money. There was no love. Finally it had to be a seaplane, once part of the fleet of Imperial Airways, now sold to the Ruler's cousin, who had nostalgic memories of Marlborough.

Boyle was used to all this; like Tully he travelled widely; but he was seldom amused, and the juddering plane, which only high-grade salesmanship had managed to shift, had shaken even his fairly steely nerves.

Motoring from the airport to Shalimar, the first thing he saw were Ranji's flags. Naturally; they were meant to be eye-catching. Nor could he uproot or supplant them, which was the first thought that occurred to him. If AIDCORP house colours flew—as he resolved they should, without delay—it would have to be side by side.

Tully was often struck by Boyle's attention to such detail, as Boyle was sometimes stricken by his colleague's indifference.

'It's a stage.' Boyle remembered Tully saying, with one of those imperceptible shrugs he found so acutely annoying, from not knowing if he was meant to see, or what. That time, too, they had been discussing flags, during a stint in a Caribbean island. 'We all go through it, and then we grow up,' he gave out his extraordinary opinion.

Boyle could not be so offhand. He remembered the conversation clearly, and firmed his resolve.

At which point, as he often did, Boyle fell to thinking about his fellow-director. Not a man one would team up with, he tended to conclude off and on, except for overriding reasons. The lustrous name, to mention one, which he badly wanted on his Board. To mention another, the respectable Copeland-Tully capital, which successive governments had scarcely been able to dent. Not to be sneezed at, in these hard times. A way with the hardware too. Invaluable in the tropics, where kicking expensive machines into functioning, or resorting to string, could incline more finely tuned

162

mortals to jump off cliffs. Also a knack of dealing with the locals—establishing good labour relations, as it was called; though Boyle allowed him this less easily.

When labour grew tired of rawhide, Boyle got hold of Tully, and Tully dealt with the rebellion. And the flurry subsided, Boyle was never sure how. Men went back to work.

Rather furtively, because his feelings on the subject were mixed, and a bit like the frail old Minister, though Boyle would have been surprised to learn they had anything in common, he put it down to Tully's stock. For it was history—and Boyle gave short shrift to Balzac's view that history was official lies, which someone had once dared to throw at him—how Britain had governed the country. One man under a peepul tree, or on a lonely bungalow verandah, holding the fate of a million or more in the imperturbable palm of one hand while dispensing justice and preserving the Pax Britannica.

Boyle was conscious of a swell of pride, when he conjured up the evocative picture. It overcame even his niggles over Tully.

Tully was aware of what lay behind that ancient, solo bravura—through his stock, and also because the subject fascinated. He had been intrigued enough to probe a little. Behind each man and his peepul stood the police contingent, the Fort, the bristling garrison. News went by pigeon, by helio, by wireless; frigates cruised, supported by a squadron of cavalry jingling ominously along the right bank; or a regiment was detached and arrived by forced marches to the music of fifes. While the locals, with a prudence the barest pirate would have exercised, had long since been stripped of their arms. By then, of course, piracy had suffered a sea-change. The Romans themselves would have saluted their equals.

Tully might know all this. He also acknowledged that no amount of stiffening behind the scenes could wholly account for the éclat of a performance that had passed into fable. Perversely, he would not say so to Boyle. He saw no need. They rubbed along, he considered, well enough together.

Some such thought was uppermost in Boyle as he debarked from the travelling crate, or People's car, in other words the oddly-named Ambassador, that had been sent to fetch him. (But the road to Shalimar was a first-rate job, a keen eye for such things had already noticed.) It reached geniality as Tully, showered, shaved, spruce (all this in five minutes flat), came forward to greet him.

'Welcome, Boyle sahib!' Pumping his hand, signalling up a

163

servant from the line assembled on Asoka's verandah, a garland descending on Boyle's gratified shoulders. And when the fuss—such a palaver, but pleasing elements in it notwithstanding—was over pulling forward a chair, pressing him into comfortable chintz depths.

'Good trip?'

'Well. You know.'

'Yes.' Sympathetically, for here they shared both language and experience. 'What'll you have?'

'What's available?'

'You name it.'

'Scotch?' Guarded, but hopeful. He had a fair amount of faith in his colleague's ability.

'No problem.'

Tumbler in hand, ruddy knuckles wrapped around the glass, Boyle began to relax.

'Well, cheers. Long time no-see, old boy. How's life?'

'Can't gripe.'

'That's the advantage.'

'What is?'

'Of the old connections, Toby. Makes this country sort of home from home, don't you think?' Sipping the reviving fluid, on Asoka's polished verandah, Boyle was quite convinced.

'Sometimes.' Tully felt obliged to sound the caveat.

'Sometimes?' Boyle would have none of it; by now he was far too cheerful.

When in breezed Ranji, loudly singing *Sheikh of Abu Dhabi* to the tune of *Araby*, the last words cunningly substituted by himself.

Ranji could have sunk through the floor.

He had not expected to see Boyle quite so soon. He had supposed, for reasons best known to himself, that the burra sahib would have been wafted off to marbled halls in Avalon by Tully. Yet here he was and no mistake—for who else could this red-faced old codger be, importantly ensconced with Tully and the cut-glass?

Boyle was not that pleased either. He did not care to be called sheikh of anywhere, especially disastrous Abu Dhabi which had been his last-but-one port of call, as he easily divined he was being. But Ranji's pain was more exquisite. Intent only on some private ribbing of the great, here he was, giving this prize exhibition. Poor Ranji paled. Military splendour might have sustained him, but, fresh from a skirmish with a Malibu, he was dressed in a bathrobe and sand shoes.

164

While getting on with the courtesies as best he could, he directed some silent fury at Tully, whom he held responsible.

Tully was blameless. He had cordially invited Boyle to lodge in Avalon, in the certainty that he would decline. Boyle had duly obliged; he shared Corinna's antipathy to being marooned on a hill, while happy to have been asked.

Goodwill established in this quarter, Tully was conscious of illwill in another, as Ranji's invective made its mark. Outshone for once, he deduced, wrongly; but what could a man in a bathrobe expect? And he gloated, somewhat, over the superior knife-edge to his own trousers. Meanwhile some latent doubts about old home-from-home had begun to nibble at Boyle, only slightly appeased by Ranji's smart accent that derived from Dehra Dun, via Sandhurst.

Being civilised men, however, the three were not incapable of rising above this private clamour; and were exchanging desperately civil trivia when help arrived in the person of Mrs Contractor.

Zavera herself, by Jove! and as plump and fair as ever was! rejoiced Boyle, and rose with some alacrity to greet her.

Dear Herbert! felt Zavera, and bore down on him, exclaiming affectionately, her evening *voile* streaming behind her.

'You naughty man! Why didn't you come sooner? No, no, no, no excuses! *We* know why you deserted us!'

'Why?' Boyle beamed.

'Because some Arabian *houri* put a spell on you! Isn't it, Ranji? But Ranji! My dear boy, you will catch pneumonia. Run away at once and change!'

Ranji hovered, also beaming. All three were. At times she would stun them silly, but joined to it was a gift for reducing a situation. Now they were in love with this woman in her poppy flowered *voile*. They adored her. They adored her froth and nonsense which made them feel as light and irresponsible as soufflés.

An amiably soufflé atmosphere prevailed.

Chapter Twenty-six

SOON Boyle was over his travel fatigue. He strode with a cluster of aides, over AIDCORP territory, an experienced eye raking over every detail of construction and development, and not missing much. Or he rode in a jeep, on extended tours of inspection. There were spot checks, and surprise descents. The atmosphere crackled—at least the infrastructure felt the sparks, though Shalimaris, who were insulated, noticed little except, perhaps, that the servants seemed to jump to it rather more when the large, heavy-jawed European was around. The rest were conscious of a kind of electricity that flowed from Boyle, that went before him like the advance warning of a storm.

It was especially noticeable on Mondays—after a re-charging of batteries over the weekend, the staff surmised. And hoisted storm cones, and whenever possible retired.

Rikki had no such Monday cares. Why should he? It was his time off. He worked weekends, and was given the afternoon off to recoup on lost sleep. Rikki would not have dreamt of sleeping, when there was a chance, in a busy and preoccupied life, of a practice with his surf-board. He sauntered, happy and idle, past Boyle who was setting off on tour, en route to Avalon to retrieve his Malibu.

These days he stored it in a godown on the hill, rather than expose this treasure, or himself, to his brother's scrutiny. His latest toy, Muthu had pronounced it.

'Just right for children,' he drew it out heavily, looking down at the slim, magical board, his full lips scornful.

'You think so?' This dull know-nothing, with his ponderous judgments. Rikki hardly bothered to hide his opinion. 'You could break your neck on one of them, you know,' he did, however, point out. Although he cared nothing for his brother's opinion.

'A dangerous toy, then.' Muthu would not retreat. He had never been known to, it was his private boast, and, he believed, his strength. He thought further, his forehead bulged. 'Specially designed for fools,' he said, 'and fools' play.'

It goaded Rikki.

'You should play more often. You'd be less of a pain, if you

166

did!' he said furiously.

'Play? When the fish are swarming?' Muthu could hardly believe his ears. 'You have lost touch completely,' he said, staring at this utter stranger.

Perhaps he had—Rikki's own thoughts were swarming.

'Just leave me alone,' he said.

'I shall. I don't know why,' said Muthu, and his throat began to work, 'just don't know why I bother with you.' His foot started kicking the surf-board instead. 'Flimsy duckboard, not fit for anything—'

Rikki felt some turmoil too, his throat was hurting. But as he listened to his brother's muttering he felt he had had enough. That same day he removed his Malibu to the godown, after getting Tully's permission.

So Rikki sauntered, and Boyle's eye fell on Rikki, and fell away as he drove past, accompanied by Tully, in his jeep. They were taking a dekko, Boyle called it. In other words they were inspecting sundry installations that modern governments insisted on.

All along the dreaming sea-board, but tucked well out of sight, lurked these guardians of the environment—filters, slurpers, booms, vacuums, ultramodern aids to deal with the very latest imperishables. All ruinously expensive to mount, and inroading sizeably into profit margins, but part of the small print that nearly drove Boyle barmy.

It had already come under discussion between Heblekar and Tully.

'You see, you're running out of things, your part of the world...jungles, playground, clean seas—you name it.' Heblekar lurks watchfully behind some kind of hood, his words come out dark and druidical.

'Who says?' Tully hits back.

'Testing, testing.' Heblekar, challenged, throws aside the hood and emerges grinning. 'But it's a close-run thing, wouldn't you say?'

'Something like that.'

'Now we,' says Heblekar, sleekly, 'aren't *that* keen to join the club.'

He does it low-key, Tully can take it from him. Besides, the past they share is such he believes something is owed to Heblekar.

Whereas Boyle comes head-on; and Tully owes Boyle nothing.

167

'All this damned gadgetry. No one bothered in my day, you know.' Boyle grumbled on, double de-clutching with unnecessary jerks.

Tully wasn't that bewitched either. He felt they were called on to do the impossible, namely, to destroy virtually indestructible matter: tubes and tubs, beercans, sardine tins, used condoms, the grisly everlasting wrack that pleasure complexes threw up on a truly phenomenal scale. But one ought to, he felt, give it a chance.

Buy anything the ad men sell, felt Boyle, convinced of his own immunity.

'I suppose you,' he said, somewhat tetchily, the climate was already getting him down, 'go along with it, member of the new generation and all that sort of thing. But new doesn't mean better than old, you know, Tully old boy. And m-o-d-e-r-n doesn't spell *excellent.*'

Tully thought it did, on occasion. He considered himself a modern man. But in the interests of the consortium he gave a murmur or two which might have meant anything.

'But we managed all right.' Boyle continued the conversation, without help. 'We got along without any of this, old boy, and it didn't do us any harm, y'know.'

By this time they had been on the go for some hours and were more or less through for the day. Someone had thoughtfully provided deckchairs—rather grand ones with fringed awnings, and directorial insignia to warn off Shalimaris who by now were out in strength; and had sited the chairs virtually irresistibly on a wheatsheaf beach, next to a very blue ocean. Into these the two men sank, after Boyle had removed the rotor arm from the jeep, as he routinely did out East, to foil the thieving endemic to these regions of the world.

When once again Rikki came past.

He had postponed his surfing, using up a good deal of the afternoon to keeping Mrs Pearl afloat. He had enjoyed it too, he had a deep and growing fondness for the old lady; but now the sea called. Sea breezes ruffled his hair, sea air filled his lungs. Rikki fairly felt the world was at his feet.

Tully, stretched out in his chair, watched from under half-closed lids.

If there was a device for Insolence, he felt, it would be blazoned on the shield of this young warrior-athlete who strides past, his bevelled craft slung under an arm. Heel and ball he swings along,

168

chin at a tilt, walking tall, lord of the entire littoral, the bunched muscles under his polished skin as powerfully stated as if flesh had been sheared open, a textbook anatomy illustration. His eye is purposeful. Careless of the homage all this bronze aplomb evokes, it is bent purely on the horizon where crested rollers are scaling up for their spectacular descent. His heels, firmly planted, throw up sand-plumes as he walks.

It was only when passing the twin thrones that this walking sculpture turned human.

Rikki, preoccupied though he was, still retained some sense, and a scrap or two of values.

Boyle got the salute he expected, Tully the usual smile and a wave, which naturally he returned. While Boyle felt grains of sand, blown back by the fresh wind, stinging his bare ankles. He leant down and scratched the spot, then spoke, when the waiter was out of earshot.

'That boy, you know.' His eye dot-dotted to the now distant figure. 'He seems to forget he's a paid servant.'

Tully would not comment, while having methods of his own. The canvas in which he was seated began to protest, the creaking sounded the louder for his silence.

Boyle found it provoking, and spoke above the racket.

'Wrong to encourage it,' he said, and then something made him take fright—perhaps it was the lines in which Tully's mouth was set, it looked quite forbidding. He left the grim man, and began on the servant-boy.

'Doesn't need much encouraging, does he. That boy,' he said accusingly, 'seems to think he's paid to be idle.'

'He's entitled.' At last Tully was moved to speech. 'He's entitled to his time off, like a paid servant. Why shouldn't he idle in his spare time?'

And settled back even more firmly in his chair after plumping up cushions, adjusting the angle of recline, tilting the sun canopy—all kinds of elaborate arrangements that underlined the absolute validity of idling.

Boyle found it disagreeable, and sought revenge.

'It's an enervating climate. I've noticed signs of lotus-eating,' he said, meaningly.

Tully struggled up. The struggle was mental; physically he was well enough co-ordinated, and by now acclimatised. And loomed over Boyle—intolerably alert, felt that man, who was, by now, sitting rather lumpily, like a sack of potatoes.

169

'I absolutely agree,' he said, and held out his hand for the rotor arm. 'Let's get moving fast, or we shall all become Hannibals, post-Capua.'

'What?'

'Go soft. But I ought to be shot, repeating ancient slander,' said Tully.

'I mean, what for,' said Boyle.

'Purification plant's malfunctioning, I've just remembered. We ought to take a dekko,' said Tully, in what Boyle could only consider a hyperactive state, and putting forward the hideous idea without blenching.

Boyle wilted—even his stout spirit. Another slog, in a haybox on wheels, at the end of the long, hot afternoon. Inwardly he felt, and undoubtedly looked a bit like, chewed pink string.

'Oh God. Can't you relax?' he said, irritably.

Tully could. He wanted nothing more. And presently—perhaps it was the time of day—was drawn into areas whose existence Boyle would have disputed: contemplative arenas where the gymnastics of the mind are more strenuous, and compelling, and breed deeper intensities of being than the most vehement deed.

Boyle also brooded, as the sun sank in the west.

It took him back to the old days. For this was the mellow hour, devoted from time immemorial to sundowners and a little agreeable gossip. Shaken by small gusts of nostalgia, he found himself wanting to commune with Tully, for all that Tully's memories would be handed down ones, and could scarcely compare with his own ripe, first-hand experience. But the man's response was uncertain. Once, early on in their acquaintance, on just such an occasion, he had been moved to remind Tully that the sun never set on the British Empire; to which Tully, repeating some flip transatlantic gibe, had replied that God so ordained it because he didn't trust the British in the dark.

Odd, in a man with his background.

Boyle, risking a glance at his quirky colleague, was struck by his looks, or at least by his face, which seemed to have been cast into an Eastern immobility. So still, under the evening sun. A profile cut in gold, of a grave, subversive beauty.

Boyle found it disturbing. He looked away quickly, as if it was not safe, or proper, to look; and presently put it down to a trick of the light.

It was a strange light, at this hour, in this country.

170

Chapter Twenty-seven

THE moment she had drawn the dust covers over her counter in the Emporium, Valli was on her way.

She wove, sinuous as a weasel, with the soft evening light behind her, to keep an assignment in the forbidden Brindavan Theatre, as they had finally re-named the Gaiety. For although the curtain would not rise for her, she could always picture it happening. So she stole, most often at twilight, squeezing time for herself between leaving the sparkling Emporium and returning to dull home chores. Then she would stand in the empty theatre, and imagine; and her breast would begin to heave, and her heels to stamp, and she would find herself whirling in skirt and bells clear across the stage.

At times the drumming was as loud as the beat of her blood.

One such day, as the clapping died, there stood Miss Carmen Alvarez from Bombay and Andalucía as billed on the posters.

A most decadent young woman, with indigo eyelids and a way of standing, four lacquered nails placed low on each flying buttress of her pelvis.

An unlit cigarette drooped from her carmine mouth.

Valli was transfixed. She would have been crushed by this smouldering splendour, except that she was too busy admiring it. She could not look enough.

Then she was really seized. For Miss Alvarez put the cigarette between her white teeth and deliberately bit it in two. And slowly began to chew. There she was, crunching up cigarette. Valli's eyes were popping, Carmen Alvarez was splitting her sides.

'It's chocolate and almond-paste. Have a cigarillo?' she said, still giggling, and offered her case to Valli. Valli took, gingerly; and it was indeed chocolate and almond-paste masquerading most cunningly as cigarillo.

'It *kills* me,' declared Carmen, wiping her eyes with a scarlet kerchief, carefully so as not to mess up the indigo. While Valli was laughing, equally mindful of the kohl as she dabbed her eyes with a corner of her scarf.

A friendship sprang up, frail enough, and conducted at longish intervals when Carmen happened to arrive early for a performance, and Valli could get away from the Emporium on the dot. For the two girls were of an age, and shared certain enthusiasms, and at least one landscape and language. It was a powerful combination, powerful enough to lower the barriers between them.

They talked about the dance, sitting in the tiny room behind the stage while Carmen applied blue shadow. Or killed themselves, chewing up almond-paste reefers in full view of some open-mouthed bystander. Or jeered at the troupes brought in to entertain at Shalimar. Typists and nurses, shaking their breasts and their skirts to the music after three-week courses, and called themselves dancers!—they could not laugh enough at these fake dancing girls, and the tourists.

'They would clap anything!' said amused, disdainful Carmen, and the two girls fell about laughing.

And then turned serious to talk again about the dance, with Carmen's castanets snapping, and her clickety heels going *tukkatukatuk!* in a circle about her as she revolved on the little round stool. Or the gauze veils swirled as Valli revolved, ankle-bells jingling, dizzy feet answering the beat of the drums.

'It has to be in the blood...A sevillana, you couldn't, unless...' said Carmen, her dark, brilliant eyes harking back to some distant Andalućian adventurer. His fire, and those vital drops; and a legend.

'Caramba! How he could dance! Everyone in Sevilla, but he was the best. That's where I get it from, you know.'

However dimly, Valli understood that it must be so. Somewhere on those bare boards the tempo of hot and dusty plains beat alongside torrid Iberian rhythms.

It was always a job, coming back. She hardly ever wanted to. So depressing—really dark, their hut, with one broken window, and the one bulb at night. So she often gave up trying, and lived instead in the Emporium, or tripped off to Spain in company with her friend.

Her mother could always tell, when Valli's spirit went wandering. That face, empty as an empty vessel, and blundering about—you could hardly believe anyone, let alone her nimble daughter, could be so clumsy.

'Can't you look where you put your feet?' As another vessel went flying.

'It's not my fault! It's so *gloomy* in here!'

172

'With electric light?' Amma could have slapped her. The fizzing pear continued to be her joy, but perhaps she was becoming accustomed or something, for it did not seem to pour out quite so brightly as it had.

But in daytime too, it seemed to her, there was a lessening of light. She was sure she was not imagining, others besides herself had noticed.

'It's that hotel,' declared Amma, in the end. 'It casts a shadow, when the sun is in a certain position.'

She exaggerated. The hotel could not have cast a shadow that long, wherever the sun was. By decree it had been kept low and circumspect. No one wanted a Manhattan skyline. After years of hankering, they had been cured, here and there.

The old man would not impugn the Asoka's height, while conscious of some psychic looming. He could not find any way to describe it, but would not accept his wife's palpable distortions.

'The hotel is not. . . is far enough away,' he said at last. It was not what he had meant to say at all. 'It is not. . . it cannot throw. . .' he tried again, and trailed away.

It was a presence. The shadow was not visible.

Is, is not, felt his wife.

'Then why is everyone saying so, I would like to know?' she enquired.

Because she was not the only one. People noticed, and were moving out. Hardly a neighbour, these days, from whom one could borrow a cupful of oil—at least one could not just pop out, one had to trudge a good ten minutes.

The old man did not answer. His eyes were fixed on a corner of the room where the golfball had rolled, after smashing the window.

When at length a diminutive caddie arrived to retrieve the ball, he received a sound thrashing. The child could not understand it. His father and this furious goat who was belabouring him were old friends. He snivelled, and between sobs gasped out reminders, and received further blows for his pains.

His indignant parents could not make it out either, their old, mild friend; and for all that Amma sallied out, and tried to put matters right, a coldness prevailed between the two families.

*

The old man was not immune to atmosphere, though he said little. The fact was, there was little to be said. He was conscious of the ineffable, the mutual exclusions in territories of the mind that

173

were given expression in those actual, physical removals of which his wife complained. He could not find the words for it. Though, once or twice, the thought did take shape that water would find its own level.

He could not bring it out.

He watched the process going on, whereby people congregated in areas where they could breathe, and feel at ease with their neighbours, and understood it was as necessary for his own people as for dwellers in Shalimar to keep a suitable distance between their reservations, until there was equalisation at all levels. That this would not take place, he also understood; or if it did, it would be in some future that he could not easily foresee or visualise.

Though there was undoubtedly traffic.

Scores of peons, beach patrols, fan bearers, pool and gymnasium attendants, earning a fat if fitful livelihood, according to season and their own temperaments, in Shalimar—all these belonged by birth and heritage to the declining fishing clan.

But, somehow, a change occurred when they clipped on their smart, blue and silver cummerbunds or badges. It was a strong dyestuff too, which, when it bled, left marks that had to be scrubbed off the skin with lye.

*

So Apu watched, and saw huts being dismantled, and erected elsewhere. But he would not move, some constitutional obstinacy stood in the way like a boulder.

There came a day, however, when compulsion became equally unendurable. His nature would not allow.

'If you wanted to move,' he said to his wife, and trembled a little, and would not look at her.

'You mean, you will?' Amma was breathless. She could have fallen at his feet.

'No, but you...' He smoothed the reeds in the faded mat. 'If you wished...I would not stand in your way,' he said.

She might almost have accepted the unusual proposition, except for the years that now began to stand in the way, now that her husband had removed himself. All those years of marriage, the weight of them. It made her unsteady.

'What talk is this?' She, too, trembled. 'My place is here, by your side. I never heard such nonsense,' she declared.

'Then I will,' he said.

'Move?' She could hardly believe.

174

'Yes,' he confirmed. For she had found the sesame that moved several rocks.

It was done quite unwittingly, but she was glad.

*

She was full of it. She had to seize each of the children, coming in from their different jobs, virtually as they crossed the threshold, and tell them. Especially Rikki, who was scarcely ever *there*.

'And you'll help when we move, won't you, Rikki?' she said.

'Of course.' He promised at once. He would have done anything for her, he loved this warm, loving woman who meant as much to him as any blood-mother could have done.

'Are you sure? Because it brings good luck if all of us have a hand in it... But you've got your job and all,' she said anxiously.

'I'll find time. I'll get leave if I have to. Now sit down and stop fretting.'

He pushed her onto the charpoy and sat at her feet, looking up at her anxious face.

Really looking, because, as he now realised, he hardly ever did. She was around all the time, she had been around for most of his life. He looked without seeing her, or saw without noticing. Now, looking, how strange this woman seemed! With her hair parted straight down the middle, and scraped tightly back into a jet-black cone, and blunt, pale nails. To his eye, which had grown used to them, the styles and tints of Shalimaris appeared far more natural. It was his mother who struck odd.

Of course it was gone in a flash. He leant his head against her knee, with affection, and relief, as she came back into focus.

Meanwhile she went on with the planning.

'The thatch must be lifted carefully. It's gone here and there, but it will do for another season or two, don't you think?'

Addressing the menfolk, who would know.

'Yes.'

'Move soon, but on an auspicious day.'

'Yes, we must make sure of that.'

'And—everyone pay attention—we must choose the site with the greatest care.'

But why? Rikki had the greatest difficulty, while trying to pay attention. Did it really matter where they pitched their hut? He could not feel that it was his concern. His concerns were elsewhere, in other worlds, on a different plane altogether.

In Shalimar. A world of villas and scented gardens, of flowers

175

and fountains, of a princely splendour where the light slipped in through milky lattices, and lay like gold leaves on the water.

There was another, at levels that at times he thought it presumptuous to enter; or, thinking of it, found his breath snagging.

Avalon.

The light was different there, it fell softer, more subtly, on those heights. An amethyst flow, shot with sun, which could melt him, into which he would melt as if he were one with some limitless ocean.

Sometimes he swayed, he was drawn in so strongly. The sense of fusion was so intense, it acquired a clarity and a reality greater than any perceived physical object. While all the time he knew, in the very middle of thoughts that he flirted with—a most gentle and tender flirtation—that there were limits to Avalon.

Chapter Twenty-eight

RIKKI had often asked Mrs Bridie, a little fearfully, he did not ever want those golden treasures to close:

'When will you go Home, Mrs Bridie?'

It was always a capital H, for at that age he mimicked her faithfully, and completely without malice.

She always took her time answering. The child could tie her up in knots, she had discovered.

'Well, Rikki, when it's convenient. It's not convenient just now.'

'When will it be convenient, Mrs Bridie?'

'Who can tell? In God's good time, Rikki.'

But presently she would pick a zinnia, or some flower flushed with petals, and intone gently, 'This year, next year, some time, never. . .' Pulling the petals off with sharp little tugs, as if she was plucking a chicken.

'Some time, Rikki,' she would say, as the last petal fell. 'Yes, some time.'

It always ended up there, whatever the flower foretold. Even he, in the end, ceased to believe her.

Now the question rose up again.

'Mr Tully,' he said, 'when will you go Home?'

Tully, a deal more involved with the present, couldn't bear to think. He was basking in the sun, lying face down on the terrace and gently toasting between sunrays and the heat steaming up from warmed stone.

'Shan't rush it. Happy where I am,' he declared.

'Why?' asked Rikki.

'Why? I suppose,' Tully had to twist his neck again to answer, 'I feel at home here.'

Every inch, Rikki had observed. And though they were such very different places, he seemed almost as much at home in Shalimar as he was in Avalon. He adapted like a chameleon.

But what if—Rikki pondered, still as any lizard—Tully's brown-gold body were hoisted up and laid on shot-silk: would his skin cope with two colours at one and the same time?

177

Some such experiment had been conducted in childhood, and had proved disappointing. The trapped chameleon, held down on a checked red-and-green square, had merely turned a muddy, all-over brick-red, probably from fury. Although when they had restored it to the silk-cotton tree from which it had been seized, the palpitating creature had changed on the bark, gradually paling to the blond hues of the branch on which it was petrified.

That some such experimental process was going on, the pores of his skin soon told Tully. He sat up.

'Now what, Rikki?'

Rikki put away the shot-silk. It would have to be put differently, he saw.

'Do you feel at home wherever you go, Mr Tully?' he asked.

'Well.' Tully was as aware of knots as ever Mrs Bridie had been, and as far as possible endeavoured to keep them from developing Gordian features. 'I try. It's pleasanter not to feel like an uninvited guest,' he said.

Mostly he succeeded. Some affiliation to a nomad, the number of places he had pitched camp. But the obverse to that wanderer was the warmth he could kindle up by any campfire, converting some bleak bivouac by maidan or jungle into a free rendering of home. Tully believed, as he said, in living free from cramp; even, with luck, with a certain lucidity. He was prepared to go to some trouble.

Boyle had virtually seen Tully, not so much worming in, as standing by in the certainty of welcome, unaware of any reason why not. Boyle had never been able to decide if it was genuine or put on. But mesmeric, such confidence, or acting, or whatever it was. Ranks opened, the outsider was merged into the circle round the fire—he himself merged. After a while even his skin did not seem to count.

Boyle could not approve. By night or day an Englishman should, he felt, stand by his colours. An age had passed, it was not the fashion, it was courting ribaldry to say so in serious in public. In private, however, Boyle understood perfectly why Englishmen had dressed for dinner in the middle of the jungle. Coquetry is a component of discipline, armies have known all the way back to woad, or gold quinces on spear butts for that matter. Boyle extended the principle. No empire had been built by the builders going native.

Sometimes, when Tully made him thoroughly sombre, Boyle

could easily picture his colleague floating around in a *djellabah*.

This was sheer masochism. Even in the heat of the Gulf, Tully would not have dreamed, any more than any other Copeland-Tully. There were no outward assumptions. If he dressed like the locals, it was more a case of inversion: the ubiquitous blue jeans culture, catching up with the locals, made them dress like him. If he sported a cod-piece, it was not a symptom of going native as Boyle decidedly feared, but a gesture of support to a local industry.

Tully's assumptions were inward.

Rikki, while not wholly shut out from Tully's communings, was following his own thoughts.

'But it just comes,' he said presently. 'You don't have to try too hard, do you, to feel at home?' For he had seen, much like Boyle, that people would make room.

'Oh, I do!' Tully protested, but not too much. 'Well, perhaps not that hard, in this country,' he conceded. 'After all, I was born here. The loam gets in, a few grains at least—at least I like to think so.'

'Does it make a difference?' asked Rikki.

'I like to feel it does,' said Tully.

'Then would you,' said Rikki, 'like to live here forever?'

'No,' said Tully.

'Why not?'

'Forever is a long time.'

'You mean you'll go Home soon?'

'Go home, yes. Not too soon.'

No capital H, Rikki noticed.

'When then?' He picked a flower from an overflowing urn, in defiance of the gardener. The man would have a fit, but Tully would talk him out of his tantrums—he banked on that. He began pulling the petals off, one by one.

'This year, next year, some time, never—?' he recited the choices as they fell, but was fully prepared to cheat.

'Not never.' Tully felt like cheating too, but pulled up there. 'When Shalimar is finished,' he said.

'Why?' asked Rikki. The way Tully looked, this wasn't a sound reason for leaving. 'Why can't you stay on, when the work is finished?'

Why not? Parked in the sun, the sound of his country dying away, Tully was charmed.

'I might at that,' he said. It would be the easiest thing in the world, the way he was feeling.

'Like the Bridies,' Rikki said, or half said.

It made Tully baulk; and now it was not so easy. A strung-up pair, the Bridies, he had gleaned soon enough. Lodged in one country, pining for another, discovering their faith could not refresh every arid stretch, strenuously offering up their labours to the Lord though they did. He might admire, but would not copy.

'I might stay on, but not like the Bridies,' he said.

And the illogicalities inherent in the two propositions became evident, without anything further needing to be said.

Now that that was cleared up, and limits clearly defined and accepted, both could relax. At least Rikki could. He had certain designs on the terrace, which he would confide to Tully when he had firmed them out in his mind. While Tully, in a mood that would have heartened Boyle, allowed himself to become obsessed by the puritan ethic.

'I ought to be working. Never get it done if I don't,' he harped, while not moving a muscle.   .

His beloved cherub, Rikki knew. Presently he sat up, and simply offered a hand.

They worked.

Rikki delicately, with concentration, a half-moon of fingernail steering the little polished fragments into place to answer what blazed in his mind. If it had thundered he would not have heard.

Tully was at work, noisily, on a somewhat gouged block in the yard that opened off the pool-room. Chipping at marble with mallet and chisel, but somehow managing to caress it at the same time, as Heblekar saw. He had come up to consult about a cricket match, but in the dedicated atmosphere that prevailed did not dare to broach even this hallowed subject. So he sat and waited for a break, as comfortably as was possible in the dusty yard, and had soon completely forgotten what he had come about, even supposing he could have made himself heard.

Chapter Twenty-nine

IT was coming to the end of that month, when Mrs Contractor began to feel a little jaded, as if she was in need of a little celebration. As she had no excuse, she decided to give herself a birthday.

'A very small party,' she told Miss Chari, who had very kindly volunteered to stay late and check over the details. 'Just a few close friends to wish me happiness. Happiness is all, is it not, Miss Chari?'

'Yes, madam. And a cake, with one candle?' said tactful Miss Chari.

'One candle,' confirmed Mrs Contractor. 'And canapés, not too many varieties—five or six—say six. That will be enough, don't you think?'

'For how many persons?' Miss Chari's pencil was efficiently poised over her notebook.

'Eleven,' said Mrs Contractor. Ten, she hoped, if she could think of some way of not asking that Nigel Patterson. Or if he could be ill, that would be helpful.

Patterson, the photographer, was often ill. He was in and out of the Spa with diarrhoea—due to the food, he said, which made Mrs Contractor feel like hitting him with a folded newspaper. Instead she took him on a tour of the kitchens, after which he took everything back, admitting handsomely that it was his nerves, he had always suffered. He was a nervy young man, tall, lanky, pale-eyed, his pale flesh often showed greenish tinges. At such times he reminded Mrs Contractor of nothing so much as blanched endive. As for his photographs, she would say nothing, except that they left her speechless.

Miss Chari could see madam was preoccupied; but it was after eight p.m. She coughed discreetly.

'The function, madam. Shall we arrange in private suite?'

'Unless you think...somewhere else, Miss Chari?'

Mrs Contractor was a little doubtful, on account of the weather.

'Well, madam.' Miss Chari was a little doubtful too. 'It is getting a little muggy. Should we arrange on the terrace?'

'A very good plan.' Mrs Contractor might have thought of it

herself.

'And a few joss-sticks to keep off insects.'

Now that she *had* forgotten.

'Yes, joss-sticks, definitely, Miss Chari.' Mrs Contractor looked with delight on the young housekeeper. 'Also—you have such a knack—if you could arrange the flowers?'

'Certainly, Mrs Contractor.' Miss Chari was delighted too. She had thought herself that she was making strides in flower arrangement.

'Just one more thing. Make sure of Das, will you? Since Joseph is unwell. For the drinks, Miss Chari. Because we don't want them spilling right and left, do we?' As newly-fledged waiters did, which was why Das and his brother had been urgently despatched from Zavera's sister's household.

'No, madam. But Das!' Miss Chari was desolate. She had already tried and failed.

'What is wrong with him?'

'He is in hosp—in the Spa, with influenza. He is not expected to recover,' Miss Chari all but wrung her hands, 'for some time.'

'Then could you not get his brother?'

'He is the same.'

'Flu?'

'Flu.'

An epidemic, feared Mrs Contractor. 'What about that boy, Rikki,' she asked, a little nervously. He made her a little nervous—his muscles, she thought, or perhaps it was his airs.

'If you wish, madam.' Miss Chari thought him slightly insolent, for his station. She was not accustomed to giving orders to fishermen, or associating with them either.

'Yes, he will do.' Mrs Contractor was relieved. 'At least he will not mix up the Mango Juice Cocktail with Scotch.'

As one of the new intake had done, unbelievably, in an episode involving Boyle. Mrs Contractor shuddered, and went over it again, to see if it could really have been as frightful as she remembered. Finally Miss Chari had to interrupt again. This time she chose to close the notebook in which she had been jotting with a little snap, which Mrs Contractor heard as she was meant to.

'Yes, that will be all. Thank you, Miss Chari,' she said, being adept at interpreting such gestures, not to mention the language of the dance.

*

A good half hour before her guests were due Zavera Contractor was ready. She fluttered about the terrace, putting the finishing touches, and hoping that dear Herbert would come early, they always had so much to talk about. And she had barely sat down in her peacock cane, and arranged her sari pleats so that only the tips of her cerise sandals showed, when there he was, the first to arrive.

'My dear Zavera! How are you? Many, many happy returns!'

'How nice to see you, Herbert! Now you haven't—you *have*, you naughty man!' Zavera was quite overwhelmed by the little crackly parcel Herbert was pressing into her hand, while kissing the cheek she offered.

'It's nothing. A little gift.'

'You shouldn't have.'

'Oh, but I should.' Boyle could be very masterful, and gallant. 'A very small present, for a very charming lady.'

'So sweet of you. . . And *just* what I wanted!' Zavera had undone pink ribbons and was exclaiming, genuinely, over Dior (not eau, but parfum!). Boyle, meanwhile, moved on.

'Where's Cyrus, the old rogue? Not still in Delhi, is he?'

'He is. He is clinching a deal.' It made Zavera sad. She loved, and missed, her husband. 'He is always busy, Herbert. Being,' she told him, although naturally he knew, and approved it in a fellow-director, 'a businessman.'

'Blest if my wife would stand for it!' Boyle was still in gallant mood. Besides, his wife was far away in England. 'I mean, on your birthday. I would have made tracks from Timbuctoo, I assure you, Zavera.'

'Well, you see,' Zavera coughed, and gestured with her hands. 'Perhaps he does not know.'

'Doesn't know it's your birthday?' Boyle was not familiar with the language of the dance.

'No. You see,' she brought it out in a little rush, 'it is only my birthday by Hindu Calendar, and he is not familiar, being Zoroastrian!'

Luckily the other guests were now arriving.

Dear Adeline, a little frumpy perhaps, but so distinguished, and Herbert's old friends the Tremletts—how old were they? they looked quite withered. But Ranji made up, so youthful, such a handsome boy. And that pleasant pair, Tully and Heblekar—so thoughtful, both of them carrying bright little parcels—but so sad, both of them grass-widowers!

'So glad you could come—but your wife, Mr Heblekar! Such a

183

pity.' Her warm, plump hands clasped the bereft young man's.

'She sends her salaams.' And the parcel, with a Delhi postmark, which he carefully balanced on the hillock on the teapoy. 'She would have loved to come...but when Delhi calls, you know.'

'I know.' Zavera had heard that muezzin. 'I, too, have to rush to Delhi every now and again, or I would be altogether homesick. I'm sure you will understand, do you not, Toby?' she appealed to him, since he hailed from an even grander metropolis than Delhi.

'Indeed. But I'm delighted to be here.'

Which here did he mean? She did wonder, but avoiding larger issues took up a small niggle. 'You should come more often! But you like to bury yourself in that hilltop, we never see you. Isn't it, Herbert?'

But Herbert was busy briefing Mrs Pearl's niece, who was young, and newly arrived in the country: another Pearl, the amused old lady said, lured to the Orient by the prospect of fishing and her aunt's rave notices. She herself was beaming upon her hostess. The two women, with little in common, nevertheless each delighted the other.

'Zavera, my dear, many happy returns. How pleasant to have a birthday party!'

'But you must have one too, it is so easy!'

'And what a good idea, having it out here on the terrace!'

'Yes, isn't it?'

Perfect, felt Mrs Pearl, enchanted by the mild evening, by air that brushed like feathers, warm and soft against her skin.

'I suppose it's to do with coming from Northern latitudes,' she said presently, when the ferment had died down, and they were mellowing, 'but I must confess I have to rub my eyes when I see us sitting out in the open like this at all hours.'

She had even discarded her shawl, after a scuffle with her Northern instincts.

'You do not find it unpleasant, I hope?' Ranji grew anxious, he wasn't absolutely sure how to take it.

'Quite the contrary, I find it blissful. In fact I find your country quite blissful.' She smiled at the anxious young man, who was known to flower when his country was praised. Even those seething with complaint shouldered their burdens and went away with lips sealed, rather than see him wasting away before their very eyes.

'So do I. I think it's fantastic,' said her niece, who was innocent and enthusiastic, with round blue eyes that easily expanded to the
184

size of saucers. She had been in Shalimar a week, and would be gone in another.

'My dear Pippa, when you've been in this country as long as I have...' said Boyle, who was sitting next to Miss Pearl, and still in the role of mentor he tapped her knee, while leaving this mysterious sentence unfinished.

'What happens?' asked mystified, innocent Pippa.

'What happens? You get to see,' said Boyle, somewhat less than compellingly, he himself realised. 'But don't take my word for it,' he rallied. 'Ask Mrs Tremlett. An old hand, you know. Twenty years in Bengal, wasn't it, Gloria?'

'Thirty,' said Mrs Tremlett. 'One got to see the seamy side.'

'The seamy side?' Ranji would not dispute it existed, except with those who dared to say so. His voice was as stiff as his collar.

'Certainly.' Mrs Tremlett soon dealt with the subaltern. 'Aspects of India which *tourists*,' she said, attacking elsewhere, an adversary in a different category, '*never* get to see.'

'I guess you're right,' said Adeline Lovat, humbly. She had tried, and failed. It would not stop her writing her book on these seamy aspects, however, aided by Dodwell and the good Abbé Dubois, and perhaps an anecdote or two from Sleeman, brought up to date.

'I think I can claim to be.' Mrs Tremlett needed no endorsement from writers. She turned to Tully. 'I'm sure your grandfather, Mr Tully—this country owes His Excellency a debt it can never repay, if you will allow me to say so—would be the first to agree, if only he were here.'

'My grandfather?' said Tully. He had two, both excellencies, in their various ways. He assumed Copeland, from the debt that was mentioned; and was gentle as memories could make him. For that consul had fallen in love with the province they had sent him to govern, and in consequence had come to learn—or possibly he was allowed to learn—more than most. While always disclaiming, as was perhaps right to do for a man not of the blood, when confronted with so vast a land.

'My grandfather,' he said, smiling, for that mild envoy had turned it into his hit party piece, 'often confessed he sometimes wondered if he ever got to see anything beyond the Cantonment and the Club.'

Mrs Tremlett thought it in very poor taste, especially in front of Americans. She also believed history was being perverted.

'Well, if you say so,' she said, stiffly, as stiffly as the subaltern.

'Well, bless my soul, he's the best person *to* say so,' said Mrs Pearl, who had been moved, though why she could not think.

'Next to His Ex,' Tully boasted, outrageously. He had got into that mood by now, besides which it took care of some distinct embarrassment. 'He used to brag about the gallons of whitewash his mere shadow could produce.'

'Something of a joker then, this celebrated Tully?' Boyle sided without question with Gloria.

'Celebrated Copeland,' corrected Tully.

'One of the most—um—popular proconsuls, if you will forgive the contradiction, ever sent out,' said Heblekar stoutly, while Ranji, who also had ancestors, now and then issued some military crossfire.

Mrs Contractor trembled for her party, listening to this civil, tribal warfare. Soon they would be at each other's throats, she felt, exaggerating as usual, unless she did something.

'Tell me, Mr Heblekar,' she said the first thing that came into her head, and it came out in a little shout, 'about the gardens!'

'What gardens?' Heblekar was caught in mid-speech.

'Akbar's?' she hazarded, rather desperately.

'Akbar's? Oh, yes.' Heblekar came to, and took pity. 'And Shah Jehan's. All of them, mad keen on gardens. But for my money, it's Emperor Jehangir.'

'Why?' asked Pippa.

'A man with an eye for beauty,' said eloquent Ranji; he was fairly sure all of them had been.

'An artist to his fingertips, in his responses,' said Heblekar.

'To what?' breathed Pippa, expectantly.

'To a bird, or a flower. Or,' said Heblekar, who had always been transported by the account, 'to a man on the point of death. Got him to pose for his portrait. You can almost see the ribs bursting out, in this sketch.'

'But how dreadful,' said poor Mrs Contractor.

'The divine detachment of an artist,' said Mrs Lovat, after quelling a frission of loathing for the frightful Turk. 'One cannot but admire it.'

'I always have,' said Heblekar, with unaffected enthusiasm.

Mrs Contractor could not. She thought it horrible. She wished only to return to birds and flowers in gardens that shimmered like Shah Jehan's, and as that was the wish of the ladies, they presently did.

Boyle, however, was not gripped, and was trying to alleviate boredom. His idle eye soon fell on the waiter—propping up a pillar, and slumbering with his eyes open, as they had a knack.

'Boy!' he called, although he was not the host, but then Zavera was coping alone, and clearly in need of masculine assistance. 'Boy! Drinks *lao, jaldi!*' And he clattered his glass loudly to wake the sleeper.

It roused Rikki, who had not been sleeping but dreaming. He was wandering in royal precincts, beside lotus pools, breathing air that blew scented over beds of wild violet in Shah Jehan's enchanted gardens. Now here was this man dragging him away by the armpits, his heels were crushing the flowers. Calling him *boy* too, which he hated being called. Rikki felt he detested Boyle.

'Coming, s-a-a-r,' he drew it out, although perfectly capable of saying 'sir'; like anyone else, he had his methods. Drawling, Boyle would have said, except that he could not believe his ears, or such effrontery.

The suppressed animosity the pair of them released into the air soon swept them all out of charming enclaves. However, as all felt they owed something to their hostess, by dint of some combined hard labour they launched themselves into the innocuous topic of picnics.

It revived Mrs Contractor. Her cheeks felt warm and pink again, as she thought of all the planning and kerfuffle that would be involved.

'It's just the right season for an outing,' she said happily. 'Now, has anyone any idea where to go? You start, Ranji.'

For she would canvass everyone's opinion before it was decided. Ranji indeed knew just the spot.

'I propose the Sultan's Thope,' he said enthusiastically. A dashing ancestor had cut a British squadron to pieces in this grove. It was recent-ish history moreover, as such things go: one of Queen Victoria's little punitive excursions, during the Pax Britannica.

'Thopes are ideal places for a picnic.' Mrs Contractor wholeheartedly approved the proposal.

'But this one's too far out.' Heblekar suppressed his junior, having perused the embarrassingly explicit commemorative tablet. 'What about the anicut?'

'What does it mean?' Pippa hoped it meant ruins like Jamshed's, or something equally exquisitely romantic.

'A sort of dam. One of our finest engineering projects, completed under the Five Year Plan,' said Ranji, and his eyes began to shine.

G   187

'Oh,' said Pippa, and ceased to flower.

Mr Tremlett now contributed for the first time. He was a somewhat silent, tortoise-like creature, when his wife was present.

'What about the cave sculptures?' he said, and flushed for his temerity.

'Cave sculptures, Basil?' Mrs Tremlett's thirty years in Bengal had yielded an abundance of terrorists, and floods; and not much else.

'Yes, Sitharam was telling me...and not far from here,' said her husband, who had not in fact needed Sitharam to tell him, but did feel some obscure need to disclaim his knowledge.

'Not far at all. Seven point five kilometres,' said Ranji, exactly.

'Rather fine carvings, I believe,' said Mr Tremlett. 'Not that I know much about such things,' he found it necessary to add.

Ranji didn't either, but was well up in other matters.

'Soon be full moon,' he informed the party, while debating if Pippa could possibly look prettier under a moon than she did already. 'What say a picnic by moonlight?'

Soon polish off the caves, and settle for a whole delectable evening, he planned.

'Yes, capital.' Even Boyle was captured. 'I know the place you mean—never been inside myself, but the countryside around there's fairly decent,' he said. He would enjoy the picnic with Zavera, and leave the caves to those who wanted them.

Zavera was thinking the same, a related idyll had already rounded out in her mind.

'Then shall we say that's settled?' she said, and composed her hands in her lap while waiting to hear that everyone agreed, not that she doubted for one moment.

When Heblekar became possessed. What else could he call it? he himself wondered, while accepting that there are many levels of possession. He was not overwhelmed himself, but the caves were echoing, he could not shut them off.

'Well, you know,' he said, 'I feel the anicut, on the whole, would be preferable.'

'I vote for the caves,' said Boyle.

'Why not the caves?' asked Mrs Lovat.

'Something of a warren.' Heblekar tried to sound rational, at least. 'I'd feel a bit responsible, if anyone got lost.'

Tully listened, and could not make it out either. He had gone round the caves with both Heblekar and Rikki, it was impossible for anyone to get lost. But as their alignment, or trust, was

188

complete, he would not hinder Heblekar.

Mrs Tremlett had no such reason to hold back. She was, besides, something of a savant in the darker subjects.

'I know what's in your mind,' she said, suddenly, and her eyes glittered a little as she focused on Heblekar. 'There was that awful case of that English girl, wasn't there. In some caves.'

'Years ago.' Before he was born. Heblekar managed a ghost of a smile.

'But I'm sure you must have heard.' Born or no, of course he would have learnt of the traumatic event.

'Yes, of course. But I'm sure,' Heblekar, well on the way to recovery, invited co-operation from comrades, 'I'm sure none of us—would we, gentlemen?—would even contemplate indulging in rape on this outing.' His smile was quite radiant.

'Incapable. Wouldn't act so dastardly.' Tully joined forces at once.

'Word of an officer.' Ranji's hand was on his heart, while a wink of one curly-lashed eye wickedly suggested he wouldn't half mind.

The men at least were laughing.

The women, en bloc, looked with loathing on these monsters.

'It's no laughing matter,' Mrs Lovat spoke heavily, 'for a woman.'

'It's not funny.' Even Mrs Pearl felt obliged to administer a caning. But then her amiable nature made her want to take away the sting, especially as she looked round the agreeable company. 'But who can say what happens?' she said. 'We're all so vulnerable, and we have these strange capacities. Strange beings, humans...quite capable of conspiring without knowing it, or imagining what isn't. We women are imaginative creatures, perhaps at times we do have fantasies.'

'Perhaps at times it's necessary,' said Heblekar. He could feel the release, some part of him that had been in spasm.

'These days?' Tully would have continued to support him, except that Heblekar had recovered. 'Where's the need? If a woman asks to be raped, she is. Not like the old days, is it? Fantasies were in vogue then.'

'Perhaps it was inevitable, given the circumstances,' said Pearl, chiding, but only a little.

'So one gathers.' Tully stretched and laughed. 'The East, at any rate...Seems to have acted like some kind of hot-house for forcing the women. Gave them all kind of wet dreams.'

189

'This girl didn't dream.' Mrs Tremlett was trembling, as old passions were kindled. She didn't care for such language either. 'The poor thing was shamefully—' she shied away from the raw word, and substituted another, 'shamefully violated, the whole station knew that. There was no excuse for suggesting anything else whatever.'

'Whatsisname put it in a book, didn't he?' said Boyle, yawning. He had not read the book. The event was before his time; and anyway he had little time for women who put themselves in that position.

'He left it up in the air,' said Mrs Tremlett, somewhat perilously. She had never forgiven whatsisname for it.

'Why? Was there some doubt?' asked Mrs Lovat, gingerly.

'It was never proven,' said Heblekar.

'It didn't have to be. Everyone knew what had happened,' said Mrs Tremlett.

'No end of repercussions,' said her husband.

'Shook even the box-wallahs,' said Boyle. He had been one himself, much later. 'As far up as Calcutta.'

'It rocked India,' said Mrs Tremlett. She meant Anglo-India.

Mrs Lovat, without a single memory of Anglo-India, was beginning to feel very left out, and American, and was getting the fidgets besides. Mrs Contractor observed, being a good hostess, and decided it was time for a break. Soon she was signalling, and the waiter detailed for such things was padding around with the vol-au-vent, and the shish-kebab, and other sizzling morsels on skewers, and the talk became general.

Rikki had nothing to do, while they ate, once he had seen to it that the glasses were charged. He squatted in a far corner of the terrace, which was far enough, the terrace being the size of a badminton court, and tried not to feel hungry. He couldn't be, he determined; he had had his evening meal; but a healthy appetite, and the spicy, golden smells, were threatening to wreck his resolution.

To distract himself he sat up on his haunches, and slotting his head between the balusters gazed down on the little cobbled piazza where the Shalimaris were gathering. It was dark by now, except for starlight. There would be no other light, by order, so that when the torches were lit—

Ah-h-h!

Murmurs as hushed as anyone could have wished greeted the torches as they were carried in, and planted in burnished sconces

190

around the piazza. They flared in the dark-blue air, strongly, giving off strong, aromatic scents of the resins in which they were drenched. People began applauding, here and there. The most blasé could not fail to respond to the reversal of darkness.

Rikki was fully absorbed. He saw the night closing in, and kept at bay. He felt mystery being created, and dispersed, but always diffuse within that circle of light. He felt himself a part of both processes.

Perhaps it was a sense of mystery, flowing from those smoking flambeaux, that affected Adeline Lovat. It could equally have been her curiosity, which had begun to smoulder while the small talk went on, that led her back to the caves.

'Tell me—' Mr Heblekar, she should have said, he being the man of the country. His name was on the tip of her tongue, when she realised the reactions she was after were European. Who, any more than she, was interested in the Indian? She had to think of her readers and reviewers.

'Tell me, Mr Tully,' she started again, 'these caves we're going to, is there a lot to see?'

'A number of carvings, yes.' The flickering light had revealed a profusion, by exuberant artists.

'Were you able to respond?'

'Well.' Tully slid away. His eye would always respond to the skills of hand and chisel, but he suspected that his mind might rest on unfirm ground. Brought up to a different idiom, capable of being stunned, and for miraculous split-seconds even beatified by the glory of a cathedral, he could not rely absolutely on its being a proper arbiter beyond its own realm.

'Best ask—' Heblekar, he was about to say: perceptions there of a high elegance and calibre, a sounding-board of chaste distinction; but finely controlled and struck through lacquer.

Whereas Rikki—

The boy stood in the gloom, and shivered. Long ripples ran, visibly, actually, down his naked spine, when they lit the single taper.

'Ask Rikki,' said Tully, and called him over.

But Rikki had never dealt in and would not talk about responses.

'They are beautiful,' he said simply.

Which left Mrs Lovat no wiser.

'Do you mean the sculptures?' she probed, 'or perhaps the

191

ambience, the—the atmosphere?'

'Everything,' said Rikki, and even went to a little trouble. 'Everything is beautiful,' he opened it up for her.

'In what way?' These bald statements. Somehow she would tease out the meaning.

'They are loving,' said Rikki. He was mellow from the torches.

When the extent of areas to be illumined became clear to Adeline. 'But what are they sculptures of?' she asked. They could be anything under the sun, of course.

'Gods and goddesses and their attendants,' said Rikki, and patiently.

'Engaged in sport?' Gods and goddesses? Was she bantering? Adeline asked herself nervously. Goddesses made her nervous, though all in favour of women. So did gods who engaged in frivolous activities.

'Yes, all kinds of sport.' Rikki was pleased with the concept, it was more than he had expected from the solemn, stick of a woman. 'You can see them playing, and praying, and dancing, and loving,' he said.

'And loving?' repeated Adeline. She was caught a little, a small tuft of teased-out wool was left flapping on the barbed wire.

Everyone seemed to be caught, or listening, love being a universal subject. The old Anglo-India hands were riveted, even a little apprehensive, following the ritual pilgrimage to Konarak which all of them had undertaken. There was a clear silence, when Rikki spoke.

'Yes, loving and joined in loving. They are—' he had to hunt for the word, 'copulating.'

No one West of Suez would have batted an eyelid; but then this was the East, its somewhat tardy heir.

These Eastern airs might once have played in a Victorian parlour, overcoming some modern feeling that they ought to be as plain-spoken about love as they had been about rape. The ladies were examining their fingernails, while Heblekar had rather squeamishly lowered his eyelids, and Ranji's ears, and the neat lean strip of flesh above his collar, were turning a dark red.

Perhaps it was the effect of bawdy in mixed company, or possibly the quality of the fustian sold by the missionary fathers. The stuff had lasted, and was proving its capacity for muffling up those reckless sensualists, the pagans, for whose decent cladding it had indeed been imported.

Rikki got the whiff, of course, that came over from the
192

schoolroom. He had thought he was done with it, with childhood.

Had Mrs Tremlett actually spoken, or was it Mrs Lovat—perhaps even Primrose Bridie, pecking at him from the grave? Rikki could not be sure, but was persuaded more than ever that their minds must be bent, or pickled.

The party, beyond mending by now, was breaking up. It was time besides, and Mrs Contractor was afflicted by gnats or something; the wretched insects seemed to thrive on joss-stick smoke.

'You must all come again soon.' Slapping away with a folded napkin.

'Love to. Thank you.' They came most evenings anyway.

While Rikki stood, and wished they would hurry up and go, and didn't care if they knew it. His belly was distinctly rumbling, and he would not even try to stifle the sounds.

Apparently incapable of anything less than the obvious, Tully saw, with amusement.

'Come with me, Rikki?' he said.

'Yes, thank you,' said famished Rikki.

No 's-a-a-r', Boyle noticed, but 'sahib' and 'sir' were missing too, and waiting for Tully to issue reminders, none came. He determined there and then to have a word with old Toby, whose lenient ways only encouraged impertinence in the ranks.

*

Rikki cleared up at top speed, but neatly enough; several disciplines operated, despite Boyle's misgivings. Not merely Mrs Contractor, but that martinet, Apu, and Bridie, and Tully, and indeed he himself, his own powerful taskmaster, would all comment powerfully if things were not done just so.

Eventually, however, after much sighing over how a handful of people could require this much paraphernalia to consume a few morsels, he was done. As he carried in the last teapoy he did spare a thought for his mother. She always pressed him to come home early. She would gladly haul out and open the heavy crock, in which she kept the salt fish, if he was hungry. But in Avalon there was a larder one walked into, and selected; and Tully had invited him.

Rikki sped round the bay—but for the current at this hour he would have swum, it would have been quicker.

'This woman,' he said, sitting in the pool-room and wolfing cold

193

roast chicken, for by now he was starving. 'Was she raped or not, Mr Tully?'

'What woman?' Tully was eating chicken too, but only to be companionable. He was thinking, not for the first time, that canapés were the devil's own, ruining the appetite without appeasing hunger.

'This woman in a cave that you were talking about.' The riddle continued to intrigue.

'Why, were you listening?' said Tully.

Rikki stopped eating. What else did they suppose he did, yanking him out of his dreaming to attend to their wants, insisting on maximum attention while they ate and drank?

And, unusually, he bundled Tully unceremoniously into the ranks of 'they'.

Tully duly felt the shove. There is a great deal of this kind of speechless relegation between individuals. And tried to retrieve his position.

'It's as you heard. She didn't know herself,' he said, somewhat woodenly.

Rikki chewed, slowly. A woman of this extreme simplicity was in like case to one who kept her virginity despite conception and childbirth, if one could accept it. Ever since the Bridies these strenuous acceptances had been a mystery to which he had never become reconciled. But he would veil his eyes, and his inability, from Tully.

While Tully caught the flicker, and tried to incorporate a rational scrap or two, or at least deal fairly.

'It's a terrible experience for a woman. Perhaps she was in no state to know,' he said.

'A terrible thing like that?' It still would not twist for Rikki. 'How could she not know?' he said.

Tully turned it over, gazing into the pool which reflected stars and clouds—rain-clouds, he hoped. He had never been altogether reconciled to piped water.

'Perhaps her mind,' he suggested. The mind was a trickster, one soon learned. It could foist its own disarray onto its simpler partner, coolly watch it writhe after transferring the load. 'Perhaps her mind was attacked, and she confused it with her body,' he said.

'But she must have known,' Rikki was stripping the wishbone, to which rites were attached, as he had learnt, 'what happened to her flesh.'

194

'If her flesh was intact,' Tully watched the Y-bone coming clean, 'that would make her virgin, are you saying?' For the boy could introduce the unspoken, not insinuating as others might, but simply allowing it to fall into place. Sometimes it thudded down.

'I'm saying if it was she would not be justified in accusing the man,' said Rikki.

'She would be fully justified, if he had not so much as laid one finger on her, if he had invaded her mind,' said Tully.

And having stunned each other with these blows, they stared at one another in silence. Tully recovered first; and more or less side-stepped.

'Well,' he said, 'you ought to know—your Emperor's grandmother did—rape comes in all shapes and sizes.'

In a shower of gold, well known to, in all times. Or slinking along a moonbeam, or descending like a dove; and the woman had to be told afterwards, and her radiance was taken for granted. (Although what woman, human or divine, would not smile upon a child whether foisted or not?)

Rikki, all smiles now, accepted it. Besides, he could just see wooden Adeline, when confronted by the moonbeam.

'Yes, I know,' he said, and held out the wishbone to Tully, who could be expected to know the rite.

Tully did of course; but his luck not being in, received a splinter.

'It's enough for a small wish,' said Rikki.

'You mean I'm still allowed?' This ritual was new to Tully, but he was more or less used to Rikki's manipulations.

'Yes. Go on,' urged Rikki.

'Well.' Tully kept it small. 'I could wish for some rain,' he said.

'You shouldn't have told! Now it won't come true!'

Rikki was appalled; he jumped into the pool to counteract the folly. In the centre stood the podium, destined for Tully's statue. He began to circle it slowly, now and then scooping up handfuls of spring water to pour libations on the column. But the pool was full of starlight, it affected his spirit. Soon he had forgotten the solemn exorcism, and was leaping and splashing in the bubbling water.

'It's like champagne!' He had never tasted this ambrosia, but had heard them exclaiming when the cork was popped. 'Come in and see,' he sang.

'I will when it rains,' said Tully, sober only through will-power.

'But it is!' cried Rikki, raising his face to the sky.

Drops clung, as Tully could see, pearling his eyelashes, glistening on his skin.

It was the heavy evening dew that was falling, but both were fully convinced.

Chapter Thirty

'BUT why bullock-carts, my love?'

Mr Contractor was baffled, when he learned of their intended mode of conveyance to some caves. He had just returned from his trip, after clinching deals in both New Delhi and Bombay, and his sojourn in these cities had inclined him more than ever towards the modern.

'They will have it so.' Mrs Contractor's note was classical, a seer who can but advise the rash.

'When there are luxury airconditioned coaches.' He alone knew the travail involved in procuring these sleek greyhounds. They projected exactly the right image, moreover, unlike what bullock-carts would do.

'I know. But—' this was the only wisp of consolation she could offer, 'the customer, you know, Cyrus.'

He did; it was his golden calf too. 'But could you not, my love. . .?' he asked, delicately, for he would not tabulate what his wife could do.

'I have tried.' Mrs Contractor all but dabbed her eyes with a wisp of cambric. 'But I have not been able to persuade them.'

They mourned together for a little. A happily married couple, they usually did things together.

However, Zavera had resolved right from the start, she might not be able to compel customers, but they would not persuade her either. It comforted her somewhat, as she rose from the breakfast table, and wrapped her housecoat firmly about her. Who wanted to, could go to the caves in carts. She would ride in an Ambassador.

The carts had been a sudden inspiration of Pippa Pearl's. She ardently felt it would be so much more in keeping, and easily won Ranji over to her way of thinking. Soon Sitharam was deputed—man from these parts, who would know what to do. That philosopher not only did, but prided himself on insights into the Western predicament. Overtaken by the Industrial Revolution, their bodies functioned briskly in the present; but the spirit had yet to catch up. He compared it to jet-lag, which found

197

expression in a hankering for the old and the picturesque. The more hardship attached the better, he would add cannily, provided it was not something irreparable like, say, cerebral malaria.

Carts were around, these days, with rubber tyres to their wheels. Sitharam's scouts were made to scour the countryside to secure the moribund variety.

And there they stood, ancient, vast, wooden, before the assembled party.

'Proper rickety old bullock-carts. According to instructions, Miss Pearl,' said Sitharam, and could not repress his giggles, despite his philosophic understanding.

Pippa Pearl could not have been happier. She stood with the blue ribbons of her straw hat fluttering, exclaiming about the size, the construction, and did anyone know how much ground one revolution of the huge wheel would cover?

Ranji, who had no idea, enlightened her, while glued to her side because of that weed, the photographer Patterson.

Patterson had at last emerged from the Spa. Greenish tinges still glowed in his flesh, and now and then his legs behaved like asparagus, but he was determined not to miss picnic as well as party.

And was met by ox-carts in which he was apparently expected to travel. Patterson stood, and wilted from the hips down the whole length of his lanky body.

'They're museum pieces!' he blurted out.

'But fun,' said Pippa, with a glint in her eye.

'Not my idea of.' Nigel Patterson did not care who despised him. 'I prefer to travel in comfort,' he said, fixing his pale eye on the waiting Ambassador.

Mrs Contractor, however, was not going to have her arrangements upset, or Patterson sharing her motor-car for that matter.

'No, no, no, the bullock-cart is best for the photography!' she cried, and bundled him into it.

The rest were tidily embarked, two ladies, two gentlemen, according to the paper she had written out. Adeline and Mr Tremlett were in the leading cart, with Philippa and Ranji; Herbert and Mrs Tremlett in the second, together with Mrs Pearl and of course the wretched Patterson. Tully and Heblekar were missing—complicity, Zavera suspected. They had gone off to a cricket match in a far village, where an AIDCORP team was challenging the local side, an event it was their bounden duty to support. Cyrus of course was a businessman with better things to do.

Presently all were in, and seated themselves on benches which had been nailed to the carts by Shalimar carpenters despite the protests of cart-owners; and waited for their guide.

*

Rikki was the guide, because Mrs Pearl had asked him.

'If you would,' she simply said. Even if he stood, almost stony with his monosyllables, it would be better than the gabbling of an official guide—there were three on the Shalimar roll. And if in sunny mood, as he could be, she would be warmed. Right through to the cockles of her heart, she rather tritely put it to herself.

'With pleasure,' he agreed at once, using the standard phrase in which they had all been drilled, but meaning it. And one or two glassy after-thoughts (of Adeline, followed by Mrs Contractor) were banished by thinking of the plush, airconditioned coaches that were usually laid on for such excursions. He had travelled in one once, at the invitation of the driver, who had once been a fisherman, and had shivered in icy luxury all the way to the airport and back.

But it was carts. His feelings equalled Patterson's. He would simply have walked off and left them to it, except for Mrs Pearl and the financial arrangements concluded with Sitharam. (Time and a half for extra duty: he knew his rights these days, and how to claim them.) But he would not ride in the cart. Not sitting beside the carter, and his back to the four of them—defenceless, and threatened, he convinced himself.

No way, he felt; and said so, shortly.

He would rather walk.

'Seven point five kilometres!' gasped roly-poly Sitharam, his town feet crept.

'Fifteen, there and back.' Rikki only did it to impress, he was not particularly bothered. That had also been the distance, he had discovered when he was older, involved in trudging to the schoolroom, starting from the time he was five.

So Sitharam stepped back, and the caravan creaked off.

It was exactly like, felt Pippa: the string of travellers, and animals, and a guide in front, journeying. She loved it, it was close to journeying overland to India in a Safari minibus as she had

199

planned to do, before various frontiers erupted. Now and then as they ground along some deep rut, or met a pothole, she slithered into Ranji, for long cushions, covered in glossy hide, had been laid on the wooden slats; and was glad to have his arm round her while she straightened her hat. Soon she began to be reminded of pioneer trails, with the waggons forming up in a laager to protect the women and children from the Matabele, or was it Red Indians? But the only Indians around were brown, and going peacefully about their business, as of course she saw; when her dippy mind swooped.

'Ranji,' she said, 'when you were small, did you play cowboys and Indians?'

Ranji had indeed played similar games. He went a dark, guilty red, but could not resist her dimples.

'No, we played cowboys and Britons,' he confessed.

'And the Britons bit the dust?' She was enchanted with him.

'Every time.'

Hugely pleased with each other, they rocked the cart with their laughter.

Mrs Tremlett, in the bullock-cart behind, was preoccupied with dust. She was of pioneer stock, and would never opt for the easy way (she had been offered the Ambassador). Had she not accompanied her husband to every posting up-country? But she could not help being affected. Her throat, particularly. She had brought pastilles, and wound a chiffon scarf balloon fashion round her lower face and head.

'It's the dust,' she said, coughing and sucking.

There was always the dust to be dealt with.

'There used to be bhistis, you know,' she told Mrs Pearl, besides much else. And that lady, who was only half listening, received a picture of beasties, rather like heraldic creatures, running mile after mile sprinkling water from mud pots, to lay the dust in front of the advancing Tremletts. Mrs Pearl felt a little sorry for, she presumed more sensibly, these humble men and girls.

'It must have been exhausting work,' she said.

'It was.' Mrs Tremlett firmly grasped the wrong end. 'Sometimes we were covered, head to foot, despite every precaution.'

In sweat, did she mean? Mrs Pearl could not suppose she would deal so vulgarly.

'In dust,' said Mrs Tremlett, getting wind of Mrs Pearl's

confusion. 'No country like it, for dust. It's what makes the sunsets, you know.'

'Makes them?' Mrs Pearl again lost track.

'So garish.'

It depressed Mrs Pearl. She could only point mutely when flamingos, pink and huffy, were flushed from a patch of green rushes as their carts ground past. Normally she would have exclaimed about the colour, the contrast, the quirky elegance of these gawky birds. The words dried up on her lips.

But as they journeyed some inner flow, that nothing could quite stop up, began to refresh her. Or possibly the dust was laid, as the landscape came into its own. An elemental landscape, that opened up tenderly to her mind, while all the time she felt the strong presences, the strong and dominating presences of, as it were, earth and water. But presenting without stridency—she came back to that. Expressed in a great, calm stillness, and even passivity—a female passivity that would speak most fastidiously, and with passion when roused, to men. Mrs Pearl smiled, for her conclusions, or illuminations, seemed to form in a pattern like the pieces in a kaleidoscope—shake, and eye to the peep-hole, and the glittering chips clatter into place like devoted guardsmen. From all accounts it had been the men who had bloomed, and the memsahibs whom the country had broken.

By now it was Tully who was taking his place, she felt quite strongly, beside her: as if he had cupped an elbow (he had a way of doing, for she tended to stray) and led her back to those men who had bloomed, and basking together in the sunshine, both of them understood why.

Tully. Mrs Pearl had to smile again, at the picture. Bareheaded, feet in sandals from the local cobbler, striding—that bossy, white man's walk—as if the earth belonged; but also as if it was a mutual emotion. He would not feel shorn if certain rights were incorporated into the deeds. In his eyes, blue, clear, at times disconcerting, a permanent consciousness of those indispensable grains in his making that he would openly and readily concede. Answering at once if approached, not a man who was easily embarrassed.

'Yes, often. Great clods, don't you feel? As the psalmist said.'

'Psalmist?'

'Whoever inspired the service for the dead.'

He made her hear those great clods thudding down, comforting the body shivering in its coffin while it waited reunion with the

201

warm earth, earth warmed by that molten, abiding core at its centre. While the frozen vicar intoned his ashes to ashes, and focused an inner eye on the baked meats to come.

Mrs Pearl journeyed on, in high good humour.

Less so was Mrs Contractor, who brought up the rear, creeping along in her motor-car in stately splendour. Directly in front was the cart bearing Patterson, and she could not help but observe that he was not behaving. She had not expected him to. She knew his passion, and his work which appeared in the most revered overseas magazines. The baldest vultures, the boniest cows, any steaming heap—and out came his wretched camera. As if there was nothing else! felt indignant Zavera. She felt like tearing off the spotty bandanna he had tied in a triangle round his face (he was moaning about odours, from behind it), and wrenching his head round to look at the fields and the birds, and other things like that.

These fields, and other bright as well as lamentable features, were engaging Adeline's attention. *Emerald oases,* she noted, *women like parakeets in red and green saris bent double in the paddies . . . the noble carriage of these smiling peasants . . .* went down on her pad, and would later confirm every image in her readers' mind of a happy, laughing, backward race.

Also, she could not help but observe Rikki, since he was walking right in front of her ox-cart, and right in the middle of the track. He had taken his shirt off, for it was warm, and screwed it up into a ball which he had balanced on his head. Walking so well, she saw, it did not unwind or wobble, and a light sweat on his shoulders across which, for some reason (she traced it to Elinor Glyn, eventually), she found herself flinging a leopard's pelt.

Rikki felt, of course, the entire epidermis being a sensitive area. However, he was not under any threat, as he would have been, he was certain, cooped up in the cart. He was walking freely, on cool, springy turf. It grew lushly on the ridge thrown up between the twin ruts of the cart track, it could have been a parapet he was walking on. When small, there had been much perilous teetering along crumbling walls and parapets in Avalon. He had not outgrown the fondness, he was discovering.

That, and the springy grass, were the reasons for his walking right in the middle of the track in front of Adeline's cart, like a bullet between the eyes.

Presently, as he teetered along, Rikki's parapet became the narrow path that had led to the schoolhouse, and it was a parcel of books he was carrying, not a rolled-up shirt. Mrs String-Bean

202

Bridie was leading, and he minced along behind her with the books balanced on his head, and she was having a job pretending not to notice his shadow, grown long and saucy in mid-afternoon sun and strutting in front of her like a turkey-cock.

But soon the shirt won, or its owner. The brilliant check was a gift from Tully, to save him from borrowing a peon's khaki drill. It was Tully now who was present. Not merely present, he was rollicking up the hill to Avalon, while Rikki marched behind to make sure he arrived.

Tully saw no need, and said so. He said he was as sober as a judge. Rikki preferred to suspect his merry mood. He toiled after Tully, who was singing, fruitily since Prospect Point, in full voice when they came in sight of the castle.

'I'm the king—' he began at the top of the scale; and stopped and turned it round. 'No. You're the king of the castle,' he sang, lordly on wine, scandalously loudly, signing to Rikki to join in.

'You know it's not mine, Mr Tully.' One of them had to be sober, for both their sakes.

'It is, it is! I'm telling you—are you telling me it's not?'

'No.' Sighing. 'You're the boss, Mr Tully.'

'So I am. I'm the boss, you're the king, and *all* this is your country.' A grand sweep of an arm took in land and sea.

'If you say so.'

'I am saying so. What's the matter with you, Rikki, you're not jibbing at your own kingdom?'

Rikki jibbed no more, it was not to be resisted. He raised up his voice and belted it out as ordered, with Tully chanting beside him.

'*I'm* the king of the castle,
'You're a bossy old—'

These splendid moments melted away the kilometres. In no time, it seemed, they had arrived at the caves.

Because it had been a hard ride, they decided on tea before anything else, also on sitting more comfortably, for all had painfully discovered bones and muscles they had never known they possessed.

The driver unloaded the boot. Bullocks and carters were banished into the scrub. The driver, putting on his picnic hat, flapped open the starched damask and arranged the cushions in a circle. Thermoses were opened.

If Tully had been present, instead of merely looming, he would have said, 'Tea, Rikki?', or 'Tea coming up!' to newer intake whose name he had yet to attach to the face; and passed the cup over his shoulder. And barriers would have dissolved, however illusively; and the illusion would have tided them over.

Or so Mrs Pearl gently imagined. She felt like doing the same, but did not have the courage: other presences defied her to follow the humane impulse. So she sat and worried at it as she sipped her tea, and hoped they would not mind as much as they ought.

Rikki did not. He was piercing the closed wicker with an eye like a rapier, to discover the contents of the bulging hamper, which he would soon be sampling. For the thing about Shalimar catering was the handsome quantity left over for everybody, and always. An entire colony could feed, and thankfully did, on the crumbs that fell from the table. So he sat himself down, under a young jacaranda that was spilling blue from every branch, and dwelt happily on the feast to follow, and must have dozed.

The caves woke him. They were echoing as they had done for Heblekar—perhaps a thought more insistently, for the lacquer was thinner. It might even have been that he actually heard. A sound that wakes one, and is heard at the instant of waking but already prolonged and complex dreams have been woven around it, in seconds that are outside ordinary time.

There was only the dreaming, but Rikki rose and went to the caves, and without surprise found the abandoned infant in the inner rock chamber, exactly as he had seen in his dream.

'What have you got there, Rikki?' asked Mrs Pearl, for the boy was being rather careful, almost cradling whatever was in the bundle.

Rikki knelt, and showed. There was not much to show, for the child was well swaddled—only a small face, and miniature fists.

These dark little scraps of humanity, said Adeline Lovat to herself, and possibly not alone. Only to be expected, she was also thinking, in a hot climate, where the arts of love preoccupied even the goddesses.

But all this was soon swept away, by the child itself. Its character, or personality, or most likely the capacity to stimulate the protective instincts that has kept the race going, was rousing different and urgent emotions in every breast. Soon the scrap turned into a baby. Soon they were passing it hand to hand around the circle, and the ladies at least were cooing.

All would have been over the moon if they could have offered some nourishment. This the child, whom their attentions had woken up, was now indicating it needed, its lips were working around for the teat. However, there was only cow's milk, and that out of a thermos, which all felt was totally wrong for so young a baby.

'It's a shame,' said Ranji, feeling thoroughly over-fed. (He had only had tea, so far.)

'A thundering shame.' Boyle's little finger, which seemed to him abominably large and clumsy, stroked the child's quivering chin. 'Whoever's responsible ought to be horsewhipped.' His sentiments, and Ranji's, for once coincided.

'It's awful—' to think, felt Philippa, feeling almost responsible. 'Those *eyes,*' she said. They squinted, the child could barely focus, but she nevertheless interpreted the blur as accusing.

She looked so tender, and concerned, that Patterson would have unslung his camera except that he, too, was moved by other considerations.

'She's a peach,' he said, meaning the baby, whose cheek indeed felt as downy and soft to his touch. He assumed it was a girl, from the pink trimming on the surprisingly extravagant bonnet.

These lavish outer wrappings were also precipitating less bearable emotions, which had to find some kind of outlet.

'You can see,' Mrs Pearl was soon compelled, 'the child's been well looked after.'

They attempted to clothe themselves with this rag, that the child had been well looked after, while they sat, and thought of the gross pressures that had worn down the mother, and were filled with a desperate guilt.

Their earlier mood, inevitably, suffered. Soon the tea grew cold, and all were yielding to the cantankerous, and Mrs Tremlett first. She had been longing to get at that Adeline anyway.

'At least, Mrs Lovat,' she said, somewhat acidly, 'you'll be able to put it in a book. It's an ill wind, as they say.'

'Yes.' The thought had already occurred to Adeline. 'Though who'll believe? *I* find it difficult enough, that these children can just be left. To live or die—it's just incredible. Though Rikki did tell me—' She looked round the company, inviting them to understand there were a great many things he told of which were past belief, she could not be blamed for her scepticism. As most of them had had some experience, most did not blame her.

While Rikki listened in amazement. What had he said that made this potty woman think what she did?

'Children are not just left to live or die,' he stated.

205

'You have not been to Calcutta.' Mrs Tremlett looked him up and down, frowning for such presumption in untravelled inferiors. 'You do not know,' she stated.

Rikki might not know Calcutta, as he readily admitted, but did know his own community.

'No one would leave a child to live or die,' he said again, flatly.

'But you told me!' said Adeline, truthfully as far as she knew, and indignantly.

Rikki retraced to discover, and concluded it had been half and half. She had asked if, as she had heard, and read in Dubois... Rikki had agreed it was possible, going by Moses who had been left or found in some rushes, not caring much what he said so long as he was shot of her.

'But how could you believe that?' he now said. It was horrible to him.

'Was I wrong to? Hasn't it happened right here in front of our eyes? Are you going to deny *facts*?' Her voice rose shrill, he was so provoking, not to say brazen.

'No one,' he said, even more flatly, looking her up and down—studied insult, his betters could have learnt from him, felt outraged, democratic Adeline. 'No one left her to die. The caves are for life, for the living. You must be mad to think—'

'Now that's enough.' Mrs Tremlett had listened, and been horrified, especially by that glance no European could forgive. Mrs Contractor was simply speechless; while Boyle, slowly going purple, was preparing his speech. Any minute now they would start on the boy, felt Mrs Pearl wretchedly. She found it unbearable.

'Come along, Rikki,' she said, mildly, and not really making much sense. Tully could work wonders, she had noticed, with some such phrases, and as she could not think of better she believed she was going about it in his way.

But Rikki would not melt for any of this crew, who could believe such dreadful things of him or his people. He was even close to believing they had brought it to pass, simply by believing. He took—virtually seized—the child from Mrs Pearl's arms, and got into the front seat of the motor-car.

No one had thought of ordering him to do this, or anything else either, or if anything of the sort occurred now, it was past them. Only Patterson retained some presence of mind. He brought out his camera, and the flash attachment since the light was going. But now they fell on him in a body, almost convulsively—dementedly, one would have said, except that it would have been difficult to believe it of civilised people.

'You must not wake the baby.'

Mrs Contractor spoke for them all, putting up quite other feelings in light, and acceptable, considerations of this nature.

Chapter Thirty-one

T H E Cave Picnic took on some of the qualities of a cameo, shelled out of time, with no perceptible beginning or end. It was set like a small, polished stone, in the mind.

Presently, however, the stone started to turn—into some kind of radioactive implant, to those who toyed with such advanced vocabulary. For rays began to be emitted, and small bleeps. People began to wonder what to do. They wondered at each other.

For no one in the colony, in which at least one man and one woman were responsible, would offer to shelter the child.

Those who prospered by Shalimar had to work at their prosperity, to keep up their standard of living. Their living was uncertain, besides. Not that they were at the mercy of the seasons any more, but there were different uncertainties. They could not trust what had not gone on for centuries, was the root of it; and following some tortuous and abiding impulse in the psyche, they titillated their minds with dark, masochistic pictures of Shalimar as an iridescent bubble.

Those stranded outside, while unworried about bubbles bursting, could not afford. They had only to look at their dingy boats, and the rotted mackerel going for manure. But they could see no reason why others. . .

Men sucked their teeth, and the women grew sullen.

It worried the old man, because they looked to their headman for answers. He had none. He felt there were none, in circumstances that had got out of control, a new and unfathomable process. But he listened to his wife, he had no option.

Amma was all het up.

'Such things.' Not that they hadn't happened before.

'But someone should find room, is that too much to ask? Or is a child simply to be cast on the rubbish heap?'

Such things were indeed unknown.

She wouldn't say so, but orphans of the storm were entitled. Would anyone have thought of leaving Rikki to scavenge around? Hadn't there been scores of offers, besides hers? Nor would she hesitate now, only she was not as young as she had been then. Her unsaid was easily absorbed by her listeners, since this is what they were thinking too.

'It's a disgrace. To the whole community.' She harped on this aspect, while picking out names of certain randy young stallions. She accused and berated them, in the bosom of her family, as she wanted no ructions such as had followed the thrashing of the innocent caddie.

But what was the point, since it came to the same thing in the end? the old man wondered, and was more wearied than ever. Rape, seduction, the act without these flourishes—were all but a single ray with the single purpose of propagation. The why of it forever unknowable, he accepted that, but part of a design of grandeur he would not oppose.

But he was very old, he could see reflected in the eyes of his family.

'Must be one of that lot, don't you think?' His wife pressed for answers, pushing him into this earthy imbroglio.

Brought to earth, nevertheless Apu would not single out or accuse any one man. Nor could he name the forces he felt were involved, while ascribing a collective, phallic responsibility to the pleasure complex.

'You can't blame...anyone,' he began to frame his thoughts.

'Why can't I?' His wife had no patience. She had named names, though in private.

'When Shalimar...' was all he was able to say, and his eye wandered to Rikki, perhaps simply because he was there. (He was trimming the thatch for their new hut.)

Looking at him as if he was Shalimar rolled up in one, and calling *that* to account, thought Rikki. Though he couldn't be sure, those rheumy eyes... But he understood that some rosette was being pinned, and turned a refractory shoulder, and bent even more stiffly over the stiff palmyra.

'The trouble is,' Amma had not yet done, her instincts rooted around the subject, 'we are losing our respect. For our traditions, that is.' But as this was difficult to prove she said simply, if crossly, 'There is no sense of responsibility any more.'

'Yes.' At last Apu could chime with his wife. Some kind of blight, he felt, had nipped. As usual, however, he could not deck it out in speech.

*

Up against India, Tully had to conclude.

Back from amiable village cricket, the two men, Tully and

Heblekar, received the dishevelled picnickers, or at least the accounts they gave were dishevelled.

'I knew it. Caves spell disaster,' said tight-lipped Heblekar.

Still in his flannels, this modern man. Tully eyed him.

'What have the caves to do with it?' he said, irritably, just refraining from swearing.

If Tully didn't know, Heblekar was not going to tell him, specifically.

'Everything,' he said, and departed without waiting for reason to be dolloped out.

Then it was Rikki.

He had given up working on the mosaic altogether. He drifted up the hill, and mooned about among the melons. Tully was determined not to ask, or to allow any excuse for the ascent of unreason. He could not avoid listening. He was out choosing a melon for his dinner, and choose one he would. No one was going to drive him indoors.

Rikki was not going to drive him or anything, but he was in a state. These days states, whether of misery, or the first covert intimations of bliss, had him ascending the hill, or aching to.

'You see, Mr Tully,' he said. 'I am responsible.' His peace, in fact, was in shreds.

Tully did not even bother to ask for what.

'Why?' Stooped over his melons, he snapped over his shoulder. 'Been sleeping around?'

'No.' Rikki was indifferent to these literal assumptions. He watched Tully prodding. 'No, not there. Press here, Mr Tully,' he said gently, and guided his inexpert fingers to where the fruit had first started to swell.

There were still vestiges of flower, papery to his touch; but Tully was losing interest in the ripeness of his melons, or his interest was being eroded.

'Then why?' he asked, this time; and slowly straightened up. Like a peasant, hand to the small of his back. That in fact was where he was beginning to ache.

'The seed,' said Rikki, and drew a long breath. His father had said, or not said. Either way he could not continue to be brushed aside. 'I have to accept it,' he said, and paused, not to excuse himself but since the accusation had been collectively aimed. 'All of us,' he said.

Tully could have attacked, pleaded for sense or demanded it, driven his defenceless opponent into a corner as he had not been

210

able to do with the experienced, and nimble, Heblekar. Since it was Rikki, that itch, too, eroded. So he simply stood in his patch, and presently saw how they grew, the melons in his field. That psalmist or whoever, whom he would recommend to the boy. Possibly he did—if not in words, something was imparted; for presently Rikki smiled and said, peacefully enough, 'Yes, I suppose.'

And as Tully had forgotten, nudged him.

'Your melon, for dinner,' he reminded.

'Yes,' said Tully, and stood without moving.

So that Rikki saw he would have to help, and sighed a little as he searched round for the best of the crop, first freeing Tully's foot which was tangled in a vine, which he could see would send him sprawling when he did move.

'Here you are,' he said, when at last he was satisfied, and severing the stalk handed up his selection. 'It smells really good,' he said.

It did. Honeydew smells were ascending. Soon it had them sniffing and exclaiming, both of them willingly caught up in these scents.

*

Meanwhile Mrs Contractor was in the dumps. The present depressed her, so much so that her thoughts flew away to the future.

'In twelve years' time, Cyrus,' she said, taking him by the sleeve to call his attention, 'there will be no problem, just think of that!'

And if her incorrigible mind hinted that in a hundred years there would be fewer still, she would not allow it to pop out.

'But why, my love, twelve years?' asked her husband. He was really curious. Close as they were, at times his wife was beyond him.

'Because, my love,' said radiant Mrs Contractor, 'in twelve years' time the cave-child can become a Moor on Shalimar establishment!'

Her spirits were quite restored, thinking of her Moors, as she called them. They were her very own, she had virtually conjured them up when the midges started. They had soaked the torches in a liquor concocted by Joseph to combat these pests, and bearers were standing round waiting for them to be ready—when the idea came to her in a flash. Soon her scouts were recruiting for sensible little boys—since the mothers would not allow their little girls—

211

with the darkest possible skins so as to contrast with the flaming torches.

It was a sensation. Mrs Contractor heard the gasps nightly when it grew dark, and the dark children trooped in. She herself loved her little giggling Moors.

'Such a picture they make,' she said with a fond pride, and sighed with pleasure, and was liberal with her presents.

There were always small boys hovering round, longing to turn into Moors.

The future being settled, Mrs Contractor felt a lot happier. She donned her morning sari, and took up her flowered parasol, and resolutely refusing to let the present upset her, set off on her daily round.

For the present, as there was no vacancy in the government orphanage, the child was lodged in the crèche. There was one, as much used as the Gymnasium, if not the Tower, and built soon after these essentials to look after the labourers' children.

In this sensible establishment Mrs Pearl was often to be found, nursing the infant. She had developed an attachment, from having been the first, after Rikki, to hold the child in her arms. She did not explain it in these words, until a past exchange with Tully brought it to her mind.

Her visit was some months old by then. Instead of diminishing, for which she was prepared, she found the country was growing on her. She also discerned—perhaps insights followed, inevitably—she was not alone. In Tully the process was not so much advanced, as in a state of being. She said so one tranquil day, without finding it in any way necessary to sound him out first.

'Yes,' he agreed. At ease with the tranquil woman, he found no inclination to fend her off, though it was a private matter. 'Yes, the country's got me. Like that gosling, I've often thought.'

'What gosling?' She was, as yet, not wholly used to these zigzags of weird lightning that lit up their exchanges.

'That got imprinted. Stepped out of its egg and saw this lumbering German, and was bonded to him ever after, poor misguided chick.'

Mrs Pearl could not see herself as a chick, but admitted there might be some imprinting. She often found she had to go to the crèche for a look, and then finding it difficult to leave, stayed on. Tully, out on field visits, often saw her, simply *there,* among the
212

slight, wide-eyed mothers and babies: large, English, slightly outlandish in the tradition of innumerable singular English women; a tradition he had no wish to disturb.

Rikki noticed too. Serving in the bar, he often saw her, sitting alone at her usual table, furiously knitting. It was a woolly shawl, and faring rather better than the jumper had done. When he brought her order she would show it off, holding it up against the light for his approval, and to demonstrate the well-knit structure.

'Coming along well, don't you think, Rikki?

'Very well.' It was growing fast. 'And not one hole,' he replied gravely.

'Quite. You take my meaning perfectly,' she said, laughing. 'Old Pearl only drops stitches when she's fuddled.'

She had never been fuddled, in his opinion, but her limbs had certainly let her down—enough to require supporting back to the Asoka. He had taken to exercising some care over what he served her.

'So there's no need to water the whisky any more,' she said.

'I never did,' he said, guiltily.

'Oh yes, took one look at the old soak and piled on the ice. But I think,' she said, looking back over those years, the bleak morass of a pointless marriage from which she had sought relief, uselessly, until it persisted as a pointless habit long after death had ended the marriage. 'I think I'm over that hump.'

He was glad. He was familiar with soaks, toddy and other brews. He wouldn't have wanted her.

She told Tully of this encounter, in a roundabout way that left out her private humps.

'He feels he has to look after me.' She had to laugh. 'At my age, imagine.'

'He keeps an eye on me too, though he allows I'm the boss.' Tully laughed too, while both understood that positions, in a quadrille, are exchanged.

That day—a fine one, but rather hot—they were engaged in choosing a suitable beach villa for Mrs Pearl, who had decided to move out of the Asoka. She loved Zavera, but Zavera's parties wearied her, she said to herself. There was no avoiding them, if one lived in the next suite. Aloud she alleged she wished to commune with nature, and even convinced herself. Where better to do this than in a villa washed by the sea?

The villas, as it happened, were all occupied. There would be

213

no vacancies until the hot weather took a grip. However, Phase 3 was now in operation, a new batch was springing up.

'You could have one of these,' said Tully obligingly, indicating a sort of skeleton, to her eyes. 'If you'd rather not wait.' For he could sympathise with these compulsive urges, from which he still suffered. Neither India, nor Rikki—and there were times when it seemed to him they were one and the same—had quite succeeded in curing him.

'I'll need more than a penitent's four walls, you know,' said Mrs Pearl mildly, and realistically, 'even if it's only for communing.' It was more than that, she was admitting to herself.

'We could rustle one up for you in no time,' he said, and factually: AIDCORP was functioning on oiled wheels. Simple and blasé alike still crossed devout fingers, but only out of habit.

'That would be lovely,' she accepted with pleasure. She could already see herself installed, and hear the sea lapping very closely. At which point she began to feel it was all her doing. As if she had conjured up her villa, like Zavera her Moors, or this desirable complex of gardens, villas, hotel, shops. Desires fulfilled, or word made flesh.

'I feel I'm behind it,' she began. It sounded so vaunting, as well as shady, that she abandoned the theme.

They walked on.

He in chaplis, she in shoes and stockings. She arguing sentimentally, from certain natural configurations, that he must have gone round in bare feet like an exemplary savage till the age of at least seven. He wondering how anyone could walk with such bunions: they bulged the leather each side of the big toe joint; but admiring her ability. And ahead of them went the unshod infant, in and out of the unfinished villas, leading them in a dance.

It compelled Mrs Pearl, in the end.

'Kali,' she said. So they had named the child, to invoke the protection of the powerful goddess. 'Where she is, she's looked after.'

'Yes,' said Tully.

'Very well,' said Mrs Pearl.

'Yes,' Tully said again. They might have been agreeing on the excellence of institutions like crèches, in particular those run by AIDCORP.

It was he who hauled them out of this bog. 'But it's not the ideal, are you saying?' he said.

'Yes.' She emerged gratefully. 'A hotel's out of the question,
214

but I could be a foster mum, don't you think?—give her some kind of continuity, in one of these villas.'

'Would you like to?' he questioned. 'Would you?'

'Yes, to both,' she answered.

'And afterwards?' he had to ask.

'Afterwards?' she answered, and serenely enough. 'I'll think about that when it comes. Just now it's like a cruise. Everyone's let off thinking till it's over. A respite one is grateful for,' she said simply, 'even if in the end there are no solutions.'

This might well be so. Tully, being a practical man, preferred to leave it there while he dealt with what was feasible.

'We'll see what AIDCORP can do,' he offered, since he was well able to commit that body.

'I'd be grateful,' Mrs Pearl rejoined.

Since AIDCORP could do a lot, Mrs Pearl and Kali were soon installed, and were often to be seen together in a rocking-chair knocked up by the resident carpenter, on the apron to the villa. Or at times there was a third, the wet nurse whom AIDCORP were paying, who sat crosslegged on the cement floor with the child at her breast, while Mrs Pearl looked on benignly.

'And who knows,' said Mrs Pearl now and then, to Kali, or anyone else within hearing. 'One of these days I might even carry you off to England with me.' And rocked, and tickled the child under the chin, lovingly, only half playing with the lovely, crazy notion.

*

Rikki often heard her, when he came to visit the foundling, or to collect her for a swimming lesson.

And would stop to listen, held by the gentle notes that entered her voice, and begin to wonder. About England, that unknown world over which he had roamed in imagination from childhood on. About whether it might be possible—here his thoughts grew tenuous, stepping most tremulously, delicate as a fawn—for him to enter. And if it was, would mists swirl as softly as they did for Mrs Bridie? The furrows were gone, in those moments, from her severe, dried-up face: even some hints of beauty, which at all other times evaded her.

These thoughts were carrying him steadily up the hill when half-way up, at Prospect Point, they began to waver.

From here it was the bay that opened up, but he found himself refusing the view. His gaze went on, up to the gatehouse from

215

which the old Sikh soldier had guarded Avalon, and when necessary charged out to strike terror in the children. They ran before his flashing sword, squealing, half enjoying the danger, part terribly afraid. But when he sat idly on his bench in the porch they crowded round, and hushed each other, to listen to Inderjit Singh who had been to England.

'To pay my respects to my comrade the Colonel,' the old man said, stiff with pride, the sun glinting on his chestful of medals.

'The Queen! What about the Queen?' They chorused in reminder.

'Of course I went to see the Queen,' he always replied.

'And did you see her, Jemadar Sahib?' They chanted, the older ones taunting, for they heard him in the toddy shop, after the liquor had let out the tawdry happenings.

'Yes. And Buckingham Palace,' said Inderjit Singh.

And sat, stiff and still, his sword laid dully across his knees, and the children gathered round felt the chill that emanated from the old man.

It was the railings, wet, cold, so cold the metal leeched to his fingers as he pressed against the bars in front of the Palace. Or was it that other place, to which they had taken him from the airport, before allowing him the cherished glimpse that had brought him over an ocean after a lifetime of saving? For it was blurred, all that time before they put him on a plane back to India, except for the Colonel.

His Colonel—no blurring there. Come up specially to see him, as soon as he heard on the wireless. Standing by him, whatever *they* said, they couldn't make him budge. His tongue, fiery as ever, lambasting the officials.

When they shook hands at the barrier they were not two old men, but old comrades who remembered they had fought together at El Alamein, and whatever comes into being between men who have fought such battles was between them, as both were prepared to bear witness.

The glow that the Colonel had kindled touched even those heedless children. Even now the warmth spilled in, radiating all the way from his childhood as Rikki re-traced.

It was a chill face, but gentled by generous memories, that Tully saw. Upturned to his, he on his way down to confer urgently with Boyle about something, but not so urgent he cannot find time for the boy.

In this liquid mood, the thoughts clustering.

216

'A penny, Rikki?' It was a half-question. Sometimes he would accept the coin; sometimes he would not tell until hours or days later, if at all.

'I was thinking.'

Tully walked on, not far when he was called back.

'Mr Tully,' Rikki said, and without any preamble, 'Mrs Pearl is taking the child with her to England when she goes.'

'Did she tell you?'

Tully was quite prepared to hear that she had. No reason why not, considering that the most curious confidences were reposed in Rikki even by fleeting Visitors. Because they were birds of passage, he had to suppose, they poured out as they might to a stranger on a bus. Or the time at their disposal allowed for profound error, but withdrew the possibility of correction. For they took him at face value: a dumbwaiter or caryatid, carved with some splendour, eyes of blind marble, there to listen and bear without comment and without emotion. A version of those hewers of wood of old, up-dated.

'She didn't tell me. I heard. She was singing to herself,' said Rikki.

Tully refused to resort to the did-you-listen vapidity that might have afforded escape.

'Do you think,' he said instead, and somewhat to his own surprise, 'she means to?'

'If she was thirty. She is,' said Rikki, gently, 'over sixty years old.'

His own youth, and the possibilities that crowned it, now lay exposed before them.

'Do you think, if I saved up, (now that he was earning such fabulous sums) I could go to England?' said Rikki.

A nuance there, it seemed to Tully, of Angle-land: not Angles but angels, in the good Pope Gregory's opinion, as he rambled in the market-place. But how long had the idyll lasted?

'To England?' he repeated.

'Yes. That was what I was thinking about,' said Rikki.

'Would you like to?' asked Tully.

'Yes.' But now the chill was welling up, all the way from Inderjit Singh. It imposed restrictions. 'If it's like you said,' said Rikki.

For in brief, rare moments Tully too would speak of his land like Mrs Bridie. *You leave a part of you behind. . . in case you forget to go back, I suppose, it's like a twitch on the cord. Yes, some part, each time you leave,*

217

isn't it unbelievable? Tenderly, and so soft he might have been talking to himself; but Rikki heard, and believed him.

'If it's like you said,' he repeated.

'It is,' said Tully, gently, for he could see what was coming. 'It is, for me.'

'And for me?' Rikki was still waiting.

How could he know? Tully asked himself; while the picture formed up of its own accord. Of the boy, decanted into the great Northern casbah dense with people, multicoloured, bewildered—a London bewilderment—walking the streets. Streets paved in grey stone, rippling with rain, smell of wet lead and damp plaster coming off houses barricaded against the cold, against the alien in its midst, no hints to the rich, and glowing, and generous interiors that still existed, here and there; and would sometimes allow entry.

'I think it would be difficult for you. It is a cold country,' he said.

'One would dress for the climate, as you said we should,' said Rikki.

So he had. Now that it boomeranged back, Tully was discovering, the ingenuous words were piercing.

'I'm talking about the climate of the mind,' he said finally, and decently. 'We are an island people.'

Capable of an icy civility veering to a contained snarling which offended their own warmer, more urbane instincts. But would such insular emotions be understood by this boy, before he was reduced to snarling back? And yet, that a gut understanding was available, was already emerging.

'That doesn't matter. You would be there,' said Rikki. 'Would you not help me?'

'Of course I would,' said Tully, and bench being unavailable—it had been freshly painted, there was a notice in large warning capitals—sat down on a tussock of grass, clasping his hands about his knees.

Hands firmly clasped, Rikki saw; the interlaced fingers long, brown, white at the roots where the sun could not reach.

'Are you sure?' he said.

What was he asking for? Tully had to wonder. It was so remote a possibility, this taking-off for England. But he answered without hesitation.

'Of course I'd help you, Rikki,' he said, and noticed that some rigidity was going, although he had not seen it overtake the boy.

Indeed Rikki was relaxing, as skins peeled back from the core of

218

his motives. It was not, after all, England he was after. Or if it had been, it was not any longer. He put this discovery to Tully as simply as he could.

'That's all, then,' he said.

'All? All what?' said Tully.

'All I really wanted to know,' said Rikki.

Flowering, as Tully saw. Knowing that someone would trouble, would care to trouble, a powerful aphrodisiac that strokes the membrane of human loneliness, a constant erotic zone.

Even in one so young. It subdued Tully, for whatever reason.

But Rikki would not allow it now. His cup was running over. He bounded up, and would have dragged Tully up with him except for certain restraints that, he supposed, ought to be exercised in view of some difference in rank. Instead he plied Tully with plans for Tully's boat, his orchard, his pool room, his larder, for all of which he was plainly surrogate owner.

Without, however, a ghost of a notion of any such thing, Tully perceived clearly enough, and with envy. Such hauntings, he could not but conclude, were reserved for those who had gorged off the apple in Eden, or the decadent. And he listened to the prodigal list of improvements and refinings, of which it appeared the bright green paint of the bench was the merest forerunner, and was himself carried away.

Boyle, accordingly, had to stew for a further hour before Tully arrived, with apologies, but no explanations whatever, as he duly registered. It left him no option but to assume yet another surrender to the East.

Chapter Thirty-two

THEN it started to be, Boyle was appalled to find, not only others but himself. Before he knew where he was, the country was nipping at him.

Nowadays while he waited, for Sitharam, for Tully, for blueprints, for ice with his lime-and-water, he found himself itching to take to an easy-chair. Sometimes he would succumb, rise from the director's upright and sink into the rudki with the wooden arms that elongated into leg-rests. But it never seemed right. Soon he would return to his proper seat, and sitting poker straight, eye the recliner, and wonder if he should bawl for the peon to remove the blasted thing from the office. But he never did, and the cycle went on.

Sometimes, as he went back and forth, there came thoughts, unpleasant, unbidden, that these shuttlings mimicked his life. For he did go back and forth, for reasons that were only partly connected with money—like others he had made his pile out East, and could have retired in comfort. Some restless urge, however, sent him on the prowl. Between Home, which was not what it had been, where he did not feel at home; and colony, protectorate, zone of influence—call it what you will, they had all once been British stamping-ground.

But neither could he relax in these familiar acres. Things were not the same—could never be, he accepted. What brought him up short, as if he had run full tilt into a brick wall, was to realise that that was how they wanted it. They had opted for their own ways; and would see to it that this time round he, not they, adapted. It was enough to bring Boyle out in a cold sweat.

And Tully would find him, crouched in his machan, eyes skinned for the tiger that stalked him in the undergrowth.

While he was forbidden to carry a rifle.

This morning, however, Boyle relaxed. He sat at his ease, and signed without hassle the papers the clerk laid before him. Presently he was done, rather sooner than usual, and pottered round to Tully's office for no particular reason, except time on his hands and a need for company.

Along with many other things, their offices were no longer the same. The old awning, whose mangy splendours had witnessed the celebration of villagers' marriages and AIDCORP's teething troubles, had long been returned to its hereditary guardian from whose protesting hands it had been wrested. At least the framework had, and some few tatters that were left, and the usual handsome AIDCORP compensation to take care of the gripes. Next they officiated from cabins, from which, as the hot weather took a grip, they fled back to canvas. . .

Now a two-storey annexe to the Asoka efficiently housed their offices. Modern, custom-built, well-mannered, the splotched greens of crotons in the ante-rooms, the low hum of airconditioning, belted peons at the portals—Boyle was by no means alone in commending the exemplary achievement. He would not crow, it was not in his nature; but found grounds for satisfaction in the respect he saw reflected in the eyes of Heblekar, Sitharam, Ranji—especially Ranji. When bedevilled, or shaken by the pressures upon him, he relied on the orderly surroundings they had created to steady his nerves. What surprised was not that it did—as much as Tully's, his nature craved order and responded to it—but that sometimes it failed him. Then it was that Boyle clambered into his machan.

This morning, all was well. Boyle strolled along the wide corridor, noted and approved the brightly polished brass of nameplates on the doors as he passed, returned the peon's salute, had himself announced, and turned into Tully's office.

'Well, Tully sahib,' he said amiably, 'how goes it?'

'As you see.' Tully grimaced at the healthy pagoda that built up daily. 'Whatever else, you can't say we didn't teach 'em,' he said, 'how to manufacture bumpf.'

'Keeps coming, doesn't it?' Boyle smiled in sympathy. He hated the paperwork as heartily as Tully, but was more conscientious in his dealings. Now he noted the numerous buff forms, converted into sub-origami shapes like boats and dunces' caps, that reposed as usual on Tully's desk; and somewhat wistfully wished he had the nerve and the know-how to copy, before moving on to other subjects.

'Well, old boy, I'm off for a breather,' he said, straightening his bushshirt. 'Ready for it I can tell you.'

'I know how you feel.'

'What about you?'

'I think I'll hang on for a bit.'

221

'Yes, well,' said Boyle, who had not expected anything else, 'I hope I haven't left you a can of worms. Done my best not to.'

'Thanks.'

'But if you find—' fiddling with a paper-knife, these things were ticklish, 'know you can cope of course, but don't think—' As well as the ticklishness of it, his conscience pricked, for Tully had been out a deal longer, right from the beginning when things were at their stickiest, as Boyle knew well enough. 'Remember I'm at the end of a telephone line,' he said.

'I'll shout, don't worry.' Tully smiled, came over, clapped him on the back—at times there was a warmth between them, genuine, bonding, that both men felt and acknowledged. AIDCORP would have thrived less well, but for this interlocking.

'Good. Well, I'm off this evening.'

'Yes. Transport's laid on. The coach'll call for you at five.'

'Coach?'

'Coach. Thought we'd send you off in style.' He and Heblekar had. Ranji had been all for the jeep; and had been overruled in committee.

'Thanks.' Little things were pleasing; Boyle was pleased.

There was no reason to, everything was buttoned up, but Boyle lingered. He walked over to the window, flipped down a slat in the blind and stood gazing at the scene, moved by it, by what had gone into it: the massive effort that went into an infrastructure that enabled people to laze on a beach. As emotion tended to embarrass him, however, he covered it up.

'Can't say,' he said, a trifle gruffly, 'we don't give value for money, eh Toby?' Which being both the equation and the key, no committal was needed. But it led Boyle on.

'I was thinking, the other day,' he said, still by the window, and gazing at what had been done, 'we ought to be thinking of some sort of show, like—what-d'you-call-it, sound and light, to show off a bit. Show off Shalimar, I mean. Like they do in Gizeh, beside the Pyramids. What—' as Tully was unforthcoming, 'do you think?'

'It's an idea.' Tully would always consider one. Though it was that much easier with the Pyramids on one's side.

'Yes. On the lines,' Boyle moved out of Egypt, 'of what they put on at the Red Fort. Have you been?'

'Yes,' said Tully.

'I've never found time to.' Delhi was always a hassle. 'But it's quite impressive, Cyrus says.'

'It is. Quite an experience.'

222

The landscape, country, coast, and sea, were crystallised, for Tully. He was back in the great Fort, within the threatening battlements, and listening to the measured son et lumière voice speaking in excellent English:

The sun, they said, would never set. . .

A pause, five weighty seconds that carried the weight of two centuries.

But it did.

And the lights flooded on, lifting the tension.

Tully stirred; and the panorama before him swirled, and settled. Out here, in this little fishing colony, sunrise and sunset would have been measured more simply, and innocently, while empires played their tunes of glory, or fell silent.

Boyle, waiting for some positive response, grew restive.

'Well?' he prompted.

'I'm not sure,' said Tully, 'it would be appropriate.'

Boyle gave way. Perhaps AIDCORP's achievements were not in the same league as whoever was building in Egypt. He would not act without Tully's backing. However, he did badly wish he could read the man's mind. This illiteracy also hit him when confronted by the Indian mind, though here he was not bothered. It was finding one's own kith and kin unreadable that was a hurtful, and unsettling, matter.

Boyle looked at his watch, grateful for an instrument that often got him out of situations which, invariably beginning congenially, tended to get glued up.

'Well, I ought to be on my way,' he said, and looked once more at the view, and found it pleasing, before getting a move on.

*

Much the same view opened out before the old man. He gazed awhile, standing in the doorway of his hut, then slowly turned and went indoors to mend his nets. An everlasting job, now that different concerns had snapped up so many nimble hands.

When he said so his wife could not agree.

'When has it not been everlasting? It's like these household chores,' she said.

Women's tasks, that never ended. She wiped the perspiration off her face, and gave another stir to the stew. Simmering herself, because where was that twinkletoes Valli? Flashing an ankle in

223

Brindavan, if not prancing around in the Emporium, never to be found when the hearth had to be swept, or a meal prepared. Well, she would find out. A girl who did not care to cook would never get herself a husband. Men expected their wives. You couldn't blame parents if they thought twice about hitching a loved son to a flibbertigibbet, however fetching her face. Coming up fourteen, it was high time Valli thought about these things.

And she tossed in some more of the dried fish, rather than the chicken pieces Rikki had brought her, for it put her in a right state to think about her daughter.

The old man went on with the mending of his nets.

'Yes, maybe you're right,' he said at last.

'Right about what?' Amma stopped stirring the pot. He took so long to answer, one clean forgot what the question had been.

'Jobs. They go on forever,' said Apu.

Though he could not remember going on so late, it was usual to stop work when the natural light went. It was best done by natural light. The knotting was that much harder, his eyes watered and his fingers became clumsy, under the electricity that fizzed down.

Or so he felt, while allowing it could be his mind that was at the bottom of his misery.

Chapter Thirty-three

IT was growing hotter as the season went by, the mangoes would soon be ripening.

Mrs Contractor fanned herself, and debated with Miss Chari if they should arrange to fly in some of the Alphonso variety.

'Because what they grow locally is so stringy, don't you think, Miss Chari?' she said, frowning, she could feel the strings catching in her teeth.

'Yes, madam,' said Miss Chari. 'But,' she ventured, 'mango is a nice change from the melon and the papaya.' She meant any mango.

Mrs Contractor agreed, not any mango, however. 'But tell me,' she said, fretfully, it was the heat, 'why do they not grow Alphonso here? It is like a lord, compared. Then there is no problem.'

'No, madam. But maybe the soil here,' said Miss Chari humbly, 'is not good.'

'That must be it. Then we must fly in. But is it justified,' Mrs Contractor wondered aloud, 'in low season?'

It left Miss Chari in a quandary. Only the best was good enough for Shalimaris. On the other hand there weren't many Shalimaris left in low season. As madam said, one must think of economy.

'You know best,' she said loyally, leaving it to madam. For herself, she did hope for imports. It would be nice to sample a variety of which she had heard so much.

Mrs Contractor mused for a week or two before deciding that to do without was the best solution. She would not have stringy mango served. Shalimar had a standard to keep up, she would not have it lowered by an inch. She sent for the chef and told him so, in case he by-passed Miss Chari, and also impressed it once more on the housekeeper, whom she was leaving in charge.

For Zavera had decided to have a holiday. Just a few weeks in their little bungalow in the Poona hills for the sake of her health. Then she would come back refreshed, all the fitter to take up her many tasks, as Cyrus said. She would take his advice. Dear Cyrus, he was so wise, and thoughtful. He knew she couldn't stand the heat, however much she tried. And her eyes grew moist, thinking of her husband whom she loved dearly, as she stood over Mary-ayah who was packing the cabin-trunk. She was a good servant, Zavera could not grumble, only now and then she forgot to put in the tissue paper between the silk-chiffon. It was important. It was so difficult to get chiffon to hang properly, once it got crushed. And would Mary-ayah, as she pointed out to ayah herself, like *her* sari hem all up and down, like scallops? Although of course it wouldn't arise, with cotton.

By the end of the month Zavera had packed and gone, by which time Boyle had settled in nicely on the Tremletts' houseboat on the Dal Lake, having been invited by his erstwhile guests. Contractor stayed. His work was his life. He had never been known to take a vacation—not even Zavera could persuade him—until a project was completed down to the last nut and bolt. For certain gildings of the lily, scheduled for construction under Phase 3, were now under way. These included an artificial lake between sea and palm fringe, an extension to the golflinks, plus clubhouse thereto—

'Not till the last brick is laid. I am a workaholic,' Contractor told Mrs Lovat, with perfect truth, and not without pride.

Adeline was not sure that she was, but was sticking it out, though her three months had long been up. One needed to sample all seasons, she felt truthfully, if hazily, to get under the country's skin. This she was determined to do, as she sweated it out in her suite in the Asoka. It was a task she set herself each time she journeyed to Asia, but had never before carried it this far. So hot, and her temples throbbing, and the hotel boomed—she might have been the last soul left in the place.

This was not quite so. There were a few around—the adventurous; executives obliged to travel round the clock and season and grateful for the break; eccentrics who thrived on heat, or the absence of fellow-men in quantity. But the Asoka's main wings were closed, the villas mostly empty, the disco mostly silent, only a few servants to attend, the rest laid off and living on stored fat while marking time.

Altogether a different place, as Adeline noted.

Shalimar resembles the desert from which it was but lately plucked, she wrote down, and strongly felt as she took her daily walk, or went along the dusty path to call on Mrs Pearl, whom she did not particularly like.

Rikki, one of the lucky few retained by Shalimar, saw her as he went about his attenuated duties; and smiled to see. Not malevolently, he was over that fevered phase; not even grudgingly, but with something approaching compassion from memories the embattled woman evoked. Outlined sharply in the white light, eyes half-shut, wiry hair very nearly twanging—Mrs Lovat summoned up Mrs Bridie.

For in the hottest month, the month of May, Mrs Bridie would go a-gathering nuts.

Nuts in May, nuts in May, she sang, and made them link hands and sing with her in the baking school compound.

Here we go gathering nuts in May
On a cold and frosty morning.

They giggled at the dotty woman, young as they were; but loved it when she told about frost, gleaning from her voice it was a thing of beauty. Her hands grew cold with love, in the height of the hot weather, they fought to place their own sticky hands in hers for the coolness. But her skin was as yellow as a dried-up leaf.

'Perhaps we ought to get away for a while,' she would say, twisting the tight gold band on her finger.

'Where to, Mrs Bridie?' They clustered round.

'To the hills. Lovedale or Wellington,' she would reply, 'where the missionaries and the Tommies go. Unfashionable places.' Smiling her nervous, bitter smile.

And they would hold her hand in sympathy, understanding she could not go to fashionable places where she would have liked to go, because missionaries were too poor to afford it.

Mrs Bridie, with her yellow skin, and her tales of Tommies who had marched away for good, and the gilt-edged books she had opened

'She gave me a lot. More than I knew. I wish,' Rikki said to Tully one day, one still day, 'I had known, at the time.'

'I don't think it was one-way.' Tully looked up, into eyes that reflected, so deeply at times that they drove him, too, to look inward. 'I think she would have known that,' he said.

Rikki drifted away, without response. Not accepting, not rejecting. In certain ways he resembled the old man, who saw them getting up and going away one by one, the oiled-gold bodies that had lain on the beach all season, and the bright beach umbrellas folded up and put away one by one, without comment or surprise.

When, however, it came to Rikki, or Rikki came to him, he said with precision, and distinctly,

'She knew what she took, and what she gave. She was not a child. You were.' For like his wife he loved his son, who was not his.

And presently as they sat together, under the unweathered, somewhat livid thatch of the new hut, the old man spoke of his own accord.

'Understanding what—what one receives, and what one gives...they say,' he said, back to his usual diffident judderings, 'is a sign of growing up. But one finds...it goes on.'

The signs came all through life. At his time, they were still coming. For it took the hot blood of youth, he felt, to fan the emotions. His own was cooling. Sometimes it saddened the old man. Mostly he was over the fury, for he saw no point in raging over what could not be helped or altered. So he mended his nets, or when his fingers fell numb simply sat on his charpoy in the waning light, and felt with gratitude the presence of his sons when it was offered him, and helped them so far as he was able.

While Rikki wandered, unseeing, through the gardens of Shalimar. Or stared at the half-empty pool so long and intently that the swimmers grew uncomfortable, and wished that the buddha brooding just above their level would go away and cease to disturb them.

Sometimes Rikki did. He forgot he was the lifeguard. Perhaps it seemed less important. He would simply get up and walk away, leaving each one to his fate. And walk along the shore, or wade into the sea and swim, and come out dripping to lie on the deserted sands, eyes closed, sun dripping gold through the lids, mind and body in labour.

Growing up. What did it mean to mind, to body?

A man's body, with the vehemence of a man. Fully developed, the crest reached, while the mind went on expanding.

And he would lie, and touch, and feel, tentatively, even shyly; and sometimes in the deep, induced languor, but sometimes in the very flood of sensations, would come a whisper that the vehemence was but an alembic. As if within it further distillings were taking place: an ultimate, profoundly stirring, that he might one day come to. Though the mind would not be exposed so easily, or forced to manifest itself. The processes were secret, hinting at the attainable, while closely guarding the way.

He accepted it, and acceptance brought sequels, garlanding him with a peace that in no way resembled the surrender of the old, waning man. His own tranquillity flowed strongly. It washed him clean, and gave his energies an edge.

After some such catharsis Rikki would sit up, and rub his eyes, and begin to see again, freshly, a freshly minted world. How blue

228

the sky was! Shells shaped a thousand ways, with polished linings to each one, revealed as he turned them over. Over by the palms a soaring light, like what might fall from an awning, all the way from the silk-cotton trees. They flared at noon, at this time of year.

He could not resist. Soon he would find himself in the grove, settled in the shade, and bring out his clasp-knife and start whittling at the blond wood. Carving out a float or two—not to keep his hand in, there was no need, not since Shalimar; nor to test an old skill; but for pleasure.

His hands, or perhaps it was his mind, took pleasure.

*

Valli was also drawn to the grove. She wandered in regions where only girls and women would go, picking up the fallen petals. At length she sat down, and fashioned them into a vivid garland, and wore it. Then she sighed a little, and waited a little, before going on her way, the petalled necklace swinging as she walked, to keep their rendezvous in the Brindavan Theatre.

Carmen was waiting in the wings. Without a word Valli took the garland off her shoulders and placed it over her friend's. The rope hung bright, and just as heavy. For Carmen Alvarez was going away. They would not see each other until the new season started. Both girls were desolate.

'But it will be nice for you to get away.' Valli echoed her friend, forlornly. She wished she could too.

'Yes. My agent,' said Carmen, 'always makes sure of my Ooty engagements. But I shall miss our little chats,' she said, generously offering the packet of dark chocolate cigarillos.

'I will too. Like anything. Although,' said Valli, 'I have my job.'

Though she did not really think much of standing at that glassy counter, now that hardly anyone came in to buy.

'And the Dance,' reminded Carmen. It was what brought them together, on a Saturday, once or twice a month.

'Yes, there is that,' sighed Valli.

'But it is really too hot to dance in the plains,' said Carmen, fixing the tortoiseshell high, over her proud, shaved nape, 'at this time of year. I don't know *how* you do it.'

'I have to.' Valli helped with the combs. 'The festivals, you see, come at any time.'

'Any time?' said Carmen, slowly opening her black lace fan. Being a Catholic, she would not know.

229

'All the year round. Hot weather, any weather,' said Valli.

'But dancers like us,' said Carmen, loyally contradicting herself, 'it really doesn't matter for dancers like us.'

And she was standing up, and the music began playing. Her skirt was silk, flouncing down like a waterfall. Her high-heeled shoes were lacquered red.

Valli was dressed up too, for the parting performance, for sometimes they dressed for each other before the show proper began.

When tabor and castanets had stopped whirling them about, Carmen tossed back her hair and said:

'I'll bring you a present, when I come back.' She was quite flushed.

'What?' asked breathless Valli.

'Wait and see,' said Carmen.

And they sat for a little, to get their breath back, and though the machines that were cutting out the lake were pounding loudly, the beating of their hearts sounded louder.

'I won't forget,' said Carmen at last, speaking low, from behind her fan.

'I won't either. The hot weather,' said Valli, also low, 'will soon be over.'

'Yes. Well, *ciao*,' said Carmen.

Chapter Thirty-four

In the peak of the heat the mangoes were ready. They were ripe, cheap, and at their abundant best. People ate heartily, on the less finicky side of the tracks, and children revived the old game of skimming. The oval stones, sucked dry, went whizzing at the oblique over the crests of the waves. In the morning the solitary off-season worker, whose job was to clean up the beach, found he was once again working for a living. His rake daily struck mango-stones, whiskery, innumerable, washed up by the sea. Sometimes, disgusted, he had to wade in and trawl for the slippery objects, in a net scoop he had finally contrived for himself.

In the Shalimar kitchens no such things were seen. The chef had his orders. He passed them on to the cooks, who kept their minions hard at work scooping out the melon-balls. While up in Poona the Contractor clan sighed over the noble fruit.

Rikki, outside these circles, had not heard of the lordly Alphonso. He had, however, seen Tully's larder, and the supply lorries. He requested his mother to purchase a basketful from the local market for Tully and Mrs Pearl, since Shalimar was denying them.

'A basketful? For two people?' asked Amma. It seemed a lot to her.

'Yes,' said Rikki.

'Are you sure?' She had to persist. Economy was ingrained in her.

'Yes. And make sure you buy the very best,' said Rikki.

She did, going to a great deal of trouble over it; and apparently it wasn't enough. For there her son was, kneeling on the floor, and the fruit all taken out of her basket and laid out for inspection on a strip of gunny.

'Do you think you know better than your mother?' She enquired, indignantly.

'No.' He flung round and embraced her, with a more than usual warmth to make up for some unvoiced qualifications in the denial.

It made it impossible for her to keep at him, though she did

231

warn:

'Rikki, you will break every bone if you hug like that!'

But really she was quite pleased. She knew that she would be really upset if he stopped crushing her like a bear.

While he released her, and went on carefully sorting, for he was very particular where these two people were concerned. Presently he was done, and went off with two smaller baskets in which he had distributed the select fruit, leaving the rejects for his mother.

Mrs Pearl, he resolved, should be first. It would save carting her fruit all the way up the hill and back. Besides which it left scope to linger on his second call, if encouraged to. For it was his day off, and Tully—well, Tully was boss, his time was his. So Rikki walked cheerfully, swinging a basket in each hand, along the cobbled path to her villa; and setting down the creaky wicker on the verandah, heard her cooing away to her infant. Low chiff-chuffs, like an elderly mother-bird—he would not have interrupted except that he had come this far.

'Mrs Pearl?' He called, cautiously. He knew her ways. He saw her daily in the pool, in her wet and revealing swimming-costume, and it did not seem to bother her. But away from pool or beach she was not happy unless she was what she called respectable.

'Mrs Pearl, are you there?'

'Yes, Rikki. I'm coming.' Mrs Pearl did indeed feel she was not quite respectable, in the equivalent of three small handkerchiefs she had daringly chosen to wear in the heat. She was obliged to get into a dressing-gown first.

'I've brought some mangoes for you, Mrs Pearl,' he said, and held up the basket, tilting the lid so that she could peer.

'Rikki, how nice of you!' She accepted his gift, after only a slight grope towards the purse in the pocket of her gown. By now she had almost cured herself of her corn-merchant habits. 'They look delicious,' she said, tilting the lid further. 'I can't wait to sink my teeth.'

'I will bring you a knife and fork,' he rejoined.

And they smiled at each other, in the shared secret. For both knew perfectly well that Mrs Pearl, despite trying, could not bring herself to sink her teeth into anything.

*

Tully was up on the Copeland battlements, smartening up an ancient 8-pounder that had been mounted there for some compelling reason, now beyond fathoming. The cannon, being sited to rake the countryside, views were naturally available of access routes to Avalon. From a fair distance he could see the advancing figure.

And wondered what it was, this time. For Rikki had a special stride, when he wished to present a crab he had caught, or impart some nugget. All manner of confidences, or gossip picked up in the bars of Shalimar, or the colony, and quite indiscriminately, came up the hill with Rikki. The basket at least suggested crab.

Now and then he would see the pair hunting: Rikki, and the stocky, somewhat lumpish figure of his brother. The one married, man and wife under the joint roof, Tully had been told; the un-private gropings in the dark he could only imagine. The other in flight, mostly. Winging up to Avalon, or working in Shalimar, hardly any anchorage within a family that had been left behind. Except that now and then, late in the evening, porphyry streaks in the surf that creamed up, he saw the two of them together, leaping and splashing as they went after crab.

The lone figure was advancing at a rate. Tully prepared to descend, shelving his cannon refurbishing. For Rikki, when he had something to impart, was apt to be imperative.

Rikki, meanwhile, was shouting; he had to. Tully could be anywhere, more rooms that one could count, in his castle.

'Mangoes, Mr Tully!'

'Mangoes.' Tully came down, wiping his hands. 'Just what I wanted, how did you guess?' he said tritely, but perfectly sincerely. For Avalon took its supplies from Shalimar, and the fruit had yet to appear on the menu, or on lorries, though the trees were loaded.

'I looked in your larder.' Rikki took it at face value, and spoke up with some scorn. 'Only oranges and grapes,' he said, 'when now is the mango season.'

'I had noticed,' said Tully.

'So I brought you some. But you should,' eyeing the oily rag, 'wash first, or the fruit will taste horrible.'

Tully had not intended to. He intended to eat the awkward fruit with a knife and a spoon, and dispense with the washing; but now remembered that these implements took away the flavour, in Rikki's view. Yielding to his superior he walked across the verandah to the yard, where a sink had been installed complete with running water, though none of it polluted the impluvium. (*That* was fed by spring-water, while waiting for the heavens to open.) Soap, towel, nail-brush, pumice-stone, all were to hand,

233

laid out neatly by servants forcibly converted into sticklers. Tully washed with soap, rinsed and dried his hands; but when he ate there was a tang.

'Is it good?' Rikki hovered.

'It would be, if I'd washed properly.'

Tully left his mango, and this time scrubbed with the pumice.

'Does it taste good now?' Rikki was getting anxious.

'Well, better,' said Tully. The tang was faint, if still perceptible, in the lemony flesh. 'The lesson is, never clean a gun before eating a mango,' he said.

The sensible precept amused Rikki, but also woke a slumbering curiosity.

'That gun,' he said, 'it's an 8-pounder, isn't it?'

'Yes. How did you know?'

'Inderjit Singh, who used to be the watchman. He didn't know who could have put it up there, though. Do you?' he asked.

'My grandfather, I imagine,' said Tully.

'You only imagine?'

'Well, I know he did.'

'Why?'

'Why? Because he had to be careful, he said.'

'Of what? What was he afraid of?' Rikki really wondered.

'How would I know, Rikki?' said Tully. 'It's ages ago, I wasn't even born.'

Rikki did not press.

But quite soon, somehow, Tully was forced to admit it was not beyond fathoming.

The gun was there, as he knew perfectly well, because they were afraid of ordinary people, that uncertain quantity. Afraid they might rise up, and topple puppets swanning it under rich and blinding baldaquins held up by British arms, and British grace and favour. Afraid of where such uprisings would lead: to the closure of the short route to loot and adventure, an end to enterprise and proud and lustrous careers. Afraid of the common people, for Copeland-Tullys had never fallen into the profound error of a Bourbon, say, or an Auckland, or a later Eden. Rightly afraid of ordinary people who could not be suborned as oligarchs were, with honours and ringing titles, one elite speaking to another in a polished tongue that both understood. Afraid of people who would one day come to know what belonged to them, and claim it back.

He said so, simply, and did not avoid looking at Rikki.

'I suppose they were afraid of people like you,' he said.

234

And the simple 'they' turned round and sank its fangs into him.

'They' included him. He, too, was afraid, when at times he looked at Rikki. Though it was not the boy he saw, but a face, pressed against a window, looking in. The face, it might be, of an entire community—a world—which a fisherboy reflected.

Rikki, meanwhile, was going over the simple, astonishing statement.

'Are you,' he said, a trifle incredulous, 'afraid of me, Mr Tully?'

It brought him back into focus for Tully. 'Of course not, Rikki,' he said. 'Those days were quite different.' And turned away to attend to the difficult mango.

While Rikki saw certain signs, a crimping that he had noticed would also overtake Mrs Bridie, usually round the mouth; and guessed he was to blame. As he did not know why, any more now than he had then, he simply sat, cross-legged on the gleaming verandah, and waited for Tully to finish the fruit. Then he said, while Tully cleaned up, rather fussily, with a handkerchief,

'It's my half-day off, Mr Tully.'

And said no more, but had a way: his design was laid out glowing like a carpet in front of Tully. And both could smell the casuarina spilling in, strong, green, incense given off by the trees when they scented rain.

'Work when you like. Any time, Rikki, you don't need to ask,' said Tully. 'But,' he said, 'it is raining.'

It was, by now. In veils, soft, Irish, pearl-grey wraps to the landscape. It had been raining off and on. Mango showers, Heblekar, not too confidently, said they were called. It roused Tully's hopes.

'With a bit of luck,' he said, 'the pool ought to fill. Well, half fill.' Since its proportions were lordly.

'Is your statue finished?' Rikki rejoined, since it was meant to adorn the pool.

'Not quite. Come and see,' said Tully, and led the way to the yard where the cherub stood. Somewhat unfinished as he had said, and somewhat dusty, and the fingers were still webbed, waiting for some hard work with the drill to free them from the marble; but where the rain had washed away the dust the marble was quickened. The half-streaked, half-glossy limbs might have belonged to a lively, grubby, skylarking little boy.

Rainfall went on creating effects. Chivvied by lesser winds it shimmied in, an undulating veil that transferred movement, or

235

instability, to the marble. It was a raffish cherub that both perceived, swaying slightly, at times perilously close to tottering.

Little soak, felt Rikki, being familiar with the genre.

'He is drunk,' he said with a smile. 'He has soaked up the water, and is drunk with it.'

Tully had to struggle to remember he was a practical man, and it was Carrara.

'If he did he would turn to gypsum, and fall to pieces,' he said, somewhat pedantically, and severely. 'But he is marble, and will not crumble unless we clog the air with sulphur and make him porous. Which is not the case.'

Certainly not, with all those vacuums and slurpers.

But Rikki could be stubborn too; and refused to be blinded by science.

'Maybe. But anyone can see,' he said, 'that he is enjoying himself. Water is right for him, as the sea is right for me.'

Tully would not argue. He set to work. Chipping away with mallet and chisel, the tapping interspersed with a faint clanging that eventually registered. The bell-buoy out in the bay, installed as a priority by AIDCORP to mark the submerged reef. One heard it when the wind blew landward. When he remarked on it, Rikki again disagreed.

'It's the bell,' he said, 'from the mission hall, where the Bridies used to have Bible reading.'

He could be right, Tully supposed. It was a Sunday evening.

236

Chapter Thirty-five

THE mercury climbed in the various gauges dotted around Shalimar that registered such things. At 37° Centigrade, which Mrs Pearl had to decode, to frighten herself, into the staggering figure of 100° Fahrenheit, it held steady for four suffocating weeks. Then it began to fall, jerkily, as if a resentful salesman was winding back on the bolt the unsold length of Nessus shirting.

Shalimar began to prepare, after the moratorium. Servants went back on the payroll, deck-chairs were given a dusting, the illuminations tested, the cobbles scrubbed. The old man, standing in his doorway, saw the beach had turned with the season. In no time at all, it seemed to him, the folded umbrellas were unfurling again, one by one on the beach. But then time, at his age, became a millrace. That it kept to its pace he could tell, by looking at his thatching, which had slowly mellowed between sun and showers.

Duties recalled people: those who had managed to get away, unlike the labour force, which stayed put.

Sitharam was back from his village, after a June he had gone through like a whirlwind, arranging matches and marriages for his numerous dependent relations. He returned accompanied by his wife, a shy Mrs Sitharam venturing into sophisticated Shalimar after much persuading. Heblekar had also come back, bringing his adoring wife, both of them euphoric from a joint win over her loving, possessive parents. These good folk, however, had clung on to their grandchild, after innumerable references to the rugged nature of Shalimar which no one remotely believed. But reunion made up for much.

Ranji, too, was back at his post, after a blissful month with comrades-in-arms, a time well spent in, among other things, wheedling a mount from the regimental stables.

So was Boyle, with delectable houseboat memories and the Tremletts. For the Tremletts, like Boyle, though ardently English could not face living in England. Unlike him they were too old to weather temporary stands in the developing world. They lived from one wangled invitation to the next, while scrupulously returning each one they received.

Zavera of course had taken up her burden, after tearing herself away from Belvista, which had brimmed with Contractors and Clubvalas. She had been a Clubvala, before Cyrus had swept her off her feet. Cousins and aunts, nephews, nieces, in-laws, whom she had not seen for simply ages, crowded round. How lovely it was! A big family reunion— 'We must celebrate!' cried Zavera, as she embraced each one, and ushered them all in, and the cooks were kept busy dishing up the *dhan sak,* not to mention numerous other delicacies.

When it was time to go she could hardly bear it.

'But I must resume my duties,' she told them. 'Duty is all, is it not?'

'It is to you, Zavera,' they sighed; they knew their Zavera.

'So au revoir, my dears,' she said, and kissed them on both cheeks, and blinked back the tears. 'Until we meet again—yes, soon-soon, I promise!'

'At Yazdegerd?' they cried.

'Yes, then, yes!' cried Zavera, and blew kisses as she drove away to the station in the taxi.

But there is sunshine amid tears, as she told herself; and soon she was smiling as she shuttled along in the train, and grew radiant when she saw Cyrus and the motor-car waiting to meet her.

How happy he made her feel! And how lovely everything was! Sparkling fresh, after the showers. Hotel and gardens spick and span—dear Miss Chari, and the gardeners.

'Shalimar is so pretty,' she said, quite tenderly.

'It is better still when you are here,' said her husband. His work was his life. Nevertheless when separated from his wife, through the exigencies of AIDCORP or otherwise, he was a lonely man.

And they strolled side by side along the little bubbling rills, which gave them so much pleasure, and then round the basin of the lake-to-be which lay close to Cyrus's heart, with Zavera's chiffon streaming behind them rosily, releasing a scent he could not place but loved.

Soon Mrs Contractor was embroiled with the chef, and the menus, and of course Miss Chari, and ordering the linen—

For bookings were brisk, the villas were nearly all taken, the Asoka was filling satisfactorily and no longer boomed even in Adeline's nervous ears.

'It is a reward, for all our efforts,' Zavera told Mrs Pearl.

'What could be nicer?' smiled Mrs Pearl, bouncing young Kali on her knee. There was a zing in things, she felt cheerfully, and amiably divided the credit between Zavera and the spring-like air.

Others were likewise affected, among them Gonsalez, leader of the Brazilian ensemble. He rolled his hips, and rocked heel-and-ball on the springy dance platform as he played his sax. He himself felt he was inspired, conjuring from his instrument airs that throbbed, and floating over the Camp from the discotheque set the most confirmed non-dancing feet a-dancing. They tapped, at least.

Mrs Pearl undoubtedly danced. She whirled, holding her partner in her arms, in her tiny villa. But then her partner made her feel so young, as she warbled to Kali, in tune with the number that came sobbing from the saxophone.

Over in the Gymnasium things were looking up too. Here it was not just the yoga class, and limbering up on the rowing machine, followed by a rub-down in the parlour. These days there was Sandhu.

Sandhu, champion wrestler of the South, all but All-India champ, had been won over by Shalimar. This giant, having pondered long and shrewdly, decided to exchange some fitful glory for a steady well-paid job. He presented his acolytes with his lesser trophies to still their cries. He retired his pride, his golden, sand-bearing camel to the nearest pinjrapole, with numerous exhortations that it be looked after well, backed by veiled threats of physical violence if it was not; plus a pension, paid per mensem, for the upkeep of the animal. He sold his leopard-skin to Mrs Lovat for a handsome sum, and wearing a breech-cloth with a studded leather apron over it, became Master of the Gym and the massage annexe.

Shalimar was pleased. It was quite something. A certain éclat, having an ex-champion. Grand trophies in niches and hung on the walls, not to mention the superb specimen. Massive, bulging arms crossed on his breast, and if he wished, the ladies at least felt, he could twirl them round with his little finger. While the men were undoubtedly revitalised. Entering flabby and despairing, they came out declaring themselves ready, as they flexed a muscle or two, to move mountains.

For Sandhu had presence, and an ability to persuade. He himself acknowledged that a proportion of his victories owed something to it. Opponents of renown had found confidence in their own prowess wavering, in face of Sandhu's powerful, communicated disdain. His encouragement, similarly, possessed mesmeric quality. It gave people faith in themselves, sometimes without any foundation. Shalimaris glowed, and performed

239

wonders, and loved their man.

But the move was not popular. The villagers felt they had been cheated. They had lost their entertainment, and their hero. They missed his drama, his prowess, his style, the fire and elegance he brought to the kill. They spoke of past bouts, and of the baby-rock. Of how villages around had clubbed together to bring on the budding champion.

What of those years, and the contributions? People came to chide, and Sandhu sat massively down, on the old ebony tripod which he had kept for sentimental reasons, and presently answered.

'It is the trend,' he said.

His eyes were the colour of horn, and if they twinkled, still everyone understood he had them in his famous half-nelson. For there were those among them, numerous sons and siblings, who had followed the trend to Shalimar, and were faring uncommonly well.

Chapter Thirty-six

MRS Contractor's concerns, naturally enough, were far removed from these matters. Of late she had begun to think that they ought to celebrate. Some kind of little show, to show what had been achieved in Shalimar, to prove to people what could be done if one tried. These thoughts clustered, and all of a sudden, she had it. She was standing by her bedroom window, gazing into the distance where bulldozers were scooping out the basin for the lake (which they would call the Blue Lagoon, she had lovingly decided) when it came to her. She had to tell Cyrus at once. He was awake, though not yet up.

'I was just thinking, Cyrus,' she said, sitting on the piped edge of the sprung, Dreamland mattress which Nargiz had so kindly sent from USA, so *much* more springy and dreamlike than anything made in India, 'I was just thinking that we should have an Open Day.'

'But, my love, we are open all year round,' said her husband.

Zavera thumped up the pillows, so that he could sit up and listen properly.

'An *O*pen *D*ay,' she said, stressing the capitals, 'to show everyone.'

'Show what?' he asked.

'*Everry*thing,' she said. She was so proud of it, and her husband. 'Everything in Shalimar, now that it is finished.'

'But it is not.' Her husband, a purist in his way, objected.

'But it will be,' said Zavera, and passed him his morning cup. 'There is only a lake, it will be ready in no time, will it not?' She had unbounded faith.

'Not in no time. But quite soon, my love,' he justified her faith in him, while sipping the fragrant tea.

*

Since it was decided, and she knew how time flew, she at once set about getting help from people. And most people did help, there was something about Zavera. Boyle, certainly, was nothing loth.

'Open Day? Splendid idea!' he boomed at her, in a way that she loved. 'Just say what you'd like me to do, Zavera. At your service, you know that.'

241

'I know. Thank you, Herbert,' she said, warmly.

'And Tully. Invaluable. Have a word, I'm sure he'll help, if you ask him,' said Boyle, robustly, because he was not that sure. If that mausoleum could spare him, he would.

'I have asked.' She had indeed. She had motored all the way up to Avalon. 'He has promised,' she said.

'What?' asked Boyle.

'To give away the prizes, at tombola,' she answered.

'Really?' He really admired her.

'Yes. You see, if you go about it in the right way, he will do anything for you,' said Zavera.

'I see,' said Boyle.

It made Zavera pause, the way he said it. What had she said? It bothered her. Perhaps she should not have.

'Of course you do,' she remedied.

But Boyle had already caught the inflection. Of late he himself had begun to wonder what had gone wrong between them. Was it his doing, was it Tully's? Sometimes he wasn't even sure anything *was* wrong. But mostly he felt, gloomily, that the country, or perhaps it was Shalimar, had driven in the thin end. More strongly than elsewhere on the globe where they had toiled together, there was a sense of wedge.

*

After Boyle there was Sitharam, indispensable man from these parts, for Zavera to woo.

Sitharam was not won over easily. He translated Mrs Contractor's Open Day into Shandy: a fair or market, but superior, full of superior tourists who would have to be treated under Shalimar rules no matter how much galatta they made. All that gaddabad, he described it to himself, sweating. And afterwards the clearing up.

He said so, differently, to Mrs Contractor.

'It is not wise,' he said, rolling his eyes. 'It will soon be monsoon,' he finished, inspired.

'How soon?'

'Soon.'

Zavera beat a tattoo with her pink oval nails. She had patience, and had noticed his eyes rolling.

'A little rain,' she said, 'does not matter.'

'Not little. Deluge.' Sitharam giggled, somewhat nervously.

'Then we will have it in deluge. No one will melt, we are not

242

made of sugar,' Zavera routed him.

'There is canvas.' Sitharam, defeated, gloomily covered his retreat. Who knew, maybe there would be deluge. 'I will instruct my assistant to arrange for tents,' he said.

'Pavilions,' said Zavera, and her eyes began to shine, as she visualised them. But remembered to translate. 'Shamianas, striped,' she said.

*

Boyle thought about the plan, and presently conveyed his congratulations to his colleague.

'Brainwave, your wife's,' he said.

'Isn't it,' agreed Contractor.

'Good scheme, an Open Day. Clever of her to think of it,' said Boyle. Actually he thought the old rogue had. Nothing like a spot of publicity for drumming up business—and you wouldn't need to tell *him* that. Cyrus—thank heaven—had his head screwed on the right way.

Cyrus had not thought of it, but his sentiments were Boyle's. It would pep up business. Contracts had to be fought for, these days there was a cut-throat competition for development projects. The firm was doing well, he knew that, but no one could afford to let up.

Presently he called for his topi, and setting it firmly on his head set off briskly for the lake site.

Despite his calling, Contractor was not a man of boundless imagination. Even when the model stood in front of him on the conference table he experienced difficulty in visualising the finished work. Now, however, in the very teeth of construction he managed to see not only the blue lagoon of his wife's inspired christening, but a lagoon alive with pedalos and similar, which hitherto had had no place to go but the sea. He would be glad. Shalimaris had a way of launching out on these cockleshells, and capsizing at first wave. They were brought out of course, always a life-guard patrolling. But when that dreamy youth was on duty—Contractor pursed his lips, for he had seen for himself it took the dreamer a little time to wake up. Not always by any means, and to give him his due a first-class swimmer, once he got going. But sometimes. There had been complaints, which both Shalimar and AIDCORP could well do without.

Should he be sacked? Contractor cogitated, not for the first time. But something in him flinched. The whole family depended

243

on the boy, he had learned from his wife, who had been told by Joseph.

Chapter Thirty-seven

RIKKI would not for a moment have denied his dreamy nature, his knuckles had been rapped too often; but it was not only that. He simply thought it folly to play with the sea. His own respect was ingrained, if not inherited. He would not treat the ocean like a pond. If Shalimaris put out on a pedalo, in a choppy sea (it amazed him, but they did), he allowed them time to regret it before he hauled them out. Unless, of course, they showed signs of drowning, in which case he was prepared to be prompt.

When it came to Tully's boat, however, he was fully alert. Contractor, no one, need have suffered a moment's anxiety. He watched over it like a hawk—mentally, the creek where it was moored was hidden away, and a fair distance from the village. When the river shrank to a trickle he had it up on the bank, caulking the seams, touching up the varnish. If a sudden squall blew up Rikki downed everything, and Tully would see him striding, slanted against the wind, to check on the tarpaulins or the mooring ropes.

Now, as he went about his tasks, Rikki kept the river in the forefront of his mind. About now it would start to rise, flushed with rain falling on distant hill slopes. And listening, he did hear, the wind carried the sound. The glut would come shortly, he judged from these preliminary burblings, but must have misheard or misjudged, for the river was already flowing strongly when he arrived. The boat was imperilled.

Tully's boat, bearing the name he had chosen.

But he had built it for Tully, selected its timbers, seen the keel laid, labours that kindled passions, pure, male, austere. He had to stand, rooted, waiting for it to subside before he could function. Swiftly enough then, in response to emotions that were hardly less strong for all that they had been in store for some time. As he saw the trim little craft in danger, but bobbing gamely in the choppy waters of the creek, for even this little backwater had not been spared.

Boatman, see to your boat!

The old cry—fishermen alerting one of their number in peril—rang in some inner region of permanent vigilance as he plunged down the bank. Old feelings flared as he reached the boat and dragged it to safety. It might easily have been his own boat's distress call that he had answered.

When he had done he had to sit down to recover, the steep bank had made it a strenuous operation. Nearby, equally breathless, a heron was giving its own version of flopping. It stood starkly on one flat foot, its topknot ruffled, its plumage flouncy, an indignant eye fixed on the watery reaches from which the turbulent current had ejected it.

'It happens to the best of us, comrade!'

Rikki, laughing, chats up this bird that is capable, between foot and bill, of expressing such ripe exasperation. Shakes his head over these extraordinary fowl that stand, hours on end on one stilt of a leg, fishing. Adroit fishers too, admired even by their human competitors. They knew it and knowledge gave them airs and audacity. Trading on immunity they stalked downstream to the brink of the fishermen's domain.

But Shalimar shattered this fine insolence. There were duck-shoots organised nowadays, and moorhen, waders, sandpipers, all had retreated from the rumpus to swampy reaches inland. The swamp had once been a hubbub of full-throated bull-frogs. The newcomers soon reduced this noisy crew, whose surviving members rapidly grew wary about how and where they did their quarking.

With the frogs dying out, the insect colony multiplied. Healthy specimens, and various new species too, could be seen whizzing round daring and unafraid in the glare of the Moorish torches. But kingfishers kept them manageable, took time off from fishing for their preferred diet to flash, blue and green, over the breeding colony, snapping up the juicy morsels.

Rikki sat, rapt. There were a hundred things, he could easily have sat all day... He was roused by the works siren, blaring faintly in the distant Camp. The evening shift was over, workers would be returning to their quarters, the offices closing. Soon, but not till after the Shalimaris had dined, he would be on duty serving coffee and brandy in the piazza. First, however, he would report to Tully that his boat was safe. And, now he thought of it, caution him not to sail. He might, he was a good sailor and he knew it; but he was not bred to these parts. Those who were, knew enough to be wary of the currents, at this time of year.

Rikki loped back, and was just in time to hop on a lorry going up to Avalon—ice deliveries were made in the evening, and Mrs Contractor had decided to send up some flowerpots for the terrace with the load. He had assumed Tully would be back, but there was no sign. He should have looked round Shalimar first, he realised, but the lorry had been on the point of leaving. Rather than just stand he gave a hand with the heavy terracotta. The ice was in a smallish container, a sort of trunk of white plastic with a chrome hasp.

'I'll see to that,' he said to the lorry driver, and heard the vehicle roaring off down the hill as he started to load the freezer compartment.

He loved the operation. He could feel himself shiver as he lifted out the ice, packed into the container in crumpled plastic bags glittery with what looked like powdered glass. Crackling cold in his hands, and dripping silver and crystal—he took his time before closing the fridge.

Then he wondered what to do, where Tully was. There was no one to ask. Tully did his own cooking, the cleaners were sent home early, the watchman was not due until nightfall.

He stood irresolute for a little, but soon began to feel himself drawn. The pool-room, as usual, was putting forward claims, and he was in a mood to answer.

On his way, however, he thought to peek at Tully's statue, to see how it was coming along; and deflecting into the yard saw that it was coming along very well indeed. The fingers had been released from the stone, the webs had vanished. The feet, which had been slabs, were arched and boned. Running an eye from top to toe, it seemed to Rikki that the statue was ready.

What its own creator might have felt flooded into him. He had to sit and worship, or at any rate gaze; and must have fallen into a reverie for he leapt when he heard his name.

'Hello, Rikki.'

'Mr Tully.' He scrambled up. 'You gave me a fright.'

'Why? Didn't you hear me coming?'

'No.'

Tully had churned up in his Land Rover. The boy must have been deep into whatever it was, he thought, not to hear. He still looked dazed.

'Well,' he said, 'no ghosts around here, Rikki—you must know that.'

'I know.'

'Nothing to be afraid of. Only a small boy,' said Tully, resting a hand on the curly marble head.

'He is ready.' Rikki recovered himself. 'It is time he went in the pool,' he said.

Tully, after subjecting his statue, was equally sure after inspection; but niggled all the same. One or two features, he felt, and a little smoothing here and there—

He pointed out a rough patch.

Rikki, smiling now, merely repeated: 'It is time he went in the pool. You can finish off, if you like, from the water. It is not too deep.'

'You'll have to give me a hand,' said Tully.

'I intend to,' said Rikki.

Used to hefting in the course of their labours, yet both had miscalculated. The statue was not to be shifted easily, like a sack, or even a slab of marble. It took them, two strong men, sweated effort, and longer than they had bargained for, to get the little boy into place on his podium.

But at length it was done. They stood back to dwell on their efforts, and the cherub. It had lost its raffish look, the air being clear and still; but still bore grubby streaks. Rikki, who had just climbed out of the pool, descended again.

'He's heavier than he looks,' he said, as he sponged off dust and watermarks. 'Whoever would think it? He looks so delicate.'

Perhaps it was some delicacy in the carving that misled; or a translucence in the stone, released as it was washed clean, and increasing. Whatever it was, it seemed to both observers that the glowing little boy would start to dip a toe any minute, as he ventured into life.

Neither heard Boyle. He had rattled up in his beach buggy (the latest thing in Shalimar) for a confab with Tully about Open Day, and perhaps a friendly noggin. Arrived, however, he found himself hesitating. The place seemed unduly quiet, though Tully was in, he could see his Land Rover standing in the portico. Nevertheless he began to feel shut out, although there were no doors shut that he could see. Here Boyle gave himself a shake, and got out of the buggy. No one to salaam him in of course—one of Tully's eccentricities. He had to make his way. Gaining the verandah he again paused, but catching sight of the yard and some dusty footprints followed them into the pool-room. Where Tully was standing and admiring his handiwork, together with that fisherboy, or waiter.

Boyle never gave any servant more that a cursory glance. Now he found he had to. Some quality to the boy's face, that he could not avoid. Worse still, when he turned to Tully he saw that

248

whatever it was, was reflected. There were reflections everywhere. In the pool, and mirrored on these two faces, and reflecting from the water to the wet, mirror-marble mosaic round the pool, and so back to the statue in the middle.

Boyle began to feel dizzy. He cleared his throat, to pull himself together.

'If you could spare a minute,' he croaked—he could hear himself; but at least it broke the infernal spell, and the mirrors.

'Of course.' Tully turned to Boyle, and his features cleared. He was his usual self—absolutely normal, felt Boyle, and whacked himself for letting his imagination bolt.

Rikki, too, recollected himself.

'I nearly forgot, Mr Tully,' he warned. 'You must not sail. It's not safe, the river is rising.'

'And the boat, Rikki?' An unnecessary question, but Tully asked it.

'Quite safe. I beached it,' said Rikki, and did not forget to salute Boyle before going off down the hill.

The night was humid, Boyle saw the land vapours steaming up white in glare of his headlamps as he drove back to his quarters. Against expectations he managed to fall asleep, but soon woke and found he could not drop off again.

It was the wasp notes of the air-conditioning, he reasoned; but turning it off would make it unbearable. Then it must be the weight of the bedclothes. He threw off the light Kashmir shawl, but it was no better. He would have dispensed with the sheet as well, except that he could never sleep without some covering. He could not sleep with it either. He tossed and turned, pulling up the sheet, throwing it off, snarling up the smooth linen into a confused drapery under which, finally, he forced himself to lie motionless.

It worked, if not too well. He fell into a fitful slumber, filled with dreams. He dreamed that he was swathed in robes, and lying on what seemed like some sort of bier, or cloud. Above him was a child, armed with an arrow which he was about to let fly; while he, on his cloud, held down by that infernal drapery, could not move, not for his life.

Boyle woke in a sweat. He recalled the swathed figure, but it was not him and there was no bier. It was the statue of a woman in nun's garb, swooning, in some kind of trance—very gradually it came back.

He was a young officer, and it was during the war, and there had been these trips to break the monotony of herding Italian POWs. And he was standing in yet another museum or cathedral, gazing earnestly at this sculpture as exhorted to, while the guide intoned about the ecstasy of the pious nun from Àvila. He had beheld only the marble. He and his companion had tittered about the ecstatic virgin, a contradiction in terms if ever they had heard one.

Now, vastly uncomfortable, Boyle saw what that guide, or sculptor, had been getting at. There was on that face an extreme purity, shot through with a voluptuous experience hardly less extreme. Somehow they existed together, in a process which Boyle began to believe he had perceived in the boy. It was he who brought it back, traces in his features recalled that long-forgotten sculpture. The same look, now that he went over it.

It was too fanciful. Altogether too odd.

Now came the really odd part, which he had been staving off. It was Tully. Looming up, and insisting on looking something like; his face reflected. *Tully?* It was too much. Boyle had to laugh, and did guffaw out loud in the darkness, and feeling a lot better, slept.

Tully, if told of it—but of course he was not. Nevertheless there were intimations, as he waited for sleep. An image of Boyle was drifting in, his face lodged itself in the forefront of his mind. Something there, he saw: bulging, a trifle outraged, eyebrows up, saying, You don't expect to get away with that bull, do you, Toby old boy? I mean we have been around together quite a bit, you know!

Tully wouldn't have expected. If told in so many words, he would have laughed and disclaimed tangentially: A nun? Never has appealed. Couldn't say why, old boy—just not my cup. Wrong sex too, don't you think?

Now he laughed in the darkness and turned over. Was not, would not particularly have wanted to claim the virtues of purity, the virtuous adjectives had long turned pejorative. Never had been a virtue, except for women, by masculine insistence, the driving masculine urge to be first on a tall peak, or first to part the tender nymphae. What man, bar Hippolytus, guarded his virtue like a fanatic?

Before and after marriage there were affairs, light, effervescent, take-it-or-leave-it when into AIDCORP's more imaginative ventures; positively life-saving when they were not. Quite a few affairs in fact—certain advantages in a nomadic life-style, not to mention accessible women. Perhaps too accessible, it took the edge off.

250

A succession, then, of encounters. Amusing, agreeable, effective, never quite satisfactory, a slight sense of glancing off, of something not there that should have been. Concluding it was the human lot, but not giving up. Always wondering if it would be different next time, with another woman, with Corinna—

He was curious to see, now that she was coming. At least there had been hints: an extravagant cable with one line on it asking if Shalimar was en route to the Linklaters in Sri Lanka.

It was. Extravagant Tully had sent his wife a full-scale map. He slept.

Chapter Thirty-eight

No cable warned Rikki.

He was weeding the melon patch, carefully unwinding a wild morning-glory from the fruit vines, and there was this woman. Slender, gold-haired, nevertheless he translated Corinna into stringy Mrs Bridie. Full of her nuts in May, to which there were sequels.

Who shall we send to fetch him away, fetch him away, FETCH HIM AWAY? she sang in her rising, reedy falsetto, and made the children join in.

He hated her. He hated being compelled to sing this song full of violence, and the force they employed to drag each other over the line she scratched in the earth with a pointed stick. He hated this woman who had come for no other reason.

Corinna saw nothing but a boy, nice looking, his features vaguely familiar.

'It's—Rikki, isn't it?' she said.

'Yes.' He continued to see Mrs Bridie in her as he stumbled up. 'Have you come to—to—'

He must have got it out, though it seemed stuck forever in his throat.

'To fetch him away?' she repeated, surprised. 'What on earth do you mean?'

'Mr Tully. But not—not yet,' he said, stammering. 'You s-see, nothing is—is finished yet.'

He meant statues and designs. She thought villas and lakes.

'But he wouldn't dream,' she said. She knew, or rather had learnt, he wouldn't budge for anyone, until he was ready. 'Bit of a stickler, my husband. Likes to be around till the curtain's actually going up, you know.'

'Yes, I know.' Slowly Rikki was coming to. 'He likes to finish things...properly, like I do,' he said.

'What things?' she asked curiously. Certainly villas and lakes were being built, but he had taken away the sense that these were important, or what he meant.

But now he backed away. He would not share with her. He could see her foot tapping as she looked down from a height. He

252

began to wonder in which godown he had stashed the gunny sacks, while he side-tracked with an apology.

'I'm sorry, I thought you were someone else, Mrs Tully,' he said, formally.

'I thought you must have.' She smiled, and wondered who; and moved on. 'And how are you, Rikki?'

'I am very well, thank you, Mrs Tully,' he said politely.

'And the surfing?' He had been keen, she remembered; it was slowly coming back, his determined tussles with her malibu.

'That's all right too,' he said, still politely, but occupied now with the garden.

'Have you been practising?' she asked, not that interested, but wishing he would stand easily. That he could, was apparent; but now he had chosen to hump himself over the vines. Not awkwardly, however. It was she who felt awkward, standing over him.

'Yes. When I have time,' he said, without even troubling to look up, and continued with what he was doing. Working most carefully, she saw; fingers loam-stained, hands quite finical, fastidiously re-routing a wandering morning-glory.

*

She recounted the conversation that evening.

'He thought,' smiling, sitting on the edge of the fourposter in her kimono, 'he thought I'd come to fetch you away, Toby.'

'Have you, Corinna?' Smiling too, watching the silky stuff sliding, really wanting to know.

'Don't think I could, darling. Do you?'

'Never know till you try, don't they say, Corinna?'

'I'm always willing, Toby.' Dropping her voice to a husky bass.

And later, rising up on rosy elbows, looking down at him:

'You look marvellous, Toby. Positively blooming.'

'Well—' lazily, 'I enjoy what I'm doing.'

'I can see. Every sign. But I meant before.'

'Before what?'

'Before this. Quite a dew on you, Toby. Noticed the moment I arrived. But I'm not asking questions.'

'No need to, actually.'

'Well I won't. But it's not—just this, what we're up to, is it?'

'Isn't it?'

'Don't know—about you—never have—but—' Between kisses, lips full on his, stopping him up. He getting clear, pinning her flat

253

so he can look at her.

'But what?'

'But I don't care. Does for me, darling. Totally. Beautifully.—Toby?'

Inviting him again. He accepting, as he wants to. Every sign, as she says; and the encounter has never been less than delightful.

However, it has to stop. Limits for a man, though not, she makes it clear, for Corinna. Besides, dinner looms: Zavera's, laid on to welcome the new arrival. He reminded her, while she burrowed deeper.

'Come on. Time you got dressed.'

'What for?'

'Dinner.'

'Don't want to go.'

'You're the guest of honour.'

He sat her up, went to check that the shower was working, turned it to cold, got her under it, grins as he hears her squall.

'You've no *heart*, Toby!'

'Have, too.'

'Doing this to me—'

'Only as I would be done by.'

Means it. Cold showers the moment she comes out, shaves, dresses, waits... Bra, pants, a dress, is all: why should it take forever?

'Because I want to be a credit to you, darling,' coos false Corinna. Eve incarnate, he knows she would titivate if she were the last living creature. But really he is pleased with the way she looks.

*

Zavera was pleased with both of them: indeed, with all of them. She liked men to be spruce, men liked to oblige her. Boyle, like Tully, would take trouble. Women, too, picked out their prettiest wear. Not to compete. The impulse died, they wanted only to please this woman who flowered almost, overflowed with affection and goodwill.

Mrs Pearl found it irresistible. She had reached that calm if rugged plateau of accepting that nothing she put on would do anything for her looks. She wore clothes as she would have worn a piece of bark, and for the same reason. Nevertheless she had sallied out to the Emporium, and prevailed upon the young girl who served to select something cheerful... And here she was in all her glory, in a tie-dye dress a-swirl with colour, with Zavera

254

showering sunshine and compliments.

'So wonderful to see you. I wish we could see you more often, but now you are not in Asoka—! But we often wish, don't we, Cyrus?'

'Yes. Often.' Simply to agree with his wife made that man happy.

'And what a lovely dress!' So lavish about it that Mrs Pearl felt amply rewarded for her trouble, while not brash enough to take full credit.

'Yes, isn't it? But I must confess it was selected for me.'

'It's beautiful! Don't you think so, er, Toby?'

'Dazzling. Local vat, isn't it?'

'Yes. A cottage industry hereabouts, I'm told. Inspired,' smiled Mrs Pearl, 'by Solomon himself, I wouldn't be surprised.'

'His touch, yes.' Tully smiled too. 'I've always been an admirer.'

Zavera felt happy, simply listening to them. How well they got on! She had asked Mrs Pearl for that very reason, although she was old enough to be Toby's grandmother. (Not quite.) And how wise she had been, she thought as she sank a prong into the creamy pâté, to keep the number small! Six was just right for a cosy little dinner-party. All such charming people, especially the Tullys. Toby on her right, his wife on Cyrus's. . .they made her sigh for her youth, for she could not but compare, and confess that she was plump, and Cyrus was portly. He had as usual left the last buttons on his velvety jacket unfastened, she could not but notice, but fondly. No, she would not wish one particle of her dear Cyrus to melt away, nor for them to change places with any married couple however slim and good looking.

And her thoughts again flew to her guest of honour. Such a pity, only a flying visit, young Mrs Tully's.

She said so.

'Next time, Mrs Tully—' she began.

'Corinna.' Corinna's smile flashed, charmingly.

'Next time, Corinna,' Zavera blushed a little, with pleasure, 'we will not let you run away so soon. Will we, Herbert?'

'We'll tie her up! But,' Boyle presumed to assume avuncular status, 'that's the trouble with Corinna. Much too popular, everyone asks her. But,' in his gallant foghorn, 'you mustn't let the old man hog you, in the short time you're with us, you know, Corinna.'

'But he should!' Zavera really thought he ought, in spite of

Herbert. In fact, it was dreadful that the young couple were parted at all, now that Shalimar was so—so livable. She would advise Corinna, since whatever might appear, women were the power behind.

'You should take your husband with you,' she said firmly. 'He has worked hard. He deserves a holiday.'

'Ah, but will he go?' Boyle chuckled richly, as one who knew the oddity best. 'Never shifts easily. Never known him to. Not till the operation's over, eh, Toby!'

'Well.' More to do with his make-up, Tully suspected, but had long since rationalised it into a care for jam on his bread. 'Sizeable investments, I like to keep an eye,' he said.

'Nonsense.' Boyle blitzed this transparent defence, and addressed the company. 'Just his way. Gets the job into his system. This time it's worse than I've ever known, now there's Av—'

Suddenly uncomfortable, he paused.

'What?' asked Corinna; her curiosity began to smoulder.

'Avalon.' Boyle had no option but to finish. 'And Shalimar of course,' he went on, more easily. 'I don't see our Toby budging till that's properly finished.'

Some echo that she caught, prompted Corinna.

'That's what he said. Rikki, I mean,' she said.

It made Zavera shake her head, in puzzlement.

'Such a strange boy,' she said. Not like the other servants, she could not make him out. Like an oyster, though some people could coax him. With them he was like Joseph was with her, she supposed. She would never have known all sorts of things, if Joseph had not told her.

'But he is so useful,' she allowed, of the graceful waiter she could always trust with the drinks, though she did not really want to talk about a servant.

And she sat, somewhat silently for her, at the head of the small table, of which the leaves had been removed because it was a cosy little dinner; and in between her hostess duties wondered at the boy. How he would come in just anywhere. Right here among the silver and the cut-glass, and her nicely-dressed and charming guests. A mere fisherboy, taking his place.

At this point Zavera bridled slightly, mainly at herself. Really, such fancies! She brushed them off her round, plump arms, as if they were mosquitoes—indeed there was an itchy sensation; but having somehow contrived to enlarge one boy, continued to feel

256

she was dealing with an invading force.

Mrs Pearl continued to deal simply.

'Useful, yes. And so obliging,' she said affectionately. 'He is a lamb.'

'Yes, isn't he?' smiled Zavera. She smiled, and nodded, and thought of the lamb-like Rikki, and how he would invade like a lion. Soon, like Boyle, and with a bewilderment not unlike, she bundled him up with the country. It was that, coming in: a smell of rotting wood and fish from those wretched fishermen's hovels, not to mention their mouldering boats drawn up on the beach like a row of herring skeletons. It all but took away her enjoyment of the fresh, invigorating sea breeze.

Boyle, amidst general agreement, and rising above these whiffs, declared the sea air was so good for one. He had strolled on to the verandah, cigar in hand, and between draws urged Cyrus to fill his lungs, and led the exercise himself. While Cyrus, breathing deeply as bidden, did debate with himself if those fishermen should not be told to move a little further off, and compensated for any inconvenience it might cause them.

Chapter Thirty-nine

NOT long after this, coming up one evening, Tully thought he saw something odd, and although slightly unbelieving, went to investigate.

But he had not been mistaken, nor was the light playing tricks. His marble statue had been got at. Still on its pedestal, it was mysteriously and unsuitably accoutred in peasants' rainwear: an enveloping one-piece cloak, constructed from stiff palmyra, that he had seen them wearing in the fields when it bucketed down. It fell from a pointed hood to the cherub's ankles, and made it resemble nothing so much as an apprentice member of the Ku-Klux-Klan. Nearby, poised for flight, stood the obvious culprit.

'Whatever for, Rikki?' asked Tully. He had to suppose there was a reason.

'In case—' looking hunted, eyes everywhere except meeting Tully's, 'it got stolen,' said Rikki.

A voodoo or talisman of some kind, Tully was almost brought to believe, since the notion of theft was ludicrous. This manifestation however was new to him, although, in common with Benjamin Bridie, he suspected that what he knew of the ways of the land might only represent the tip.

Rikki, of course, could not divine this. He thought he saw unbelief writ large, and spreading. Guilt was having its effect too.

'Not stolen. I mean,' he gabbled, 'in case it rains.'

'But that's the point,' said Tully. Of that oblong, purposely left for the heavens to pour in. Of the cherub stood in the middle, on whom it could pour, for whom water was right, according to Rikki. 'That's the whole point,' he repeated.

Rikki stood somewhat sheepishly, gazing at his handiwork, thinking that perhaps he had gone too far. It was really foolish, when he thought about it. He was working up to saying so, when Tully spoke again.

'Isn't it?' he said.

Rikki simply stood. Tully never insisted, he let things go. This new behaviour disoriented him, he felt he did not know which way to turn. It did not prevent him ferreting out causes. Soon, somewhat darkly, he succeeded in placing the blame on Mrs

Tully. She was the force that moved Tully to put him in this corner.

While Tully felt slightly ashamed. Making a thing of it, he felt—there was even a feeling of rooting into another's privacies. He was about to make amends, when Rikki recovered. Movement, if not speech. He snatched up the palmyra, and scrunching it up as small as he could, departed.

*

Neither of them, of course, could let it rest. Tully had to consult Heblekar about this voodoo or talisman, Heblekar was totally unfamiliar. He told of what he did know.

'They put a lump of camphor on this—this—' Then he could not think of the name. 'On this thing like a ladle,' he said, feeling unutterably foolish and inadequate, 'and then they light it, to ward off jealous Powers, if there are any. If something is more beautiful, or gifted, or loved, than it has any right to be. Women do,' he finished, to save face.

Tully, an expert at this, saw through.

'Don't you?' he said.

Heblekar did, sort of. His son was a rather handsome infant. His wife, and he, thought it not unwise to light camphor, occasionally. Put in a corner now, he could have been nimble, being expert at this. However, something about Tully stopped him wriggling out.

'Well, there's something, isn't there, about those whom the gods love, they take,' he said, somewhat lamely.

Or words to that effect, which of course nobody really believed, except for a chip of deathless silicon inside them that went on throbbing and believing, having stubbornly developed an existence of its own. Heblekar hoped Tully would subscribe to this, and it would deflect him from pinning on the offensive labels; and strangely, Tully did. The mantle of wherever he was tended to fall on him, and he tended on the whole not to twitch it off his irritated shoulders. Where he was now, of course, was Heblekar, but overwhelmingly Rikki terrain.

Rikki's worry stemmed from a practical reason. The palmyra rainwear had not been his to scrunch up. Almost on the threshold of their hut he remembered it belonged to his sister. He had borrowed it from her, judging it nearer the cherub's size than his own; he would have to return it in a reasonable condition. Sitting

259

down he tried to remedy the damage, wishing he had been less ruthless, or the palmyra more pliable. For the thing was quite wrecked. Cracks and rifts ran right and left, from top to bottom of the rigid fabric. Palm-fronds flew up in crisp flakes as he thumped and wrestled to get it back into shape. There were hideous, splitting noises.

'What are you doing, Rikki?'

Valli, rounding the corner, and about to dance in, discovered her brother.

'It got broken. I'm trying to mend it,' he said, abandoning the attempt.

'Broken?' said Valli, arrested by the sight of the mangled object. 'However did you break it like that, Rikki?'

'I just did.' The explaining one had to do, in the course of simply living. It was beyond him. 'I'll get you another. Select whatever you like,' he said, grandly, to hide his confusion. 'I'll buy it for you.'

'Oh no, Rikki,' said generous Valli. 'You mustn't waste your money. You know I never use that thing,' she kicked the palmyra wreck, 'nowadays.'

For nowadays she never had to lend a hand in all weathers, she had her lovely little job in the shop.

Besides, there was the parasol.

It was a present from Carmen from Ootacamund.

'From Spain,' said Carmen, to add lustre. 'As you can see,' she said, waving a languid hand at the senorita on one panel, embroidered in silk by herself. Actually she did not know where it came from. It was one of six, all presented by an overseas mandarin, a manufacturer of sunshades and umbrellas and an admirer of the dance.

But it was handsome by any standards. It had been made in Hong Kong by young girls who compulsively infused cherry-blossom tones into the worst tat that they churned out in the sweatshops. The handle was curved and polished, the ribs were scarlet, the frippery was of lace as beguiling, and about as permanent, as foam. Valli had never seen anything so pretty. She furled and unfurled, and held it dizzily over her head and sashayed along, pretending to be a tight-rope walker, and it would have been difficult to say which of them was most delighted, by the effects she achieved by twirling the dainty parasol against the footlights of the Brindavan Theatre.

'And you remembered me!' breathed Valli.

260

'I said I would. I made a *promise,*' said Carmen, fingering the rosary she always carried with her, and feeling very solemn and Catholic.

'I know, but—' Remembrance was the sweetest thing, felt Valli with a swelling heart.

She, too, had brought a gift—humble, but solicited. She whisked the cloth off the pottery bowl and presented it to her friend. She herself did not think much of what it contained, which could be had freely, one didn't even have to pay for it in the market. Since that was what Carmen wanted, however,

'I pounded it up fresh for you,' she said.

'Is it what you use?' asked Carmen, prodding the henna-leaf chutney.

'We all do, when we need to have colour,' said Valli. As she did, for a forthcoming festival. She opened her hands to display her stained palms.

'But I don't know how. You must show me,' said Carmen gravely.

'Now?' asked Valli.

'Yes. I have a few minutes to spare,' said Carmen, glancing at her jewelled watch.

'It's quite easy,' said Valli, applying the paste to the coin-size circle Carmen drew on her forearm with a wetted finger. 'But in a few minutes it won't take properly,' she warned. 'There won't be much colour.'

There was, however, enough for Carmen.

'I love it. I love new things very much, don't you?' she said. She was quite smitten with the pale coral moon that just showed up on her skin.

'Yes, I do,' said Valli.

'That's why I adore to travel, I always learn something new,' said Carmen, 'and it broadens the outlook completely.'

'I'm sure,' said Valli.

'Except my mother,' laughed Carmen. 'She has travelled widely—Ooty and all—but she is so narrow-minded—man, you won't believe. But,' she said, leaning confidentially towards her friend, 'you know what the old folks are like.'

'Old-fashioned,' laughed Valli.

'One doesn't know whether to laugh or cry,' said Carmen.

Valli agreed with all her heart. Her eyes were bright with tears and laughter as she picked up the parasol, and balancing it daintily, wove her way home.

Apu watched his daughter from under his eyebrows as she tripped along.

'Now what's the matter?' asked his wife.

'It's not...right,' said the old man, after unravelling his emotions. 'It does not seem right,' he corrected himself, because things were not as clear and steady as they had once been.

'For what?' she asked.

'For her...station in life,' he answered.

'Let her enjoy. We are only young once,' said Amma. She felt her own youth slipping away, and blamed it on her husband.

'Yes, only young once,' said the old man, gently; after a long interval.

As if he had just discovered that, thought Amma rancorously; and watching Valli twirl, compared it with her own dowdy existence, shut up in a hut with this old, hopeless man.

Chapter Forty

CORINNA, far away in Avalon, was also driven to dwell on life, being lumbered with time and little else to do. For the Linklaters had—let her down, she almost felt, by contracting some tropical ailment. She had had to postpone her visit, and prolong her stay in this isolated and mouldering—she convinced herself despite some meticulous evidence to the contrary—castle of Toby's. Or mausoleum, as Boyle called it under his breath, but sometimes openly, when it provoked him beyond endurance.

She shared his feelings, in more than one way. She, too, began to be conscious of distance, or division. A sense of wedge between herself and her husband, more pronounced than she could remember, for she could not honestly pretend it had not manifested before. But hardened, while running alongside the incendiary unions that sequelled, as usual, their separation.

She too was made to wonder, as Boyle had been: was it her, was it him? And she found herself, a little to her own surprise, watching the man she had married as he went about his life. In Shalimar. In Avalon. Lying on the terrace, absolutely still, as still as the landscape at late afternoon. Or up on the battlements, sniffing up scents, alongside the ridiculous cannon; and inviting her.

'Smell.'

'I can't smell anything.'

'Yes you can.'

'Well, hair-oil, or whatever you put on that thing.'

'No.' Braced against the gleaming barrel while he squeezes the breath out of her, crushing her diaphragm with determined, even violent, hands. 'Not oil. Casuarina. Now—' letting go, 'breathe deeply.'

She did, she could not help. She gulped in air, but no casuarina.

Then she decided it was him, although was-it-him was-it-her continued to flicker. Under a spell, as Boyle hinted. Sufficiently under to imagine what was not there, or create out of dust some splendour that he needed, that was pleasing to his nature. She said so, more or less.

'It's got you—all this, hasn't it, Toby.' Indicting Avalon with a wave of her arm, and rather spitefully, because she felt it excluded her. The air solidified into bars when she tried to enter, and by his doing, she came near to believing; although it could simply have been a hardening of attitudes. Physically, of course, she was over the threshold.

'Perhaps it has. Why not?' he smiled and agreed, while extending the boundaries of what she meant.

'It's only a *place*, Toby.' Her jealousy flared. She would not have minded a woman, flesh and blood; it was part of the freedoms they allowed each other, and within what she could cope with; unlike this citadel that evaporated before her when she would have challenged its bastions.

'It's wrapped itself round you,' she said, resentfully. 'Do you realise?'

'Like a boa-constrictor, d'you mean?' he laughed.

'Exactly like.' She would not be laughed out of it. 'It's squashing you into a different shape, Toby.'

'But nice?' he suggested.

She melted. 'Very nice, darling. That's not altered, not one bit.'

For they could still play together, and rather well.

They kept to these areas.

She content with what does for her, totally, beautifully.

He agreeable, as always; except that suddenly one day it was not enough. Suddenly, then, he wanted more than the high-grade technique she was offering him. Face aloof, body rampant. He, striving to wring from her whatever was missing, that was making him ache. Grasping her throat, to get her face up.

'*Look* at me.'

'All right.'

Obeyed him, bringing up her luminous, moon-white, moon-blank face to his. Speaking drowsily.

'Something wrong, darling?'

'Don't you feel there is?'

'No. I feel great. Sweetie, what's the matter, can't you—' opening drugged eyes, offering the only explanation, 'make it, properly?'

'Is that all there is to it?'

'Isn't it enough?' It used to be, she felt, piqued; and turning her back on him spoke out of a mounting resentment. 'But don't ask me, Toby. You're the man, you ought to know.'

And of course he was, and did; and so would continue to

question.

It was outside the playground that she found it dull and stifling. As she walked around, kicking at stones in her way, or slashing at the scrub with an ancient coachman's whip she had unearthed in the disused stables. Or sat, bemused, on the bench half-way down the hill, staring at the arid slope of cactus. Or stood in the pool-room, on the sacking, and never once caught a glimmer; though certainly those dun, unreflecting thicknesses were a hindrance.

She had to bring it up, in the end.

'Do we have to coop ourselves up here, Toby?'

'Don't have to, no. But,' he said, 'I don't feel cooped up.'

'Not at all?'

'Not at all. I feel—' he thought of 'exhilarated', changed it, '—relaxed, if anything,' he said.

'Really?' Because she felt strung up.

'Yes, really,' he said. 'I find it appeals to me.'

'What does?' she asked, starkly.

Sprawled on the bed, plucking at the bobbles on the counterpane, as he saw. And was moved to try to move her.

'Well, there's something about the place, isn't there,' he said, less than adequately.

It would not have moved a stone; Corinna was not persuaded. Cold as a bone, and about as lively, she felt; and certainly the Carrara that had lain dull and ruinous around the compound over decades did have to be taken in hand and warmed before it would gleam, and recover its serenity.

Corinna experienced only the glancing coldness.

'It strikes chilly around here, sometimes,' she said, with a shiver.

Then it came through clearly to him, what the man before him had felt, those decades ago, lying perhaps in this very fourposter. The intimacies of that marriage were unimaginable, incestuously so. The emotions, however, spilled over, as he tried and failed to coax a single ember from the woman to whom he was tied. So he lay, and puzzled over why it had taken him this long—eight years of marriage. Suspicions coming all that time, that what she had to offer would never be enough. Well, perhaps it did take time, and place, to strip away the legendary seven veils. Here, now, it was becoming transparently evident.

Well into his privacies, she saw. She did not care. She would take herself off down the hill.

*

265

Rikki, perforce, had to be circumspect how he came and went, now that Mrs Tully was once more in residence. And indeed, curbing the free and easy ways encouraged by Tully that Boyle so deplored, he had exercised the utmost caution for several suffocating weeks.

But that day it so happened that Miss Chari had broken a jasper vase. Madam had entrusted it to her, to fill as she thought best, and place to one side—not the side where the telephone was—of the polished counter at Reception. Miss Chari filled it with tiger-lilies and ferns, and had almost reached the counter, clasping the vase to her bosom with both hands for it was a large, and precious, object, when it happened. On the verandah. Polished like glass, as she had told that donkey, the chokra, a hundred times not to. She kept her balance, just, as she skated along; but the vase shot from her hands and exploded at the foot of Reception. Miss Chari trembled and gulped, amidst the shattered jasper and the tiger-lilies.

Rikki was admiring the Asoka's brimming urns. He usually detoured on his way back from pool duty for this purpose; and ran up the stairs to help.

Miss Chari was feeling too miserable to disdain help from any quarter. She even felt a little guilty when she saw him kneeling to deal with the fragments, for she had no time, and had often made known these feelings, for hoity-toity fisherboys.

'You there, be careful you don't cut yourself,' she advised him for his own good, overlooking the criminality of using a Shalimar cummerbund to sweep the debris into.

He hardly heard her. In any case he was being very careful, for among the ruins were fragments of a certain rich garnet which he needed, and had been on the lookout for, for some finishing touches to Tully's mosaic. These he collected, leaving it to others to deal with the rest of the disaster, as Miss Chari observed. Because she was beholden, she would not say it out loud, but muttered about doing things properly, if done at all, as she supervised the servants who had by now arrived in strength.

Rikki did not hear these utterings, or was not greatly concerned. The shards were burning in the cummerbund he had re-wound round his waist, the sharp pieces digging into his flesh from being tied on so tightly. He simply sped, without a thought in his head beyond getting to Avalon, and trying out the garnet.

Momentum swept him up the hill and to the portals of the crystal room, and he was about to burst in when he realised it was

266

occupied. Even then he did not so much see, as feel presences. And stood, outside the glass, while Tully and his wife slowly came into focus. They were standing side by side, as he had once seen them, long ago. Except that this time nothing suggested they would kindle if they touched, nor fly apart. Both possibilities were done with. The two he saw, were burnt-out people, insofar as they affected each other. They were standing quite close together, gazing at the pool, but the impression he received was of distinct space between the two figures that were, in actual fact, touching.

All this took, of course, only split seconds. Bare soles are not soundless. There were reflections. Rikki had to breathe, after his pell-mell ascent. Tully turned as he advanced into the room.

'Hello, Rikki. You look a bit bulgy?' he said.

'Yes.' Rikki unwound the cummerbund carefully.

'What is it—treasure?' smiled Corinna; he was being so, extraordinarily, solicitous; but there was also something tender in it that touched her.

'Yes,' said Rikki, rubbing the crazy-paving pattern he could feel through his shirt, which the shards had left on his flesh.

'Well, let's see,' said Corinna.

Rikki held back, briefly; but then discovered he did not mind. He laid the cummerbund down obediently, and unrolled it to reveal his loot—the jasper in fragments, but the garnet pieces smouldering on the blue-and-argent silks of Shalimar. There were brighter flecks too, as Corinna noticed.

'You've cut your finger, Rikki,' she said.

He had noticed, but was more intent on contemplating the engaging effects the stains were producing.

'Rikki,' she said again. 'You ought—'

This time he did answer, disregarding the band-aid he heard her suggesting.

'It doesn't matter, it's just a scratch, Mrs Tully,' he said cheerfully, although to oblige her he did suck his finger; but she was dwindling, while he concerned himself with colour: namely, if his blood, or at least some similar pigment, would improve on the garnet if sparingly employed.

He would experiment, although time was limited. He reckoned he had about a month for trials and refinings—two, if he was lucky; for naturally Rikki had no access to the peremptory schedules of AIDCORP.

Chapter Forty-one

TIME was a concern that Zavera shared.

'We shall never be ready in time,' she had taken to declaring, on waking of a morning, to her husband.

'We shall,' soothed that man, who, unlike his labour force, was privy to AIDCORP's schedules.

'The Blue Lagoon you mean, Cyrus?' she queried anxiously. It was essential, if they were to have pedalo races on Open Day.

'The Blue Lagoon I mean, my love,' replied Cyrus calmly, adjusting his eye-mask against the raw dawn light, before sliding down the pillows for another half-hour. As he felt he could afford to. The lagoon might exercise his wife, but the final completion of Shalimar, lock stock and barrel, was not until well after Open Day junketings. In fact precisely two weeks after, in compliance with their programme. A lot could be done in a fortnight, apart from which they were well ahead of schedule.

Cyrus slept, while his wife wondered how he could, with so much waiting to be done; but she was too considerate to wake him up again.

While time raced for anxious Zavera, Corinna felt only its longueurs as she waited for the Linklaters to recover. Rather than kick her heels around the place, she retrieved her pony, which had been rusticating, plumply, in an animal shelter run by a pair of English. And rode down the hill as she had promised herself, with her hair tied back in a broad yellow band. And one fine day there was Ranji.

Handsome, cologned, beautifully booted, magnificently mounted on the splendid chestnut coaxed from his regimental comrades.

She casual in denim and plimsolls, riding well, though not as well as Ranji, nowhere as well mounted either. In fact on a jutka hack.

The young lieutenant thought it abominable, as he reined in, and saluted her.

'Mrs Tully.'

'Hullo, Ranji.' She smiled, in a way that would bring him to say Corinna, eventually. It usually took him a good half-hour. 'Going

268

anywhere special?'

'Nowhere special.' He was inspecting the shoreline, but would be diverted from far grander enterprises, if she suggested.

'Then may I join you?'

'Enchanted.'

Ranji was; he was very susceptible. He wheeled his horse round to join her.

They rode along the beach, following the curving coastline, Corinna holding her own, just, against what she could see was a superb horseman. She could hardly say so to a cavalry officer, as she had discovered Ranji was, even if brisk modern winds had whisked the regiment into a tank corps. There was, however, his horse. She transferred the compliment.

'Lovely horse, Ranji,' she said, admiringly, and totally without ulterior motive; so that she was taken by surprise by his next manoeuvre. For Ranji, trotting a little ahead of her nag, which was not difficult to do, had swung round smartly into her path; and brought her to a halt.

'Whatever are you doing, Ranji?' asked Corinna.

'I insist.' Ranji dismounted, and rather flushed but determined, led his charger to her side and delivered up the reins.

Thereafter Corinna would find horse and groom waiting patiently in the portico, to take her for a morning ride. Or if they rode together, Ranji would soon be off his horse, and insisting.

'But you can't ride an old hack like this,' she tried saying; but if she could, he would, declared the adamant young cavalier. In the end she gave way, and gracefully. She saw it gave him pleasure. His youthful face expressed a quite transparent pleasure as he jogged along on the jutka pony.

In return she took his surfing in hand. For Ranji, though keen on the sport, was resigned to being an indifferent performer. He saw himself as a legionary, when not a hussar. 'A land animal, not much good off terra firma,' he told her sadly. It would take genius of Caesarean proportions to transform—not him, but the ocean into a field on which he could do battle unbeatably, and with glory.

'Nonsense,' said Corinna.

'Do you mean that?' asked Ranji, gingerly. He dearly wanted to believe.

'Yes. I'll prove it, if you like,' said Corinna.

'Could you bear to?' asked Ranji.

Corinna could and did. Soon the lieutenant was sea-borne. Soon he was balancing finely, and turning out creditable

269

performances routinely, instead of by fluke.

'At this rate you'll scoop up the prizes,' Corinna told him, generously, as he came ashore after a particularly impressive glide. This was some weeks after he had begun surfing in earnest, and was perhaps as much due to her inspiration, as his rising mastery of an unruly element.

'What prizes?' asked dripping Ranji, turning dark red with pleasure.

'Aren't there going to be any, on Open Day?' asked Corinna. She thought there ought to be, there were prizes for tombola, for example, and for the pedalo race. By now she had given up on the Linklaters, and resigned herself to being around—perhaps even till Open Day.

If she thought so, then there would be, resolved the lieutenant; and set about organising an event to fit.

Zavera, naturally, was only too happy. Open Day was her brain-child, she co-opted and welcomed allies, especially one as enthusiastic as Ranji. Meanwhile she herself worked tirelessly to make it a success. Unable to fluster her husband, she turned to others like Sitharam and Joseph, who were more obliging.

'*Everyone* is coming. The whole world,' she declared, 'will be watching us.'

It gave Sitharam nightmares, not to mention his shy young wife.

Heblekar, unconvinced that the world would make tracks, refused to be overwhelmed. Nevertheless he felt the thing was getting out of hand, for here were requisitions for grand pavilions, garlands by the metre, silver shields, silver cups—he sent for his assistant.

'What is all this, Ranji?'

'For Open Day. For Shalimar,' said Ranji, standing to attention.

'I know, but is all this absolutely necessary?'

'Absolutely. Any show we put on, worth putting on properly, as befits our great nation, sir,' said Ranji, disdainfully, and clicked glossy heels, and went.

Showcase, Heblekar felt; and supposed in a way that was it.

Less obvious, deeper emotions would mark the completion of Shalimar. Open Day was a gala, a public affair. They would also commemorate, quietly and privately, the culmination of months of endeavour, principals to lowliest labourer setting their own private seals on a common and by no means facile (in any sense) undertaking.

270

Chapter Forty-two

ONE week before Open Day, late in the evening, Heblekar took the path to Avalon to make a presentation. He had been contemplating it for some little while, and at length wrote, and had the portfolio of drawings mailed to him from his flat in Delhi.

The collection had come down to him from the old Dewan, who seemed to have a passion for masonry, which his descendant shared only to a limited extent, and that mainly for filial reasons. But the before-and-after scenics in which the old man had indulged did at times appeal to his heir. In this package, then, were sketches of forts, knocked down by the British, built by them; of Palaces similarly ruined, and rescued from ruin; of Residencies flattened by furious mobs, urbanely restored when the fury had abated; of citadels of proconsular splendour, often incorporating rubble of the consuls' own making.

Among this pageantry, executed by an unknown artist, was a watercolour of the Copeland mansion, built on land half wrung, half coaxed from the Dewan in the Copeland heyday. Enfolded therein was a facsimile of the relevant charter, which was as much to do with land rights as with an endorsement of qualities each had perceived in the other, and of certain values to which both the Dewan and his opponent the Resident subscribed. Both firman and fading aquarelle had, perhaps because of his own perceptions, acquired value for Heblekar.

A lifetime ago (it seemed: it was much less) he had brought out the watercolour to show Tully, and Tully had been moved, and Heblekar had seen that he was. In the great gentleness that can come into being between men who have worked together, or who have looked upon whatever it is and shared an emotion, Heblekar was moved, on this eve, to part with what he, too, held in affection.

Avalon: as Heblekar walked, reflective, up the finely cambered path. Avalon, with its towers and dreamy terraces and the vigilant cannon, as had been envisioned by the man who built it, and captured in its flawed magnificence by that unknown artist's hand. Impermanence, it went without saying, in all structures: an imperative, and vital, obsolescence woven in. Nevertheless within that evanescent frame a palpable influence, whether standing in splendour, or in ruin (for that state too had been within an ace), or beguiling, or haughty, for all these aspects could present in turn. Like a Mughal garden, or a peremptory Roman road, it affected what came after, compelling a respect that time would turn to softer emotions. Time, an incomparable alembic, in which the resented effusions of pomp and power were subdued into a heritage. Perhaps it was Tully's influence, but there were glimpses of the initiation of that process in Avalon, or so Heblekar had come to believe.

So far he had been walking easily and with a purpose, the tubed watercolour like a spy-glass under his arm. Now, however, the gradient levelled out, hinting at a need to pause for breath, leading without insistence to the bench on which PROSPECT POINT was incised. Heblekar was hardly winded, but he was tempted, despite some instinct that urged him to resist. And, taking his seat, naturally Shalimar figured in the panorama that opened out before him.

Shalimar.

Long ago (again that illusory lifetime), he and Tully had come here, and sitting on this very bench much the same view, ravishing, disturbing, had seized them both.

Then Heblekar, somewhat shaken, understood it had indeed been a destructive impulse that had led him. And rose, castigating himself, and the devil for tempting, and the view for good measure, before resuming the ascent.

Tully, on the verandah with an after-dinner coffee, heard the familiar footfalls and walked down to meet Heblekar.

'I thought you might come,' he said.

'I thought you wouldn't mind,' said Heblekar.

Tully ushered him up the steps, pushed forward a chair, a comfortable rudki with arms and cushions, pulled up its companion for himself.

'I could do with some company,' he said.

If Heblekar had some inkling, being a married man, he kept it to himself with a conventional enquiry.

'Corinna?' Tully also played by the rules. 'She's having an early night. Said she needed it, after coaching Ranji.'

'She would, after Ranji. He tires *me* out.' Heblekar laughed, and they talked of this and that as people do whose minds are on other things, before broaching them. Presently Heblekar was
272

confessing to flutters which, he now admitted, as much as the aquarelle had directed his steps.

'Butterflies?' Tully repeated, watching the slender fingers flare to illustrate distracting wings—as if he needed such graphics. 'We all have them,' he said.

'You too?' Heblekar said, more than asked. He would not be surprised to learn—though nothing showed, and he would have been surprised if it had.

'Well, no one's immune, are they,' said Tully. And side-stepped slightly, stepping out of the present which was growing unmanageable into the past, to tell of a valley.

Between hills, scooped out like a soup-cup (but by infinitely patient, superfine craftsmen), it was eyed as if it were just that, and custom-made to boot; and they turned it into a cistern to provide drinking-water for thousands, plus a spot of sailing for a few.

That, too, had been AIDCORP, and it was not a far country where one built and bolted, but in a democracy where every man had a say. And having said, found like many another that he might have saved his breath, in a wilderness that rang with unheeded cries.

But it had been a beautiful valley, and there had undoubtedly been butterflies, which the chapel had undoubtedly multiplied. For they could not shift it like the animals and the people and the lesser habitations. There it stood, it could do no less, any more than Luther. And if the demolition squads triumphed in the end, still its sturdy, stovepipe chimney, whose fire had warmed choirs, and kept the damp off the Sunday school infants, saw to it that the edge was taken off. It rose, tall as a witch's hat, above the tumbled blocks of masonry. When they were drowning the valley it was the last to go under, and it went painfully, protesting every step of the way with the shrill, convulsive vehemence of one who dies unwillingly.

'It was mesmeric. Everyone,' said Tully. The thirsty hordes, winners, losers, money men, the lot. 'Everyone suffered twinges.'

Heblekar took it on trust that they had.

However, by now they were wondering—Tully as much as he—what connection there was between Shalimar and a faraway, flooded valley. Heblekar could not, without trying, see any application, apart from the butterflies manufactured in common. Shalimar had not swamped anything, neither valleys nor chapels. No one could have designated anything that had actually been

273

taken away. It had bloomed where there was more or less nothing, with a beauty of its own which no one could deny. As he was not willing to make the effort to connect, he merely said,

'I suppose it's the human condition.' The suffering and the tears, some crocodile.

'I suppose so,' agreed Tully.

If they were not altogether satisfied with it, they let it rest there, not wishing to be saddled, or melancholy. Instead they allowed what they had, essentially simple, to take effect. The fragrance that rose from the cona, from berries picked barely a stone's throw away, freshly roasted, hand ground. From company which had taken on a dimension that neither had foreseen, despite promising beginnings in a basement bar called Shiraz. From the night, of a width and magnificence that Tully had not experienced elsewhere, and understood he would not elsewhere be able to match. Leaving out the ineffable, he remarked on the actuality.

'Yes. One becomes aware of it, in a place like this,' said Heblekar, whose own vistas—those of a city—were generally cluttered.

'It gives one hope,' he thought to add, with a clean sweep of an arm that took in the entire panorama. 'So immense, we could keep on repeating our Shalimars as much as we wanted, it wouldn't even notice.'

And it was the *it* that stood out. Impersonal, neutral, untouchable, unlike the frail creatures who scuttled around in its shadow, who were demonstrably capable of being crushed. Rather than enter this territory, Tully preferred to be kept in thrall to the night, and indeed it was not difficult.

'It's what I shall miss most,' he said, avoiding the personal, 'after Avalon.'

'Which reminds me,' said Heblekar, and laid what he had brought on the table.

It looked like a diploma or charter, for Heblekar for reasons best known to him had fastened it with a bow of red ribbon; but Tully had a fairly clear notion.

'I couldn't. It belongs to you,' he said.

'No, I don't think so. Not any more,' said Heblekar, carefully, and carefully interposed Open Day and other such charivari so that Tully should not dispute.

Tully did not, but could have. He sat on, after Heblekar had gone, the scrolled vellum spread open in front of him, one hand and the table-lamp keeping the charter and its attachment from

274

springing shut. While the faded watercolour confirmed a feeling that more than one quartz, and emotion, and intention, and lucidity, had gone to the raising of Avalon; and into its loving embellishment.

No, not his. Not entirely, whatever Heblekar might say.

Heblekar had not meant to look back, but at a certain point, beyond which verandah and terraces would have gone from view, he did turn and look. And saw Tully, head bent, still sitting at the table. Table of satinwood, brought to a satin finish. On it a lamp, shaded in glass, dark-blue, brilliant, streaming blue and blue-black and niello on to the head and shoulders of a man in—

But it was too private. Heblekar turned quickly and walked on.

*

The next morning, at breakfast time, Boyle came up to consult.

A working breakfast, he called it, although really there was nothing left to work out, so close to completion. They had been over most things pretty closely anyway.

However there he was, and a plate laid for him, and a starched linen napkin over his knees to catch the crumbs. They were at the civilised, second-cup stage, before Tully invited, in the broadest terms:

'Well, Boyle sahib?'

Boyle was prepared, and brisk. It was the wave-machine. It was hiccuping again. Swimmers liked waves in the pool, but not being swamped. The question was this. Should they call on the manufacturers, or fix it themselves which would be more satisfactory bearing in mind the time factor; but by this act they would void the guarantee. They threshed it out, and came to a conclusion; and Boyle then wondered if there was a spot more coffee. The cona was obliging. Boyle stirred, and sipped, and remarked on the marvellous aroma, and at length said, rather shyly,

'Got it off the ground, eh? Wouldn't you say, Toby?' A sweep of an arm, not without pride but restrained—an Anglo-Saxon restraint—taking in the wide arc of coastline occupied by the Shalimar complex.

'Yes. Yes, I would.' Tully was happy to go along, and equally restrained; after all he, too, was an Anglo-Saxon.

'Yes. Well, let's hope,' said Boyle, and slipped into what he was really thinking, and indeed hoping, for he genuinely retained scraps of feeling for whatever they built. 'Let's hope they don't wreck the whole caboodle, after we've gone.'

'Wreck it? Why should they?' asked Tully simply.

Put like that it looked insane, even to Boyle. He shifted around in his chair.

'Well, you never know out here, do you,' he said vaguely. 'I mean, one can never be absolutely sure with these bods.'

And realising it was a bit vague, cited examples, some quite dated, like Corinna's lamentable taxi in which Corinna had not arrived; and succeeded in driving Tully out of the Anglo-Saxon stockade.

'Why not?' he asked, mildly. 'After all, we made sure, way back in '47. We trained 'em before we left, as a matter of policy. That's why we hung on as long as we did, surely.'

'I know,' Boyle agreed, while suspecting the generation gap was getting the upper hand. 'I know they've learnt from us. Good learners, I'll give you that. But sometimes I can't help feeling it's a case of Western top-dressing. I mean, one never knows out East, old man, does one...'

'No. Not easily,' said Tully.

Boyle, still sunk in imponderables, hardly heard.

'Maybe I'm wrong, and the graft has taken,' he said, 'but then again, it could be skin-deep, the science out here. Who knows? Quite on the cards,' by now he was becoming convinced, and waved widely, 'it'll all go to rack and ruin the moment our back's turned.'

'I hardly think so,' said Tully, with reason. 'I mean, why would anyone ruin what they've spent good money on?'

Boyle got up. He was in a mood for sympathy, not reason. He definitely blamed the generation gap, playing hell again.

'Well, if they do, no skin off my nose, or yours,' he said—handsomely, considering; and complimented Tully on the coffee and the melon, before driving off in his buggy.

Tully followed, but on foot and leisurely, for it was a nice morning, and still early enough for dew, and birdsong. First, however, he climbed to the little casuarina copse, and circled this redoubt for mere pleasure, before starting to descend, walking, now, between wheel tracks left by the buggy. The impressions were distinct, for it had been raining, one of those sporadic storms that seemed to blow up overnight and blow themselves out; and perhaps they directed his thoughts, for as he walked between the Firestone treads, Boyle's conflicts were transmitting. The implications repeated, in regions inaccessible to gravity, or reason.

276

Good learners, I'll give you that. . . but you never know out East, old man, it could be a case of Western top-dressing.

In fact, a con by the locals, to avoid offending their imported gurus. A case—it amused Tully to flirt with the scene—of suited natives by the million sneaking off home to kick off leather shoes and prostrate themselves at household altars, the reverent syllable OM reverberating from a thousand hearths. Although reasonable men might reasonably expect all sounds to cohere eventually, the dissonant notes struck from diffuse bell-metal starting to melt and shimmer, silver clapper to silver bell, stabilising at some kind of acceptable harmony.

But what if—as the piquant picture developed panels, a cold triptych that made him flinch—what if the sticking qualities of an applied culture are as stated?

It is abundantly demonstrable, gentlemen, that in time the graft will take, and without fear of rejection. Now if you will direct your attention to this limber youth, in his smart livery of argent-and-blue—

At which point Tully had to chuckle, for it was reducing to absurd proportions. For Rikki was not to be constrained by anything as flimsy as livery. He seemed to burst out of it. Or rather was sufficiently contained—a self-containment that made one vividly aware of nerve, muscle, tendon, spirit—all of them implicit under the skin, and inescapable.

Still smiling, yet there was something else. Frissons of—whatever it was, passing coldly at the far edge of consciousness. Footsteps over one's grave, they called it when they were children, to rouse up the tingles. Tully shook it off, he was in no mood; and casting around for the culprit fixed, unfairly, upon Boyle. He continued to transmit, through those ponderous tyre welts, raised up on either side of the path. But looking for them, to spill some active venom on, he saw that they had vanished. For by now he had reached the beach, and buggy tracks had given way to—

Tully stands and admires: to daring chevron designs that zigzag madly up and down the sandy coastline. Some bold rebel of a beach attendant, stoned by routine, gone on the rampage with his rake. The littoral far and wide is scored with the dizzy signs of revolt. Alongside, here and there, are sturdy barefoot imprints. Friday: his mark. Tully grinned, and followed for a bit these anarchist tracks that march off into the sunset, for all that he knows. He would have liked to go that far, to find out; but, needless to say, there were other things to do. Presently, and sighing much as Rikki might have done, he turned off in the direction of the offices.

Chapter Forty-three

THERE were always things to do in Shalimar, and these grew and were accentuated now that there was to be a fête, or fiesta, shandy, bunfight—people gave different names to Open Day. Accordingly staff were recruited on a temporary basis.

One week before, to buff and polish and prepare; one week after, to clean up.

Muthu was one of the new ones. He had no wish to be, but was pushed. Easy money, his mother said. Then she jangled the tin in which they kept their savings. 'And that only coppers,' she said, significantly, distributing her glances, and her indignation, between her son and this penniless ancient. The old man, sunk in his own thoughts, roused himself, and in his son's view, capitulated.

'What harm?...a day or two, no matter, one way or another,' he said, and avoided looking at the man whom he was addressing, while dodging the glances of his wife which tended to lodge, cruelly, somewhere low down his spine.

So Muthu beached the rickety boat and applied; and was taken on as beach cleaner for the fortnight; and sometimes in the course of his duties wondered: what afterwards?

More frequently he was moved to think of his brother, whose weight, as a boy, his shoulders had carried.

'What will you do, afterwards?' he asked, eyes fixed upon the battered tin-can he had raked up, rather than look at Rikki. 'After Avalon', he added, from a sense that it was what counted.

Rikki could not say.

Except insofar as he had accepted there were limits to Avalon, he never thought ahead. In his Bridie days Mrs Bridie had been fond of saying, sometimes with pinched lips, but at times in a perfect tranquillity, 'Sufficient unto the day, Rikki. What was enough for Our Lord is surely enough for us poor mortals.'

He found it was. He repeated after her, 'Sufficient unto the day'; but leaving out the evil thereof, substituted happiness.

Sufficient unto the day the happiness thereof.

And so he never bothered his head about the next book he would read, until he was through with the one he had last purloined from the envied pile locked in the woodshed. Time enough, when he had turned the last page, to go in search of what Mr Bridie called his 'box of tricks', to which he had allowed him free access. Tools of delicacy and precision were to be found there, among the unused hammers and wrenches, of celluloid and supple wood designed to construct and lever ships into bottles. They were equally good for picking locks.

'I'll think about it when I have to,' Rikki answered his brother.

Nevertheless, as a result of this prodding, at times he fell to wondering.

*

Invited to inspect his vines, or his boat, or while they worked in the pool-room, Tully was aware of being gravely eyed, but was not subjected to a single anxious or inconvenient question. Yet Rikki could ask; his style and character inclined to the cavalier. If he did not, it was from instincts that would have graced a Carmelite, felt Tully. His own temperament, despite the urgencies of AIDCORP's programming, inclined him to live in the present; except that here there was one besides himself.

Rikki, the invader, as Zavera might have said.

He shared her emotion, without those whimpers of protest that rose in her throat. The boy did invade: Tully had experience. He had a way of coming in, though never without invitation; touching him, nevertheless, at every turn.

In the end, he had to ask. It was at the creek. They had walked down to inspect Tully's boat, at Rikki's suggestion. He wanted Tully to see it, fresh from its latest overhaul. He had caulked it within, and varnished it without, and brought the timbers to the polished brilliance of a mirror. Tully could see himself reflected in the shining hull. Rikki could see him sitting, slightly crouched, on a driftwood spar, for all that the sand was white and warm and clean, and usually Tully could not resist it. He had grown out of middlemen by now, and would simply abandon himself to earth or grass, whatever was available. But now he was crouched.

Rikki kept his mind on this aspect, while he replied.

'What will I do afterwards? Sufficient unto the day,' he said simply, but also like an adviser.

'Yes, I know,' said Tully, who had not expected the book to be thrown at him this early. 'But I'm bound to ask,' he said.

If he felt bound, it was because of him, Rikki could not but conclude. He had some notion of weights that could bear down,
280

extracting answers to suppressed emotions.

'Ask what?' he said, to gain time while he thought of how to remove the burden.

'About afterwards,' said Tully.

'Afterwards,' repeated Rikki, and despite every effort felt his own mind beginning to slip, towards the unknown. 'Do you mean after I finish your design, Mr Tully?' he asked, 'or after you leave Avalon?'

Although both were connected, in ways he would not go into.

'I suppose I mean both,' said Tully, still sitting on driftwood.

Rikki looked at him; and then at the sand, which was appealing, everything one could wish for. And he could not endure it any longer. He wanted nothing, except that Tully should stop crouching and enjoy the day. If Tully did not, he would not, either. He lifted the picnic basket out of the boat in which he had deposited it, and carried it up, swinging it as he came, and inviting.

'Would you like to eat now, Mr Tully? While everything is nice and fresh?'

Flapping open the blue check cloth, for he had learnt well, and these days would set out a picnic or a barbecue in style. There would be dressed crab, Tully knew, and floury rolls, in place of the spartan sandwiches that had once stunned frogs, and bunches of rose-scented grapes cosseted in crushed ice—all needing time to arrange, and arranged to deflect him.

If he saw through this, still Tully would not insist. Persecution had never possessed immoderate appeal for him. He smiled, and gave way, understanding he was being spared himself, as much as he was sparing another.

'I'm famished. I'd love to eat now,' he said, and slid off his perch to help. While Rikki, also kneeling on the fine white sand, carefully constructed a little cairn of pebbles at each corner of the cloth, which had begun to flutter in the gentle breeze that was blowing.

Chapter Forty-four

THE last few days sped, like a runner on the last lap making his final sprint. Sitharam felt, like that runner of his imaginings, quite spent by the time Open Day dawned. It was not only the thousand-and-one trials of organising it, but the possibility of inclement weather that distracted. The weather stations along the coast had been warning of inclement weather. Not cyclones—Sitharam quivered, remembering wretchedly the deluges he had so irresponsibly and frivolously predicted to Mrs Contractor (whatever had come over him?)—but high winds, and a possibility of storms. There had been storms overnight, intense but short, dying out by morning. However, no one could have complained of the days.

But it never did to be confident about anything, life and solemn treatises had convinced Sitharam. Waking early on the morning he nervously hoped, like Boyle, nothing would wreck and ruin all that was done. He prayed as well, adding a fervent plea to his usual devotions.

Prayers made him feel safe and cosy. Soon he forgot his trepidations, and his spent condition, and set out briskly to inspect what was on display.

And walking along, he was cheered by everything around. The air was clear, the wind was light. Even at this early hour the Shandy, as he had morosely dubbed the event, seemed to partake rather of a carnival in the People's Park, which he had always thoroughly enjoyed. Sitharam saw with a new, bright eye the vivid striped pavilions, the tents for refreshments, the tethered balloons, the bunting. He had seen it all before, hardly anything had missed his beady inspecting eye; but now there was a distinct atmosphere.

Mrs Pearl was certainly influenced. She woke feeling cheerful, and it mounted as, making herself respectable, she stepped out onto the little apron of her villa to sample the morning. For it was a nice day, the flags were out, the gulls were in full voice, and, no doubt about it, Zavera had succeeded in permeating the whole atmosphere with the fizz and nonsense of a fair.

After breathing in deeply a dozen times, as per her daily ritual, Mrs Pearl went back in to tell her companion, and bring her out to

282

enjoy with her. Kali invariably did. She was a good little baby, and now that she could focus would gaze with intense interest on whatever was available. Mrs Pearl was persuaded of a great acumen in this, and would always share a view, or point out something pretty; and invariably regretted that she in turn could not share the wholesale experiences of her charge, who would put any bright bauble that pleased into her mouth for exploring in the round.

Having told, Mrs Pearl washed and dressed them both, and rather carefully, for they were to be on show. Then they breakfasted, Kali first for, though good, she had no patience. The bottle (she had graduated from the wet nurse) had already arrived, corked inside a wide-mouthed thermos, with the usual Shalimar efficiency and the compliments of the Management. Next Mrs Pearl had tea and toast, for nowadays she liked to keep it simple, with the aim of working up to the simplicities of the country in which she was hoping to become a permanent fixture. Then they were ready to sally forth. Mrs Pearl brushed off crumbs, and perched the baby astride one ample hip as the Indiennes did, and as they sauntered along she pointed out the balloons, and the pretty streamers that were fluttering everywhere, and other such engaging trifles.

Ranji, naturally, had taken charge of standards and banners. The flags of many nations floated—indiscriminately, Boyle felt. Ranji knew what Boyle felt. He did it to annoy, chiefly, but also to make the point that his country, a free country, would deal with whom it pleased. He curled a lip, and would inform anyone who questioned that they could jolly well do as they liked, and those who still dared were left with a distinct impression of duelling pistols in the young man's capable hands.

Heblekar was less juvenile. But he, too, savoured a certain satisfaction in seeing the lines drawn, not according to those laid down by foreign potentates, but by those whom it concerned. Unlike what it had been within living memory. Different indeed, then: with the barriers up against free trade and ominous alliances, the silk route sealed, the caravans from Persia, Cathay and Arabia—all this ancient, natural flow—halted to allow the wares of Manchester and Birmingham to flood in, past frontiers arbitrarily raised by remote, but shrewd, and powerful, consuls.

Like Copeland-Tullys.

Courtesy would not allow it out, but the thought flickered; and communicated. It was Tully (he had come by invitation to be fortified for the day ahead) who voiced it, after Ranji and Boyle had taken their running feud elsewhere.

'Quite a change, isn't it,' he said. 'Every flag you care to name.'

'Used to be only one, overall. It was,' said Heblekar, and drew a long breath, 'a rather forced orientation.'

'Yes. It must have been,' agreed Tully.

Yet neither these two, nor Ranji for that matter, had direct experience of the drama and spectacle of empire. Born after that curtain was rung down, they were fuelled by memories, some bequeathed with strict injunctions not to forget; and responded to them and to history. Heblekar could feel, from the past and impersonally, some slight suggestion of thumbscrew in its working. So could Tully, when he tried. Now, after a pause, he put it in words that rejected gloss.

'It must have felt like having your head wrenched round to face West,' he said.

When the thought came—the merest flicker—that something of the sort could be said of Shalimar. Like Heblekar, he did not voice it; but now communication had ceased, or possibly at this point they parted company. At any rate Heblekar did not take it up.

Instead he held up the prized vial he had specially brought. Squinted at it, dished out hospitality from this special flask, passed it cordially to Tully.

'Here you are.'

'What is it?'

'Nerve tonic.'

'Just what I needed.'

Tully accepted gratefully, tossed back the home brew, gasped as it flayed his throat.

'Christ, what is this—paint-stripper?'

'Jungle-juice, compliments of the Coconut Grove. Liquor, actually,' Heblekar descended from these heights, 'from under the counter.'

Luckily there was barely an ounce apiece: steadies the nerves, doesn't touch the head.

*

Waiting for the Day to get into its stride, the ladies gather in little posies in the grounds. The men have gravitated to the bar: Boyle, Heblekar, Tully, Contractor, Ranji the Bold, Tremlett the

Silent who is once again part of the scenery, Patterson the hairy one, back with his camera for another stint. A caucus of free enterprise, shattering techniques at their fingertips, capable singly and jointly of operations of hair-raising finesse, yet they are individually and collectively suffering tremors from just thinking of the social melée ahead.

'It feels, sort of *hollow*, just here,' reports the lieutenant, slapping an agreeably incurved solar plexus. 'Like going over the top, in war,' he adds, unwisely, never having done so; but then Ranji often and easily imagines battles.

'What war?' Boyle won't let it pass. The man is blathering, as usual. No wars in *his* lifetime. His temper is not sweetened by the soft drink which is all the bar has to offer at this time; and he can distinctly sniff raw alcohol on at least two in the company. 'Do you mean,' he says, meanly, '*field* exercises?'

'Well,' Heblekar, with a touch of belligerence—country liquor is acting—rises to defend. 'We have had our little border disputes, you know.'

Though he knows for a fact young Ranji was not embroiled in any.

Boyle does not know, but waves a dismissive hand.

'Oh, those. Skirmishes,' he says, 'you can't begin to compare. The Desert War—now there was a war if you like. No tanks, no ammo—nothing. Until Monty, of course. But we fought. Did we fight, we Rats! Not for me to say so, but—'

But they don't give him the chance. Tremors forgotten, racial affinities ditched, the heartless cabal disbands and flees as soon as it decently can.

*

Heblekar, rosebud in buttonhole, making the rounds with Tully, is joined by Sitharam, who has lapsed into worrying. He often does, when the serenities of orison and litany wear thin. His present worry stems from the crowd: not the crowd of Visitors, who are orderly, but the villagers who will not be, he is fairly certain. They have come to have fun, and to his mind—he thinks along Shalimar lines—their fun means rowdiness, and tossing their rubbish around to the ruin of these raked and spotless precincts.

'You see, sir,' he gesticulates, and addresses Heblekar. 'Our people are so *excitable.*'

'Yes, I know. But what,' asks Heblekar philosophically, but

285

unhelpfully, 'is to be done about it?'

Sitharam licks his dry, vermilion lips, which are clamouring for betel-nut, but cannot be indulged; and goes off to harangue these people who are indeed excited. There are to be boat races on the lake, they have heard, and also a wrestling contest, in which their ex-champion Sandhu will star... Some half dozen coastal settlements are emptied.

'Well, after all,' said Heblekar, the thought was flushed out, by this chance shot of Sitharam's, from somewhere in the pit of his stomach where it roosted. 'It is their territory, isn't it?'

'Yes.' Tully, not keen to follow this line of thought, strode along.

'I mean,' Heblekar could not leave it alone; a fine sweat, squeezed up from the roots by some sudden lurch of certainties, pearled his brow as he continued, 'it belonged to them in the first place, didn't it?'

'It did. It still does.' Tully, not wanting to be lumbered, strode along, like an ostrich now.

Heblekar caught up.

'Does it?' he croaked, baldly.

'Of course. Look, Heb.' Tully, soul of reason as ever, set out to stun them both. 'This is a democratic state, it's modelled on ours, no question whatever of them and us. Everything's wide open to anyone, same as it is back home.'

'These *villas*?' It stunned Heblekar.

'These villas. No one's barred, you know that,' maintained Tully, stoutly. 'All you need is the necessary.'

'What?'

Tully finds it insufferable, this Oriental craze for plainspeak. Even, he feels crossly, one's rosebud-sporting chum. Heblekar's feelings are the same, in reverse.

They are rescued from each other by Mrs Contractor.

Zavera is circulating happily, in fuchsia chiffon, in an effusion of ladies swirling softly about her in similar aurora hues. She is pointing out various delightful features, while they wind along the Walk that curls into a rose-pergola, when she spies the two who are where they should not be.

Zavera cannot allow pleasure to interfere with duty. Overcoming a dissident who is clamouring for rose-bowers ('Presently, Mrs Mukherji, we will *all* see what is inside the pergola. I will conduct you round myself!'), she alters course and bears down upon the two delinquents. At least she means to, but

286

cannot help floating, in the centre of the bright ellipse of ladies that swirls along with her, like a brilliant, transparently harmless Portuguese man-o'-war.

'Now, Mr Heblekar,' she addresses him formally, to sound as severe as she can.

'Yes?' Heblekar, smiling, innocent, is entirely at her service.

'Mr Heblekar, our guests are waiting,' she reminds him reproachfully, 'for you to draw the raffle.'

'Of course. Just going.' Heblekar is suavest when he is lying. 'On my way, as a matter of fact.'

'Not that way. In the CHANDRAGUPTA tent.' Zavera stifles a sigh, and points him in the right direction, and turns to Tully. Such a charming scatterbrain, just like the other; but she also suspects the two egg each other on.

'Now, Mr Tully.'

'Yes?' He too, it appears, is entirely at her service.

'Mr Tully, you remember you agreed to present the tombola prizes.'

'So I did.' (Whatever possessed him?)

'In the AKBAR marquee. I *hope* you won't forget.'

'I shan't. I'll be there. Look, I've put a knot in my handkerchief.' (Boy, the things one does for a living!)

*

Meanwhile Shalimar, being on show, was also coming under the microscope.

'Good show, Jagdish.' A magenta Colonel, just down from his retreat in the Nilgiri hills, barking at the subaltern (one of Ranji's cronies). Dragooned in, but conducting himself handsomely, the smart lieutenant stands exquisitely attentive over the Colonel, who barks on. 'Yes. Excellent. Showpiece too, eh?'

'In what way, Colonel?'

'Well, my dear chap...airline, hotel, luxury tourist complex. You fellows behave as if you've money to burn. But what about your slums, eh?'

'Cleared quite a few, sir.'

'Cleared 'em? Don't know what you're talking about, m'boy. Now look at all this. No expense spared. Now a *tenth* of what's been spent here would have cleaned up Bengal.'

'Doubt it, sir.'

'Calcutta, then. But you will insist on your showcase. Sheer lunacy, but you all go in for the same thing. Every new state. Point
287

of honour, what?'

'Absolutely. But I wouldn't call it a *new* state, sir. Would you? I mean—'

Impertinent young pup, one pip on his shoulder, republican army what's more, if one pauses to think. One's weapons and weapons-training trained *against* one these unthinkable days, Poona to Persepolis. The Colonel marches off, rumbling, to lock antlers elsewhere.

While Tully, proceeding tortoise-like to tombola, is soon engaged by a wisp of a girl in a whirl of cyclamen sari.

'What would you say, Mr Tully?'

'About what?'

'About the state of the nation.'

'Well, one does get a bit out of touch in Elysium—' smiling at the provocative slip, a little sorry for her because this has been lobbed at him before and he is prepared, '—but at a guess I'd say it's not doing too badly.'

She rewards him, smiling up doe-eyed, murmuring, a drawing-room murmur straight from a long vanished Kensington. 'Too kind, Mr Tully...'

Tully returns her smile, moves on to where the softest cudgels are out, stops to listen. Voices slub-textured, with a Welsh lilt, musing on the nature of aid and the strings that come attached to such packages.

'But please don't think...we perfectly understand these unfortunate necessities...but grateful, yes, most...wouldn't know what to do without...'

The fairest speech, laced with ice-floes, perceptive slivers that slide around, shy, elliptical, in warm, friendly, darkly eloquent eyes brimming over with Eastern charm.

It's all right, we understand: your savvy for our raw stuff, harbours, bases, crude, and when we've caught up—but that'll be another story.

Though nothing like as crude, out here. Out here it's always been a thought different: a touch of softly-softly...

It captivated Tully.

*

Over in the de-luxe shamiana they are dealing with the ice. Huge chunks, like what the Tremletts, after 30 years in India, insist on calling the Himmer-layers. Hauled here on sledges, tipped into vast vats, chipped off into more manageable containers

288

by white-coated servants, slid chill and steaming white vapours into glasses.

Glasses and drinks in all colours, circulating on trays among Visitors and guests, among them ex and neo colonials. They stand around sipping strange flavours, one eye on opportunity, ready to clinch it with hard currency, on which the natives have fixed *their* eye. Aussies, Americans, Madrassis, Punjabis—Zavera's whole-world-is-coming was not entirely off target. There is a fairish sample. Talking with each other, not communicating, separate haunted landscapes pressing darkly behind the dapper exchanges.

Cut off from the masque by language and script, a clump of Russkies are eyeing the bottles: used to vodka with the breast-milk, bemused by Kola.

'Where is the bar?'

Leafing through the phrasebook, enunciating slow and care-ful-ly.

'The bar is closed at this hour, comrades, by law.'

Answering loud and clear-ly. One is dealing with a lesser-known tribe.

Closed? Only Russian vernacular can cope with the crescendo of Russian fury. Infernal laws! Infamous land! Unmatched for alcoholic chaos except by effete Britain! Evidence of cast-iron strength here that Britannic theories STILL permeate the liberated colonies—their short-cropped hair almost stands on end.

The Yanks, CIA-briefed, keep their cool. Their informed eyes slide around, grown soft and radiant with reflections of moonshine. Must be some, some place. Never a period in the most bigoted history that the stuff wasn't available, some place. Problem is to find it. India is newish, uppish territory, one doesn't know where to start asking. Whereas these English s.o.b.s, been around a couple of centuries, certainly know but aren't letting on.

And their eyes fasten on the English s.o.b. who has just drifted in, looking, as they always look, as if the whole darn place belonged.

Tully gets the loaded drift, which carries right across the crowded pavilion: hoists a courteous shoulder to convey regrets. I feel for you. Bottom of my heart. But that, friends, is the way it is.

The simmering posse departs, to snoop around elsewhere, watched by Tully who is so engrossed he fails to notice in time the coachload from Scandinavia that now descends on him. A party of Vikings, used to Northern lights, to winter in six-month slabs, blinking up at blinding awnings, crowding fellow-blond Tully who has been pointed out by the guide.

'This joint is surprising, yes?'

'Yes. In—er—what way?'

'So war-rm!'

'So glad you like it.'

As Tully sees, they do. They stand around clutching discarded anoraks, in love with new latitudes, longing to give themselves, not quite ready. Airlifted in seven hours flat from Ibsen country (whatever their notions on the subject), it takes time to adjust. But the sun will melt these snowflowers yet, coach good learners into modes of liberty and laxity, exact prostration from them and in return for these extravagant forms of worship lavish its own gifts in high-grade finishes to skin and perception, burning the fondant colours into deep golds and browns. No one switches more expertly than the Europeans: it awes even the native practitioners.

But then, Europeans worshipped the sun before they turned, and are turning again, as the wheel comes full circle, into what they were. Pagans, unalloyed. As the Bridies had long ago pronounced sun-worshippers to be, according to Rikki. Strange, Tully reflected, how often this unknown pair would interpose, speaking, perhaps, more truly than they knew.

Tully would have liked to linger; but now a wild baying—Bingo! Bingo!—reminded him of Zavera, and duty. Leaving the marquee reluctantly, he set off for the Akbar tent, and tombola.

'Toby. If you're not too busy?'

'Not frantically.'

Tully, still en route to tombola, deflects without a qualm. He is always prepared to make time for Mrs Pearl, this unusual woman who has set sail blithely for India on some private quest, and seems to have found whatever grail she was seeking. As they sometimes did, from all accounts, in the old days, just the few, odd ones.

'Well, come and say hello to Kali.'

'Love to.'

'She's such a good baby.' She hands him the gurgling infant, tenderly, tenderness turns her into a madonna. Blue rinse, lumpy figure, she overrides it all to become, indisputably, a madonna. 'And she's done rather well, don't you think?'

'Extremely well.'

'But—poor Rikki—he was dreadfully upset at the time, do you remember?'

'Yes, I do.'

Permanently cut, this intaglio: of the desperate boy, dragging up the hill, saddling his totally innocent loins in some mad kind of psycho-paternity. But then, innocence is notorious for playing the most terrible roles.

'And, you know, it seems to be working out. She's a happy little thing, don't you think?' says Mrs Pearl.

'She looks as if the world belonged.' He is diverted by the little girl, who is chuckling, one fist—it takes a whole fist—clutching his thumb. 'Yes, she's charming.'

'She's up for the Bonnie Babies Competition. You're not,' says Mrs Pearl earnestly, retrieving her infant from his arms, which do by contrast look like a gorilla's, 'one of the judges, by any chance?'

'No, I've been spared. But don't tell me,' laughing at the fond woman, 'you'd be shameless enough to subvert a judge?'

'I would, but I shan't need to,' says radiant Pearl. 'I'm sure she'll win in her own right, aren't you?'

He would like to reassure her, and himself, but now they are close to the Akbar tent, and the cries are louder and wilder than ever. Bingo! Bingo!

*

The old man heard them revelling. He was used to it, even if this was something special. It would go on, and cease in the early hours, at which time it was right and proper for him to rise from his pallet.

Except that there was no need, since they would not be putting out to sea.

Still, he would have liked to sleep, and wake refreshed, but the shindy they were creating prevented him, he tried to believe. But the truth of it was, one did not sleep much, at his age. Only, he would have liked to close his eyes, and perhaps nap for a little. . . So the old man sat wavering, and nursing his resentments, or trying to but not finding it easy, these extravagant emotions were beyond him; and slowly cracked his jutting knuckles one by one.

Alone, in his hut. Wife and daughter gone off in finery to feast their eyes, the woman bewitched as much as the child. The two men, his sons—

Muthu, the beach cleaner.

Rikki, the waiter. But see him in water, or at sea, and the boy—yes, then you saw him in his full, true beauty. The old man's eyes softened, and his heart was wrung.

291

Chapter Forty-five

RIKKI, in point of fact, was not waiting on anyone. He had gone down to the beach, and given himself up to the sumptuous solitudes of ocean and sea-shore. Strictly speaking, there were no such solitudes. There were people about, refugees from the fair and pavilions, some in the sea, sporting with surfboards. The beach was patrolled—divided with military precision by Ranji into half a dozen sectors, each under a life-guard (he was one). But he had always had resources, which Shalimar had developed: ways of ensuring the solitudes of mind that he needed, a means for the manufacture of invisible, insulated domes to shut off in which at times he craved, as ardently as it distracted those debarred from entry, who could not get at him when they wanted to.

Under this transparent bell-jar he quite soon forgot cares and compulsions. Quite soon, following his mood, he had absorbed himself in the play of water, the fun it was having, wavelets were tumbling about on the shore like very young puppies.

'But they tug at one, you know, Rikki!' he could hear Mrs Pearl protesting, accusing even the smallest waves, when, infrequently, he enticed her into dipping a toe.

'I'm here, I'll look after you, Mrs Pearl.'

'I'm sure you will, Rikki, but it's me.' Standing gingerly, holding her skirts up as the sea scoured round her ankles, laughing at herself. 'I'm a proper old ninny, I'm afraid.'

She was really afraid. He could never persuade her to walk in boldly. She would stand in shallow surf, and shading her eyes look into the distance where the sea, it was easy to imagine, tumbled headlong off unknown precipices.

It did not, and this was less readily acceptable. It rolled on, this restless ocean spread at his feet, round the world to—where? Exactly where, he had once again forgotten; but there was a map pinned to the wall in Tully's office. He was on his way when he remembered—or rather was jolted into remembering by one of the beach guards, whose boggling eye spotted him sloping off—that he was on duty. Waking up, slightly, he returned to his sector and plumped himself down on his malibu, which had once been Mrs Tully's.

292

He had brought it out boldly, he was no longer afraid of her, or that she might snatch it away from him. The sense of her power, which had once been able to dislocate him, was lifted, and perhaps had owed its existence purely to his imaginings. So he felt safe, and removed the malibu from the shed in which he had stowed it out of her sight, and had taken to storing it in the open, upright in the cluster of Shalimar surfboards and as glossy and head-up as if it had every imaginable right to stand there.

When he thought about it, he knew he was as good as any Shalimari who rode the waves; but now, well into his bell-jar, he was not particularly concerned.

*

'Rikki?' Valli picked her way delicately, lips tremulous on two grounds. Was she allowed here? Would he respond?

'M-mm?' He emerged. Never so under he wouldn't, for his sister.

'For you, Rikki,' said Valli, holding out a flower, but rather shy. Brought up with him all her life and most of his, but shy of kin touched with the sheen of Shalimar. Distances, like the stuff of dreams, come spinning off such looms.

'Wherever—?' For it was a special bloom.

'Where do you think? A cactus flower?'

'But that's not for a long time yet!'

'A long time has gone by. The thickets are in flower again. You're out of touch, Rikki.'

Was he? He could not tell, of a state to which there were so many variables. Once, long ago—so long it could not be matched in with time—he had been so out of touch with Tully that he had thought to buy him with the gift of a flower from the sacrosanct thicket.

Now there were only gifts.

'Rikki?' Valli could see he was slipping away.

'Yes?'

'Shall I tell you something?'

'What?'

'What I think. What we all think. You're better than anyone in Shalimar, Rikki.'

'I'm sure. But,' laughing at his extravagant sister, 'in what way, specially?'

'Every way,' said loyal Valli, and her little pointed face was loving, 'but especially in the sea, when you're—you're—' she gestured at his board.

'Surfing?'

'Yes, surfing. If they let you take part, I'm sure you'd win the prize. If you think about it,' said Valli warmly, 'you're better than *any* of these Shalimaris, you know, Rikki.'

He had thought about his skill with the board, and had not been concerned. Now, however, the silver cup was sparking as he sat, and heard Valli say she must be off or someone would have a word, and watched the sand feather up behind her curved, vermilioned heels as she fled.

Still sitting on his malibu, with his knees drawn up, and his chin sunk in the bony vee.

Presently he began to feel cramped, and getting up off the board hoisted onto a stook of rope to watch the surfing. This perch provided excellent viewing. He could see the surfers in the troughs, as well as when they rode the crests of the breakers; and feeling the spray fly, would have liked to take part equally, and win prizes. As he could not, he began to fray and burn, all of it an interior molestation; and tried to get back under his spun-glass, but now it had become the most difficult thing in the world to do.

*

Tully, elsewhere, was enjoying the satisfactions of duty done. Stint over, he emerges blinking from the strobe lights of the tombola tent, stands for a bit to get the tic off his retina.

Overhead the sky is flecked blue, has been since dawn. The afternoon is balmy, fanned by a fresh wind that rasps lightly through the palms, fluffs up the small striped-canvas kioskery. It trifles with hair and clothing. Stoles are slipping from delicate shoulders, sequined scarves unwinding, escaped curls dance wickedly round girls' demure young cheeks. Duennas watch, eyes glinting, saris, passmenteried in the grand manner, stiff with gold lace, swinging open in full toreador splendour—a flourish of Castilian insolence as they pass by stately on their way to afternoon tea. There is the chink of china from the tea pavilion.

'Tea, Toby?' Heblekar passes by, cheerfully, on his way to sustenance after the raffling.

'Dying for a cup. Be with you in a moment.'

He wants a blow first; or perhaps to investigate what bulks in his line of vision—already he is headed for the beach, and this still figure.

Still as a monument, the boy on his rostrum of twisted rope.

294

One leg dangling, one bent, a brown heel laid on a bare thigh, the grave beauty of unmoving stone in his limbs, eyes driven frantic.

'Hullo, Rikki. Anything wrong?' said Tully.

And though he was used to almost anything in this quarter, was unprepared for the envy, pure, abstract, that struck like flint from the cold granite effigy. A bent look, from a height, from the boy.

If it had not been visible to Tully before, it was not for want of looking. He had inspected narrowly, nerves tensed for the first flicker; unnecessarily. Rikki moved sweetly, with clean instincts, through the muted splendours of Avalon or the extreme indulgences of Shalimar, with only the odd, frank jackdaw pounce on something bright that took his fancy. But then, things start small. Oak trees. Man. His cancers.

Tully was reduced to silence.

Meanwhile Rikki managed to see who it was. It loosened a muscle, he jumped down.

'Nothing is wrong. Everything, Mr Tully,' he reported, 'is in order.'

Standing attentive as a sentry, perhaps by intention, nothing would get past him. Tully did not even try. He moved conventionally. Shading his eyes, looking out to where one or two contestants were practising runs, he said,

'Great sport, surfing, don't you think, Rikki?'

'I was thinking that,' said Rikki, paused, corrected himself. 'I was thinking I would like to have the silver cup,' he confessed, quite forgetting about standing guard.

Once again it defeated Tully. Rikki had never coveted silver. There was enough around, tableware and ornamental, in Shalimar. Once, in Avalon, he had dug out of a godown a vast punchbowl redolent of regimental glory, pride of some mess, left behind to moulder in one of those periodic, precipitate withdrawals. Rikki had come beaming to present the find. Breathing on the crater, buffing up the acanthus and the laurel-berries, it had him exclaiming generously on the deftness of the silversmith.

However, if Rikki had cravings, Tully could have bought him a dozen silver cups without breaking the bank. He came perilously close: all but pumping in money, ready with this Western nostrum for all ills, no amount of failure cures the fatal delusion. He caught himself in time. It would not do. More was at stake, and for both of them.

'I don't think it's real silver,' he said, to allow breathing space.

295

As far as Rikki was concerned, it could have been a corn dolly.

'That doesn't matter,' he said. 'It would prove—' something important to him. Rikki hunted for words, fruitlessly. 'I could win,' he said at last, and added, 'if I tried,' so as not to appear vain. And smoothed his limbs in which—Tully for one was aware—the will and grace, and certainly the ability, resided. 'But you see,' he explained, 'I am not allowed.'

He was a fisherboy, paid for other things, not for competing against cosmopolites. As of course Tully knew, but was wrung all the same, as the old man had been; and as helpless. Avalon—there had been indications—might have given Rikki quarter. Shalimar was a new and different proposition. Some difference in conception, or even in the building, had worked through both, and varied their responses. Shalimar, at least, would have no time to brood, and glimmer, and give way, and enfold. It had no time to spare.

They stood side by side and exchanged this solid nugget. But as nothing much else could be done, they turned their attention to the sport. The two still standing side by side. Tully, trained in Cornish waters, a surfer since so high; Rikki sea-bred, with his inherited, internal gyro; both fully capable of appreciating the finer points.

'The sea looks good, for the surfing,' remarked Rikki.

Tully agreed, and would have lingered, but now his presence was required elsewhere. A bearer had arrived with a summons from the tea tent.

*

Ranji, meanwhile, was suffering. He had abstained from tea, in order to be fighting fit for the surfing contest; and what with the tang of Pekoe and Darjeeling, and the triangles of crisp gold pastry stuffed full of heavenly ingredients, he was feeling decidedly hungry.

There was that; and there was Tully.

Although he was three tables away, the lieutenant began to be very conscious of his presence, and even more so of the beautiful, absent Corinna. Thoughts began to assemble.

Not done, hogging a man's wife, he said to himself. (Though that was all he *had* done.) And he had not been—like Heblekar, say. He had been unlike Heblekar, to a man who was a guest in his country. Distinctly un-civil, at times. (Past pin-pricks opened like potholes in the lieutenant's conscience.) And hogged his wife. Ranji sipped hot water, and felt wretched, for he was not only susceptible, he was also very young. Soon he could endure it no longer. He rose, and carrying his cup, and dragging a chair which he intended to squeeze in somehow, he went over to the packed table.

'Nice day,' he said, and wedged himself between Zavera and Tully with no idea of what next, but with the diffuse intention of making amends.

Tully agreed it was. Their paths had crossed more than once that day, and each time they had agreed about the weather; but patience was one of his strengths.

'And good for the surfing,' he added, conventionally enough, but since the lieutenant was keen, and known to be aspiring.

'Yes,' said Ranji, and began to feel quite hag-ridden, and showed it, and didn't care who saw. Tully did, and enquired.

'Don't you feel well?' he asked, humanely.

'I feel hungry,' said Ranji. It happened to be true, but it was not at all what he had intended to say.

'Then you should eat,' said Tully, who had these blunt ways despite everything the country could do to refine him; and passed a plate of fodder.

Ranji recoiled, and temporarily forgot his misery.

'Out of the question. Couldn't possibly compete on a bloated stomach. I'd lose my balance,' he said, indignantly.

'A cucumber sandwich,' Tully held up the wafer, 'isn't likely to sink anyone. I've never found it disabling,' he coaxed.

'But you—' now Ranji was acutely envious, 'have so much more *experience*!' he said.

'True. But you've made up. Corinna's quite impressed,' said Tully, truthfully. 'She thinks you stand a good chance of winning.'

'Did she say?'

'More than once.'

'If I do, due to her entirely.' Ranji was transported, but still hag-ridden. 'Super guru, your wife,' he said, cautiously.

'I'm glad she could help,' said Tully.

It gave Ranji thoughts. Handing over his wife like that, his eye said plainly, if dodgily.

Not quite like that, even in the West, replied Tully, wordlessly. Out East, as Boyle might have said: under its burning glass things showed up more, that was all.

Before anything else could be worked out between them, Corinna was there, in a bright beach wrap, weaving her way
297

between the tables.

'*There* you are, Ranji,' she called as she came up to them. 'I've been looking for you everywhere!'

Everywhere, that is, except in the tea tent; for Ranji, unwilling to hide his light under a bushel, had made known his intention to fast. Now he rose, looking red and guilty, and somewhat ostentatiously put down the mug of warm water.

'Ready when you are,' he announced, which was patently untrue. He was still in full regimental finery.

'But, Ranji, you haven't even changed yet!' said Corinna.

'Will do. In a jiffy,' said Ranji.

Corinna intended to make sure.

'Come along, Ranji,' she said, firmly; women did tend to take charge of the young man. 'Things are moving. First heats, it should be fun.'

And led him away by the hand.

As the surfing event was one of the highlights, as soon as tea was over Zavera assembled her little court about her and set off for the beach. Cyrus she could not persuade, nor Helen Pearl; but Herbert was with her—what would she do without him? And that dear young couple, the Heblekars; and Mrs Mukherji, who was proving something of a leech; and Toby, whom she kept by her side so that he could tell her all about the surfing. She even linked her arm in his, to stop him escaping, but after an old-fashioned look from Mrs Mukherji—. Zavera sighed, and withdrew her arm, and felt a teeny bit cross with old-fashioned people, but it was not in her nature to be put out for long. Soon she was cheerful again, and commenting cheerily on this and that, including the sea, although she was never very sure of that element apart from its simpler aspects.

'Just look, the sea,' she ventured. 'So pretty, isn't it, Herbert?'

'Bang-on, for surfing,' said Boyle, who had never done any, and did not intend to if he could help.

It was, in spite of eulogy, a moderate sea.

The breakers came in triple formation, building up from the swell, cruising majestically along on the huge water-bed to the point of perennial ruin. At this fatal apex, a pause, a waver—and the swelling base on which they are rolling stalls and pitches them forward—Vroom! They crash, still skirmishing madly, in cascades of milky spray.

Surfers are in their element, in all this. It made Mrs Pearl

298

shudder. Nothing would induce her to watch the surfing contest, except from a distance. She wrapped up her curls in a scarf, for the wind was brisk, and let the brave do what they would, while she retreated to view in safety from the heights, and distance, of the Asoka.

All this exhilarated Ranji. Like all converts, the new religion had him knife-keen; and moreover there was Corinna's heady opinion. In less than a jiffy he was stripped for action. In even less time he had sprinted back, and joined the small group of contenders for the silver cup, among them Corinna. For she was good enough, and determined enough, to compete in what had begun as the men's event.

'Sea looks good. Don't you think, Ranji?' said Corinna amiably.

A hand shades her eyes against the sun. Her fingers are a closed fan, through which the light filters. It is enough to show up some stunning workmanship, the finely turned bones are clasped in a webbing of palest glazed coral veined with running vermilion.

Ranji was quite bowled over.

'What? Oh the sea, yes, see what you mean. Brilliant!' he babbled.

The scene is. A brilliant sun, breathing on enamelled claws, illustrates brilliantly why it is fit for worship. The sea is raked goldfoil. The wind sand-grained, but pleasing, is whipping up white horses, but not too close. People, pleasure-bent, are out in strength: not only Shalimaris, but coastals and countryfolk. Views can be had from anywhere, the coast stretches. . . In yellow and red, in saris and sarongs and sophisticated pared-aways, they prepare to be dazzled by the spectacle.

The judges are soberly attired: shorts, white shirts with short sleeves, one tenderfoot in sand-shoes, all befittingly solemn, each of the three from a different part of the world, to ensure equitable judging.

'The three best wave runs.' Fricker, elected spokesman, announces once again for the benefit of late arrivals and those, like Zavera, who are not *au fait* with the sport, but love it. The quorum sits upon a little rigged-up dais on the beach, watching keenly, each a practising member of the guild, ready to inscribe mystic squiggles on notepads balanced on knees that will later decode into points for or against the contestants.

Zavera could not make head or tail, although she peeped; but did not allow it to worry her. She was simply happy that everyone was enjoying. She too was enjoying. She smiled and clapped, and

now and then covered up her eyes when it made her dizzy to look.
It was a dizzy sight.

Each man, one supposes, carries in himself the centre of gravity
which he has to hang on to, to keep his balance.

Corinna and Ranji, and others of their calibre, in turn
demonstrate that it is not strictly necessary.

They play with gravity. They manipulate it. Masters of finesse,
they walk the plank, stall at breakneck point and weighting and
unweighting at speed bring the board back into trim for hair-
raising changes of direction. Raft and rider swing between sheer
brass and vertiginous spectacle, criss-crossing the curling lip of the
ocean just one shade off disaster, just one shade ahead of the
pursuing wave.

But subtler themes accompany the drama: long slow flawless
glides, languid, low-profile meanders of armature-precision...
The crowd grows delirious.

Elsewhere, gambling adds spice to the spectacle. Someone has
set up shop, the betting is brisk. Valli, who has bet on the
lieutenant, is wild with excitement. She jumps up and down, she is
sure he will win, she can't *wait* to collect. Sandhu's money is on the
Englishwoman. He thinks she will triumph, because the besotted
officer will let her, for by now it is clear the prize must go to one
of these two. Sandhu's horn-coloured eyes are shrewd and
calculating.

Zavera thought that everyone should win. Rather like Tully
earlier, she felt like purchasing a dozen little silver cups so that *all*
the surfers could have one, as they deserved to.

'Everyone is simply wonderful, don't you think, Toby?' she
said, turning to him; and found that she was addressing thin air.
Where had he got to? Zavera was slightly put out. He should have
been in their little group, enjoying with them. Looking round to
see, she spotted him at last. He was with that Rikki. Lounging
beside him, his back against a bundle of whiskery ropes, chit-
chatting. Zavera's smile faded a little. It was not what he should
have been doing at all. She felt like taking him by the arm, despite
Mrs Mukherji, and marching him back, but was unsure of
success. He would smile, and see her point, and agree he ought to
do whatever she suggested, and somehow continue to do whatever
he wanted. Zavera gave up the idea, and turned her attention to
Ranji, who was doing superbly as even she could see.

Ranji had not meant to. He fully intended to lose to Corinna.
Like Sandhu, however, he miscalculated just a little, in that he

forgot about his training. Armies are not trained to lose, on the whole. Ranji could not help but try to win. Naturally so did Corinna.

Delicate decisions are left to the judges. Heads down, checking up on the arithmetic, they come up again with the same score. Ranji and Corinna, Indian and Englishwoman, have tied. Each has a precisely equal number of points. Trust the country, rises unspoken. It can rustle up problems without even trying, out of an inexhaustible fund.

'Can't have a tie. Only one cup,' grunts Boyle.

'Your problem,' said Fricker, his shoulders narrow with loathing.

'One half-point would settle the matter.' Boyle's voice is notching up to querulous.

'No way. Can't fiddle the scores,' says the frigid judge, and enlists the support of international jurists.

Surfers stand around, dripping, half-naked. The restive crowd, hearts bleeding for these waifs, starts hurling barbed advice at advisers huddled round the deadlocked quorum. For two pins Boyle would send these mutinous tribunes packing, but alas! those powerful days are gone beyond recall.

'One deciding run,' he says, backsliding towards reason.

'No way,' says rigid Fricker, licks a finger and holds it up in some arcane ritual. 'Wind's blowing from the wrong quarter.'

'Too blustery.' Colleagues back him.

'No other solution,' snaps Boyle, returning to form.

'Well, it'll take time,' Heblekar strokes a serious nose, one hand resting on the shimmering rim of the presentation cup, 'but we could smelt down. Enough mineral here for two smaller trophies.'

The juvenile Ranji falls about, while Boyle, simmering, resorts to ripe commentary, and Zavera worriedly looks around for someone to pour oil now that principals, who should know better, are engaged in ruffling the water.

When the absent Tully sprang to her mind.

The moment she thought of him her spirits picked up, and she marched off at once to fetch him, and this time without hesitation. But he was not lurking behind the rope-bundle, as she had convinced herself. He had gone. The beach patrol claimed he did not know where.

'Are you sure?' asked Zavera firmly, but less firmly than she intended. The boy, as usual, affected her. She could not deal with him as she could, say, with Joseph or Miss Chari. She put it down to his eyes, they looked at one in such a way as to turn things

301

topsy-turvy. Now, for instance, he was making *her* feel tiresome for insisting, whereas *he* was being tiresome by not knowing.

'Yes, quite sure,' answered Rikki patiently. He did not know for certain, but gazing at her harassed face he did wonder that she could not guess. Where would anyone go at the end of the day, except home? Tully was probably in Avalon, or on his way. To oblige her, however, he peered about to see; but the light was going, the folds of the hill were already sombre.

*

These sombre hues affected the old man. He sat in the darkening hut, still in his corner, complaining to himself that he could hardly see. Usually at this hour his wife would remark on the gloom, and wipe her hands on a clean rag she kept handy, and reaching up for the switch, click on the dazzling pear.

Where was she? Gallivanting out there with her daughter, leaving him with an unlit pear. He had no liking to, nor would he deal with it. He would wait for his wife, it was her duty and pleasure. He stared at the object, dangling from the rafters, grey and ghostly at the end of the wire. One click, and if you happened to be looking directly it hit you in the eye, you could not see anything except that pear, for a time. And even after, the light streamed harsh and grainy.

Presently, as evening waned, Apu was put in mind of the old lantern, which his wife had relegated. When lit, it lifted the darkness like a curtain, rather than ripped it apart. Its light did not rasp his eyes, it had never left a feeling of grit under the eyelids. Then an impulse began throbbing, which he tried to still; but it would not rest. So at length he rose, and stole like a thief to the opposite corner where the lantern was stood, and squatted down beside it. It was grimier than ever, but he wiped off the worst with the handy rag. Then stealthily, and feeling bold and criminal, he raised up the glass shield and applied a match. Light poured from the lamp, soft and radiant as he remembered it. Apu blinked once or twice, he had got into the habit from the nightly onslaught, but soon he was soothed. His head began to nod.

*

Tully, as might have been guessed, was indeed making tracks. He had his needs. Up and about since dawn, sociable since an early breakfast, these were making themselves felt. There are times, after all, when the most social animal needs to hole up.

302

En route then, to his hole. Not that anyone—not even Corinna—could call Avalon that by any stretch of nerve or imagination. Not with Copeland-Tullys for builders. A retreat however. Built to order, burnished by desire, a place of lofty space, costly seclusions, with views to rooms...all this magnificently reduced in the Copeland manner and treated, mildly, as a corner in which to unwind. The piquancy never ceased to entertain Tully. Although both were incorporate in him, he had always been able to comment, and had never been deterred from commenting, in separate vein on the Copelands and the Tullys.

Each in turn had contributed an inlay, a lamina in mother-o'-pearl, to his corner: a vanity, or flourish, in personal signature, not that far removed from the persistent graffiti scratched into ancient walls. His own was unfinished. Not the pool, which had been taken over, but the hand-carved, custom-made cherub. His labours showed, he continued to be convinced, where ideally they should have been invisible. The emery, vigorously deployed to impart the sheen of flesh, had not been plied too well. Rasp marks, like scratches in the marble, continued to be visible to an eye which, meticulous over Shalimar, grew ardent over Avalon. He intended to see it right, before leaving.

With Open Day ending, the evening stretched. He thought to put in an hour or so, before the Contractors' gala dinner.

He said so to Rikki, and waiting until the dizzy Zavera had closed her eyes for an instant, headed for the bay.

'Going to rain, sahib.'

A life-guard, in the last sector before Shalimar's jurisdiction ceased, passing the time of day.

'Yes, looks as if it will.'

He nodded, and returning the man's salaam walked on. Along the tousled sands, dodging the usual confetti of galas tossing around in the breeze, walking briskly to arrive early and make the most of the light.

But on his way up, his intention began to slip. Rikki haunted the pool room. He would be there—not physically, the patrols were under strict orders not to budge until the beach was empty, which would be a while yet. His presence. About now, in the glut of light that often precipitated darkness, the boy would come hurtling up the hill, an oriole in flight, to test out a colour or a pigment against the incandescent crystal. Lately it had been the garnet of the fragmented vase.

Yes, Rikki. Permanent intruder, come to take up the

permanent niche chipped in the marble between them. Tully had never been averse, was not now; but was not in the mood for company, even of this tender order. Perhaps, with a fortnight to go, it came too near the bone.

The beach, as it happened, was handy.

So he sat. Contemplating: a fraught occupation. Like a Buddha, or a Jesuit. Or a soldier of fortune, or come to that his counterpart the multi-faceted master-builder. Squirming out of the wire-cage, now and then, to wonder what was a-building, or stepping down from the viewing-platform now and then to look up at the stars, wonderingly, or down, with an equal wonder, into a quenched valley. Aware as never before of sound, and light.

A hammered light, here in the open, streaked flint and pewter coming off anvils of dark stone. Under a dropped sky, clouds jostling, no flamboyant slashes of things to come, up those dense sleeves.

He had taken off his jacket and rolled up his shirt-sleeves in expectation, but now rolled them down again. Rain was not far off, the wind getting up and beginning to bluster. Squalls struck at foundations, butting at the little tethered tents, rocking the illuminated traceries of Shalimar, shadows like corybants. From way below a carborundum uproar from the corrugated palmyra.

It carried clearly up the hill, and was presently overtaken by the demented hee-hawing of the emergency klaxons.

It woke the old man, who had fallen soundly asleep, abruptly.

Chapter Forty-six

THE sirens, routinely installed by AIDCORP, were set off by the lifeguards. They left the rescue to the old man's son. Best swimmer on the coast, he himself bragged; and they knew it to be true. Also, he happened to be nearest.

Rikki was minded to wash his hands. He felt he had done his duty by warning Mrs Tully. To begin with he could hardly believe what he heard, or that she meant it.

'One last run, Rikki,' she said. She had come back specially to make the most of the last few dregs of light. 'Keep an eye on this thing for me, will you?'

Handing him her silver cup (Ranji had insisted) while she selected a surfboard from the cluster he was sheeting up.

'The current, Mrs Tully', he said, forbiddingly. He had no liking for those who played with the sea, in this mood. 'The wind is blowing strongly.'

Blowing off the land, it took a hand in wave-size, the flow of water, in the currents that formed below eye-level, in the clash between onrush and backflow which surfers of calibre could turn to their purpose, riding out on rip tides if sufficiently accomplished.

'Current?' Corinna was highly accomplished. 'The rip is a bonus, Rikki. Surely you know?' She was sure he did, she had seen him skimming out on his plank.

'Not now,' he said, and as it was too much to go into, he proposed instead. 'Another day, Mrs Tully,' he suggested.

'Won't be one. I'm leaving tomorrow.' She was slightly high, after the charged day. Perhaps, too, some destructive impulse, less uncommon than supposed, led her. 'It's now or never, Rikki,' she said.

This time he did not hear her. He was listening, to sounds ferried in by the wind, of the glutted river tumbling down to the sea. If she had been a boat he would have beached her high and dry, out of harm's way. As it was he watched her walking, slightly lopsided with the weight of the board, down to the sea.

The sea ruffled, showing white crests here and there, not too formidable. What was formidable, did not show. Somewhere at unseen levels drag-currents formed, white, cold, where sea and river fought, the river whipped by a high wind rushing headlong into the sea, the sea resisting, the two threshing it out on the huge sea-bed.

Somewhere on the sea-bed, caught in cross-currents, swirled the dust of his father. That barely remembered, unforgettable man: his own blood and bone.

It made him run after her, but when he had caught up there was nothing he could do. He could not, after all, lay hands on her and drag her back bodily. What was left, he did, while hating her for making him.

'My father,' he said, 'was showing off too.'

And the wind blew chill, as it had done off and on for most of his life, from the time he took in what had left him an orphan. He glimpsed it in their eyes, while they laboured over the half-invented furies of the sea with which that wanton man had diced, and lost: a conspiracy an entire community had entered into, to spare the vain man's son.

It was the utmost that could have been asked of him. But for Tully, nothing would have dragged it out. What was owed there, made him.

Corinna did not know what he was talking about. She also felt, unusually for her, that he was forgetting his place, suggesting she was showing off.

'Well, if I am, I am,' she said, coolly, and turning her back on the servant, strode into the water.

She was still in her depth when the current seized her. Very gently, silk-cord wound round her limbs. At that stage she was not afraid. Nothing there she could not handle. Moments later she came upon the truth, which was that she was being swept out to sea, and it was out of her hands. She began to scream.

It woke the life-guards, lulled by lack of incident into more or less slumbering with their eyes open. It wrecked Rikki's first reaction, which was to let her drown. He could not. The screams were too raw. His own strong impulse, he recognised in time, was corrupt. So he went after her, in the wake of the crazy diagonals in which cross-currents were dragging her. While the galvanised guards raced for the alarm and the lifeboat.

There was one, with customary AIDCORP efficiency. It was launched, also efficiently, by men who had left their calling, but not so long ago as to have forgotten how to cope. It was, besides, more than familiar, being a converted fishing vessel.

Then there was nothing to do but wait.

All of them waiting, simple and blasé alike. Streaming out from their huts, the pavilions, from the Asoka, the shore dark with people freely or forcibly embroiled.

Kitted out in stormwear, for it had started to pour, a frontline of Shalimaris. Nerves jumping, demonstrably extraneous, but not to be deterred. Some indomitables with cameras at the ready, of the same kinky stock that would cram into cars and race along the highway to the scene of the crash, urged by unadmitted lusts to participate in death.

Death was in the air, chill, penetrating, numbing the closely grouped coastals. Re-enacting a timeless play, this silent chorus assembling to watch and wait. A time-worn waiting, by some sea-lashed coast for a sighting, waiting cowled and shawled for the streaming forms to be carried ashore, the dull, leaden waiting of people used to repeated blows like beasts of burden. A peasant people cowering before the thunderbolts of heaven, joined now by sophisticates.

Them. Us. One of each.

They clung together, the old man and his wife.

Contractor could not bear to look. He could not see much either. It was raining, and his spectacles kept steaming up. But he understood, the message of the klaxons was loud and clear. He had come as he was, still in his silk suit, and somehow in the confusion found his wife. They stood together, in their group, under the bucking parasol she did not realise she was holding up. Presently he said, precisely, and for the record, of which he was proud,

'Not one. Not one single casualty in all our operations. We take great care, you know, Zavera.'

And he took off his spectacles which had again misted over, and polished them carefully before hitching them on again.

Zavera could not speak, her throat hurt too much. She clung tightly, with her one free arm, to her husband.

Heblekar did not have the courage either. He huddled into his group, in his smart city mackintosh, and veiling his eyes made offerings to Tully, who had arrived in shirtsleeves and was drenched.

'Here you are.'

'I'm all right.'

'Shivering like that? Come on, put it on.' Jollying him into it like a nanny, Tully reduced to a child, hands like ham-fists catching in the waterproof's sleeves, Heblekar having to ease them over.

'There, that's better.'

'Feels better.'

'No sense in getting pneumonia.'

'None.'

'That youngster, you know, he can swim like a fish.'

'Yes.'

'Like a dolphin.'

'Yes. Sharks eat dolphin, don't they?'

'Sharks? What's the matter with you? No sharks in these waters.'

'In deep water, where they are. Bound to be.'

'But they're not. They're in the boat. Look, Toby.'

At this juncture Corinna was. Rikki was bobbing alongside, while they jockeyed, perilously close to the reef, to get him in, when the rogue wave came at him. It smashed him into the side of the boat, dragged him off it, and repeated the performance before they could haul him to safety. He was still conscious, but clogged with water. Eyes, lungs, streaming off his limbs, his hair. They would have to pump him dry at the very least, he felt.

Chapter Forty-seven

THE storm did not blow itself out overnight as everyone expected, but kept on. It was not unduly violent, people with quite short memories could recollect much worse. Nevertheless a good many structures, and people, took a battering.

In the general disarray the colony came off best. Elbowed away from its superior neighbour—some, indeed, thankfully retreating from the lush sea-fringes—it escaped the full onslaught of the ocean. Apart from which, it was no emperor's city. It could survive on basics.

The choice coastal strip, groomed for the opulent, fared worst, in some rare arrangement of divine nicety. Taking the full brunt, it was flooded, washed by sea-water of unquenchable blues—an accompaniment to states of mind now, inundated, as ever it had been at its swept and garnished best.

The reflections were intense.

*

It was the fifth day before the sedated Rikki registered the ebb and flow of light. He also felt he was alive, and checked with the nursing orderly to make sure before settling down for another sleep in the incredible bliss of his bed in the Spa.

Elsewhere, too, people emerged to take stock. Boyle first of all, and the storm barely subsided, for delays were worrying and costly. But inspecting the bedraggled complex, he soon saw that the damage was well within AIDCORP's competence. Structures were sound, foundations well laid—the consortium had never gone in for building on the cheap.

'Basically a case of cleaning up,' he said to Contractor. Tully was not available.

'Do you think?' Cyrus, in crisis, forgot about understatement. He only knew, as did Boyle, that sewers were awash, the power supply erratic, the fans and freezers out of action—that the vital infrastructure of civilisation stood on the brink.

'Yes, I do. I rather hope,' said Boyle, 'to keep to our original schedule. No reason why we shouldn't be able to,' he added, to carry his leaden colleague along with him.

309

'In nine days?' That was all they had left of the original fortnight. 'Is it possible?' said Cyrus.

'Oh, entirely so,' said Boyle, not vauntingly but simply, because he understood the potential of AIDCORP more absolutely than his partner. Being human, however, he would have liked to have some backing. A little support from associates, he felt rather wearily, would not be out of place.

'Nothing we can't cope with,' he said, to encourage the other. 'Not insurmountable, surely, a bit of flooding? Ought to have the place spick-and-span in no time.'

'Yes, I suppose,' said Cyrus, gazing at vistas that opened out from the office verandah, while the scenes began to tumble like counterweights up and over in his mind. Shalimar spick-and-span. Shalimar, a zone of disaster. Both views were coming up, so that he said, wearily,

'Floods, no floods, what difference does it make? It is all one. All is in the mind.'

'What?' said Boyle. Sense, he felt, had somersaulted out of the window. 'What is the matter with you, old boy?' he asked.

But Cyrus was too far along this path to retract.

'It is illusion. All is Illusion, or Maya,' he said.

'You sound,' said Boyle, with the freedom possible between old associates, and by now out of patience, 'like a bally Hindu.'

'Yes.' Cyrus, a committed Zoroastrian, did not protest; his fingers, that usually beat brisk tattoos, rested passive on the windowsill. 'Yes, it seeps in. The airs of Hindusthan,' he said, 'which is the proper name for India.'

The tunes it played, were sounding plainly.

Boyle dismissed them; he was too fond of the old rogue not to. He spotted reasons, and made excuses for the man.

'It's getting you down, the mess. Same here, Cyrus. Loathe it. But we'll soon clean up,' he said, kindly, and with a genuine concern. 'Come along, I'll buy you a drink.'

And soon the slurpers were in action, the pumps vacuuming powerfully, the clean-up operation in full swing with double shifts at work.

Elsewhere, too, they set about patching and cleaning up. Rents in the thatching, and those immemorial puddles, and bulging mud walls here and there which needed shoring up. There was not much to be done, however, about the electricity, which had failed. It lay with others, who had their hands full elsewhere.

310

Apu was thankful. He could not have borne to look at his wife, in the merciless light that fell from the pear. He would have been glad of the lantern, however, but they had run out of kerosene. So he sat in the pitch dark, and longed for a glimmer, and wondered how soon Muthu would return with a little borrowed oil, and the two women from the hospital, while the darkness began to press down. When he could endure no longer he rose, and feeling his way to the door undid the thong and let himself out into the evening, where under a wide sky the dark would not oppress.

Outside, settled on his string cot, and looking about him, the night seemed to the old man to shine, bright as a young woman's hair. He could not make it out, and rubbed his eyes to clear them, but then he saw it was a brightness of stars, suspended in the air like a fine, shiny dust.

He had grown unaccustomed, since Shalimar. It lit up at night, and then one did not see stars or starlight, only the illuminations. His wife and daughter often went out to look, they were enthralled even now. It would distress them, not having anything to look at, the old man thought with a pang on their behalf; but then remembering where they kept vigil, allowed that it did not matter.

*

While AIDCORP dealt with Shalimar, Heblekar, man on the spot, took on the colony. Its needs were real, but small and essentially simple. For Heblekar, IAS trained, IAS authority as well, and accustomed to catastrophe on a grander scale, it did not present intractable problems. His lanky figure could be seen, folded into a jeep, chugging off to town; or there was Heblekar, wearing his crafty hat and flanked by the military, namely Ranji, cajoling AIDCORP eminences, or village worthies. And soon AIDCORP lorries were rumbling in loaded with palmyra thatch wrested from villages with surpluses, and roadside depots doled out the kerosene and rice.

Help poured in from other quarters too. Word had gone out from the Bridie Mission, as it was still called. The Bridies had long been laid in their graves, but their powerful presence was not to be routed by the somewhat colourless pair to whom the torch had been handed on. Word went forth from the Bridie Mission, and in no time Christian Succour were organising relief. Soon, no less than a two-ton truck was fitted out, and filled with supplies, and put in charge of their energetic, and experienced, Mr Applebee who had volunteered to deliver it.

311

Mr Applebee, an enthusiastic and dedicated worker, did not approve of multinational corporations like, say AIDCORP. Prudence restrained him from saying so, since they were a good touch for philanthropic ventures, but privately he considered them downright immoral. However, as he drove along the splendid highway that led to Shalimar, and incidentally to the coastal settlements, he fairly admitted they had their uses. The two-ton truck he was driving would have bogged down up to its axles—being experienced he was fairly sure—on the usual muddy country track. As it was...Mr Applebee felt the wind whip through his rippled blond hair, and sang as he belted along.

Shalimar had been alerted, and the Asoka chosen as the distribution point. Accordingly lemonade and cool moist towels were waiting to greet the dusty envoy as he swung himself down from the cab.

Also Zavera. As soon as he was refreshed she joined him, and presently, beaming with gratitude and goodwill, she stood beside him in the courtyard to supervise the unloading.

But as it went on, her smile began to fade, and by the time the truck was empty, it had gone.

'Tell me, Mr Applebee,' she felt like saying, as she ran a shrinking eye over two tons of offerings. 'Tell me, what shall we do with all these sigris and blankets?'

Instead she addressed Joseph, suspecting he would answer more reliably, after Mr Applebee had driven off.

'Tell me, Joseph,' she said, 'what shall we do with all these blankets and cardigans?'

Joseph did not know. Not one for looking a gift horse, however, he soon came up with a solution.

'Ooty merchants, memsahib,' he suggested, 'is giving good price.'

'But, Joseph.' Zavera was stern with the reprobate. 'These goods are not for sale. They are gifts to our poor unhappy people.'

'Yes, memsahib, for poor people only I am saying,' swore Joseph. 'They are not requiring warm things, but memsahib can sell and give the money, then they will be happy.'

And they spent the hot, steamy afternoon superintending the loading of the goods into godowns, to await the arrival of traders from cold regions, after Joseph had abstracted a few dozen assorted items to flog on his own account.

However, Joseph was not alone. Zavera, too, had picked out a sweater. Knitted in striking, even lurid, wool, she felt the vivid garment would please that poor boy in hospital. Something of a peacock, as she had remarked more than once, and a lively eye for colour. So she folded it up, and put it away in her almirah, until such time as the doctor's verdict came, when she looked forward to making the presentation.

Chapter Forty-eight

AND so things got back to normal, insofar as that dimension could apply; although there were fluid times, usually at night, when the sturdy concept tended to waver in many people's minds, a little like illuminated seaweed in the flowing darkness. But mostly things were normal.

Shalimar, fulfilling every promise made, was as good as new; and if Visitors had flown, dismayed by tropical excesses, the flow was being reversed. Zavera was happy, cosseting the newcomers, and showing them scars where the blows had fallen, even if her attentions were divided. Soon they would be moving to pastures new, Cyrus was already in Delhi finalising; and shortly she would follow him, leaving Shalimar to new incumbents with a good conscience and the knowledge that it would go from strength to strength. Already there were plans for expanding. Rumours had reached that the powers-that-be had expressed interest in Avalon. After the lease had expired, of course. A guest house or similar, but like a Maharaja's Palace, only the most distinguished Visitors and exclusive Tour Companies.

Zavera herself might have been tempted to stay on, except for Cyrus. She thought of him now, as she directed Mary-ayah who was packing the cabin trunks for sending on in advance, and her lips were soft from the inward dew. No, not for anything would she be parted. She could not bear it, after what they had been through.

Boyle too would soon be on his way, and hoped Tully would be ditto. They were due in Doha by the end of the week for top-level consultations; and AIDCORP's boast was that it kept its appointments come hell or high water. This time, he felt, there had been both; but Boyle was conscious, and proud, of having surmounted every obstacle with the sole exception of Tully. Not that Boyle had given up here entirely. He intended to have one more go before throwing in the sponge. He chose the bar, to nerve himself, and bought a round before attempting.

'Any idea, Toby,' he said, reasonably, 'when you'll be leaving?'

'None, I'm afraid,' said Tully—unreasonably, he himself realised. He constructed a hapless matchstick man out of toothpicks on the counter.

314

It got Boyle down. He tossed back his chota-peg.

'Surely you must know,' he said—if Tully didn't, who would?—'when you'll be leaving?'

The trouble was, Tully didn't.

'Who knows?' he said.

Like yet another bally Hindu, it sounded to Boyle's offended ears. He had not yet forgiven Cyrus.

'Well, you ought,' he said, shortly, and glinted over his glass. It made Tully exert himself.

'I really don't know yet,' he said.

'Weeks? Months?' Boyle slumped against the bar for strength, and only just stopped his eyeballs rolling heavenwards: how, in the name of reason, could a corporation be expected to function?

Tully, if aware, was indifferent, or wanton.

'Could be. I really couldn't say,' he repeated, and lighting up, blew smoke rings, an art he had neglected of late. Smoke drifted across the room, blue, quoit-shaped, moving to ellipses in softest greys, callibrating finely to clarity. 'I'm not leaving till I've seen Rikki on his feet,' he said. Then, as Boyle's face grew outraged, he added what was acceptable. 'Least I can do, considering it was Corinna,' he said.

'I suppose. But,' Boyle grunted, dragging at his lower lip, 'that could be come Christmas.'

'It could be. But I'm sure,' Tully placated, able to now that his own indecisions were resolved, 'you'll be able to hold the fort?'

Boyle was sure too; but that was not the point.

'So long as you bear in mind,' he underlined, 'that we're due to start up again in a matter of weeks.' Since AIDCORP did not thrive by sitting on its butt.

'Where?' said Tully, from whose mind, by now, it had slipped.

'Where!' said Boyle, glassily; and read his associate a lecture. 'Well, case of stick a pin on the map, old boy. Growth sector, you know, holiday camps. Any spot on the globe you care to name, provided it can afford our services. But actually,' he said, 'I'm talking about Lagos. We're due—'

But actually Tully didn't care, Boyle saw clearly, and his voice began to falter. Well, you could afford not to, if you were a Copeland-Tully, he tried to tell himself. However, he had a clear notion it did not have much bearing.

*

Ranji too was leaving. Stint over, he was off to rejoin his

L   315 regiment. But for the farewells, he would have been quite bucked. But there it was. He stood like a ramrod in front of his superior, and extended a hand.

'Goodbye, Mr Heblekar. It has been a pleasure to work with you,' he said, correctly.

'Same here,' said Heblekar, and warmly wrung the hand that was proffered.

'I'm sorry,' said Ranji, unbending a little, and voicing one or two hazy suspicions, 'if at times I've been a trial to you.'

'You haven't. You've been a help at all times,' said Heblekar, and clapped him on the back, and sent the young officer glowing on his way.

Then it was the Tullys. Mrs Tully, in particular.

Ranji rode up the hill, handsome as ever, even more cologned and gleaming to tide him over the fraught occasion, rehearsing his farewell speech as he went. When he was ushered in, however, and saw her lying on the rosewood fourposter, he fell in love all over again and all his faculties deserted him.

Corinna had to help out.

'Hullo, Ranji. How are you?' she said, and offered him her hand.

Like a bruised flower, pale and fragile as a lily, the blue wounds showing—if he could have transferred his own bouncing vitality to repair the damage, Ranji would have not thought twice. As it was he took her hand between his own, and crushed it.

'It's you,' he blurted. 'How are *you*, Mrs Tully?'

'Corinna,' she reminded.

'Corinna,' he said, tenderly.

'I'm fine, Ranji.' She was moved, as many were, by his transparent emotion. 'But tell me about you. I hear you're off soon?'

'Yes. Rejoining tomorrow. Regiment's been posted to Simla,' said Ranji.

It might have been a posting to the Gobi, except that Corinna knew better.

'But you'll love Simla, Ranji. You know you will,' she encouraged.

'Will I?' The lieutenant was not to be parted from sweet melancholy so easily.

'Of course. Brimming with girls. You'll be the beau of the ball.'

What did Ranji care? He cared only for Corinna.

But Corinna was skilful, and gradually the young man

316

brightened up, especially after she had given her word to look him up, the very next time she happened to be passing. He was almost restored, by the time he came to join Tully on the verandah, as invited to.

'Mr Tully,' he said, stalwartly. 'Goodbye.'

'Goodbye, Ranji. Take care of yourself,' said Tully.

'And you. I hope,' said the lieutenant, a phrase from his speech coming to his aid, 'you'll come to our country again.'

'So do I,' said Tully.

'Really?'

'Really.'

'You'll be most welcome. Don't ever think,' said Ranji, earnestly, 'otherwise.'

'Why should I?' asked Tully.

'Well.' Ranji's flags were haunting him. 'You might feel—some rotters around, utter scum—don't exclude myself—myself above all!—might make you feel you weren't. What I mean is,' he said desperately, 'if we—if I—have made you feel less than welcome—'

'You haven't. You've made me feel—terrific.'

'You're not just being polite?'

'Why the hell should I be?'

'Well, you might.' Squirming, loving free speech, its utter brutality.

'Well, not with friends. I've loved being here,' said Tully. 'Loved every minute.'

'I'm so pleased. Couldn't be more!'

It unmanned Ranji too, so that Tully had to give him a leg up, there being no syce handy. Normally he would have vaulted into the saddle.

Possibly it was the lieutenant. An essence lingered, impulsive, generous, releasing something that had been in spasm between them. At least Tully felt so as he came back into the room, and pushing aside the chair from which the smitten Ranji had worshipped, for the first time since the night of the storm sat on the bed beside his wife.

'How are you, Corinna?' he said.

'I think I'll live.' She smiled. She too felt that something was being broken down; and said quite simply as she was now able, 'I'm sorry, Toby. About Rikki, I mean. It was unforgivable. I must have been mad—'

'We all have fits.' He was over his own; he had wanted to mangle her. Only the knowledge that he could, coming in the nick

317

of time, had in the end saved them both being crippled. 'But,' he said, 'Rikki's mending. He asked me to tell you. All in one piece, he thinks.'

'Is he?'

'I believe so.'

'I'm glad. I know he—' she frowned, mystery was seeping back, she could cope only by admissions, '—means something to you, Toby. I don't know what, but something.'

She would never know. Rikki, or perhaps the country he was bound up with, were equally outside her reach. Nor did he deny, or attempt to flesh out so elusive an emotion. It would have needed a return to childhood, and a child's preposterous simile: the coils of a python, which had been thrown round others besides himself. It would make no sense to grown-up people.

Different emotions, too, were being kindled by the evening sun, slanting through fanlights. And as the silence had ceased to be destructive, Corinna could question, without abrading.

'What has happened, Toby? To us?' She could no longer pretend that nothing had, when the sword, or wedge, was palpable. It lay between them, where once they would have fused.

He accepted past fusion; but in prolonged pacing of the labyrinth had come upon deeper passages. The marriage was flawed. They had explored each other, and fired each other to incandescent union without ever lighting up the secret places. Lacunae remained, and had been pointed up in a different climate, that was all.

He did not answer. She did not press. There remained residues of tenderness from the past in which both of them were lingering. While evening slipped away, and the light streaming in drew fire from the rosewood. An unusual light, she saw, and saw him touched to an unusual beauty as Boyle had seen, but did not look away as he had done. She could have been lost, or melted into the gold carving, except that now the light was being withdrawn.

Enough remained, however. He saw the purple bruises. They had had to bludgeon the panic-stricken woman with their oars to prise her fingers off the boat, to save them all from drowning.

He took her hands in his.

'Does it hurt, Corinna?'

'Not as much as you'd think from looking. It's just that I bruise easily.'

'I know.'

They were smiling at each other, and their memories. Some-

318

times she would accuse, pointing to plums and outrageous blue strawberries ripening on her milky skin; and wring promises of reform in a complicity in which both knew she loved the marks he left on her. So she smiled at these reflections, while allowing her hands to rest in his. Rather fine hands, she had always acknowledged; and saw no need to change these convictions.

Then there were things to do, as soon as she had recovered. Rikki to make her peace with (she did, with an unassumed humility, and courage). As for him, he found he could not continue to hate her, now that she was leaving. Then there arose the old question of what to do with the pony. In the end she drove him in a horsebox to the horse-loving English pair, and saw him comfortably settled in his stable. On her way back she shopped in the Emporium for gifts for the Linklaters. This durable couple had once again invited, and Corinna saw no reason for not accepting. Nor did Tully. There was no reason, really.

They drove together to the airport. On the journey it was of the boy they spoke.

'Thank heaven he's mending.'

'Yes.'

'I'd never have forgiven myself if—. Keep me posted, will you, darling?'

'Of course.'

When they kissed at the barrier their lips were affectionate, but cool. So cool and unimpassioned that Tully momentarily rebelled, furiously charging the country with extracting its last pound of flesh; but as this was not true, as indeed he knew, the fury died even as it was kindled.

Chapter Forty-nine

RIKKI would mend. That was the kernel of all the reverberating pronouncements that came out of the cool, white-walled hospital. The old man clutched it for strength, when at last he went to see his son. He clung to his wife too, and for the same reason: he would not have dared these precincts, if he had not had her to bolster him. Not just for the first visit, but every time he went, he had to have her beside him.

It made Amma impatient, her broken reed of a husband; but she humoured him because she saw the marks of his suffering. It would not restrain her from scolding, for his own good.

'What is there to be frightened of? A grown man like you!' She elected to conceal her own dread, when confronted by the fearful contraptions, the glary white walls, the click of cold machinery. If she gave way, what hope for him?

'And everyone so kind,' she hissed. She didn't want anyone to overhear, as she propelled him along the corridor. 'You ought to be ashamed of yourself.'

The old man felt no shame, nor anything else either. He was too numbed, as he sat on the chill, white-tiled floor, and listened to the sinister clicking, and stared at the muffled-up figure lying on the bed. It was of course the bandages and plaster, but it seemed to the old man they had taken his son away from him, and substituted this grotesque changeling.

But at length the pulse grew strong. There were stirrings, and recognisable features beginning to show up, Apu conceded it was indeed Rikki and not some dummy they had planted in his place; and sometimes, when he gazed long enough, could almost have believed he saw the ocean mirrored once again in his son's grey-gold eyes. Then his own would mist over, knowing himself beholden; and one day it had to be given expression.

'They have looked after him well,' he said, and smoothed the spotless white sheet with a finger. He could not bear to contemplate what they would have done, he, and even his strong wife, if there had not been this hospital on their doorstep to see them through their time of travail.

His wife sniffed. 'Not one good word to say, till now,' she

reminded.

The old man was not put out. It was no more than the truth, which had impelled all his utterances. Though it was never easy to light on truth. Or untruth for that matter. Especially when the reflections rose so strongly.

*

It was not just Apu. The reflections were everywhere.

They came off the sea, the Blue Lagoon, off the swimming pool on the lip of the ocean. They had scoured it out, and refilled with dredged and purified water that ran, from the tiling, to more delirious turquoise hues than the permanent, placider dyes of the ocean.

It was the ocean that Tully saw, from the terraces of Avalon. What engaged him were the tracks in his mind: dolphin trails as of one who, out of patience, or from motives of the purest pleasure, would shear across the waters of the bay.

For Rikki it was the pool, which he could glimpse, if allowed to crane, from the ventilator in the sick-bay. He saw the glimmer, and also, quite clearly, its links with his standards of living, planted and growing like a row of stately trees. He wrung promises, as soon as he was able.

Mrs Contractor was unprepared. She had gone to visit, taking a jar of sweetmeats and the brilliant pullover to cheer up the poor boy; and expecting only thanks, also received this surprise.

'Can I have my job back, Mrs Contractor?' he lobbed at her, having some idea that Tully's power was passing, in this sphere.

'Rikki—' Zavera was stricken. It was early days, and as she looked at, and away from, the deadweight of plaster she was far from sure what would eventually emerge. 'Rikki, if—' she faltered, in her distress.

'I can. I shall be able to.' The strength was pouring from him. Zavera felt it, but then she had always thought he was a strong, strange boy. She could not withstand him, or hold back the promises demanded. Going beyond her writ, and closing her eyes firmly to the enormity, she pledged the new administration.

It was, she strongly felt, the least that she could do.

It was a common emotion. No one could do enough for the boy. He seemed to encompass wrongs done, if any. As no one could be absolutely sure, he was converted into a scapegoat cum Christ-figure. Not that anyone believed in these either. Radiating uncertainties in an age of reason, the conversion was only accomplished by stealth. Most people believed that most ills were curable without having to resort to extremes. They were rational about it, while simultaneously accepting that there could be problems without solutions. Created, insoluble. A bit like matter, a few felt furtively. Once created, indestructible. And dodgily, their thoughts would go to the different kinds of creator.

*

With ripples so widespread, Heblekar could not escape wholly, but did his best. He did so by the simple expedient of dodging locations where the reflections crowded him, like, for instance, a certain point on the ascent to Avalon where the bench was thoughtfully provided. He would get out his motor-car for the short run, and roar up the hill to keep some crucial appointment for a game of chess, or to collect a melon that Tully was nursing along for him.

'What's wrong with walking?' Tully said finally. 'This rate your legs will atrophy.'

Heblekar preferred to take that risk. He continued to drive up, but on his final ascent threw caution to the winds, or the night beguiled him.

His last night, moon at the full, sheen coming off the sea, silver moonbloom on the gift bottle.

Heblekar walked, reflecting, unavoidably, as people did who walked. Walking delicately, as people tended to on this hill, but without stopping anywhere until terrace, and its occupant, came into view. Then he paused, and called:

'Toby?'

'Yes?'

'Can I join you?'

'Any time. Come on up.'

'Right away. At the double.'

Heblekar did, as Tully watched, leant on the gleaming baluster rail, listening to crushed stone going crnch-crnch-crnch under his nifty feet. Feet in sandals, flying up the slope, soles as thin as chapathis. But arrived, Heblekar turned sober. Breathing evenly, speaking prim and proper as a judge.

'I'm off tomorrow, Toby.'

'I know.'

'So I thought I'd say goodbye at a decent hour. No. Not goodbye. Au revoir.'

'Au revoir, yes.'

322

'Meet up again sometime, someplace.'

'Sure. What the hell, Heb,' enquired Tully, 'is the matter with you?'

'It's these blasted farewells.' Heblekar sank onto a step, wiped sweat off his nape, confessed. 'Ten in one day is too much.'

'Too much for man or beast.'

'Knew you'd feel the same. So I brought us this. Can't go wrong with Napoleon,' said Heblekar, and brought out this treasure, dark, mysterious, cobwebs and grape-bloom on the ancient glass, leant the noble bottle up against his forearm like an expert sommelier for Tully's approval.

Tully gazed, awed.

'Where on earth—?'

'From Ranji, from Pondy.'

'Pondy? I thought he said Simla.'

'Pondy first, to stock up. A raid on some old caserne Ranji knew of—some mouldy ancestral memory.'

'Some story.'

'His. Vaults stashed skyhigh, according to him. French life-absolutes.'

'Trust the frogs.'

'Yes. Vive la France.'

'Vive l'Empereur.'

They mellowed together, as they were used to doing, with the noble fluid helping, and without the intrusions that Heblekar's strategy had routed. While time slipped by, there was that tryst with a plane. Heblekar rose, reluctantly.

'I ought to be moving,' he said.

They took the path together, Tully carrying the bottle, since it was only half empty. And the slatted bench playing at Lorelei as usual, neither could escape it. Inevitably the very harmonies that Heblekar did not wish to hear, were sounding. He began to harp.

'Untouched coasts, Toby.' Waving a hand at a coast that was far from. 'Shouldn't be touched, is how I feel.'

'I know how you feel.' At an hour like this both were of the same persuasion, but Tully's head was clearer. 'Still, there it is,' he said.

Heblekar could not accept, or only if it was unavoidable, like destiny.

'It shouldn't be. One shouldn't lay a finger, not one little finger. But that,' he said, heavy with the fumes, 'is fate. Their fate.'

'Whose?' Tully had lost him.

323

'Virgins'. Happens,' said Heblekar, 'all the time.'

'Does it?'

'Yes. Virgins sacrificed *wh-rr-ip*! on the altar.'

'Not any more, surely?'

'They *are*.' Heblekar was convinced, and convincing. 'Girls, mostly. From the dawn of time.'

'Why girls?'

'Law of nature, and the boys don't come forward.'

'Doesn't seem fair.'

'That's why,' said Heblekar, crooking two fingers for the bottle.

'Why what?' said Tully, handing over, because he wanted to find out.

'It's Mother Earth,' said Heblekar, twisting like Houdini. 'If it were Father Earth one would think twice.'

'That's quite a thought.'

'Isn't it?' Heblekar too was charmed. 'Mother Earth, universal common or garden,' he said, comprehensively.

'How I feel, Heb.' Their community of thought impressed Tully. 'Exactly how.'

'Don't we all?'

'No.'

'Yes we do. We only act impious.'

'Impious? What does that mean?'

'Mean? You mean you don't speaka da lingo? It means we act like baskets,' said Heblekar, translating well, turning contemplative as the sea brings him round, insistent, rotating him towards itself, towards a horizon resembling polished moonstone. 'Isn't it magnificent?' he said.

'Yes. That,' said Tully, 'is the whole point.'

'Of what?' Now Heblekar was lost.

'Selecting this spot.'

'For this bench?'

'For Shalimar, I meant. Meant to lure.'

'What?'

'People.'

'People, yes.' Heblekar paused; and tumbled headlong off the polished beam. 'But places before people.'

'In what way?'

'The way it works out.'

'I don't know,' said Tully. He didn't want to, either.

'In the end,' said Heblekar, insistently, dangerously, he felt himself edging round some lonely crag, its dark side.

324

'I don't know, I *said*.' Tully would not tread here. 'One's got to give it time.'

'Can't. Time's running out.'

'Impossible. Goes on forever.'

'Put it this way. *We're* running out of time.'

'True. We shan't be around too long. Not that long before R.I.P. goes up on the headstone.'

'Oh God.' Heblekar reeled, put on a face, senile, bewrinkled—a great actor has been lost in this man. 'You make me feel old.'

'*I* feel old.'

They fell back on Napoleon, taking alternate swigs.

Time flows, like aqua vitae.

'Your turn,' said Tully.

'I pass,' said Heblekar.

'Why? You can't,' said Tully, squinting hard at the spirit level: a good inch to go yet, 'take it with you, you know. Except this way, you blot it up into the tissues.'

'Is that so?' said Heblekar.

'Yes. Come on. Last drop. Never say no to the last drop.'

'Is it?'

'Word of honour.'

'All right.' Neckhold on the bottle, tilting it steeply, griping afterwards. 'But you know I'll *never* get on that plane.'

'You will. Put you on it myself, if necessary.'

'That's rich.' Heblekar gets to his feet, waits till the firmament steadies, throws down the gauntlet. 'Come on. Stand up.'

'Why?'

'Go down to the sea. Send a note to the world in this bottle.'

'No.'

'Why not?'

'Might fall in.'

'Won't.'

'Not worth the risk.'

'I'd like to try.'

'You go ahead.'

'All right, I will. You watch me.'

'I will.'

Heblekar goes off down the path, swaying a little, cradling the empty against his slender, minaret frame. Tully takes the path up, for a view from the terrace. The terrace moonlit, stone urns spilling milky blossom over pewter brims, bergamot smells. Far

325

below a mineral sea, silver-ash sounds and colours barely molested by chapathi crnch-crnching, until ruptured by sudden emotion.

Heblekar has made the beach. Touched by the moon he starts to yell—*ul-ul-ull-ah!* resounding muezzin cries, whirling like a dervish as he hurls his bottle.

Tully watches, leaning on the polished rail.

Heblekar must believe in his note: he is dancing on the sand, some wild tribal dance, to egg on the bobbing bottle.

Chapter Fifty

M R S Pearl watched the ripples spread, serenely. She would sit by the swimming-pool, its shallow end; and if it happened to be untenanted, toss in a surreptitious pebble to amuse herself, or Kali. She would not go in, until she had learnt to swim, and that would not be achieved until Rikki was able to resume tuition. Mrs Pearl was content to wait. She did not feel, at her age, like entrusting herself to new instructors (who were available); nor, so calm and still was she, the slightest urge to rush at things. There was time. She was staying on, and without neurosis, she hoped with some confidence; and while waiting for endorsements, bit by bit went native, insofar as that natural state was achievable.

She had moved out of the beach villa now, into a thatched hut. It was custom-built, true, and several cuts above the ordinary, but she felt it was a step in the right direction. Mrs Pearl was a tranquil woman as she waited, or watched Rikki demonstrate his skills on or off crutches; or settled down to pen a few lines to Zavera, in answer to violet-scented effusions that told of Zavera's longing for news about Shalimar, which continued to be twined round her heart—like honeysuckle, she wrote.

Tully too was vouchsafed stretches: a relief resembling peace as he studied the medical bulletins. From these he learned of strains, of future stresses (which could not be quantified at this stage) of bones upon the plate (one had been inserted); notwithstanding which the patient's prognosis could be said to be favourable.

What this reduced to—Tully reduced it—was that the body would be whole. He could hardly ask for more. He too would take it step by step.

And now Avalon began to murmur again. One could, if one listened, hear the turtledove notes reviving. Tully resumed his occupations. He inspected his orchard, and restored a wall that was crumbling, and chose his melons—not anyhow, but expertly as he had been taught. Ascending to the turret he buffed up the gun's ornamentals, and tended his boat when reminded to by Rikki. The cherub he left. There was much to do elsewhere.

In particular, a purposeful trip to the little freshwater creek where the boat was moored, and still lapped in a precarious seclusion. Tully took this path, meandering, easy, made by cattle combining a desire for water with a loathing for unnecessary toil. Arrived in peaceful frame, he sat down on the white sand to review the boat's fate; some vague pretence of considering what to do with it, while he knew perfectly well it would go where it belonged. It belonged with Rikki.

A case of possession, pure and simple: nothing whatever to do with money transactions, as he saw quite clearly. For Rikki's had been the moving spirit. He had selected the timber, presided over the keel-laying, bought coconuts with the lavishness of the newly rich and broken them over the hull while he prayed, painted it with the passion of an artist, and finally fallen in love with his creation, also like any artist, from the moment it was launched.

And Tully, aiming for a late sail, would come upon him in the evening, after pool duty, standing in the prow, singing. Not film hits, which he favoured, but one of those ditties, haunting, slightly tinny, that, early on, one heard the women singing when the fishing boats rode in.

Yes, Rikki. He would add it to his prized possessions, of which he had compiled a list, which he read out without the least encouragement at every opportunity. Completely open about such reprehensible avarice, but also reciting with cadences, as if it were a sonnet.

One radio cassette
One pair green frog flippers
One chronograph, LED, quartz
One boat with sea-serpent painted—
although at this point he would halt, and primly explain it was not his, only cared for as if it were his own.

Tully was smiling as he rose. Rikki had always had the power. The boat belonged to him. Tully would bequeath it to its proper owner, a proper resolution of at least one equation.

*

But problems generally were reducing. Time saw to that. By now even the clanging of the bell-buoy failed to molest him. The day came when, cautiously enough, he swam through the banded sea, turquoise, green, a laced sapphire above the hidden reef, and round the reef; and that too, he discovered, had been miraculously exorcised. Thereafter he resumed his early morning swims, as religiously as before, and with an edged pleasure from the lifting of
328

that particular cramp.

He was in full flight one dawn, towel streaming over a shoulder, when he almost ran down Mrs Pearl who was ascending.

'Toby, I've won. I've won!' She was hallooing, and also a little breathless. It was a stiff climb, for her.

'Roulette? Bingo? The pools?' Recovering his balance, he enquired.

'No, no such luck. But,' said elated Mrs Pearl, 'I'm staying on!'

As she had made no secret of it, he waited for more. She supplied, refusing to allow him to water down her triumph.

'Officially,' she emphasised, waving a buff, official sesame. 'Mr Heblekar has arranged everything. They're going to let me stay. No difficulty whatever, can you imagine?' She had imagined Himalayan hurdles, going by what went on back home. 'Isn't it marvellous?' she said.

'Yes. I'm so glad.' He was, for her.

'So am I.' She fell into step beside him, he modifying his usual ostrich to accommodate the dumpy woman as many people, surprised, did find themselves doing. 'I would have stayed anyway,' she said frankly, 'only now I feel they don't mind me belonging. It's so—I don't know, but I feel I can breathe freely. Enjoy the air, and the scenery, so many new vistas—at my age, isn't it incredible? But it's lovely, I feel like that giant on a mountain.'

'What giant?' Her zigzags would make him, too, flounder, much as his ziggurats often left her stranded.

'Or whoever it was, standing on a peak in Darien.'

'Actually,' he said, 'we're at sea-level.'

'You're ribbing me, Toby,' she said equably, 'but I deserve it for raving.'

'I rave too. Frequently,' he confessed.

'It's the sea-air.' She conjured up explanations for both of them. 'And just look at this sea.'

'Glorious,' he agreed. 'Join me?'

'In this?' asked Mrs Pearl.

Casting an eye, he saw the tentage: a voluminous caftan of striking Madras check.

'Just peel off,' he said. 'I'll look the other way.'

'Peel off!' A little yelp from Mrs Pearl. 'Ah, Toby, all very well for you young people, but for me—'

'For you too, try it and see,' he urged. 'Nothing to lose but your chains, you know.'

329

'I know,' She smiled. 'But I don't think I'm quite ready to cast off yet. And to be perfectly honest, Michelin ladies aren't quite built for such freedoms.'

And she sighed, so heartfelt he virtually saw the entombed sylph aching to climb out of blubber. But then, he amused himself by thinking, sylphs were everywhere, shut up in human flesh as much as in marble, ears pricked for the tapping of mallet and chisel.

If he saw, she too caught a glimmer. A hint of lacunae, well concealed by loving-godmother gifts of looks and wealth, under .flippant or urbane exchanges. In a man whose inner resources were of an order, as she had seen, that would keep him fulfilled, in close converse with some bedouined desert, or marooned on an isolate hill. She could only guess at these riches, as she could only guess at the loss, without indulging either pastime. It was by a process of osmosis that both were communicated, although the signs, or lesions, were evident.

Parked on the beach with her knitting and the baby, she would see him stride past; and smiling over his ineradicable, bossy, white man's walk, also notice his hands. Brown, fingers white as the roots, stained yellow with the nicotine as he worked out of the nervous spell. Sitting on his own, crushing out half-smoked cigarettes in saucers. Eyes unseeing, focusing inward, at times haunted by ghosts not all of them gentle. A man undone by his own quality.

And at times, moved, she would join him: leave the child in the crèche and come up to admire the amaryllis, or to share a coffee on the terrace. On one such occasion, the cona bubbling between them, she thought to ask about the mosaic. Rikki had crowed over some recently-acquired pebbles, which had brought it to her mind.

'The mosaic? Come and look,' he offered. 'It's rather grand, as you'd expect.'

'Yes.' Both understood that Rikki had been ambitious, as well .as impassioned. 'As befits Avalon,' she could not but add.

'Yes,' he agreed, and when their cups were empty took her arm. They walked up the steps together, across the verandah, past the crystal and into the pool room, and whatever Mrs Pearl was expecting, was transcended.

She stood, with the crystal light pouring in, and gazed upon what she might have called an Eden, except that the milder notes were transfigured by an ample use of blazing golds and blood-reds. At which point Mrs Pearl paused, and asked herself to behave like a sensible woman.

Not Eden then. But perhaps she would settle for a paradisial garden, such as some Caliph might command of his local Capability Brown? But even as she pondered the scene was refusing the frames she had in mind. It came at her, in all the innocence of a primal garden, shot with a grandeur and a violence of an order also to be glimpsed in Avalon.

It surprised Mrs Pearl. She had toiled up to this mansion many a time, without such glimpses. She had come, and admired the charming and elevated enclave, and had never once encountered vehemence, for which watch-tower, gatehouse, the imposing battlements, had seemed only past evidence. Even the cannon had been no more than a piece of decorative but unalarming ironmongery. But now as she looked about her, she could not doubt it. The founding stones were flagrant, no less so than the threat implicit in the cannon, or the ruthless conduits cut in the hill to pipe in water from the springs.

However, it was soft rain-water that filled the pool.

Mrs Pearl concentrated on this. She slipped off her chaplis (she had given up shoes: another step on the route to her nirvana), and sitting on sumptuous tesserae lowered her bunions with some relief into the limpid depths. Then she was able to comment on Rikki's labourings.

'It's striking,' she said, inadequately.

'Grand. I told you.' He concurred, more or less.

'But it's not quite finished, is it?' Getting over the dazzle, Mrs Pearl spotted the sacking that covered off a rectangle.

'I've no idea,' he answered.

'Haven't you peeked?' She admired without stint; she knew she could never have resisted.

'I haven't dared.' He laughed. 'Never know what kind of dragon's hatching under those wraps. I'll wait till Rikki gets here to tame it, before I open up.'

Had he, then, perceived the laced violence, which Rikki's instincts had spotted, and incorporated, fittingly enough, into this blazing design? Mrs Pearl wondered, but was not prepared to delve. Instead she splashed about, uninhibitedly, with the caftan drawn up at least to her knees, sluicing the little marble statue standing in the middle. Water was running smoothly down the polished limbs as she sloshed, except, she noticed, where it had not been properly sanded. Rasp marks showed, in a rough patch along one gleaming flank, which interrupted the fluid movement. The

331

water seemed to judder here, as it went over the uneven bed. She wondered that he did not finish off, there was so little to do; and was about to ask, but then she saw no need. Many things in life, inevitably, were left unfinished.

And so she was brought to think in these easy stages of Rikki. At seventeen, or so, the moulding had some way to go yet. Avalon would burnish further, if he was lucky with the newcomers. If not, Shalimar would; though its polish would of necessity be of a different order. Neither love, nor hate, went into its fabric. Meticulously built for selling itself, it fulfilled that purpose. Shalimar went whoring after money.

Here Mrs Pearl pulled up, to rebuke herself. It was altogether too strong, and wrong, a description. Shalimar did nothing of the sort. Its wiles were more courtly, those of a courtesan. However Rikki, she rather hoped, would not fall for these alluring, but lesser, charms. She would wait and see.

*

Apu, too, waited. He squatted in the doorway of the hut, or leant against a wall, and one or two passing would pause and enquire of the old man.

'I am waiting,' he answered them. He did not know for what. Except that sometimes, of an evening, when he brought out his charpoy for a breath of air, and sat gently rocking on the slack strings—sometimes all knowledge and understanding were vouchsafed him. Then he would know he was waiting for his sons, all his sons, and see them setting forth in the dawn that was breaking just over the horizon, in graceful craft neither more graceful nor strong than the men at the helm. At the same time he understood it was a vision. But he would cradle it to him, and rock, and answer gently enough if he was questioned: I am waiting.

*

Adeline was of those who noticed Apu. He had once been pointed out to her as the headman. She stood and looked, and Apu looked back at Mrs Lovat. Impenetrably, as far as she was concerned, and not for the first time was vastly irritated. People here were like brick *walls,* she said to herself.

She was leaving, finally. Tropical excesses, and the people, had worn her down.

'I've had it,' she told Mrs Tremlett, for want of a better crony.

332

'Up to here.' Holding the flat of her hand up to her chin.

She overcame these feelings to visit the sick.

'I hope, Rikki,' she said, and perched an envelope, with her cheque coyly concealed inside, on the locker beside him, 'you'll soon be better.'

'So do I. Thank you, Mrs Lovat,' said Rikki, civilly, in spite of feelings he had never got over.

'I'm leaving. I have come to say goodbye, Rikki,' said Adeline.

'Goodbye, Mrs Lovat,' he rejoined, and waited for her to go.

'Yes, I must get on.' Standing by the bed she fired her parting shot. 'I want to finish my book. And don't be surprised,' she said archly, 'if you find yourself in it.'

'I don't want to be in it,' said Rikki.

'Why not?' She had expected him to be flattered.

'I know what you would make me look like,' he replied.

'What?' She was startled into asking.

A clown, he was about to say, but a clown belonged to the human family. He was not sure Mrs Lovat had ever admitted him.

'A funny object,' he said at last, flatly.

However, as he would never read her book, he was not too worried.

There were closer concerns. He was recovering now, the process engrossed him. Soon he was badgering the nursing orderlies, and even the august doctor; and one fine day, sooner than these cautious people liked, informed them he had no further need of their services.

Then he had to think. Not far ahead, to where oceans tumbled off precipices. He never thought that far, Mrs Bridie's Sufficient unto the day had never made more sense than at present. But he thought a little ahead, to the time when he was due to take flowers to lay on her grave. The anniversary was approaching.

It was also time to keep what he thought of as a promise, made to Tully.

Long ago, when death had abruptly sealed off his expanding horizon, and Bridies (before Shalimar or Avalon were fully unfurled) had been the meridian, he had offered to conduct Tully.

Tully had been tepid. Over the heathen world, graveyards bore witness to untiring missionary zeal. He found them pathetic places, the burial ground of simple, poignant convictions finally faltering before the onslaught of invincible and inconvertible heathen seas of profound faith.

But faced with the boy's eagerness to conduct him, he agreed

333

that one day, when he had time. . .

For Rikki the time was now come.

Leaving the flower-procuring in the hands of his reliable sister, he turned for advice to Sandhu the ex-champion, in whose hands he had an equal faith. Stretched out on the slab in the massage parlour, he asked.

'Can you walk fifteen kilometres?' repeated Sandhu in amazement, and stopped pummelling the pelvic arches, whose articulation was not entirely to his liking, in order to say No. Finding he could not bring himself, he palliated. 'Where's the sense?' he said. 'Forcing it, it'll only start up the ache. Give it time, lad, give it time.'.

Rikki could not. Time, that once plentiful commodity, was in short supply. It placed him in a quandary. Twinges resulting from forcing it he could put up with, but what if he started to limp? Tully striding, himself dragging along like an old man instead of striding too, as Tully liked to see, quite plainly, he never bothered to hide his liking. This picture he thrust aside, roughly. He could not bear it. He could not bear for Tully to see him limp.

He would have to ask.

The request made sense to Tully. Whatever atrophy might threaten the non-walking Heblekar, he did not see himself hiking that many miles to visit a graveyard. Moreover Rikki's reckonings of distance, as he knew from many a conducted tour, tended to be on the conservative side.

He got out the beach buggy that Boyle had bequeathed him, and they drove. The two of them in front, the flowers stowed with great care in a pail on the back seat.

For Rikki of course it was a familiar journey. Right through childhood he had come this way, hugging the coast, splashing through the surf until the point where one turned off down the path that led to the Bridies. Or if he was impatient—a ship due for launching, or a raid on the bookstore imperative—he would cut across country, careless of thorns, not feeling the scratches until Mrs Bridie applied the iodine. He might still be making that journey, it came to him, if the Bridies had not feasted on salmon. As they approached the Mission he said as much.

'I might still be coming here—' for he understood the seam had not been exhausted, '—if they hadn't died,' he said.

'Would you have liked to?' asked Tully, keeping his eyes on the bumpy, barely visible track. As Mr Applebee had found, assiduous highways built by multinationals rarely ran to the rural

334

hinterland.

'I don't know,' said Rikki, truthfully. There had been so much in between: all manner of forces had tugged. He had no means of sorting out.

They drove on, bumpily, and presently Rikki was able to point out.

'There it is, Mr Tully. The Bridies' bungalow.' And schoolroom, and chapel, and house of meringues and devotions. Much was incorporate.

Tully slowed, stopped in front of a pair of rickety gates set in a crumbling wall, turned off the engine, gazed. In this place, fires had been kindled.

This ramshackle edifice.

Present incumbents, doing their utmost, had still been unable to make much impact on past neglect, which they considered had been of ungodly, and upsetting, proportions.

Tully, too, cringed a little before driving on.

Even he, however, could not fault the little walled-in cemetery. It was small, neat, white, tended, trim, pebbles, as clean as if washed and rinsed, keeping down the couch grass.

'Who looks after it, Rikki?' he asked, as he followed his guide to the Bridies' grave.

'Mission children,' said Rikki. They had been smartly despatched, when Mrs Bridie lost patience with their fidgeting; and departed willingly since anything was better than droning over her verbs. 'I don't know if they still do,' he said, for he had never been back to the schoolhouse. Oddly, it was the cemetery that was free from hauntings; he could scarcely believe it was tenanted.

Except that the writing proclaimed it.

BENJAMIN AND MARTHA BRIDIE it said, in letters of flaking gold, engraved on local stone for Bridies could never aspire to Carrara, or even Flanders marble. Under the stone, the two who had advanced his twin palanquins, each decrying the rival, Mrs Bridie's foot tapping as she looked down upon her absurdly rich, extravagantly scroll-edged verandah. But Mr Bridie had fits of allowing his wife some credit. 'Keep at it, Rikki,' he would say, loudly, winking behind her angular back. 'Essential for a fisherboy, English grammar.'

Alone, he could be generous. Smiling at the memory, Rikki shared it with Tully.

'Mr Bridie used to say,' he said, answering that brigand's wink, and mimicking faithfully, '"the old girl's right. It's a powerful

335

world-beater, the English language. You keep at it, my boy, it'll take you a long way.""'

Tully, his reverie interrupted, looked up.

'Seems to me you've come quite a way, Rikki,' he said, smiling; while unable to stop some conjecture as to what that destination might be. The grave, inevitably, prompted. In the end he had to give in, and ask.

'Would you,' he said, 'like to go back, Rikki?'

'Go back?' repeated Rikki. He had gone forward, from mangy hut to schoolhouse, to Shalimar when it blossomed, moved on to Avalon, its grave, rich heights. 'Where to?' he asked.

That was indeed the question, which Tully should not have asked or answered, except that the sea flooded in, and swamped his usual clarity. Visions were encouraged, in this beclouded state, not dissimilar to Apu's; and although a world divided the two men, took shape for similar reasons.

'Back to fishing,' he said.

'Fishing, yes,' said Rikki, preoccupied in arranging the flowers to Mrs Bridie's liking, while squatting on the tombstone under which she was laid. Not disrespectfully, though she would have judged it so—he could readily hear her offended voice primly telling him to mind his manners. As for Mr Bridie, he would have slapped his thigh, and come out with something, as coarse as he could think, to test his wife's endurance.

By now both presences were strongly beside him. More than ever he was sure they were not battened down, but dispersed in the elements, which he would always respect. Part of air, and sea, which Tully was trying to hand back to him.

Rikki would have liked to please him by accepting, but there were obstacles, and objections. He began to ache with thinking, the twinges came strongly.

'I would need a boat,' he said, at last.

'I would get you one,' said Tully.

'You already have,' said Rikki; while both knew that it would not do.

'Not a river-boat. A fishing sloop—something seaworthy,' said Tully, pumping in money like life-blood, perfectly aware that transubstantiation could not take place. Reality was slipping, to suppose it could.

It refused to, for Rikki. The reality was that people, as much as boats, had to be seaworthy. He avoided this, and said instead, 'No. My job is all fixed up. In Shalimar.'

And was entangled, the softest tendrils curled up from the syllables.

'Yes, Shalimar,' he said, lulled, and saw the light flowing milky through the latticed screen and lighting up the scarlet roses.

'I see,' said Tully. And he too glimpsed the rays, and would have seen they were refracting and corrected them, but for his state. Weighted, lead-heavy, he saw Shalimar reflected. Its brilliant trawl, which had netted a boy. Looking at this boy now, it seemed to him he was looking at a youthful, Caravaggio androgyne. The same ambiguity on this face, a washed innocence inflecting towards licence, the venal seeds were present.

This was a bought boy. Sold on Shalimar, wherever he might pasture, his soul—

It struggled out from forgotten keeps, thrusting up fresh as a daisy between the couch-suppressing pebbles. An ancient text: the words of some classical ruminant which the young Tully had been set to construe from the Latin. Long submerged, it surfaced now, more trenchant than ever that eleven-year-old could have imagined. *His body might go anywhere, but his soul was taken hostage.*

'Yes, I see,' he repeated.

And Rikki was winged. The grapeshot of opinion was grazing his skin, leaf-thin where relations with Tully were involved. It bewildered him, and made him brutal.

'It's no good, just one good boat,' he said sullenly, and cantankerously. 'You'd catch maybe two sardines and one grey mullet.'

It would not amount to a living, which needed a fleet, not that row of hulks with their ribs bursting out. He did wonder that Tully could not see it.

But Tully was beginning to; his customary clarity was returning. He saw it as a way of life; and from a distance heard the voices of children, those reliable cognoscenti, chanting. Not all the king's horses, nor all the king's men, could put it together again.

Meanwhile the Caravaggio, which had threatened, was giving place. In any case, which would he have preferred?

Leaving this, he offered:

'Shall we drive, Rikki?'

'Where to?' asked Rikki.

'Nowhere special. Wherever you like.' Since Rikki liked driving, and would cadge a lift at the slightest excuse from the coach drivers, or even the lorrymen who brought supplies up the hill. 'You choose,' said Tully.

Rikki did; and could hardly have picked better. The buggy, built for precisely such rumbustious excursions, let itself rip. It zipped along the beach, it churned through deep surf without a hiccup. In all Boyle's somewhat neurotic tenure of the vehicle it had not behaved as well. But then, it had not been driven like this either.

Both Tully and Rikki were revived, then exhilarated, then becalmed as, turning inland, they drew up once more at those rickety, compulsive gates.

Rikki's mood was of the tenderest; and was presently revealed.

'Mr Bridie,' he said. But he could not leave out the suppressed, yellow stick of a woman who, when such things were possible, had taken him on her lap and read from her tome, encircling him with a bony, long-sleeved arm. The two of them had brought him Avalon, and Tully.

'Mrs Bridie too. They made things possible. I was lucky,' he said.

Riches had flowed, Tully was being told. He was not a man who would fence with the truth, he did not do so now; but to be told, pierced. While he also heard the whispers which were rising. A murmur from a trout stream, wry, haunting, not as distant any more as it had once been.

'Subtle country, my boy. The minx knows—' over a shoulder, busy with the rod, 'what she's given, and how to give back, in exact proportion.'

And, as Tully perceived, the mix being returned was befittingly adroit. He could not for his life have sorted out the aloes from the honey.

Chapter Fifty-one

THEN time began to race.

Rikki set the traps overnight, and by dawn was back with his catch; and woke his sleeping mother for her to deal with it in her matchless fashion.

Amma obliged, not because of the flattery, but because it was Rikki, and she knew it was for Tully.

Tully had been out early, though not as early as Rikki, for his morning swim, and after changing and packing came out onto the terrace to lean on the polished baluster rail.

A spot of some attraction this, overlooking an indigo bay, as well as the dizzy path up which had hurtled an oriole in flight. Down it the sweet Sophie had fled, pursued by admirers; and he in turn had followed, speeding down, towel streaming, for his daily dose of sun and sea. Coming out to be dried off by the breeze, walking glowing up the hill escorted, one fine day, by a smart detachment from the casuarina copse. Two trim birds, cocky young blades playing anything-you-can-do all the way along before swooping down and up into a treetop where they sit and sing.

The terrace was flooded with their song.

In the diminuendo he heard, and saw, the oriole, soberly ascending. The basket, well laden, was creaking loudly. Mangoes, could it be? Another season come round again, so soon, when it seemed only the other day—?

Tully waited.

Rikki, having gained the plateau, revealed mangoes and much else besides.

'It is a picnic for you, Mr Tully,' he said with a flourish.

'That's marvellous, Rikki.' Tully was enchanted, and showed it. 'But it's not done, a picnic for one. Join me?' he suggested, in a way that Mrs Pearl would wholly have approved. She admired his ability, and often tried to emulate, but somewhat resignedly, saying to herself you either could or you couldn't.

Rikki was agreeable. He always was, if asked properly.

He spread the cloth and laid out the food in high style, and they sat by the orchard wall, sharing it with a young espaliered almond.

339

Blue cloth, coral lobster, claws soon stripped clean between them.

'Was that good, Mr Tully?' asked Rikki.

'Excellent.' Tully polished off a last flake from a finger, as Rikki had not brought implements. 'Haven't tasted better.'

'Because it's fresh. I wish,' said Rikki, 'it wasn't your last picnic.'

'So do I,' said Tully.

Since it was, they lingered.

Lemon scents, sound of surf on shingle carrying up clearly. On the wall sea-glimmer, reflecting all the way from the ocean, a cat's cradle of light. Far below the brilliant crescent of beach, just slipping into shadow, hyacinth in the shadows sealing off the bay.

'I must go,' said Tully.

'Why? asked Rikki, who had forgotten.

'Plane to catch,' said Tully.

They packed up the basket, neat and orderly as Avalon required of them.

'Will you come back, Mr Tully?' asked Rikki, when they were done.

'I wish I could,' said Tully.

'Cross your heart?'

'And hope to die.'

As ever it enchanted Rikki that Tully could follow him through all these ins and outs; but he also understood they shared a language that went beyond English, and was outside the scope of mere words. As, of course, did Tully.

They walked back, carrying the basket between them, and Rikki helped to load the buggy.

'Want a lift?' asked Tully.

'No, thank you,' said Rikki.

'Well, so long, Rikki,' said Tully.

'So long,' said Rikki, and turned away his face so that Tully should not see him crying.

Not that Tully would have looked, except that he could see, without looking. Grief smears on cheeks too young, really, to take them. He too was having difficulty, as he let in the clutch. He would not have thought it possible to feel such pain. Bunched, like a fist, in his throat.

When the buggy was out of sight Rikki went back to the empty house.

Empty as he had known it would have to be, in the end. He had always accepted there were limits to Avalon. Except that Tully had invaded too strongly to be silenced now. The permeated fabric returned him, the halls and corridors were echoing, the mansion throbbed with his presence.

Rikki wandered in and out of the rooms, looking, listening, not really surprised by what he heard. Tully had given Avalon life, it belonged to him. The throbbing was a measure of what it was giving back, a natural return.

And so by easy stages he was brought to the pool-room, and stood there for a while, gazing at the mosaic he had designed and executed. It was not finished, the sacking reminded him; but that did not matter now. Going into the yard, he fetched the implements he needed, and presently began levering up the little polished tesserae with as much care as he had laid them in position.

He was acting purely by instinct, without knowing why; but as he worked he began to accept that it was a sure instinct. Because the mosaic had been laid down for Tully, it could go to no one else. Because something was over, a time had passed.

There was a time, and a season, for everything. A time to sow, and a time to reap, as Mrs Bridie had been fond of intoning in her thin, cracked voice.

That-yellow-stick-of-a-woman! he ground out between the hammering and the chiselling, but did not interrupt his labours. And all the time as he worked the tears flowed, uncontrollably, because his blood, after all, had gone into the pigment.

At length it was done. He swept up the pieces neatly, ready for sacking in the morning; and after a last look at the jewelled heap went onto the verandah and down the steps and away down the hill from Avalon.

His cheeks were still wet, he realised as he walked. He wiped them dry, wondering as he did so why he bothered. It was quite dark by now, there was no one around to see. Then as he walked he saw he had been wrong. It was not quite pitch. There was a faint light visible, a pearly sheen on the distant horizon. The false dawn, they called it, forerunner of dawn proper.

Rikki's step quickened. He would hurry, and get to Prospect Point in good time, and settle down to watch. The views from there were matchless—not to be had from anywhere else, as he and Tully had often agreed.

341